MARRIED BY MIDNIGHT

SHANNON McKENNA

SNOWED IN SECRETS

JULES BENNETT

MILLS & BOON

First Published in Great Britain 2022
by Mills & Boon, an imprint of HarperCollins*Publishers* Ltd
1 London Bridge Street, London, SE1 9GF

www.harpercollins.co.uk

HarperCollins*Publishers*
1st Floor, Watermarque Building,
Ringsend Road, Dublin 4, Ireland

ISBN: 978-0-263-30390-2

1022

This bo

For n

Printed a

MARRIED BY MIDNIGHT

SHANNON McKENNA

One

There he was again. Mr. Mysterious was giving her that wickedly sexy smile again from across the room.

Who was he? The reception that followed her keynote address was by invitation only. Invitations were for big donors. Ronnie could have sworn she knew all those people, by sight, at least. She would have remembered that guy.

Look away. Breathe. Veronica Moss smiled at the man in front of her and tried to remember what they were talking about. Franklin Dodd was a kindly old gentleman with a wispy white goatee who chaired the board of directors of the Kitsup Foundation, which supported scientific literacy in children. They were talking about policies to support math instruction in early childhood education.

Pay attention. Act intelligent. Look alive. Hard, with her bandwidth all taken up by the effort it took to not turn and stare.

She'd first seen him from the stage during the keynote

speech she'd just delivered at the Future Science Conference in Las Vegas. It had been the challenge of a lifetime to her concentration, but she had not screwed up. Then, during the standing ovation, he'd locked eyes, kissed his fingertips and blown the kiss at her.

She had felt that kiss on every inch of her skin. That terrible flirt.

She managed an intelligible reply about educational policy to Dr. Dodd and turned to wave at a passing acquaintance. He was still smiling, waiting for her to gawk at him again.

Stop this girlish crap. She was a grown woman. She had made her life choices. The biggies, anyway. She and Jareth had obtained their marriage license yesterday at the Clark County Courthouse in Las Vegas. At midnight, she turned thirty, and to keep her promise to her aunt and cousins, she had to be married by then to ensure that Moss-Tech, the huge biotech and agri-tech company founded by her uncle Bertram and her aunt Elaine, did not pass into Jerome's hands.

She had put herself into this mess with her own hands.

Ronnie bitterly regretted the childish impulse that had come over her at her cousin Maddie's wedding. She'd been so angry after Jerome, her dad, tried to ruin the event. He'd been spitting mad ever since Ronnie's aunt Elaine legally mandated that her three grandchildren—Ronnie's first cousins, once removed—be married, Caleb and Marcus by age thirty-five and Maddie by age thirty, or else watch Ronnie's father, their uncle Jerome, take control of Moss-Tech. A dreadful prospect.

Then, on Maddie's wedding day, Jerome somehow hid the papers that had to be signed after the ceremony. Once the clock ticked over to midnight on Maddie's birthday, it would be too late. But Maddie and Jack had gotten secretly married beforehand, just to keep their asses covered. Curses, foiled again.

Then there was that shady stuff her dad pulled on poor Marcus and Eve, setting them up so that it looked like Marcus had betrayed Eve. It was sheer luck for her cousin and his bride that things had gotten ironed out, and trust restored. She'd been so sick of it. Personally, too. Her dad had been harsh and critical ever since she could remember, and the night of Maddie's wedding, her rage had boiled over.

Ronnie hadn't been a part of her aunt's mandate at first, being only a niece. That honor had gone to Aunt Elaine's grandchildren. Her aunt felt guilty for having raised them to be workaholic overachievers, and her solution had been to manipulate the three of them into matrimony by waving the threat of Jerome over their heads. But after her dad's embarrassing performance at Maddie's wedding, Ronnie had begged Aunt Elaine to put her into the documents, too.

At the time, it felt like the perfect way to hurt her father. Deny him something that he actually cared about; i.e., controlling MossTech, wielding power, making money. It wasn't like she could punish him by estranging herself. He wouldn't care, or probably even notice. But this? Oh, this, he would definitely notice.

It took a while to convince Aunt Elaine, but Jerome had given her a terrible scare, so she let Ronnie talk her into it. Same terms. Same punishment if she failed. Controlling shares of MossTech would pass immediately to Jerome. A fate dreaded by all.

Of course, for her, the marriage mandate wasn't as fraught as it had been for her cousins. She was a sure thing, safely engaged to one of the producers of her TV show. Jareth was handsome and smart, extremely competent, personally interested in her career, and wealthy in his own right. She'd been flattered by his offer, though she'd dodged setting a date for months. There always seemed to be some pressing reason to wait a little longer.

Not anymore. She turned thirty on the stroke of midnight, and the mandate had to be honored. Or else.

She'd get a video of the ceremony, held in a cheesy wedding chapel, officiated by the flashiest Elvis impersonator she'd been able to find, and send it to her dad. Ka-pow. The final blow. It was hers to deliver, after all the hell he'd put her through.

Then she'd go no contact forever.

Not that there would be much to miss. Derision and contempt. No tenderness that she could remember.

But she was okay. She'd learned to live without it. God knows, Jareth wasn't the touchy-feely type. He'd been genial and flattering at the beginning, but as the months went by, bit by bit, the flattery had faded away. Jareth was all business. Constantly working, constantly hustling.

But she didn't hold that against him. As a Moss, she had a deep respect for hard work and dedication. It was childish to expect the man to make a constant fuss over her. He'd made her show a huge success, after all. What was good for Jareth was good for her. It really was.

The problem was, after the heat of the moment faded, her gesture toward Dad had started to feel small and spiteful. She could have left things as they were. Dad would still have lost his chance to get control of MossTech, but she wouldn't have been the one to strike the final blow.

Too late for regrets. She had to see this through, like her cousins had done. Spectacularly, too. It had been a last-minute miracle for Caleb, Maddie and Marcus to get married in time. And not just married. They were crazy in love. Over-the-moon happy. All three of them.

It made her feel almost...well, jealous. Left behind.

Which was silly. Jareth Fadden was a perfectly good

fiancé. Tonight, he would become her perfectly good husband. Jareth had a lot going for him. He was creative, successful, ambitious, energetic. All qualities she admired. She had no cause to envy anyone.

Dr. Dodd's talkative wife joined him, and over Mrs. Dodd's shoulder, she saw Jareth keeping a sharp eye on her from across the room. As always, checking to make sure she was paying attention to the right people. He was forever scolding her for getting into conversations with people who in his estimation were not worth her precious time.

She gave Jareth a reassuring smile and wave, signaling that she was on top of it.

"Franklin, let's visit the buffet," Mrs. Dodd said. "I'm light-headed from the champagne. I need actual food."

"Of course, my dear." Dr. Dodd gave Ronnie a gallant bow. "Dr. Moss, can I get you a plate from the buffet as well?"

"No, thank you," she said with a smile. "Go on ahead. I'll see you in a moment."

The Dodds linked arms and made their way toward the buffet. Over their heads, she saw Mr. Mysterious take a champagne flute from one of the trays circulated by the catering staff. He raised his glass to her. God, that smile.

Now that he was closer, she saw how tall he really was. He towered over the people around him. His shoulders and chest and face were broad, his jaw strong and square. Intense dark eyes under heavy dark brows. That grin was drop-dead sexy.

She smiled back, and lifted her hand with her engagement ring, fluttering her fingers so that the huge diamond winking there would catch the light and send its clear, sparkling message. *Already taken. Done deal. Sorry.*

Mr. Mysterious's smile turned rueful. He smacked his hand against his heart, as if mortally wounded. Clown.

She turned away, spotting another caterer with a tray of glasses going by, and reached for some champagne. She definitely needed to fortify herself.

Bridal jitters. This kind of thing always happened when one made a commitment to any course of action. It was just Fate, tormenting her with the lost possibilities, paths not taken.

She wouldn't let it rattle her. The marriage license was in her purse, with two white gold wedding bands. She'd been wearing Jareth's engagement ring for months now and had the snagged and ruined sweaters and scarves to prove it. The setting of the jutting diamond was pure destructive hell for her cashmere wardrobe pieces, but it was a magnificent stone, and life was a series of trade-offs.

"Hell of a rock you've got there," said a deep voice behind her.

Ronnie spun around. Mr. Mysterious, at dangerously close range. His aftershave was warm and citrusy and delicious. "Excuse me?"

"Sorry. Was that too personal a comment?" he asked.

"I'm not sure yet," she hedged. "Your wording was ambiguous."

He held out his hand, and she offered her own before she could think better of it. Not an intelligent move, she realized, as his hand enveloped hers. It was warm. His calloused palm felt supple, like seasoned leather, like hand-polished wood.

"Not ambiguous at all," he said. "I was referring to the rock on your ring finger. I have mixed feelings about it."

I am not interested in your feelings about me, my ring, my rock. That was what she knew she should say, but all that came out was a wispy little "Oh."

"I'm sorry to see that ring," he mused. "But I don't see a wedding band."

The nerve of this guy. Ronnie gazed into his smiling dark eyes. “Have we met?”

“No. I’d remember if I’d seen you before in the flesh. I’m Wes Brody.” He shook her hand, which he had never relinquished. “I know who you are, of course. The photos in the conference booklet don’t do you justice. I’m a big fan, by the way. I’ve watched every episode of *The Secret Life of Cells*, many times. It’s brilliant. And so are you.”

Ronnie withdrew her hand, with a tug. “Thanks.” She tried to keep her voice cool, but it ended up sounding prim.

“Your presentation was amazing,” he said. “I could listen to you forever.”

“You’re very kind,” she said. “I saw you in the audience.”

“Yeah. I had a prime seat.” His grin widened. “You don’t even want to know the shady stuff I pulled to get a place right at the front.”

“No, I really don’t,” she agreed. “Let it be shrouded forever in secrecy.”

“So.” He paused. “Could I buy you a drink, afterward?”

Ronnie shook her head. “No. My fiancé and I are getting married this evening.”

Wes Brody’s eyes widened. “Tonight?”

“Yes. A wedding chapel, an Elvis impersonator who sings while we sign the paperwork, the whole shebang. And I do have a wedding ring. His ’n’ hers. In my purse.”

“Ronnie!” It was Jareth’s voice, with that sharp, dictating tone that made her hairs stand on end.

She could not snap to it in front of Wes Brody.

Brody’s eyes narrowed as he gazed over her head. “That’s the guy?” he asked. “The one who’s bellowing at you right now?”

“That’s him,” she said. “Well, then. It’s a big night for us, so thanks for the—”

Tweeeeet. A deafening whistle split the air. She flinched. Damn, Jareth. Here?

God, how she hated that habit of his. Hated it intensely.

"He *whistles* for your attention?" Wes Brody looked appalled. "He has the freaking nerve? In public, at a reception given in your honor?"

"Not your business." Her face was hot.

"My mother would've had something to say about that," Brody said. "She had clear, articulated ideas about how a man should behave around a lady. I didn't always measure up to her exacting standards, but I tried. I knew what side my bread was buttered on."

"Good for you," she said, inanely.

"Ronnie!" Jareth's voice got louder as he approached. "What is the matter with you? Have you gone deaf?"

Wes Brody leaned closer to her. "Pro tip," he whispered. "Don't marry that guy."

Ronnie looked over her shoulder at Jareth. When she looked back, Wes Brody had melted into the crowd. A neat trick, for a guy his size.

"Ronnie?" Jareth scolded. "You're in a daze! Are you deliberately ignoring me?"

"Do not whistle at me ever again, Jareth," she said. "I am not your dog."

Jareth looked startled. "Whoa! Since when did you get so damn sensitive?"

She set her empty glass onto the tray of a passing caterer and turned back to him. "I always disliked it. I should have told you before. But I'm telling you now."

Jareth lifted his hands. "Okay, okay! Simmer down. I was trying to get your attention, while scrambling like a bastard to serve your interests. Samuel Whitehall invited us to the Observatory tonight, his luxury retreat in the mountains, and he's offering us a ride in his helicopter.

Just twenty people are invited, the who's who of our business, and thanks to me, he's interested in *The Secret Life of Cells*! Whitehall could take us to the next level."

Ronnie craned her neck, scanning the room one last time for Wes Brody. She'd met Samuel Whitehall a few times. Not her favorite person. He leered and stared, he made suggestive comments, he was an "accidental" toucher and an enthusiastic shoulder-massager. He was also immensely powerful in the TV world.

But compromises had to be made. Or so Jareth constantly reminded her.

"Who are you looking for?" Jareth asked impatiently. "Did you hear what I said? Are you even connecting, Ron? This is Samuel Whitehall I'm talking about!"

"That's great, but we have other plans tonight, Jareth, remember? Personal plans."

Jareth rolled his eyes. "Ron, Whitehall's bringing us into his inner circle! We cannot blow this event off. It's important for both our careers."

"We're getting married tonight!" she insisted. "This has to happen before I turn thirty! You know that!"

Jareth sighed. "Seriously? This symbolic stunt to piss off your dad is more important to you than the biggest networking opportunity we've ever had?"

"It is extremely important! I've explained it more than once."

"Fine," Jareth said lightly. "It's early yet. We to the Observatory for dinner, and then head back to Vegas and get married. Easy-peasy, problem solved. Let's go. Samuel's waiting in his own personal limo to take us to the helipad."

"Helipad? We won't have any control over the timing if we're dependent on someone else's helicopter! Let's get married first, and then drive to the Observatory. They can toast to our wedding after dinner."

"No," Jareth snapped. "Catching a ride in the helicopter is part of the scene, Ron. It has to be spontaneous. Samuel's parties can get pretty wild." He cast a critical eye over her elegant ivory suit. "I wish you weren't dressed so primly."

Whitehall's parties tended toward the depraved side, which was not her scene. Maybe she was prudish, but in her heart, she was a hopeless science nerd.

"You don't have a spontaneous bone in your body," she told him. Ronnie crossed her arms over her chest, chilled. "I know you work hard on my behalf, but when it comes to our plans for tonight, it's simple math, Jareth. If we take a helicopter to Whitehall's party, we won't be back in time to get married."

"Of course we will," Jareth scoffed. "Don't be silly."

"I'll go to Whitehall's party," she said. "But only if we go to the wedding chapel first."

Jareth's reassuring smile faded. "Ron. You're being irrational."

His eyes had a chilly glitter. A sinking realization took form. "You never meant to go through with this to begin with, did you? You organized this, just to have an excuse for getting back too late to get married by midnight."

"Don't be such a drama queen. Everything is not all about you, you, you."

"That wasn't a denial," she said. "So it's true?"

"Goddammit, Ron, that's the wrong question to be asking!"

"Answer it anyway," she persisted.

"All right, fine. If you insist." Jareth leaned forward. "You're too blinded by your anger at your father to keep your own best interests at heart."

"*My* best interests?" she repeated.

"Yes, Ron! Yours, mine, ours! It's my job to put the brakes on this idiocy. I hoped to do it in a way that would feel like it wasn't anyone's fault, but that was too much to hope for. With you, nothing is simple. It has to be a big, fat, complicated production."

"You can't be serious," she said blankly. "You can't do this to me."

"Take the larger view," Jareth urged. "Go to the Observatory with me. Network with me. We're an unbeatable team. Let the deadline pass. Tomorrow, we'll wake up and take stock of our new prospects, which will be brighter than they have ever been before."

"Prospects?" she said.

Jareth sighed. "You're being deliberately obtuse. If Jerome gets those controlling shares, he'll take MossTech public. Ultimately, the payday for you will be phenomenal."

"No! I promised Aunt Elaine! She only put me into the paperwork because I urged her to! And I only did that because you'd already suggested we run off to Vegas and arrange a party later! I thought you were on board with this! You've tried to get me to elope to Vegas more than once!"

"That was before. You hadn't loaded this huge agenda on top of it," Jareth said. "Your aunt is an adult, Ron. Let her take responsibility for her own actions."

"But I gave my word! To her, and to Caleb and Marcus and Maddie!"

Jareth gave her a thin smile. "Maybe you did, Ron. But I sure didn't. I want to marry you, yes. But not on these terms. So let's change the terms."

Ronnie took a step back, on rubbery legs. She had the strange, disorienting feeling, as if a spell had been broken, and she was seeing the real Jareth for the first time. "You've seen what I stand to inherit when we did the prenup," she said. "It's a crap-ton of money. You have plenty of your own to begin with. So why?"

He shrugged. "So why not write a few more zeros on the end of that number?"

"Because it's a betrayal of my family, and I love them!"

"Excuse me for putting our own interests, and our future children's interests first," Jareth said. "I'll marry you, Ronnie. Gladly. Just not before midnight tonight."

"It's tonight or never," she told him.

Jareth shook his head. "Don't play power games with me," he said. "You won't win."

"It's not about power," she replied. "It's about integrity. I can't compromise on that!"

"Then you'll find yourself alone, with nothing but your principles to keep you company. Not even your show. I have final say on renewal for Season Four, remember?"

She sucked in a startled breath. "Really? You'd play that card?"

"Certainly. I'll manage your emotional excesses any way I can, Ron. At this point, I know how to handle you."

"Handle me. Really." Her face burned. "Manage this, Jareth," she said, through her teeth. "Fuck off."

Jareth rolled his eyes. "Oh, come on. We'll talk tomorrow when you've calmed down. You'll thank me later for thinking ahead on your behalf."

"Get away from me," she said.

Jareth pulled out his phone and placed a call. "Walt?" he said into the phone. "Yeah, it's me… I wanted to give you a heads-up. Looks like *The Secret Life of Cells* won't make it into the lineup for next season… Me too… Huge disappointment… Long story. I'll save it for when I'm back. We'll grab a drink. I'm trying to salvage it, but it doesn't look good. Women, am I right? Can't live with 'em, can't shoot 'em… Yeah. We'll be in touch. Later, Walt."

Jareth closed the call. His gaze was triumphant. He made a scissor-snipping gesture with his fingers. "Free and clear, Ron. Your bridges are burned. Your showbiz career is going nowhere without me and Fadden Boyle Productions."

"Tell me one thing." Her voice shook, to her dismay. "Was this all just about money for you?"

Jareth looked annoyed. "Of course it wasn't, Ron. I admire you. You're bright, beautiful, talented, accomplished. You're too volatile and emotional, but I was hoping that you'd grow out of that—"

"You see me as a child?"

"You act like one," he snapped. "Adults consider every angle. If you change your mind about having a husband, or a career, call me after you turn thirty."

He strode away without looking back.

Ronnie stood there. Rooted in place. She wanted to retreat to her room, but her room was the penthouse suite that she shared with Jareth. It was no refuge.

Get another room. Go to the check-in desk, talk to the staff, pull out your credit card. Move through space, dammit. Left foot, right foot.

But she was too disoriented. She stumbled through the hotel lobby, out onto the street. She wandered down the Vegas Strip, dazed and blinking in the blazing sunshine.

She'd never thought that Jareth had MossTech on his radar. She knew that he liked money and did not mind the fact that her family had it. But forcing her to betray Aunt Elaine and her cousins?

When they first got involved, she'd liked that Jareth was rich. That had been very reassuring, since she'd been beating off would-be suitors who were sniffing after the MossTech billions since she was an adolescent. When she met Jareth, he'd been a driven TV studio executive, in a field light-years distant from biotechnology and agriculture. He barely noticed what her family's company did, what it was worth. He'd been far more interested in how he could monetize Ronnie's own talents. But it had all been an act.

She'd destroyed the only family she cared about, and for what? A chance to spite her father. Score a point. Like a spoiled, stupid child. Jareth was absolutely right about that much, and she was ashamed of herself.

She turned thirty at midnight. No stopping the clock. She'd made a horrible mistake. Jerked around like a puppet by anger and spite, kind of like someone else she knew. The apple didn't fall far from the tree. Maybe that was what she had to look forward to. Her father's life. Poisoned by bitterness and rage. Estranged from everyone, even his own child. The world despised him. What a prospect for her future.

But at least she wouldn't be married to that lying, conniving bastard, Jareth.

Tears overtook her. Jareth hadn't been perfect, and she'd been well aware that he was too domineering, but she'd thought she could manage it. Hah.

One of the big casino hotels loomed over her, blocking the Vegas sunshine, so she went inside, wandering through slot machines. She sat in the quietest bar she could find and ordered a lemon drop, huddling behind her hair as she sipped it.

"Excuse me," said a deep, velvety voice. "May I join you?"

Ronnie froze for several seconds, her heart thudding madly, before she turned.

Yes. The face that went with that gorgeous voice. Mr. Mysterious. Wes Brody.

"It's you," she said.

His smoldering, dimpled smile flashed. "Yeah, last I checked."

She studied him for a moment. "Are you following me?"

"I'm not tailing you from place to place like a maniac, if that's what you mean," he said. "I saw you walk in here, and I followed you inside. I don't mean to be creepy. Or make you uncomfortable in any way."

Ronnie was too numb to register discomfort, or creepiness. "It's okay," she said.

Brody studied her for a moment. "Are you all right?"

"No," she said. "I'm wrecked."

"Does this have to do with the guy I saw? The colossal butthead who whistles for you? Did you fight with him?"

"Big understatement," she said. "We had a catastrophic difference of opinion."

"I see. I know that this is none of my business, and that it's a bad time to chat you up. But if you'd like to talk, I'm all ears."

"Not smart," she said. "I will not sparkle. In fact, I'll probably snivel."

"Warning duly noted, but your misery doesn't scare me. What did that son of a bitch do to you? Want me to flatten him for you? I'm up for it."

"Never mind him," she said. "It's a long, weird story."

"If you tell it to me, will you be late to your own wedding?"

"No," she said. "The wedding is off. Forever."

His eyes lit up. "Damn, Dr. Moss. That's the best news I've had in a long time."

She couldn't stop laughing. "Call me Ronnie. It's terrible news. For me, anyway."

"Then call me Wes, and why is it terrible news? I think it's awesome. I could tell across a crowded room that guy was a massive jerk. You're well rid of him."

"Maybe so, but I had to get married today," she admitted. "Or else screw up the lives and careers of the people I care about the most. And now it's too late to fix it." Her face dissolved. "And I did it out of spite. I can't believe myself."

Wes pulled a pack of tissues from his pocket. He tucked one in her hand and laid the rest of the pack on the bar. "Sounds like a hell of a story," he said. "I'd love to hear it."

Ronnie blew her nose, mortified. His eyes looked so warm. Sympathetic, fascinated. Not judging. "Really?" she said. "This story does not reflect well on me at all."

"I'm as curious as hell," he said. "May I sit?"

She nodded. Wes sat next to her, and signaled the bartender, pointing at her drink. "Two more," he called out. He spun on the stool to face her. "So? Tell me everything."

"It starts with my dad alienating everyone in my entire family," she began.

It took a few rambling false starts, but Wes's questions were intelligent, and the wheels were liberally greased by two more lemon drops. The story soon poured out of her.

"Anyhow," she concluded. "That's it. In a nutshell, I really love my aunt, and my cousins are like siblings to me. And I screwed them over and let my dad win."

"Ouch," Wes murmured. "Harsh. But I don't get why you asked your aunt to include you in this mandate to begin with. What did you stand to gain?"

"Nothing," Ronnie said bleakly. "Not a goddamn thing. I did it out of spite. I wanted it to be personal. I wanted him to know that when he had his prize snatched away from him, that I was the one who had done it." She winced. "Ouch. Not my finest moment."

"But besides that," Wes mused. "Seems like a huge risk, just for a jab at Dad."

"That's the thing," she wailed. "I didn't think it was a risk! I thought I was safe! I thought Jareth and I were solid. He'd tried to get me to elope before, so I knew he was fine with a Vegas wedding. It never occurred to me that he'd crunch the numbers and decide to screw me over." She paused. "Which makes me not only spiteful, but gullible, too."

"We've all miscalculated a time or two when it comes to love," Wes said.

"Yes, I know, but other people will pay the price for my miscalculation," Ronnie said. "Which horrifies me. And there's absolutely nothing I can do."

"So you turn thirty on the stroke of midnight," Wes mused. "Does this mandate stipulate that your marriage has to be specifically to the whistling butthead? Or would the conditions be met if you married someone else?"

The question threw her. "Ah… I suppose anyone would do. But I turn thirty in a few hours, Wes. It's a little late to go husband hunting."

Wes put his hand over hers. "I'll marry you," he said. "Where's the chapel?"

Two

The fateful words popped out of Wes's mouth without the benefit of reflection. Raw instinct, like a hawk diving for prey. Time stopped. He heard the jingle and hum of the casino hotel doing its thing, but the two of them floated alone in a bubble. Veronica's lips were parted. Her brilliant blue eyes were fixed on him, full of confusion.

As well they should be. He was a flirtatious stranger. She should tell him to get lost. He wouldn't blame her. But he'd said what he said. He'd wouldn't walk it back now.

One part of him was electrified by what this might mean for his secret investigation. The other was just electrified by Veronica Moss herself.

He wished it were all about her. Her splendor would have been enough to justify what he'd just said. He might have lunged for this chance even if he hadn't been burdened by his agenda. Why not jump up to save the gorgeous damsel? Solve her problems, be her hero and score a killer excuse to be close to her, 24/7. Close enough to smell her shampoo. What was there not to love about that scenario?

Just the truth he had to unearth from the Moss family history. About what had really happened twenty-three years ago, at that lab in Sri Lanka, and who was ultimately responsible for the lives that had been destroyed there.

One step at a time, though. Veronica was already traumatized from being used, manipulated and lied to. This enterprise was going to be tricky, and damn distracting, with his racing heart and his glands on overdrive.

God, she was beautiful. He'd admired her on her hit TV show about cell biology, but he'd assumed she'd been helped into that state of perfection by a team of professional makeup artists. But she needed no help. It was all her: dewy skin, delicate bone structure, sharp cheekbones. Rosy, sensual, kissable lips. Huge, startling blue eyes, smudged with mascara. That cascade of tousled, fiery hair. Her body, too. Slim, luscious. A dancer's posture. The whole package: beauty, intelligence, charisma. He'd started watching her show because he was obsessed with the Mosses, but soon he watched it just for her.

What better way to gain her trust? Earning her gratitude? He was being tongue-kissed by Fate…if he could land this opportunity. A very big *if.*

She didn't look trusting or grateful right now. She looked scared.

He wished he weren't so conflicted about it. A functioning conscience was an inconvenient burden.

"Not a good joke, Wes," Ronnie said.

"I'm not joking," he said.

"Of course you are. I don't know you, and you don't know me."

"Maybe not, but with me, you'd be doing better than

that last guy," he offered. "I would never whistle for you. I would treat you like a queen. A goddess, even. The utmost respect."

Her eyebrows climbed. "You're not very subtle."

"You don't have time for subtlety," he pointed out. "You told me that your male cousins arranged business marriages to satisfy the mandate. How is this any different?"

"Caleb knew the woman he was getting married to from years before. Marcus picked out someone who had been vetted and cross-checked. They knew both of those women far longer than…how long has it been? Less than an hour, over drinks in a casino bar?"

Wes shrugged. "I don't think your cousins had the same time crunch," he said. "With me, you can save your family company, keep your word to your aunt, keep faith with your cousins, put the shaft to your scheming dad, protect MossTech jobs, and also, incidentally, flip the bird to your venal, butthead ex. All in one smooth gesture."

He realized, with a thrill of excitement, that she was actually considering it.

"Too dangerous," she said. "You know too much about MossTech. I just spilled my guts to you. I don't have a prenup to protect me. I don't even know if your name is really Wes Brody. I don't know you, and I don't know anyone who knows you. You're a smooth talker, but you could be a con artist, or a bank robber. Or a serial killer, for all I know."

He laughed out loud. "I'm not a serial killer. But I'm happy to address your concerns. It's true, I know that you're rich, but I don't care because I'm also rich."

"News flash," she said ruefully. "That was what I thought about the last guy, too."

"I'm not like Jareth," Wes said. "If I want more money,

I'll make more money. I'll show you my company website, my tax returns, my stock portfolio. I have my laptop."

"Really," she murmured.

He pulled his wallet from the inside pocket of his suit coat and pried his driver's license out of its slot. "There," he said, presenting it to her. "See? That's me."

She studied it. "Weston Robert Brody," she said. "Nice picture. New York?"

"Sometimes," he said. "I have a house in Manhattan, in Chelsea. I also have a place in Montana. I recently bought a villa on a cliff over the Amalfi coast. I have to get it renovated, but it's got beautiful stonework. It's got a tile terrace overlooking the sea, and lemon trees. I'm always knocking big, juicy lemons off the trees with my head."

"Sounds luxurious," she murmured. "I love lemons. Do you have pictures?"

"Hundreds of them," he assured them. "On my phone. I'll even show you the deed. It's in Italian, but we could find someone to translate it."

"A driver's license can be faked," Ronnie said.

The gleam in her eye hinted that she was messing with him. "I have a passport in the safe in my room. A passport is hard to fake. I'll show you my tax returns, the deed, my investment portfolio. Come up to my room."

"Oh yeah? Will you show me your etchings?"

He grinned. "I'll show you any damn thing you want. Here." He pulled a laptop out of his briefcase and opened it, pulling up the home page of Brody Venture Capitalists. "I own a venture capital company," he told her. "I employ over a hundred people. That's me. Weston Brody, owner and CEO."

She glanced at the masthead photo, then at him. "Impressive."

"No criminal record," he said. "No secrets. Deep pockets. I got an MBA at Harvard Business, and started as an equity research analyst specializing in biotech. I've left a huge digital footprint. Here's the page with some of the start-ups I funded. Any of the people I partnered with would vouch for me. Do you know any of these names?"

She studied it for a moment. "Yes, I do, actually."

"Excellent. Make some calls, or have your people make them. Ask any of the people on that list if I came through for them. I'll wait."

She looked away from him for a moment, biting her lip. "Wes," she began. "Your intensity is gratifying. I appreciate the bona fides. But what do you get out of it? My cousins made bargains that gave a benefit to both parties. But if what you say is true, then you're rich, well-known, successful in your field. You don't need me. So why do such a random, risky thing? What do you get out of it?"

He laughed to hide the discomfort. "Come on," he said. "If you have to ask."

"No," she said. "I absolutely do have to ask. You are an incorrigible flirt. I'm sorry to say this out loud, but it has to be said. Any marriage of convenience that I might undertake would never presuppose my sexual availability. Never, ever. Got it?"

He gave her a courtly bow. "God, no. The very idea."

"This is serious, Wes."

"I'm not taking this lightly," he said. "But I'm trained to recognize opportunity. If I feel it, I go with it. I'm not infallible. I've made some bad calls. But my track record does not suck. When I see a once-in-a-lifetime opportunity, I don't hesitate. I grab it."

Ronnie's mouth trembled. "I don't feel like such a stellar opportunity right now," she said. "I feel like a hot mess. If I were you, I'd back away slowly."

"Not a chance in hell," he said. "Full steam ahead."

She looked away. "Well," she said. "Thank you, Wes. For the vote of confidence."

"So? Are you going to call your people?"

She blinked at him, sniffing into the tissue. "Call who?"

"You know, the lawyers, the accountants, the private detectives. Get the process started. The background check, et cetera. And there's the small matter of a marriage license." He gave her an encouraging grin. "If I check out, of course."

"I have a marriage license, but it has Jareth's name on it," she said.

Wes glanced at his watch. "We have some time yet. Your people can work on the background check and the rest while we go to the courthouse and get ourselves a fresh license. Good thing your amazing keynote address was a morning event."

"But it's not that simple. I had a detailed, ironclad prenup with Jareth. I can't do a fresh one on the fly, without the help of my lawyers. It would never be valid in court, and I can't marry you without one."

"We'll do a new one," he suggested. "Let's find an online notary. Get your people to draft something simple. My assets are mine, and yours are yours, unless we feel like legally changing that in a postnup. We'll video-record the whole thing. Your people can send us the forms to sign. We do an online interview, sign it in real time in our recorded video call. Witnessed, signed, stamped, notarized. It's doable, Ronnie."

Ronnie shook her head. "You are a piece of work."

"I want you to have hard proof that I am for real, and not on the grift."

She gazed at him with searching eyes. He returned her look without flinching.

"You know what the problem is, Wes?" she asked slowly. "Why I'm so uneasy?"

"Tell me," he said swiftly. "So I can fix it."

Her lips twitched. "I'm the only one who needs something," she said. "The power balance is off. The stakes are higher for me than for you. That makes me nervous."

"There's no power play going on," he assured her. "I'm fascinated. I'm excited. I'm entertained. For me, that's reason enough."

"It's dead serious for me," she said. "Not entertainment."

"I'm useful to you, even if I'm entertaining myself, aren't I? I'm fulfilling the terms of your aunt's mandate. Whose business is it but ours if I enjoy myself in the process? Who am I hurting by being titillated?"

She rolled her eyes with a snort. "There you go again. And speaking of hurt. You don't have a string of disgruntled lovers who will get their feelings bruised, do you?"

"I'm free as a bird. My parents are both gone, so there isn't even anyone to feel hurt that they weren't invited. No strings. Just a new friend, holding out a helping hand in a time of need." He extended his hand. "So take it."

Another breathless, charged silence. Seconds of frozen waiting…

Ronnie reached out, clasping his hand.

Joyful excitement blazed through him. Discomfort in equal measure, for everything that he hadn't told her. Lying was not the way you treated a queen.

But in his case, lies were a brutal necessity.

"It would be temporary," Ronnie told him. "If the background check comes back okay. I would need you to stay married to me for five years to satisfy the terms of the mandate. Would that be acceptable?"

"I can do five years," he said promptly.

"Of course, you can do anything you like in your personal life, as long as you make the marriage look good for the duration of that term."

"Sounds doable," he said.

"So…really? This isn't a joke, or a trick? You're willing to do this?"

"Really. Go on, make the calls. Do the checks. Have your lawyer draft the prenup. Give me your lawyer's email address, and I'll send him my stuff. Tax returns, investment accounts. Anything he wants to see."

Ronnie pulled out her phone. "What's your number?"

He read it out, waiting while she tapped it into her phone. His own phone chimed with a text.

"My lawyer's email," Ronnie said. "Now you have my number."

He set his laptop on the bar. "I'll send stuff while you make the calls. Then you pick out an online notary and set up the appointment. We better get cracking, or we won't get to the courthouse during business hours."

"Okay," she said. "Excuse me, then."

She retreated to the other end of the bar to make her phone calls. He kept a close eye on her as he sorted through files for documents to send to her lawyer's address.

Ronnie appeared to be having an impassioned argument with someone on the other end of the line. Evidently, her lawyer thought that marrying a random stranger she'd met in a Las Vegas casino bar was a shitty idea. Uptight bastard had no sense of humor.

He wished he had no secrets to hide, because he had absolutely nothing against that radiant creature. He never wanted to hurt her. Veronica Moss deserved reverent awe from every unworthy guy who dared to raise his eyes to her. And even if the Mosses were guilty of the crimes he suspected, the new generation who ran MossTech now was blameless. What their parents and grandparents had done wasn't their fault.

And yet, he couldn't let it go. Because the Moss family had achieved its outsize success at his dad's expense. Wes's father had paid the tab for that family's meteoric rise.

He'd paid for it with his life.

Three

As Fate would have it, the woman who helped them at the Clark County Courthouse was the same one who had generated a wedding license for Ronnie and Jareth the day before. She was a round, stern-mouthed lady with rhinestone-studded glasses. She looked at Ronnie, looked again and looked at Wes. Her eyes narrowed in puzzlement.

"Weren't you in here yesterday?" she said suspiciously.

Ronnie steeled herself. "That's right."

"But not with him." The red-haired lady scowled at Wes.

"Nope," Wes said. "Different guy. A much better one. If I do say so myself."

"Humph." The woman's eyes slid to Ronnie, brows climbing as she waited for an explanation. Which she was not owed, dammit. It was none of her business.

"It didn't work out with the other guy," Ronnie finally said.

"I see." The redhead clucked her tongue. "That was quick."

"Pretty much," Ronnie agreed.

The woman harrumphed. "Well, I've seen it all, believe me, but I think you beat my personal record for waffling. Maybe you should think this through, miss. Marriage is not entertainment. Ask any married couple. They'll tell you. And it does appear that you two have been drinking. Just sayin'."

Ronnie drew herself up to full height. "I didn't ask for your—"

"Hell, no!" Wes cut her off. "After all the trouble I went to, prying her away from that mouth-breathing troll? She and I were meant to be together. Don't wreck this for me, ma'am. True love stands before you. Please, don't get in its way. It's bad luck."

The redhead snorted. "You do seem more enthusiastic than the last guy, I'll give you that," she said, turning to her keyboard. "I'd call it a step up."

Ronnie couldn't argue with that, though she did not appreciate the commentary. In fact, Jareth had balked, up to the last minute. He'd tried to persuade her that she'd regret not opting for a big wedding. No flowers or photos, no feast, no cake, no fabulous dress, no emotional ceremony, no memories to treasure.

When she held firm, he'd finally signed the paperwork, muttering something about having his balls squeezed in a vise.

Wes Brody did not look like a man who felt that his balls were being squeezed in a vise at the thought of marrying her. He looked like he'd scored a huge win.

They walked out of the courthouse with the fresh license safely tucked into her purse. She pulled off Jareth's showy engagement ring with an effort and tucked it into her purse, and took out the old marriage license. She tore it into several pieces, flinging them into a recycling bin.

"That looked cathartic," Wes said.

"Absolutely," she agreed. "Good riddance."

"Amen. So have your people checked me out?"

"Yes," she said. "My accountant, my lawyers, the PI firm. A team of experts have been poring over your life. You look great on paper."

"Ah," he said, smiling. "Nice to know."

"It makes them crazy, that they can't find anything bad. You're rich, successful and on the level, as far as they can tell. Your VC company makes money hand over fist. Your luxury properties in Montana, Manhattan and Amalfi are all on public record. The only bad thing that can be said about you is that you're hedonistic. You deny yourself nothing. Gossip magazines babble about your wardrobe, cars, motorcycles, high-profile romantic liaisons—"

"I haven't had any of those in a while," he cut in.

"Poor Joseph made so many phone calls, trying to find someone who would say that you're a liar and a loser, but nobody would oblige him," she said.

"Excellent. So? We've done the bona fides, we've got the license, we have the prenup notarized. What else is holding us back? Shall we go to the chapel?"

"What about me?" she asked. "Did you check me out? It seems only fair."

"Certainly I did." His voice was silky. "At great length. With great pleasure."

"Oh, stop it," she scolded. "I mean, seriously."

"No need," he said. "You're a celebrity, and MossTech itself is the corporate version of a celebrity. You're a household word."

"Oh, please. I'm hardly a household word. Unfortunately, my people are in an anxious tizzy."

"I don't blame them. They don't want to see a rare gem cast before swine. I approve of their zeal and concern." He lifted her hand, and bent over it, in a graceful, ceremonial bow. "And though they can't hear me say it, I solemnly promise to treat you with gentleness and respect." He pressed a kiss to her knuckles.

Her throat clenched. She let her hair fall forward as he held the limo door open for her. She got in, surreptitiously brushing the tears away. This was ridiculous. She was so damn needy, after a lifetime of Jerome's criticism and indifference, and now Jareth's betrayal, too. She was so hungry for the slightest kindness, all Wes had to do was be gallant and nice. Just baseline politeness, and she melted into mush. *Oh yes, please, please, be nice to me, please.*

That made her terribly vulnerable to predators. No wonder Myra and Sam and Joe were so worried. They knew Jerome and Jareth. It was probably written all over her, how compromised she was. Predators could smell that.

Then Wes Brody slid into the limo beside her, his big, powerful thigh just inches from her silk-clad leg. His big hand clasped hers, and the contact sent a deep, beautiful thrill rippling through her. That smile. Those eyes.

His admiration might be an act, but what an amazing act it was. Too pleasurable to resist. In her life, such thrills were not thick on the ground.

Screw it. She'd done what she could to protect herself, legally and financially. She'd survive a worst-case scenario. If he proved to be on the take, at least Aunt Elaine and her cousins were safe and protected. She'd just forgive herself right now, in advance, for all the humiliation and legal hassle that would ensue.

And in the meantime, she'd enjoy the warmth of the contact with him, glowing against her hand. His delicious, focused attention. His charming conversation.

Tonight, Wes Brody was her best bet—and she was betting it all on him.

Wes was glad to see Kenji, his personal assistant, waiting for them outside the wedding chapel, as Wes had directed. Kenji held a box in one hand and an armful of flowers in the other. The younger man's dark eyes were curious as the limo pulled up.

When Ronnie got out of the limo, Kenji gave her a once-over and glanced at Wes, impressed. "Not bad, boss," he said under his breath.

"Didn't ask you, but yeah, I know. Did you take care of the things we discussed?"

"Yeah," Kenji said. "All arranged." He handed over the small box to Wes.

"Excellent." He turned to Ronnie. "This is my personal assistant, Kenji Miyota," he told her. "Kenji, Dr. Veronica Moss. My bride-to-be."

Kenji shook her hand. "I'm a huge fan, Dr. Moss. I've seen that episode about photosynthesis six times. Every time my mind is just..." He mimed an explosion around his head. "You make me feel like I actually understand all the science stuff."

"Aww. How sweet of you. Great to meet you, Kenji. Call me Ronnie." Her smile dazzled Kenji, who kept helplessly shaking her hand.

"Ronnie, could you try this on?" Wes opened up the box, and pulled out the wedding ring he'd asked Kenji to get, hoping to God it would fit. He'd just eyeballed her slender hand, and taken a guess at her ring size.

"But I already had rings!" she protested.

"I didn't want to use them," he said. "Seems unlucky. Wearing a ring bought for the whistling butthead? No, thank you." He handed her the ring.

She slid on the glowing golden band and held out her hand. “It fits perfectly,” she said softly.

“Excellent.” Their eyes locked, and his heart started to thud. “I’ll…um…take that back, then. For the ceremony.”

She passed it back, smiling. Wes cleared his throat. “What else have you got for her, Kenji?”

“Ah, yeah. These are for you.” Kenji took the wrapping paper off the flowers and presented her with the bouquet that Wes had specified. White calla lilies, orange orchids, floating in an ethereal cloud of baby’s breath. Perfect with her red hair.

Ronnie looked startled and touched. “How gorgeous! You didn’t have to, Wes!”

“All brides should have flowers. And there’s this.” He indicated the big box.

Kenji opened it, and Ronnie’s mouth fell open as Wes lifted out a beautiful, filmy, lace-trimmed bridal veil, attached to a wreath of fresh rosebuds. The fine, sheer fabric billowed in the faint evening breeze.

“Oh, wow,” she whispered.

Wes crowned her with the wreath, draping the veil around her shoulders. This was no job for a future husband. That honor should have gone to her mother, or another significant female relative. But Fate had decreed that Ronnie face this strange milestone alone, with a stranger, on a busy, noisy street in front of a wedding chapel. She looked like a fairy princess. No, actually. She looked like a goddamn angel.

“Wes,” she whispered. “That’s sweet. I… I don’t know what to say.”

Neither did he, which was not normal for him. He always had a line for any occasion. But he was struck dumb by awe and dread. A looming sense that he was misusing something that he'd only just realized was precious. Even sacred.

"Ah…yeah," he muttered, strangely flustered. "Kenji, take some pictures. Her alone, and then the two of us together."

Kenji took dozens of pictures of them on the steps, the brilliant colored lights of Vegas behind them. "I'll take pictures inside, during the ceremony if you want," Kenji offered. "Or video the whole thing. You tell me."

Wes looked at Ronnie. "Didn't you want to video this? To send to your dad?"

"Oh, no. I'm embarrassed I ever planned to do anything so mean-spirited. At this point, I just want to forget that part of it. If I'm lucky, my dad never has to know how spiteful I intended to be."

"Ah. So the thing about doing it right before midnight—that's off the table now? We have some time. We could stall for a while, if you wanted. Get a drink."

She checked the time. "If I wait, with my luck, you'd get struck by lightning right before we go into the chapel."

Wes swallowed his laughter. "I'll try to stay alive until then," he said. "No lightning bolts until the papers are signed, I promise."

She laughed nervously. "Sorry."

"Why delay? The sooner we tie the knot, the sooner you can relax." He turned to Kenji. "Just take pictures of the ceremony. And send me the ones you have already."

Wes scrolled through the gallery of Kenji's shots as they walked into the chapel. They were great. Ronnie Moss was photogenic as hell. The floral wreath and veil and the flowers in her arms made her look fey, magical. The veil looked perfect with the starkly elegant white pantsuit. The goddess of spring, in spike-heeled pumps.

But his face looked afraid. Probably he was the only

one who could see it. On the surface, he was smiling, confident. But in his eyes, he saw fear.

He didn't want to use her or disappoint her. He wanted to be worthy of her.

But he had to be worthy of his own father, too.

His dilemma began three years ago, when he put the house that his father had owned in Colombo, Sri Lanka, up for sale. The people who had been renting it for the last seventeen years had moved back to London, so he'd decided it was time to simplify. Let go of the past.

Then the agent handling the sale told him about boxes of old papers that had been hidden behind some furniture in a wall closet, forgotten for twenty-three years. Wes had been traveling in Asia at the time, so he'd flown down to Colombo to check it out.

That was where he found his father's journal, and the lab notes, describing an outbreak of toxic mold in a strain of MossTech drought-resistant millet. It had sickened and killed sixty-two people, twenty-eight of whom had been children.

According to his dad's journal, someone had been aggressively covering up the disaster, trying to make the whole thing go away with bribes and intimidation. His father had suspected Naomi Moss, Ronnie's mother, and the rest of the Mosses as well. The data looked bad. In spite of his dad's dry, laconic writing style, Wes could tell how unsettled Dad had felt.

The last journal entry was dated the day of the bombing, twenty-three years ago. John Padraig, his step-father, had a meeting with Naomi that day. He wrote that she thought someone was following her, and she'd sent home copies of all the documentation, just in case. She'd promised to tell him everything she knew.

That was the day they both died. A bomb had destroyed

the lab complex where they were meeting. After, when the toxic mold and the cover-up came to light, it had been pinned on Wes's father. Who had been conveniently dead. Unable to defend himself.

It had broken Mom's heart. First losing him like that, and then having him maligned and falsely accused. Mom had fought for years to clear his name. She'd given up in exhaustion, and died soon afterward.

The journal and the file were the weapons his dad could have used to clear himself, if he'd lived. Now it fell to Wes to follow through. He had to keep all of that firmly in mind. Particularly when Ronnie Moss was making his pulse race.

The Elvis waiting for them was chubby and florid, eyebrows penciled heavily in, sweat beading his forehead from the synthetic white sequined pantsuit. He had a deep, plummy voice with a Tennessee accent, and he smelled of Old Spice and bourbon.

Proceedings got underway. The ceremony was campy and kitsch, but Wes did not feel like he was participating in a joke. He felt like wire with the casing stripped.

He realized that Elvis was asking him to recite his vows. "Excuse me?"

Elvis rolled his eyes. "Do you, Weston Robert Brody, take this woman, Veronica Maud Moss, as your wedded wife, to have and to hold, from this day forward, for as long as you both shall live?" he repeated.

Ronnie had legally specified five years, not a lifetime, but for a brief second, he hesitated to lie to the guy, even though Ronnie had specifically asked him to do so. As if perjuring himself might bring bad luck.

He shook the emotion off by sheer force, and got back to business. "I do," he said.

Ronnie exhaled, giving him a relieved smile, while Elvis turned to her and recited the vows again.

"I do," she responded softly.

"I now pronounce you husband and wife!" Elvis announced. "You may now kiss the bride!"

Wes froze. They hadn't discussed the kiss, and he wasn't making any assumptions with this woman, whose hand he scarcely felt worthy to touch.

Elvis looked impatient. He made a get-on-with-it gesture with his heavily beringed hand.

Ronnie took matters into her own hands. She wound her arms around his neck, pulled his head to her face and kissed him.

Everything lit up when their lips touched. Everything he thought he was sure of was instantly called into question. Everything he believed was impossible might turn out to be real after all. Magic and mystery, bring it on. Anything was possible. Bring on Santa and the Easter Bunny, what the hell. He'd make room. There was infinite room inside him. He could see all the way to forever.

God, her lips were soft. Sweet. Her body felt pliant, hot and vibrant against his, head tilting back, the silky fall of her hair draping over his wrist where he clamped the small of her back, his fingers digging into the fine ivory silk of her suit coat.

He could kiss her forever. Feel the sensation of her high breasts, pressing against his chest, her mouth opening. That low, startled, questioning sound she made—

Elvis cleared his throat loudly. They swayed apart. Her face was red, lips parted. Her mascara-smudged eyes were full of complicated emotions.

What in holy hell had come over him?

That kiss had blown his mind so completely, he'd forgotten about his dad. The long years that Mom had mourned him. The pain and stress of his dad's disgrace, which had brought on Mom's premature death from heart failure.

Wes had been furiously angry about that. For years.

Now look at him. A brief kiss from a beautiful woman could make him forget everything. His sacred mission, *poof*, gone. Thinking with the little head.

God help him. Like he needed another thing to feel guilty and conflicted about.

Four

They signed documents as Fake Elvis belted out the second ballad she'd chosen at random to a distorted karaoke track. The man had a beautiful singing voice, deep and rich and resonant. She couldn't make out why she felt like this. Perched on the edge of a cliff so high, she couldn't see the ground.

The song was so overused, it had become meaningless. Or so she'd thought. With Wes next to her instead of Jareth, her perception shifted, and she heard it as if for the first time. The simplistic lyrics now seemed not trite, but poignant. The song sounded like a plea, a promise. It was full of hope, like a tiny candle flame in an immense darkness.

And it was making her cry. Damn. She couldn't get sappy, not with a guy she didn't know, who might be completely unbalanced. A guy who was doing her a dangerously lopsided favor, which put her at a huge disadvantage.

For nothing more than the entertainment value, and the vague hope of getting laid.

Ironic that she'd chosen this song, about tenderness and love and fidelity. She'd been so cut off from her own feelings. Tenderness was the key. It always had been. It was her missing piece. Her secret wound.

She'd gotten many things in life, wonderful things, to be grateful for. Wealth and privilege and opportunity, even a certain measure of fame and celebrity. But no tenderness. Not from her dad—that was certain. And she'd freely chosen Jareth, who wasn't tender either. After a while, he hadn't even pretended to be.

Why would she do that to herself? No wonder that song had always seemed silly to her.

Then Wes Brody appeared on the scene, teasing and clowning, paying her lavish compliments, kissing her hand, garlanding her with flowers, draping her in lace. Offering to help solve her complicated problems. Asking nothing in return but the pleasure of her company. Some men were just like that. They flirted, in the same unconscious, habitual way that they breathed.

Still, that kiss had shaken her, soul deep.

The last chord of the karaoke track faded away. The colorful disco lights ceased to spin. Ronnie tucked the bouquet into the crook of her elbow and clapped vigorously.

"Thank you," she told the singer. "That was beautiful. I'll never forget it."

Fake Elvis looked gratified. "My pleasure, Mrs. Brody."

Yikes. Mrs. Brody? That felt strange.

Outside the chapel, she looked up at the sky, breathing deep as the constricting, oppressive fear finally lifted. She'd done it. At what cost, she didn't know yet. But whatever the cost, she wouldn't force her cousins to pay it. Thank God…and Wes Brody.

Her phone buzzed, and she pulled it out. Speak of the devil. Twelve unanswered messages. Eight unanswered calls. Aunt Elaine, Caleb, Marcus, Maddie, Caleb's wife Tilda, biting their nails, as well they might be, with Moss-Tech hanging in the balance.

"Are they checking up on your marital status?" Wes asked.

She nodded and opened the group chat, entering, Safely married. Breathe easy.

She showed it to Wes. "Short, sweet and nonspecific," she said. "I'll tell them about you later. I don't feel like dealing with histrionics right now."

"One thing at a time," he said.

"Myra and Sam and Joseph all threatened to call my family, but I told them I'd fire them," she admitted. "Not that I actually would, but I put on a good show. They're furious with me. But I'm used to fury. I grew up in a house steeped in fury. I barely notice it."

"You don't deserve that," he said.

"How do you know that?" she asked, with a teasing smile. "I could be completely wicked. You don't know."

"Oh, but I do," he said. "You're as good as gold. I'm sure of it."

Her face went pink. "That's very sweet. And so was all of this." She lifted the veil, the bouquet. "White lace and flowers and rings. And just marrying me to begin with. You saved me from disaster and disgrace and life-long guilt."

"It was an honor and a privilege."

He sounded like he meant it. There she went again, all sentimental because of a few offhand, gallant remarks that cost him nothing.

Jareth had never pretended that marrying her was an honor or a privilege. He'd been too busy reminding her of what an honor and privilege it was to be chosen by him. What a lout. And this was the first time she'd finally seen it clearly. What in the hell had she been thinking?

Ronnie lifted the veil off her head, trying not to damage the flowers, and folded it over her arm. "Well. Guess I'd better go back to the hotel and get myself a new room. It's late. Shall we meet tomorrow morning for breakfast?"

"But you should celebrate," Wes said. "You pulled it off. Against all odds."

"No, you pulled it off," Ronnie said. "You saved my bacon."

"But you had the nerve to seize the opportunity," he insisted. "That was brave."

"You put such an attractive spin on everything," Ronnie said. "My lawyer saw it in a very different light. The poor guy almost had a stroke."

"How's this for an attractive spin? Come up to my room for dinner. No expectations on my part. Call your people, tell them where you'll be and the room number. Have them check in on you periodically. All I want is to wine you, dine you and make you laugh."

She giggled. "You're overdoing it, Wes."

"We should mark the occasion. We'll call the front desk and book you a new room. They can run a fresh key up to you while you're relaxing over your appetizers and wine."

Oh, hell with it. Agreeing to dinner seemed the least she could do, considering the hellfire and brimstone that he'd saved her from. "Just a glass of champagne," she hedged.

"Whatever. We've got a lot to talk about, now that we're husband and wife."

As if it were choreographed, his limo pulled up. She slid into the cushy leather seat. Wes joined her and took her hand. "I bet you haven't had anything to eat since before the speech."

"Actually, not since dinner last night," she admitted. "I'm always too wound up before a speaking gig. Just coffee. And those drinks we had at the bar."

He looked scandalized. "Good God, Ronnie. I'm surprised you're on your feet at all. Let me feed you."

"I am a bit hungry, now that I think about it."

The ride was short. On their way through the hotel lobby, Ronnie was grateful not to encounter anyone she knew. Her ugly interchange with Jareth had been horribly public. Word had certainly gotten around. People would draw their own conclusions as to why a recently dumped woman would return with a fresh man in tow, and none of those conclusions would flatter her.

But to hell with them all. She was a married woman. And even if she weren't, anyone who wanted to judge could sit on it and spin.

Wes pressed the button for the penthouse suites. The elevator had mirrored walls, showing every angle of her ravaged face. She dug into her bag for some makeup wipes and cleaned off the worst of the mascara smudges before the door slid open.

He used his key card to open his door, and beckoned her in.

Ronnie stopped short, and gasped.

The main room was lit up with what had to be a hundred candles. It was the only light in the room, other than the blaze of city lights in the picture window that opened onto the terrace. A lavish feast was set out on the table. Wine, champagne on ice, platters of tempting starters, silver lids covering up the entrées, fruit, salads.

There was even a wedding cake. It was miniature, three tiered, with a tiny bride and groom perched on the top. An enormous flower arrangement was the backdrop for the cake. The pale carpet was thickly strewed with white, pink and red rose petals.

"Wes," she whispered weakly.

"Kenji outdid himself," he said. "Do you like it?"

"Of course I do. It's romantic. Magical. It's just that… well, what part of 'business marriage' did you not understand, Wes? Did I give you the wrong idea?"

"How many times does a person get married in their lifetime? The occasion should be marked. A fuss should be made. I just married my celebrity science crush. That's worth a few rose petals. Shall we break out some champagne? I texted them to deliver dinner as we got into the limo, so the food should still be hot."

Ronnie was dazzled by the look in his eyes. Not just lust. She got plenty of that. Wes's gaze looked deeper, and some part of her couldn't help but hungrily look back.

Watch yourself, girl. Don't throw yourself over that cliff. You don't know him.

"Um… Wes?" she murmured. "You're not going to make me say it again, right?"

"I'll be the soul of propriety. Just let me pay tribute to your splendor. I see you, and my instinct is to fall to my knees and give thanks to a benevolent universe."

She laughed at him. "You are so full of crap."

"You betcha," he agreed cheerfully. "Blarney, my mom called it. The goal was to make her smile, at any cost. It wasn't always easy. I had to work like a bastard sometimes to make it happen."

Ronnie hesitated. "She had…troubles?"

"After my dad died, yeah. There was a long stretch with no laughing. But I kept at it. I made it my business to make her smile. I had it down to an art."

"What a good son," she murmured.

He popped the cork on the champagne bottle and

poured. He passed her a glass with a flourish. “Can I take your jacket? I’ll get you a plate of starters.”

She hesitated before she let the jacket slip off her shoulders. Beneath it, she wore a low-cut ivory silk camisole with delicate lace insets. The room was warm, but she felt so bare, so vulnerable. She instinctively shrugged her hair forward, like a shawl.

The appetizers were delicious. Seared langoustines, morel mushrooms, foie gras croutons, delicately pan-fried crab cakes with mango-papaya salsa. Every bite tasted divine. The champagne was delicious and fizzy and cold.

But what she really wanted was more about him. He was a tantalizing mystery.

She licked the fruity salsa off her fingers and studied his face. “How old were you when your dad died?” she asked. “If you don’t mind me asking.”

“Almost ten,” he said.

She winced. “I’m sorry you lost him so soon. Same with me and my mom.”

“How old were you when it happened?”

“I was seven,” she said.

He nodded. “That’s very young to be motherless.”

She nodded. “I had to fight for my memories. My father was furious after she died. He thought she’d betrayed him in some way, so he didn’t want to remember her, or to let me remember her. He burned all the pictures of her, and all her personal things.”

His eyes widened. “Good God, Ronnie.”

“But Aunt Elaine and Uncle Bertram had some pictures, and some home movies they’d filmed that featured her and me, as a baby and a toddler. They made a video for me. So that I would at least know what her voice sounded like.”

“I love them for doing that,” he said.

She savored a wild mushroom. "Me, too. Do you remember your father well?"

"Not as well as I would like. Certain things. He was a tough guy. Kind, but stern. We butted heads. I got into trouble as a kid. I broke windows, got into fights, went places I was told not to go. We got into it. After he died, I felt guilty for a long time for being such a naughty little jerk. I wished I'd been a better boy for him."

"He wouldn't have wanted you to feel guilty. If he was kind, like you say."

"I like to think so. I know how hard it is to keep a memory vivid. Now it feels like one of those stars in the sky that you can only see when you're not staring straight at it. I'll get a random flash. The way the light hits a room, a familiar smell, a man wearing a hat like Dad wore, and for a second, I've got him. Then poof…gone again."

"Yes," she said. "Yes, that's how it is for me, too."

He served her the next course, as tempting as the last. Warm artichoke panache, poached green asparagus with balsamic vinaigrette, baked lobster and squash manicotti. Every bite superb. Her appetite had awakened. No sound but the clink of forks.

"I had no idea how hungry I was," she said.

"I'm glad you're enjoying it," he said, refilling her glass. "I chose the hotel for the chef. Hedonist that I am."

"You do treat yourself well," she said. "How did you get started at being a venture capitalist?"

"My dad's life insurance was the seed money," he said. "It was a generous payout. Mom managed it well. It covered my education, and there was some left over, so I played with it." He gave her a crooked smile. "And for the most part, I won."

"Lucky you," she commented.

"I guess." He looked at the locket at her throat. "Is the locket a sentimental piece?"

She touched the trinket that always hung at her throat. "Yes," she admitted. "And if it looks like something a seven-year-old might wear, that's because it is. My mother gave it to me before she left for Sri Lanka. That last trip." She snapped open the latch and showed the photo of Naomi Moss that her mother had cut to size and tucked inside it. "So that I could look at her anytime I wanted and remember how much she loved me, until she came home. But she never made it back."

He looked away for a moment. "Damn, Ronnie," he said.

"Sorry," she murmured. "You asked."

He wiped his eyes. "I did," he agreed, leaning closer. "May I?"

She nodded, and he lifted it up to look at the photo. "She looks exactly like you."

"So they tell me," she said. "I can't see it. But I suspect that's why my father has so much trouble with me. He looks at me and sees her."

Wes snapped the locket shut and rested it against her throat. "That's unfair."

"Maybe so, but I have now exceeded my quota of bitching about people who have done me wrong," she said. "They will not define my life. I'll be fine, even without *The Secret Life of Cells*."

"Without it?" He sounded alarmed. "What do you mean, without it? They're not canceling the show, are they? Why would they do that?"

"Jareth was one of my producers. He's the Fadden in Fadden Boyle Productions. He canceled it to punish me."

"What an asshole! He'll regret that."

"I hope so," she said. "I had ideas and scripts ready for

another three seasons' worth of shows. Who knows, maybe I can eventually take it to another production company. I need to meet with my entertainment lawyers, and pore over my contract."

"Go to all lengths necessary," he said. "I don't know how you do it, but you make cell biology sexy."

"Thank you," she said. "I loved doing it. It seemed like I could do more good by fostering science literacy in kids than I could working in MossTech's research and development department. I loved that feeling. Like I had a real mission."

"You have to continue," he said. "The world needs it. And I'll make it my personal business to see that you do."

Heat rushed into her face. "Gee, thanks," she said demurely. "One thing at a time, though."

He nodded and stroked the wedding ring on her hand with his fingertip. "It looks nice on you," he said.

"Yours, too." She smiled at him. "It's certainly more comfortable than Jareth's engagement ring. I'm so grateful that I don't have to wear the damn thing anymore. I have to get it back to him, ASAP."

"You didn't like that ring?" He sounded surprised. "It was such a big, impressive rock."

"Sure it was, but the setting ruined all my favorite clothes," she said. "And it never felt at home on my hand."

"Out of curiosity, if you were to pick the perfect ring, what would it be?"

"Pearls," she said promptly. "I love pearls. They're alive. But Jareth hated that idea. He said, 'Pearls just don't pack a punch.' Now that I think of it, that's why I prefer them. They don't glitter. They glow, like the moon. They're formed inside a living organism. I'm a biologist, so I love it that a sea animal created something so perfect inside its own body. It makes me feel connected to the sea, and the animal world."

"Pearls," he murmured. "Duly noted."

She was alarmed. "I wasn't hinting that you get me a ring! Don't even think about it. I'm already far too much in your debt and I have no way to repay you."

"Don't worry about it," he soothed. "It's a random question. A get-to-know-you game. Like that stuff you do on social media when you're procrastinating. Take this quiz to see what jungle animal are you, what flavor of potato chip, which kind of cheese, which Beatle, which Hogwarts House. That kind of thing. I'm just establishing your baseline."

"Ah." She settled into her chair again, cautiously mollified. "Okay."

Wes refilled her champagne glass. "A toast," he said. "To last-minute fixes. To eleventh-hour solutions. To unexpected saves."

She raised her own glass. "To new friends."

"Hell, yeah." They clinked glasses. The sweet bell tone of the crystal glass was diamond sharp, like all her heightened perceptions.

Their eyes locked, and her face heated. "No giving me that look, Wes."

"Sorry," he said. "How about we distract ourselves? With wedding cake?"

She was grateful for the change of subject, and the wedding cake was a marvel of miniature artistry. Three tiers, the bottom around eight inches in diameter, then a five-inch, and on top, one the size of a cupcake. All three were clothed in chocolate fondant, dark, milk, white and ruby chocolate, marbled together. The miniature bride and groom on top, the size of plastic toy soldiers, held hands. Smiles were painted on their tiny faces.

"It's adorable," she said. "A shame to cut into."

"Inside is a dark moist chocolate cake of smoked Peruvian chocolate with a hint of rum. Sounded decadent and good. Just one more little detail, since it is now—" he glanced at his watch "—midnight plus three minutes." He opened a little box next to the cake, which was full of tall, thin white candles. "I asked for them to provide thirty," he said, inserting them into the perfectly marbled frosting until the small cake had a close-set crown of candles. "Tonight, it's all about candles."

Ronnie was moved. Jareth never thought to mark her birthday, and certainly her father hadn't, so it never occurred to her to celebrate it. "Wes, that's so sweet!"

"Oh, but it will be." He used the candle lighter the hotel had provided to light them. The flickering ring of delicate, ethereal candles looked beautiful, like flower stems.

He smiled at her over the flickering light. "Make a wish."

The wish made itself, but she pushed it away. It was childish, unrealistic. It should be enough to just enjoy a lovely evening with an attractive man who made her feel good. It would be silly to grab for more, even in the privacy of her mind. She had to let tonight be tonight, and just enjoy it. She blew the candles out.

Wes laid out two dessert plates that had been provided and passed her the knife. She took out the candles, and sliced two wedges from the bottom tier, offering one to Wes.

"Don't we have to do that ritual where we feed each other wedding cake? Isn't that a ceremonial necessity? About nourishing each other, and all that good stuff?"

She lifted an eyebrow. "We don't need to put on a show for anyone."

"So let's put on a show for ourselves. Don't we deserve to be entertained, too?"

Hah. She was more than entertained. Wes Brody was walking seduction. If she started hand-feeding him bites of dessert, she would be taking one more shuffling step toward the abyss. Or more like a giant, stumbling stride.

But she was in the game now. "Hold still," she said, scooping up a bite of cake. It was tender and goopy, and she had to get both cake and frosting on the end of the fork.

Wes accepted the bite. His eyes closed, and he let out a growl of pleasure. "Oh, wow," he murmured. "Sensual. Complex. Aromatic. Addictive."

Everything she could say in response felt suggestive and flirtatious.

Wes scooped up a forkful of cake and held it up for her.

It was a marvelous burst of flavors. The chocolate was deep and bold and smoky, the cake melting, tender and buttery, the frosting creamy, with delicate aromas of cinnamon and rum, and behind it, a faint hint of fiery pepper and sea salt.

But she kept her eyes shut. She couldn't look at him. It felt like total exposure. As if she were naked, letting him watch while she touched herself intimately.

Where did that erotic thought come from? That vivid thought was the final step. Over the cliff she went. She wasn't going to deny herself this experience.

She opened her eyes and stared at the naked desire in his face. Unafraid of it, because it mirrored her own.

It was a moment outside of time, outside of the rules and expectations that had governed her life; the *should*s and the *can't*s and the *absolutely not*s. They melted away into nothing as shimmering awareness filled the air. It stole through her, lighting her up. Making her feel weightless, buoyant, larger-than-life.

The movement was imperceptible, but suddenly they were closer to each other. So close, the slightest movement would make them touch.

She liked this distance. The glint of beard stubble, the faint bump on his nose, the sweeping line of the hairs of his straight eyebrows. The sexy points of his square jaw. His lips were full, well shaped, sensual. His lashes were thick, on heavy-lidded dark eyes.

She couldn't resist any longer. She leaned forward, pressing a swift, exploratory kiss against his lips, and rocked back, shocked at herself.

Just a brief contact, but her lips felt a hot, tingling glow, and a sweet ache for more.

Wes looked startled. "Ronnie," he said. "This isn't what you said before."

"I changed my mind," she said.

They gazed at each other for a breathless moment, and then he slowly reached out to her face. He cupped her cheek, slid his hand into her hair, making a sound low in his throat, an incoherent groan as he pulled her close and kissed her.

It started out tentative, and then bloomed into something hotter, sweeter, wetter. Hunger surged. It made her want to whimper and cling, to plead for more of him.

Wes let go, unsteady. His face was flushed. "Whoa," he said. "We have now reached the far end my self-control, so you should get in touch with the front desk. Get yourself a room. We'll talk tomorrow, in the café, over coffee. Where it's safe."

"Not necessary," she said.

His eyes narrowed. "Meaning?"

She felt brazen, reckless. She'd blasted past all her limits. She was out in no-man's-land. Free to be anything, do anything, all night long. "I'm not going anywhere."

"Help me out here, Ronnie," he said.

"You said it yourself," she said. "How many wedding nights does a person have in one's life? The occasion should be marked, right? A fuss should be made."

He cleared his throat. "But this is the direct opposite of what you said before. So I just need to be sure that you—"

"I'm sure," she said.

"I feel like I've always known you," he said. "It's like I've been waiting for you. I know it sounds corny, like a cheesy pickup line, but I swear, it's true. No blarney, no bullshit. I have never felt anything like this."

"I feel it, too," she said simply.

"But that doesn't mean we have to race forward top speed," he said. "We can take it slow. You can't walk this back, once we do the deed. It could be like a massive landslide. We could wake up and find ourselves in a different life. All the rules changed."

She placed her hand over his. "I like the way that life looks."

"You won't feel like I pressured you, after? I don't want you to think that I—"

She put her finger on his lips. "Just kiss me."

Five

Wes was under her spell, commanded by some absolute authority deep inside him that could not be gainsaid. He'd once gotten caught in a riptide while surfing. This felt similar, but this time, he wasn't struggling to swim free, or fighting to stay above water. He was letting the wave pull him wherever it wanted him to go.

Take me. Own me.

The kiss was urgent, desperate. Like they were dying of thirst, and this was the first water they'd seen. Her lips were sweet and ardent. He stroked the perfect, elegant curve of her spine, the flare of her hip.

She pulled back, tugging the silk camisole out of her pants, and pulling it off over her head. She flung it away, and tossed her hair, her eyes dazed with arousal. Lips red from kissing, parted from panting. She kicked off her shoes. Her body was so perfect. Those high, plump breasts in the flesh-toned satin bra begged for his palms to caress them.

"You're so beautiful," he said. "I just can't help bleating that out over and over. It blows my circuits."

She looked him up and down, her gaze lingering on the erection straining against his pants. "The necessary circuits appear to be working just fine."

"Nope, no problem there. I don't have any diseases, by the way. I don't expect you to trust my word, but I could fish my last bloodwork results out of my email, if you want, and show you the—"

"I trust your word," she said.

Her words reverberated inside him like a bell. He was moved by her trust, but the more she trusted him, the worse it would be when his hidden agenda came to light.

Tell her. Just tell her now. Everything.

It trembled on the tip of his tongue. But as he opened his mouth to blurt it all out, Ronnie laughed. "Good heavens, Wes. You look like you're afraid of me. I don't bite."

"You're perfect," he said softly.

She let out a snort. "You'll know the real me soon enough." She seized his tie. "Until then, bask in my fictitious, fleeting perfection. I'll enjoy it while I can."

There were so many ways he could reply to that. He wanted to tell her that she could be perfect without having to be perfect, but that sounded ridiculous. She unhooked the front of her white trousers and let them drop to the floor.

She unfastened the front clasp of her bra and lifted it off. Sweet holy God. Her breasts were rosy and high and pointed, little hot pink nipples, taut and hard. She hooked her fingers into the side of her boy shorts and tugged them over her hips. She had a sweet, ginger-toned swatch of ringlets over her mound.

There she was, in just a wedding ring, and her mother's locket.

Her eyes were full of amusement as she waited. "Well, Wes," she said. "As opening gambits go, I don't know what more to do to convince you that I'm up for this. Short of tying you to the bed."

He cleared his throat as he wrenched his tie loose. "That won't be necessary."

"I also have a clean bill of health and thank you for bringing it up. Before I came to Vegas, I thought it right to check my health status before I got married. Fresh starts, new beginnings, that kind of thing. I haven't been with Jareth since months before that, for various reasons. Also, I'm on the pill. So there's that."

"Wait," he said. "Months? How on earth?" His mind had seized upon the most incomprehensible bit of random information in that list.

"I haven't seen him in a while," she admitted. "We've both been extremely busy professionally."

"You were wasted on a self-satisfied clod like him," he said.

"Hmm. I can't say I disagree, but I'm afraid of what that says about my judgment."

"Nothing," he said. "The spell is broken. We hereby close the door on him. This is a private party, and he's not invited."

That earned him a smile. "Charming, as always," she said. "And yet, despite all your brave words, you're fully clothed. What gives, Weston Robert Brody?"

She shook her hair back. The locket gleamed, and the candlelight painted the tender curves and hollows and swells of her body with a dim, gold-toned glow.

He jerked open the buttons of his shirt, his fingers

clumsy with eagerness. "Just letting you take the lead," he offered.

"That's a lovely thought, but don't lag too far behind. I wouldn't want to lose you." She reached out and pulled the buckle of his belt loose. "Pick up the pace, mister. You have husbandly duties to perform."

Oh, sweet, sweet husbandly duties. He got the cuffs loose and unfastened his pants. Ronnie drifted around behind him like a graceful ghost, moving silently on bare feet, and lifted his shirt off his shoulders. She let out a sigh, her smooth fingers running over his shoulders, sending shivers over his skin. "You're beautiful," she whispered.

He shucked his pants and briefs as he turned to face her. Stark naked.

Ronnie's gaze slid along his body. Over his shoulders and chest, his belly, his groin. His aching erection, jutting hopefully in her direction.

"Well," she murmured. "You look ready for anything."

"I've been fielding this erection on and off since the moment you walked out on the stage this morning," he admitted.

Ronnie laughed softly. "Aw. How sweet."

"Not the adjective I'd choose, but whatever."

He took her hand, and lifted it to his lips, pressing a kiss against her knuckles. Then he pressed it against his chest. "You're safe with me," he told her. "Absolutely in control. This is all for you. All for your pleasure."

Her eyes dropped, the brilliant blue veiled with the long, sooty dark lashes. "All?" she said, her voice throaty, as her hands slid lower, and then lower still, into the tangle of dark hair between his legs, grasping the shaft of his penis and squeezing it tenderly. "There's…um…a lot of you."

"Not much I can do about that," he said, and then caught

his breath, choking off a groan. He wanted her to feel powerful, pampered, adored. "But I'll make it work for you."

Wes kissed her hungrily, stopping from time to time to gasp for air at the wild sensations that jolted through his body with each slow, sensual caress. He could hardly believe she was real. So warm and smooth. Over her shoulder, he admired the stunning view reflected in the picture window. That hair swinging at the small of her back. The curves of her bottom. Perfect.

She let go of his penis to wrap her arms around his neck with a low, incoherent whimper of need. Wrapping her leg around his thighs. He followed her lead and lifted her up, holding her backside so that she straddled him.

Best feeling on earth, to have that deliciously scalding hot, secret, wet female flesh pressed against his aching rod. He held her right where she needed to be, so she could move, stroking the tender pleasure points up and down his shaft. A tantalizing taste of the deeper contact that would follow. She arched, in trusting abandon, reaching with one hand to grip him. Holding him more firmly against herself as she pulsed her hips against him. "Can I?" she asked, breathlessly. "Do you mind if I—"

"Please," he choked out. "Best thing in the world. It's killing me, but don't stop."

She laughed under her breath, through the panting eagerness as she voluptuously pleasured herself against him. Head flung back, eyes shut, her lower lip caught between her teeth. Her panting turned to whimpers as the tension built…and built…

And broke, explosively. She arched and he caught her, holding her tight as she abandoned herself to pleasure. Sobbing at the wild intensity of it.

He watched her come with fascination. It was long and

delicious, and it finally faded to a subtle, rippling throb. Her body was limp and soft, trusting.

The intimacy made him feel awestruck, humbled. And so aroused he could barely breathe.

"My God," she whispered. "My God, Wes. What the hell was that?"

He nuzzled her neck, licking away the sweat. "I'd call that a promising beginning."

Finally, she lifted her head, and stroked his flexed biceps with a low murmur of approval. "Aren't you getting tired of holding me up like this?"

"I could hold you up forever," he said. "But I'd like to use my hands to touch some other parts of you. Not that holding your ass isn't absolutely the high point of my entire life. It's silky and round. Perfect as a peach. But there are other places I want to explore."

"Do you have any particular destinations in mind?" she murmured teasingly.

That smile on her face made him euphoric. "I intend to leave no part untouched."

"Well," she said, "in that case, put me down."

He set her onto her feet, and sank to his knees, nuzzling her belly. It felt right, to be in this position, unthreatening, paying tribute to her beauty, passionately appreciative. As a bonus, he got a good, close look at her beautiful smooth thighs and that swatch of hair. Her sweet, hot scent. Intoxicating.

She looped her arms around his neck as he embraced her hips, pressing her closer. His face to her belly. He put his hand on the inside of her knee and stroked slowly upward, glancing up. "May I?" he asked.

She gave him a jerky nod. Her hands shook as his fingers brushed her slick, hot core. He caressed the whole length of the seam of her labia, up…and down. Slowly, tenderly massaging that taut little bud of nerves hidden in her secret flesh.

He slid his fingers inside her clinging wet warmth, swirling and flicking with his thumb. Swirl…and flick. "I want to lick you," he said. "You're the most beautiful thing I've ever seen. Is that all right with you?"

"Do you want to go to the bed?" she asked. "My knees are like jelly. I don't think I can stay on my feet."

He swept her into his arms, which made her laugh. Every giggle felt like a win. So did every orgasm. He'd just keep racking up points, as long as he could. Until he…well.

For as long as he could. He'd just leave it at that. He shoved the painful and unwanted thought away and slammed the door on it.

The king-size bed in the next room was heaped with rose petals, the bed turned down. A long-stemmed red rose lay on the pillow. Nice touch. Kenji knew his stuff.

He set her on the sheet and shoved the puffy comforter to the side, sending petals scattering in every direction. He stroked her hair, draping it over the pillow. Her eyes were shadowy pools of mystery. Her locket gleamed in the dim light.

Their eyes locked. They were completely in tune. If it weren't for his secret agenda, this would be perfect. A peak life moment to burn into his memory forever.

Her brows drew together. "What is it?" she asked. "Is something wrong?"

Damn, now she could read his mind, too. "No," he lied. "Nothing's ever been so right. I just feel…unworthy." True enough. All things considered.

But Ronnie shook her head, smiling. "You're wonderful," she said softly.

He hid his face against her throat. The locket felt hot and smooth against his lips. Her skin was so cloud soft. He kept his eyes shut as he made his way hungrily along her sweet body with his lips, taking his time, exploring every curve, every hollow. He lingered for a long time at her breasts, licking and sucking them delicately as he stroked between her thighs. Seeking out the spots that made her sob with pleasure.

She came apart around his hand, clutching his fingers. Best sensation on earth.

Well, almost the best, but only one thing could top it. And he was getting there. Taking his own sweet time, doing it right, making her come, making it count. Over and over. That was the way. Keep the bad thoughts away. Allow nothing but pleasure.

She was so limp and relaxed after that last orgasm, she barely noticed him parting her legs, folding them high and wide so he could admire every detail of that perfect flowerlike female beauty. He settled between her thighs and put his mouth to her sweet, tender bits, worshipping them. Lapping up her magic balm. His senses overwhelmed. Systems on override. He couldn't think about inner conflict. He couldn't think at all.

That was the trick. Just spend all his time like this. In heaven.

Time slipped loose of its moorings and they drifted in a dreamlike state. Intoxicated with her flavor and scent, her texture, the sounds of her low voice vibrating through her body as he pleased her. Her silky texture. The tiny shivers of delight that vibrated through her.

The energy was slowly building to another climax. He settled in to make it an explosive one. Building her up, then easing her back, again and again. Letting her hover near the brink, over and over, until finally she'd had enough torment.

She grabbed his hair, silently demanding that he finish,

so he did, with passionate enthusiasm. Fireworks, delicious and pulsing, right against his mouth.

She cried out, shivering with her helpless response.

He cuddled up afterward, gathering her limp body into the shelter of his arms, pulling the comforter over her. His body throbbed with urgency, but he was goddamn well waiting until it was the right time, the right move. With this woman, he would take nothing for granted. He would treat her like blown glass.

He buried his nose in her fragrant hair and inhaled her sweet scent until her pulse slowed, and her breathing calmed. Finally, she shifted, snuggling against him.

"And?" Her voice was dry and husky from the panting. "What about you?"

"What about me? I'm in heaven. You're spectacular. I love making you come. It makes me feel like a total sex god. I love it. I could specialize in this. Sign me up."

She chuckled as she slid her hand over his belly and then tangled her fingers in his pubic hair. She stroked his stiff, aching penis.

"And what shall we do about this?"

He dropped a kiss on her forehead. "Whatever you feel like doing," he said lightly. "Your call. Do what you want with it. Or not. You could sleep now and I'd still be happy. Or you could use me like your own personal sex toy." He rolled over, putting his hands behind his head. "Like I said. I'm at your service."

She tilted her head thoughtfully. "Are you playing games with me? What is that?"

"I'll tell you what this is," he said. "One, it's me keeping my ass covered. Two, it's the fulfillment of my wildest dreams. You, climbing aboard me, pleasuring yourself with my body…yeah. If that's a game, then yes, let's play games. I just intend for you to win every last one of them."

She tossed the comforter off, and climbed on top of him, throwing her leg over him. "I will take you up on your generous offer to be my sex toy."

Wes looked up at Ronnie, swaying over him, backlit by the candlelight, and the spangled city lights outside. Her hair brushed and tickled his belly, his chest.

He struggled to keep his voice from shaking. "I'm all yours," he said.

Six

Ronnie stared at him, stretched out beneath her. He clasped her waist with his huge, strong, but exquisitely gentle hands, waiting for her cue.

She felt so odd. As light as air. Lit up and floating, like a lantern. Every bit of her glowed with a hot, total awareness, as if every cell of her body was sexually aroused, from her toenails to the tips of her hair.

And it felt so good.

So different from her other experiences. Not that there were many. She'd concluded long ago that she must be one of those people for whom sex wasn't a top priority. Which, oddly enough, was one reason she'd originally thought that a match with Jareth might actually work. Because it had soon become evident to her that it wasn't much of a priority for him, either. He was a busy man, lots on his mind. So she thought, okay. They'd be a cerebral couple. A marriage of the minds.

She felt anything but cerebral with Wes. She felt hot, carnal. And she loved it.

Wes cupped her breasts tenderly. “You’re so gorgeous.”

“You’re pretty fine yourself,” she told him, touching that stiff, thick phallus lying against his taut belly.

Wow, that was a lot of aroused man, but she wasn’t intimidated by his size. She relished it. He made her feel hungry. Greedy.

Wes gripped himself at the base, holding his shaft up. “Like this?”

“Perfect,” she said, poised over him, sliding her hand over the smooth, hot surface of his glans, making him shudder and groan. “It’s okay?”

“Heaven,” he ground out. “Everything you do. Perfect.”

Well, great. So she could do no wrong. She swayed over him, undulating as she captured him. Petting herself with him…and then slowly…slowly…sinking down…and taking him deep inside.

The two of them made the same sharp, panting sound, between a sob and a moan.

She braced herself against his chest, unable to move, but Wes instinctively shifted, making it all perfect, effortless, delicious for her. He gripped her waist, angling himself, and they settled into a slow, pumping rhythm. Gliding, slick, fabulous.

She melted around him. His thick shaft caressed her inside, a slow, sensual lick, caressingly stroking over and over her unexpected new sweet spots. Maddening, tantalizing, sweet. It drove her wild.

Her nails dug into his chest. She incited him with whispered gasps to pick up the pace. He gripped her hands, deepening his strokes as they both sought that tantalizing promise of bliss, like a shining trail that glowed in her head, brighter and brighter, terrifying, inevitable.

It crashed through her. She was lost to the world. Pure delight blazed through her, body and soul.

After, her face was pressed against his damp chest. It rose and fell, but she still heard his heart, thumping madly against her cheek.

She lifted her face, gazing into his dark eyes. He looked somber. No dimples, no joking around.

"And…how are you?" she asked.

"Flattened," he said. "It's never been like that for me. I mean, I love sex. Always have. Tons of fun. What's not to love? But I never, you know. Felt myself dissolve into stardust or anything like that. I think I passed out. That was wild. Deep."

"Me, too," she admitted. "Is that a good thing? For you? The stardust, and all?"

His lips twitched, and his penis, still inside her, stiffened afresh. "I'm great."

"I love it," she told him.

His arms tightened around her. "Thank God," he said. "The stakes felt so high."

She felt moved, realizing that he felt insecure, too. He seemed so confident.

She shifted on top of him. "Do you want to go for round two?"

"I'm always ready, but I don't want to get greedy," he said. "Let's not overdo it."

"And leave me high and dry?" she teased, her body clenching jealously around him. "Though I'm anything but dry." She slid off him, lying on her side, her thigh flung over his, and tugged at him. "You on top this time," she told him.

"You sure?" he asked.

"I crave it," she said. "I love how hard and solid and hot

you are. I want to hold you with my arms and legs. Give in to my voracious desires, Wes. Don't make me wait."

He rolled obligingly on top of her, still mostly inside, and reorganized their bodies. Him on his knees, her arched back, legs folded wide. Stroking her clitoris cleverly with his thumb as he thrust inside her.

She shivered and sighed, abandoning herself to pure sensation. Bracing her feet against his chest as he skillfully teased her into another orgasm.

After that, he kissed her slowly and sensually as he pulsed slowly inside her.

"You okay if I finish now?" he asked.

That was a question she'd never even known a man could ask. Wes had a level of skill, self-awareness and self-control that she'd never encountered before.

"That's fine," she said. "I'm in a state of perfect grace. I just want to watch you come. The last time I was too overcome to even pay attention."

"You got it," he said. "Tell me if it's too much."

And they started up again, eyes locked. Bit by bit, the movements deepened. Urgent, slick, hot. Against all expectations, she felt that charge of pleasure start to build.

Wes sensed it, of course, and shifted, instinctively hitting just the angle that she needed to nudge her closer to the brink, stroking her while he stared into the depths of her soul. That marvelous, melting vortex was opening up for her, pulling her into a wild, chaotic storm of passion.

Sometime later, she stirred against him. They were a damp tangle of limbs. She dropped a kiss on his big shoulder. "Um…" she murmured. "I think a shower is in order."

"Can I join you?"

She started smiling at him and realized she couldn't stop. "Sure."

The shower in his suite was huge, faced with black marble, with multiple showerheads at every angle. She tried twisting her hair up into a knot as she sudsed up under the jets of water, but it came from every direction, plus she was wildly distracted by the glorious spectacle of Wes Brody, naked and wet. All that lovely width and breadth and bulk of him, all that cut, defined muscle. To say nothing of his magnificent erection.

He followed her gaze. "Down, boy. Think of it as a tribute to your female power. It doesn't matter how tired I am. One glance at you, and whammo, I'm ready."

"Do you want to—"

"No, no. We'll take a rest. There's more where that came from, and there'll be more tomorrow, too. And the day after that. Here, let me rinse you."

His clever hands, slick with foamy soap, caressed her expertly under the pounding water. Before she knew it, she was squirming around his hand, her hair clinging to her shoulders, soaked in the spray as she worked herself into a deliciously melting climax.

She was floating, weak in the knees, clinging to his shoulders as Wes rinsed off the soap. He toweled her off, still dripping, dragging the fluffy towel carefully all over every inch of her skin before he dried himself off.

"Sorry," he said into her ears. "That was a crime of opportunity. You felt so good. Hot and pink and perfect. All that slippery soap. Too much for me."

"I forgive you," she told him.

"Hey, it just occurred to me that there's a whole lot of tasty food on the buffet table, and the champagne's still in the ice bucket. The food's cold, but I don't care."

That idea sounded excellent, to the point of daring to put weight on her wobbly knees. They swathed themselves in the terrycloth robes the hotel had provided and made their way through drifts of rose petals and scattered clothing to the living area.

The food was even better the second time around. The icy cold champagne tasted like the elixir of the gods. Artichoke tarts, peppers rolled around creamy cheese, red olive paste spread on crusty bread, the tray of cheeses, the leftover manicotti…delicious. Her usually spotty appetite felt like a blast furnace. Between the two of them, they polished off most of the food, and nibbled on another piece of cake. So good.

Afterward, Ronnie opened the door to the veranda, and strolled out to lean on the railing, looking at the wild, clashing colors of Las Vegas.

Wes followed her and leaned on the railing beside her. She glanced around, taking note of the architectural design that protected them from the view of anyone else on the top floor of the hotel. Luckily. Considering what she had in mind.

"So," he said, in a neutral, careful voice. "Do you feel as if the occasion of your wedding night has been marked appropriately? Has an adequate fuss been made?"

She gave him a teasing smile. "What do you think?"

"Not what I asked," he countered. "I'm sticking with my original question."

"Are you feeling insecure, Wes?"

He shrugged. "Maybe. I'm human, and this is important. Tell me how you feel."

She leaned against his shoulders. "I have never felt like this in my life," she told him. "I didn't know sex could be this good. But this is the thing."

"What's the thing?" he demanded.

"You've awakened some part of me that's sexually insatiable," she informed him. "Now, you have to deal with it. You'll have your work cut out for you, satisfying my voracious appetites."

He looked delighted. "How voracious are we talking? Just to get an idea."

"Ravenous," she said emphatically. "A panther on the prowl."

"Awesome," he said, as she jerked the sash of his robe loose. It fell open, and she closed her hand around him, enjoying the throb of his heartbeat against her palm.

"I know you think it's more gentlemanly to let me rest," she said. "But I don't want you to be a gentleman right now."

"I'll be however you want me to be."

She shrugged off her own robe. She felt so hot, the chilly breeze against her damp hair was intensely stimulating. She turned her back to him. Bending at the waist, arching her spine. Parting her legs. "So?" she prompted. "Fulfill me."

"You got it," he rasped, reaching for her.

Seven

Something tickled Wes's nose as he floated up to full consciousness. Light, against his eyelids. With every breath, he felt a faint tickle.

He opened his eyes and saw rose petals fluttering as he exhaled.

He was alone in the bed.

He sat up quickly, looking around in irrational panic. Ronnie wasn't in the bedroom. He didn't hear movement in the front room. He didn't hear water running in the shower. Just silence. Shit. She'd panicked. Bolted.

The intense depth of his disappointment startled him.

He slid out of bed, hesitating for just a moment before heading into the main room.

That night had been astonishing. White-hot. But he'd known she might panic and withdraw from that intensity. It was a classic move.

They barely knew each other, after all, and last night

had laid them bare. He'd felt more known and seen by her than he'd ever felt. Dangerous secrets notwithstanding.

He kicked away bruised rose petals as he strode through the room. The candles had burned down over the course of the night. It was late morning. Evidence of their late-night feast was everywhere. His clothes were still scattered around the floor, but Ronnie's shoes, pants, jacket, purse, all gone. His heart sank lower.

The towering flower arrangement and rose petals seemed to taunt him. She'd left the bridal bouquet behind, still in the vase that Kenji had selected for it, as well as the box that held her folded flower wreath and veil.

Evidently, she didn't plan to conserve it as a keepsake. That hurt.

The bathroom door flew open. He spun around with a gasp.

Ronnie stood in the bathroom door, looking dewy and fresh, dressed in yesterday's white suit. Her hair was brushed out, loose and wavy and gleaming.

She looked bright-eyed and rosy, considering how little sleep she'd gotten.

"Good morning," she said. "You look startled. Were you expecting someone else?"

"I just thought..." His voice trailed off.

"Thought what?"

He shrugged self-consciously. "You were nowhere to be found, and I didn't see your clothes or purse, so I thought..."

"That I panicked? After the most fabulous night of my whole life? Hah. You'd need a crowbar to pry me away." She held up her purse. "I took my purse into the bathroom because it had my makeup wipes and brush and mascara and emergency lipstick. And I had to rescue my clothes from the floor and recycle them."

"We could order you some clothes," he suggested. "If you want fresh stuff. There's a boutique in the hotel. More than one, I think."

"What I want is to retrieve my suitcase from Jareth's room. But I don't want to engage with him right now." She took her smartphone out of her purse and scrolled on the screen. "Yep, eight calls from him last night. Texts, too."

"What does he want?"

"To know where the hell I am, and when I'm coming back," she said.

"A) none of his goddamn business, and B) not in this lifetime," he said.

"Exactly. But I will try to be classy, if I can," she said.

"I bet you he's not in the room," Wes said. "He's out prowling the hotel, hoping to run into you. He's realized that he miscalculated, so he's too agitated to sit in his room. He's been awake all night, worrying about it. Now he's trying to track down his errant heiress. He wants to herd her into the barn, where he thinks she belongs."

She winced. "Ouch. I suspect that's a pretty accurate assessment of his attitude."

"Let's go now," he suggested. "I'll knock, and if he answers, I'll say I'm delivering the travel crib that he requested for his baby. If he doesn't answer, just go in and grab your stuff. I'll stand guard outside to make sure he doesn't surprise you."

She looked troubled. "Why do I feel like I'm stealing?"

"Because from his point of view, you are," he said. "You're taking back something that actually belongs to you. Something he thought he owned. Your life, your choices, your freedom. He's liable to be ugly about it. By the way, who booked the room?"

"Me. It was my idea, and therefore, my expense. Jareth isn't much for treating."

He grunted in disapproval. "All the more reason to check him out of the room. Freeloading asshat." He pulled on some jeans. "I'll get dressed, and we'll get your stuff."

He tossed on a sweatshirt, shoved his feet into some shoes, and they were on their way. In the elevator, he took her hand. It was cold and clammy as they went up to the penthouse floor. He hated it that she felt nervous about running into that worthless tool. He wished he could take Jareth aside for a talk before she saw him. Give him a remedial lesson in manners. A pointed lesson.

She stopped by one of the doors in the hallway and pulled out the key card.

Wes knocked, waited a few moments, knocked again. Nothing. "You're clear."

Ronnie lifted her key card. The door flashed green. She went in and got to work, scooping stuff out of the closet and cramming it into a hanging bag and a large suitcase. She disappeared into a bathroom and came out with a beauty case and a bouquet of brushes and combs.

Then, the electronics. She coiled the cables, gathered up chargers, packed up her laptop and tablet and stowed them all in a large leather computer bag.

"All done?" he asked, his eyes fixed on the elevator.

"Almost," she said. "I just need to leave…this."

She took her wallet from her purse and extracted the diamond ring from the pocket where she had stowed it the night before. She tucked it into a black velvet ring box.

"I feel as if I should leave a note with it," she said. "But anything I could write to him would either be scolding or insincere. Neither is particularly classy."

"Silence is fine," Wes said, loading up with her suitcase and garment bag. "He'll hate that. Silence gets my vote."

Her mouth twitched. "Agreed." She set the box on the bed. "All done."

They returned to his room with the bags. "It's official now," he said. "That chapter of your life is over. Congratulations."

"Thanks." She sank onto the couch, staring into space. "I am so glad that I didn't marry him. Why couldn't I see it? It would have been a miserable, suffocating disaster, and it would have ended in a horrible divorce. It's so clear to me now."

"I'm glad that you were spared all that," he said. "We should celebrate."

But Ronnie didn't look quite ready for celebration yet. "It's a good thing that I forced Jareth into a corner," she mused. "It's the only way I would have seen who he really was in time to bail."

"You would have figured it out," he said.

"But at what cost? I can't believe how blind I was."

The troubled look in her eyes was making him nervous. "Are you okay with how all this went?" he asked. "It's a lot. All these massive changes, and then me, all up in your face, demanding your attention."

"I'm fine with the changes," she said. "I'm just…not sure what happens now. My whole life, I've had a clear path in front of me. First it was getting good grades in school, then doing well at university, then at grad school, and then getting the fellowships, the grants, etc. Then the research and development job at MossTech. Then it was the show, which absolutely consumed me for the last few years. I haven't stopped to breathe since it all began. I had a mission, and suddenly it's gone. There's no path anymore, and it feels…strange."

"You'll find a new path," Wes said. "You're not the type who can stay pathless for long. And your mission hasn't changed. The mission chooses your path for you."

"You're probably right, but I still feel lost."

"I have a suggestion," he said. "It might seem suspiciously self-interested but hear me out. The perfect time for soul-searching is when you're pathless. It gives you an ironclad excuse to do things you otherwise would never let yourself do. Fun, frivolous things. Run away with me. I stole that guy's bride, and his wedding, so why not go three for three, and steal his honeymoon, too?" He paused, studying her face. "You were going on a honeymoon, weren't you?"

"No," she admitted. "Jareth had to be in LA by tomorrow, for some meeting or other. There was just no time for it."

"I see," he murmured. "Well, lucky me. I have the time for a honeymoon."

"Really?" she said. "Aren't you a hotshot venture capitalist with your fingers in scores of pies? I would have expected a guy like you to be constantly on the go."

"Oh, I hustle plenty," he assured her. "But I had already planned some downtime for myself, as it happens. I had some business meetings to take care of here in Vegas earlier this week, then I hung around to see your keynote address. After that, I was going to do something fun. Maybe climbing in the Rockies, maybe go to Amalfi, to get the renovations for the villa started. Or Greece. I love Greece. I have a yacht docked in Argostoli. I could take you sailing. We'll hug the coast of Kefalonia, sleep on the boat, stop at all the hidden coves and beaches, skinny-dip in bright blue water, eat fried fish and moussaka and red olives and tzatziki and gyro flatbread, and wash it all down with cold, crisp Robola white. My local favorite. You'll love it."

She looked impressed. "Sounds wonderful. You go all-out, don't you?"

"Why hold back? Life is short. But take your time. What are your dream destinations? Anything your heart desires.

What setting would make Veronica Moss relax enough to start dreaming up what's next on her path? That's the question. And whether the answer is snorkeling in the Great Barrier Reef, or climbing Machu Picchu, or floating under the Bridge of Sighs in a gondola in Venice, or trekking in Nepal, I am up for it."

She looked intrigued. She had no clue how passionately willing he was to follow through on this. Showing Veronica Moss a good time sounded like the most fun he'd ever had in his life. He'd go to any lengths to persuade her.

"Sounds decadent," she murmured.

"Oh, it is," he told her. "Your people warned you that I was a hedonist, right?"

"They did," she said. "And you proved it last night. Beyond a doubt."

"I could prove it again right now," he offered. "I could keep proving it all day. Or all week. Indefinitely. I am so inspired."

"Sounds like great fun," she said. "But first, coffee."

He brewed her a fresh pot while she called the front desk and checked out of the room that she'd shared with Jareth. After that, she accepted the cup of French roast, and gave him a thoughtful, assessing look. "You've finished your business in Vegas?"

"That is correct."

"So have I. Vegas has served its purpose for me. I'm no gambler."

"You gambled on me," he pointed out.

"Good point," she murmured. "Time to cash in my winnings, then."

That look of sensual speculation in her eyes made hunger surge inside him. "I like the sound of that," he said. "Say the word."

"Come with me to Seattle. If you want to," Ronnie offered. "I'm not quite ready to leave the country with you yet, but I'd enjoy the process of being persuaded. In the meantime, we can have some honeymoon fun in the Pacific Northwest. It's as beautiful as any other vacation destination. Let me check some flight times."

"Don't worry about flight times," he told her. "I'll fly you to Seattle."

"Fly me?" she said, startled. "You have your own plane? Here?"

"My pilot is standing by. Tell me where you want to go, and I'll take you there."

"Impressive," she murmured. "Okay. First stop, Seattle."

"That's where your family is based?"

"Yes. I've been back and forth to LA for the last few years, and I rented a nice apartment there, but I kept my condo in Seattle, even though Jareth tried to persuade me to sell it. I like having my own space when I'm in town. All of us Mosses were born and bred in Seattle. MossTech is there, so my dad lives there, my aunt, and my cousins. Though technically they're my first cousins once removed. My father was ten years younger than my uncle Bertram, and my mother was fifteen years younger than my dad, which makes for some confusing generational mixing. But all my cousins are older than me, Maddie by a couple of months. They feel more like siblings. We're very close. They're wonderful people. You'll like them."

"Will I meet them when we get to Seattle?" He held his breath for her reply.

"Maybe Maddie and her husband, Jack," she mused. "The boys are both traveling right now. Everyone is extremely busy, but Jack and Maddie are more available than the others, mostly since they can't seem to stop honeymooning. They're both between jobs, too, so they're taking their time and living it up."

"Sounds like fun," he remarked. "We should try it."

That earned him a luminous smile. "Right now they're spending a lot of time up in Cleland, this gorgeous little town in the Olympic rainforest. Jack just bought a beautiful house in the forest that I love. Minimalist cubes of glass, in the woods, in a cathedral of mossy trees, right on a river canyon with waterfalls. And when they're not there, they're at the beach house my aunt Elaine gave them as a wedding present."

"Living the dream," he said approvingly. "What about your male cousins?"

"They're in Southeast Asia right now. Tilda and her little girl, Annika, had to go to a friend's wedding in Jakarta, so Caleb decided to go along. Marcus is on one of his trips to Indonesia, and his brand-new wife, Eve, is off at some genetics think tank with her team, working on taking Corzo, her grain project, to the next level. And my dad's in London, thank God. Everyone is scattered to the four winds. The only family member that I'm sure that I can introduce you to is my aunt Elaine."

Wes felt a rush of guilty relief. Maybe he wouldn't get busted right away.

"Let's get moving," he said. "I'll pack up. We'll grab a bite and get on our way."

"Sounds good," she said. "I've worked up quite an appetite, hanging around with you. I'll just get some fresh clothes and change while you pack."

Wes stared around the jumbled bedroom, the wildly disarranged bed, his scattered clothes, drifted rose petals, burned-out candles, and started throwing stuff into his bag, more haphazardly than usual. He felt too excited and jittery to be methodical.

Under the circumstances, he shouldn't feel this excited, but Ronnie exerted a huge gravitation pull on his mind, dragging him into the present moment. Away from anger and pain. The fear of what would happen in the future.

But it was all still there, lying in wait.

After that horrible incident with Tilda and Caleb last year, his window of opportunity would be brief. Once Caleb heard his name, it was all over. He'd have only hours in Seattle to search for whatever documents Naomi Moss might have shipped home from Sri Lanka in that container twenty-three years ago. The truth was in those files, if they still existed.

One thing was certain: if this gambit didn't work, he'd have to apologize to the souls of his dead parents, pray that they forgave him and suck it up. Accept that he would live the rest of his life not knowing. And then get the hell on with it.

Last year, he'd been in a different headspace about it. Much more angry and punitive. The Mosses had been trying to do a hostile takeover of Tilda's father's company, so he'd given Tilda Riley a copy of his father's file so she could attack the Mosses with it.

That had been an unqualified disaster. Far from ruining the Moss family, Tilda had joined forces with them. She'd fallen in love with Caleb Moss. She'd married the guy, for God's sake.

Tilda had never used the file because she hadn't believed what was in it, and she hadn't wanted to destroy the family she'd just married into or betray the man she'd bonded with. So she'd sat on it. And when Wes showed up to do the job himself, she stole his original documents and burned them. To protect the Mosses.

Which left him with no hard proof. Nothing but the copy of his dad's journal, which he'd transcribed himself. There had been a sheaf of lab notes that went along with his dad's journal, but all of them were gone. Incinerated in Caleb Moss's fireplace.

The disaster had culminated in Wes getting attacked by Caleb Moss in a hotel room. Caleb had concluded that Wes was having an affair with Tilda. So Wes opened the door, fresh out of the shower, and found himself in a no-holds-barred fistfight. Not his finest moment. It was safe to say that Caleb would remember his name.

But if Tilda and Caleb hadn't mentioned him yet, he might have a window of opportunity before the Moss family sent him straight to hell.

Not that it would matter. When Ronnie found out, he'd be in hell already.

Eight

"You're attracting a lot of attention," Wes said. "Is this normal for you?"

Ronnie glanced around and saw six pairs of eyes snap away. "Pretty much," she said. "Maybe they recognize me from the keynote address or the conference program."

"I thought of the hotel restaurant because it's excellent and conveniently close. I forgot about you being a celebrity. I should have taken you someplace more secluded."

"No." Ronnie squared her shoulders, meeting the gaze of anyone who had the nerve to stare at her full on. "Let them stare. I'm finished with being self-conscious. Last night just burned it all out of me, and it feels great to be free of it."

Wes made an approving sound. "You can hardly blame them for looking. You're on fire. I couldn't look away if I tried."

Good, because that was exactly how she felt. She was

glad that it showed. "Don't try," she said, throatily. "I like when you look at me." She took a fat, ripe strawberry, and scooped up a generous, quivering glop of Chantilly cream with it, then ate it slowly and sensually, in unhurried bites, licking away creamy goop, and then licking each of her fingers in turn. "I can't get over it. Everything tastes so good today."

She caught her breath at the fierce blaze of hunger in his eyes.

"You are merciless," he said softly.

"It's all your fault. Yesterday, I was a harassed, mealy-mouthed people pleaser, scurrying around and trying to keep the world from getting mad at her. Today, I'm a naughty, hedonistic, selfish bad girl, intent on my own pleasure." She stroked his finger with her own, a long, slow caress. "And I'm going to let you help me. Because you're oh…so…good at it."

He cleared his throat. "Ronnie. Not fair. We already checked out of the room."

"There will be other rooms," she said. "And it'll keep."

"That's for sure," he said fervently. "The question is whether I survive the wait."

They finished their coffee and headed through the lobby toward the exit as Wes checked his phone. "The limo is waiting, bags stowed. We can head to the airport."

"Ronnie!" A sharp, angry voice called from behind them. Jareth's voice.

This was going to be interesting. But she didn't feel that sinking dread she had expected, buoyed up by Wes's warmth. Like he said, she was on fire.

Ronnie turned, bracing herself. Better sooner than later.

Jareth strode toward her, eyes darting suspiciously between her and Wes.

"Where in the hell have you been, Ronnie? You had me

worried sick! You didn't answer your phone, you didn't answer my texts, you weren't in the room—"

"I didn't want to talk to you," Ronnie said. "I still don't."

"That's too bad, because we still need to talk about our future," Jareth lectured. "Being part of a couple is all about compromise, finding a solution that works for both people, and you just don't seem to get that. I regret upsetting you yesterday, but you drove me into a corner, Ron. You left me no choice."

"There's always a choice," Wes commented.

Jareth fixed Wes with a gaze. "Excuse me? Did it look like I was addressing you?"

Wes smiled and shrugged.

Jareth snorted and turned to her. "Get it through your head. Going forward, I won't indulge your irrational impulses. Especially not when they affect our future."

"We have a problem, then, Jareth," Ronnie said. "Because irrational impulses are kind of my thing right now."

Wes gave her a grin, which Jareth caught. He turned to Wes. "Whoever you are, this is a private conversation," he said sharply. "Buzz off."

"No, actually. I'll stay right where I am." Wes's tone was implacable.

"What…?" Jareth glared at Ronnie. "Do you know this person, Ron?"

"I do now," Ronnie replied. "Jareth, this is Wes Brody. My husband."

"Husband?" Jareth's face darkened. "If this is a joke, it's in extremely bad taste."

"My bad taste is no longer your problem," Ronnie said. "I will never embarrass you again, Jareth."

"But I…" Jareth's mouth worked. His eyes moved frantically between her and Wes. "You couldn't have. You didn't actually…"

"Marry him? Yes. I already had the chapel booked, after all. I used the same time slot that I booked for you and me. We just got a new license at the courthouse."

"But who *is* this person?" His voice got louder.

"A new friend," Wes said. "Ready to help out in a tough spot. Your loss is absolutely my gain."

Jareth's mouth twisted, and for the first time, she realized his uncanny resemblance to her father. God, she'd come so close to yoking herself to this. Falling right back into the miserable trap of her childhood. The nearness of her escape made her dizzy.

"You slept with him?" Jareth's voice cracked with outrage. "You married the very first man you saw, and then just…just took him to bed? That's disgusting, Ron!"

"Watch your mouth," Wes said evenly. "If you want to keep your teeth in it."

Jareth shook his head. "A complete stranger? You have multiple degrees, Ron. I know you're not a stupid woman. But this is idiocy! He'll take you for every penny he can get, and it will serve you right!"

"I had to keep my promise to Aunt Elaine," she said. "You let me down, so I had to improvise. I'm lucky to have found a solution, thanks to Wes."

"You won't be thanking him for long," Jareth said. "And when this bites you in the ass, I will be watching the floor show and slow-clapping, Ron. Because he's got an agenda, too. Everyone does. Always. You're too goddamn innocent to grasp that."

Wes took her arm. "This sounds like our cue. Let this clown eat our dust."

"Yes," Ronnie murmured. "I can't say I'm enjoying this."

"I'll make it my business to inform everyone in the business how crazy you are!" Jareth shouted after her. "No one will work with you! You're finished in television!"

Ronnie stopped and turned, drawing up to her full height. "Are you threatening me, Jareth?" she asked. "Is it time to get MossTech's legal department involved?"

"If you do, play them a video of this conversation," Wes said. "As soon as I saw his face, I hit the record function." Wes held up his phone and touched Play.

Jareth appeared on the screen, shot from below, at Wes's waist level. His flushed face looked grotesque from the strange angle as he harangued her.

"...in the hell have you been, Ronnie? You had me worried sick! You didn't answer your phone, you didn't answer my texts..."

Wes stopped the video. "I've got every word that comes out of your mouth. All the way to the end, where you threaten her with career-ending slander." He tapped at his phone. "Saved to the cloud. Ass officially covered. So, you were saying?" Wes gave Jareth a thin smile. "Or are you rethinking it?"

Jareth's mouth worked. He looked at her. "I thought you were better than this," he said.

"I thought you were, too," Ronnie replied.

She let Wes take her arm and lead her away, mortified by the tears blurring her vision. He drew her through the big revolving doors at the front entrance of the hotel. Dammit, why? Jareth wasn't worth her tears.

Wes opened the door of the limo that idled at the curb, and helped her in, then slid in beside her, his leg pressed against hers. He wound his fingers through hers. "I'm sorry you had to go through that," he said. "I should've taken you out a side door."

She laughed. "And sneak away like a fugitive? I have

nothing to be ashamed of. And it's not your job to protect me."

"Actually, it is," he said thoughtfully. "Protecting each other falls under the umbrella of the spirit of marriage vows. And you're well worth protecting."

Ronnie squeezed his hand. "Aww, a lovely thought, Wes, but getting embroiled with Jareth Fadden was my poor judgment, not yours. That unpleasant conversation had to happen. I'm glad it's over."

"Well, for the record, you were amazing," he said. "Indomitable."

She looked at him and snorted. "Sweet talker."

"No way," he insisted. "You were calm, elegant, polite. You never lost your cool. Your voice was smooth and golden. You were in complete control of yourself. Whereas he degenerated and had to be put sternly in his place. Which you did, like a goddess."

"Quick thinking, to record him with your phone," she told him.

"As soon as I saw his face, I knew it would get ugly," he said. "A record of his bad behavior will keep him honest. Force is the only language a troll like that understands."

Ronnie shook her head. "I don't know how I got myself into that." Her voice still uneven. "He was nicer early on, but after a while… God. I don't know. I guess I was just so used to Dad being cold and belittling. I didn't notice anything out of the ordinary when Jareth was, too. It just seemed, you know. Familiar. I knew I could survive it because I always have. And he seemed to value me. For things that I could do, the way I looked, my ability, my credentials." She paused. "And MossTech," she concluded. "Mostly MossTech."

"Bastard," Wes muttered.

"Thanks for standing by me," she said. "It would've been harder alone. Particularly if I were still unmarried."

"I'm honored to help."

The warm, tender look in his eyes made emotion swell inside her, and when her phone rang, she was so flustered, she hit Talk before she saw her cousin Maddie's name on the display. Whoopsy-daisy. Another intense conversation, hard on the heels of the last.

"Maddie?" she said.

"Ronnie! Do you know how many times I've tried to call you? Where are you?"

"I'm on my way to Seattle," Ronnie said. "And you're a fine one to complain. You've let me stew in my own juices for weeks at a time without answering my calls or texts when you get into one of your moods. Remember when you ran off to Hawaii?"

"This is different," Maddie said. "Since you insisted on inserting yourself into Gran's marriage mandate, that means you have to endure our scrutiny."

"Fine," Ronnie said. "Scrutinize to your heart's content."

"So you're married? That's what you said last night in the group chat."

"Sure am," she replied, leaving it at that.

"So how is it that when I called Jareth to congratulate him, he told me that you guys had a huge fight, and that you stormed off, and that you weren't married at all?"

"Maddie, what on earth possessed you to call him?"

"Why not? I figured, the guy's like my brother-in-law now, and I have to make an effort, right? I was trying to be nice. I am so confused right now."

"You haven't said anything to Aunt Elaine, or Caleb, or Marcus yet, have you?"

"Um...not yet," Maddie said. "Not that it matters, babe.

If you're not married by now, you've missed the deadline, and that's that. Happy birthday, by the way."

"Thanks," she said.

"Look, Ron. I get it, if you choked at marrying Jareth," Maddie said. "I just regret that you wrote yourself into the mandate to begin with. Bad time to criticize, but that move was as dumb as a box of rocks. But there's just no point in lying to us about it."

"Listen up," Ronnie said. "Short version—I am married. Legally married, shortly before midnight yesterday. I'm just not married to Jareth."

Maddie was quiet for so long, Ronnie started wondering if the connection had broken. "Maddie? Are you still there?"

"Wait. Hold on. So you're married to…who?" Maddie's voice was small.

"His name is Wes. I met him yesterday. He offered to help me out. A last-minute save, to keep MossTech out of my dad's clutches. So I took him up on it."

"And this was after you stormed away from Jareth?"

"To be precise, he stormed away from me," Ronnie said. "He refused to go through with the wedding. He wanted Dad to get MossTech and take it public. He was thinking of the eventual payday. I was on my own. Then I met Wes."

"Ron." Maddie sounded subdued. "That's so risky. You know that we care much more about you than about MossTech. I hope you haven't gotten yourself in trouble."

"Not at all," Ronnie assured her. "The situation is under control. He's coming back to Seattle with me now."

"He is? That's interesting." Maddie harrumphed. "Hmm. So Jareth turned out to be venal, calculating and self-serving, eh? Goodness me, Ron. I'm shocked. Shocked, I say."

"Don't start," Ronnie begged. "I'm already so embarrassed, okay?"

"I'm not scolding you," Maddie soothed. "It's just a relief that now I can freely tell you what a condescending butthead he is."

"Um...yes," Ronnie agreed. "He tried to coerce me by putting *The Secret Life of Cells* on the line. I wouldn't back down, and he canceled it to punish me."

Maddie gasped. "That bastard! Your beautiful show! Annika will be crushed."

"Yes, but I'm glad it's over. He would have destroyed me, by inches."

"Well, none of us ever liked him. We all hoped that you'd come to your senses in time, so we were appalled when you put yourself into the mandate."

"It was stupid, yes," Ronnie admitted. "But you know what? I think that things are looking up. I think my luck might be changing."

"Oh, really?" Maddie's voice changed. "Do tell! Is it the new guy?"

Her eyes flicked up to Wes, who was looking away from her, trying not to smile.

"Can't really talk right now," she said. "Please don't say anything to Aunt Elaine or Caleb or Marcus yet, okay? Give me a minute. Let me breathe."

"On one condition," Maddie said. "Dinner, tonight. I want to meet him."

"Maddie, it's a little early to start inflicting my relatives on—"

"The hell it is! You're married to the guy! Meet us for dinner, or I call Gran right now. What do I call him?"

"I called him Mr. Mysterious when I first saw him," Ronnie said.

Wes's smile stretched into a grin. "Cool," he said.

"Aren't you guys still up in Cleland?" Ronnie asked.

"No, we're at my place in the city. Jack had meetings, and I had a client consult. Let's go to that place down the street from you. Café Kuna. Can you get there by eight?"

"I think we can manage that."

"Great. I'll book a table. Can't wait to dissect your new husband. I just hope he's worthy of you, and that you have an ironclad prenup. You do have a prenup, right?"

"Yes, yes, I have a prenup," she soothed. "Signed, witnessed, notarized, filmed for posterity, and already in the possession of my lawyers. Have no fear. My ass is covered. And I really dodged a bullet, Maddie. I feel… I feel like I'm floating on air."

"Is that so?" Maddie sounded like she was smiling. "I like the sound of that. I haven't heard you sound that way since we were kids. I look forward to meeting the guy who can make Veronica Moss bubble and froth and float on air."

"I do not bubble or froth!" Ronnie protested.

"We'll see for ourselves tonight. Till then!"

Ronnie let the phone drop. "My cousin Maddie and her husband are meeting us for dinner tonight. Hope that's okay. They intend to grill you left, right and sideways."

He grunted. "Fun times."

"Actually, it will be," Ronnie said. "Even if you're being grilled, Maddie is always fun. She's like a sister to me, and Jack's a great guy. You'll like them."

"I'm looking forward to it. Will I meet your dad, too?"

"No, he's in London, and will be for a while yet, if the Fates are kind. I stay as far from him as I can. I got my own place as soon as I could. A condo on the waterfront. I never could get comfortable in Southern California. I'm an Emerald City girl."

When they boarded, Ronnie was impressed with the luxurious interior of his Fabiolet Eagle.

"I love to fly planes," Wes confided, as they strapped themselves in. "But when I'm in business mode, I get someone else to fly me."

"Very nice," Ronnie said. "So it's true. You deny yourself nothing."

"Nope. I know it's extravagant, but I invested in the company, Fabiolet Eagle. Cutting edge eco design. As of the time I bought it a couple years ago, it had the most efficient thrust-to-weight ratio of any plane on the market. It uses sixty percent less fuel, emits fifty percent less carbon. It's a great little plane."

"My cousins Caleb and Marcus would love it," Ronnie said. "I can't wait to introduce you."

Wes picked up the bucket of ice on the shelf and set up two champagne glasses. "I'm looking forward to it," he said. "I've heard tales about them."

"Yes, they do tend to make the news," she agreed.

"You must have the celebrity gene in your family," he said. "Along with the good looks. I've seen pictures of them. But you look completely different. Just as good-looking, but no family resemblance at all that I can see."

"They say that I look like my mom," Ronnie said. "Any luck that I had on that score can be attributed to her."

He popped the cork of the champagne. "And your dad?"

"I've seen pictures of him when he was young," Ronnie said. "I suppose he was a good-looking man. But his face is so pinched and severe now, you can't see it anymore."

"Last night, when I was helping drape your veil, it occurred to me that it should've been your mom to do that," Wes said. "But maybe she was there. Watching over you."

That gave her a sharp pang of longing. "I like to think so," Ronnie said.

"So, you said that your dad burned all her stuff, right?" Wes touched her locket. "This is all you have left?"

"I have a few things that Aunt Elaine salvaged for me," she said. "Some photographs, some fine jewelry, a couple of scarves, a few of her favorite books. Old, dog-eared paperbacks. And those home videos that I told you about."

"Did they ship her things home from Sri Lanka after she died?"

"They must have," she said. "I was only seven, so I didn't have much of a grip on the details. But I'm sure that Dad threw out everything she'd ever touched." She paused. "But now that I think about it, my aunt must've dug that stuff up from somewhere."

"You should ask her," Wes said, pouring out the champagne. "A couple years ago, I was selling property that had belonged to my dad. I found a box of old files, and it had a journal in it. Dad's last journal. It was amazing, the way it made me feel. Like he was right there with me. I could hear his voice in my head. So if there's anything to be discovered, I recommend making the effort. As part of the new project. Veronica Moss, seeking her path into the future."

"That must have been an incredible feeling. What did the journal say?"

"It wasn't so much the content, which was mostly about his job. It was his distinctive way of talking. Now and then, he mentioned me and my mom." He lifted her hand and kissed it. "Ask your aunt if there's anything to look through. You might find something meaningful. It's worth a shot."

"It's a good idea," she told him with a smile. "I will."

Wes lifted his champagne flute just as sunshine slanted through the window, illuminating the sparkling wine into a brilliant, crystalline glitter. "To reconciling the future with the past," he said.

"Amen," she said.

She glanced out as the plane banked and turned, looking at the blue sky and the pale brown desert scrub below, now giving way to dry mountains. She felt so light.

Life was so shockingly different from yesterday. She'd been preparing to marry Jareth Fadden and braced for a long week of meetings with the production team to plan Season Four of *The Secret Life of Cells.* She was used to eighteen-hour days, sleepless nights, constant multitasking. She had a killer work ethic, like all the Mosses.

All that was gone, and she was sipping champagne, soaring over the desert in the private plane of the most attractive man she'd ever met, after a night of delirious pleasure. On the brink of a wild adventure. It felt great. She'd never been the type to put pleasure or excitement at the top of her list of priorities, but then, she'd never spent a day and night with a man like Wes Brody either. Call her frivolous, but this uncharted path into the future was a hell of a lot more fun than anything that had ever come before.

She finished her champagne and shook her head when he moved to refill her glass.

"Do we have privacy in here?" she asked.

"If I latch the cabin door," he said. "Do you have something in mind?"

"How long until we land?"

"Maybe another forty minutes before we start the descent," Wes said.

Ronnie set aside her champagne glass. "That's long enough," she said, unfastening her seat belt. A few steps took her to the cabin door, which she swiftly closed and latched.

"Ronnie," he said, looking intrigued. "What's up?"

"You, Wes," she said, in a low, husky voice. "Very soon."

His eyes widened as she sank to her knees in front of him, gripping his thighs. "Last night, you rocked my world," she said. She reached out, and tugged his belt, pulling the buckle loose. "Today, I feel like returning the favor."

He sucked in air as she unbuttoned his jeans and reached inside to stroke the stiff, thick shaft trapped in his briefs. Stroking it. Squeezing it. Freeing it.

She took her time. Slow, twisting strokes that made him arch and gasp, shuddering with sensation. His response made her feel powerful. Intensely aroused.

She took him in her mouth, savoring the groan of helpless delight that vibrated through his body. She wanted to melt him down. Drive him wild with pleasure. Exactly what he deserved, after what he'd done to her last night.

Luckily for him, she was a firm believer in balancing the scales.

Nine

Wes admired Ronnie's waterfront condo while she got ready for dinner. It was a beautiful space, comfortably decorated, overlooking the busy waterfront. It was open plan, with an airy living space dominated by huge picture windows that looked out at the water and a beautiful terrace with a view of the water. There was a comfortable grouping of rust-colored, crimson and slate blue couches and chairs and beautiful Persian rugs scattered over the gleaming plank flooring.

Twilight had given way to evening. Ronnie was freshening up while he paced, nervous as hell for this dinner date with the cousin.

He distracted himself by looking at her pictures and knickknacks, but he was too anxious to focus. This might be the moment of truth. Ronnie hadn't said his last name to her cousin, but she would when she introduced him. Everything hung upon whether Caleb and Tilda had told the rest of the Mosses about his dad's file and journal.

And the fistfight with Caleb in the hotel room, of course.

Tilda might have kept it quiet. That incident didn't reflect well on her, though he understood her motives. Sneaking, stealing, corporate espionage, destroying evidence—it wasn't the kind of behavior a person wanted to advertise. And Caleb wouldn't be quick to admit where he'd gotten the black eye and the split lip. He'd probably told everyone that he fell off his bike. Macho idiots did stupid stuff like that. He knew that for a fact, being a macho idiot himself. But at least he was self-aware about it.

Of course, once Caleb and Tilda got back to town, the jig would be up. His best-case scenario was to get a handful of days to find out what he could about Naomi Moss's papers. Anything she might've sent home from Sri Lanka.

But the more time that he spent with Ronnie Moss, the less important the past seemed. He was using the most desirable, intriguing woman that he ever met in a way that was manipulative and dishonest. Mom and Dad would not have approved. If their positions were reversed, he would feel furious, humiliated. But what could he do? The damage was done. There was no going back. They'd made love. His fate was sealed.

He'd put himself squarely into the lying-scheming-bastard category.

Even if he came clean, and confessed everything to her right now, she would feel betrayed. He would lose her anyway. Along with his last shot at the truth.

He might as well hold out a little longer. Salvage something from this.

It was a long shot in any case. Jerome had burned Naomi's things. Ronnie didn't live in her family home, or even go there often. It was a lost cause.

And yet, here he was.

He wandered around looking at what she'd hung on her walls. There were a lot of candid shots of Ronnie's cousins. Then he came upon a column of three similar framed photographs of three extremely good-looking couples. Her cousins, paired up with their respective mates. Formal photographs.

That was Caleb with the blonde, ethereal Tilda, that one was Marcus, and there was Maddie. Three entirely different, distinctive types of extreme good looks. Maddie's husband, Jack, was Hollywood handsome in his own right, and Eve, Marcus's wife, was a stunner. Those big, luminous gray eyes, that gorgeous smile.

All three couples looked happy. Too happy to be stiff and self-conscious while getting their pictures taken. Laughing. Trusting their partners. Excited for the future.

Ronnie was the kind of woman Mom would've liked. That made it worse. His parents would've wanted him to be happy. They would have wanted him to take an opportunity like this and treat it with the reverence that it deserved.

He pushed the thought away, moving on to a photograph of Ronnie's parents. That was Naomi Moss, on the deck of a large sailboat, dressed in cutoff shorts and a bikini top, her red hair flying in the wind. A man was next to her. Dark haired, barefoot, in rolled-up linen boat pants and a loose shirt. He was laughing.

Jerome. Wes could barely see some subtle resemblances to Ronnie. The tilt of the eyebrow, the firm jaw. Ronnie was right; he'd been a good-looking man, in a sharp, chiseled sort of way. Ronnie wasn't in the photo. Maybe she wasn't born yet.

He moved on to the shelf over the fireplace, admiring the Emmy she'd gotten for Season Two of *The Secret Life of Cells*. He'd watched the awards ceremony on TV. There were shots of Ronnie, receiving the award, in a sequined black gown, her hair a mass of luxurious curls. And other pictures of her, receiving other awards: Excellence for Women in STEM, another for fostering scientific literacy in youth. She truly did have a mission, and she was fulfilling it with brilliance and generosity. She was a gifted, top-quality woman, and she deserved better than this duplicitous bullshit from him.

That reflection made him utterly miserable.

"Hey, there," Ronnie said, from behind him. "See anything interesting?"

He turned. She stood in the entryway to the corridor. "It's all interesting," he said, gesturing at the photos. "Look at you, rubbing elbows with the A-listers and stars. So you were in *Metabolize*? The Pixar film that won best animated film?"

She laughed. "Yeah, I voiced Molly the Mitochondria. That was fun. I met some movie stars. Going to those events is grueling, though. The expensive dress, the cameras, the scrutiny. It's stressful, but great publicity for the cause, so whatever."

"No, you crush it," he corrected. "These couples on the wall, are these your cousins and their spouses?"

"Yes." Ronnie's eyes softened. "Aunt Elaine insisted on formal photos for everyone, and they turned out well. They all look so happy."

He pointed at the sailboat photo. "And these are your parents?"

She moved closer, bringing a fresh, springlike whiff of flowers with her. "Yes, that's Mom and Dad, on their honeymoon. She was already pregnant with me. I think that's the only picture I've ever seen of my father smiling."

"I'd be smiling, too, if I were him. She's gorgeous."

Ronnie's hand went instinctively to her throat, touching the locket. "She looks larger-than-life to me," she admitted.

"Like you," he said. "And speaking of which, you look great. As usual."

She dimpled at him, smoothing her hands over her dress. "Flatterer."

It wasn't flattery, just a statement of truth. Ronnie wore a clinging gray sweater dress that hugged every perfect curve and swell of her body, a black belt accentuating her narrow waist. She had on black knit stockings and short black boots, and her hair was twisted up into a glossy knot on top of her head. Her eyes looked shadowy and mysterious, and her lips were cherry red. She looked gorgeous, vivid. Happy.

He wished he could enjoy that. That this thing between them could have made them both happy. Wildest-dreams happy, if not for his secret agenda.

Ronnie's smile faded. "Are you okay? You look tense. Subdued. For you."

"Just nervous about the grilling, I guess."

"Are you kidding?" Ronnie rolled her eyes. "Rest easy. Aside from saving me from the consequences of my silly choices, you just saved MossTech's collective butt, and my cousins' careers. You saved Uncle Bertram's legacy, and you saved my aunt Elaine from her own folly. You're golden, Wes. They'll love you."

Hardly, when the truth came out. He plastered on a smile. "Shall we call a car?"

"No need. It's a five-to-ten-minute walk, depending on how high my heels are."

"And how high are your heels?"

She struck a pose and gracefully kicked up one foot,

showing him the moderately high heel. "Six-point-five minutes, by my calculations," she said.

"Lead the way," he said.

After the blazing sun of Las Vegas, the damp wintry chill of Seattle made him turn up his collar as they walked toward the restaurant. But he was grateful for any distraction from that sucking hole of dread in his belly.

If Maddie and Jack recognized his name, his idyll with this woman would be over.

He wasn't ready. He never would be. But into the doghouse he would go, and there he would stay, for the rest of his natural life.

Café Kuna was a small and elegant place, with a mellow, hushed decor. They went inside, but before the host could even speak, they heard an excited voice ring out.

"Ronnie!" They turned to see a gorgeous woman hurrying toward them, smiling widely. A handsome man with blue eyes followed her. She had smooth, golden-brown skin, a halo of tight black bouncing ringlets. Big amber eyes, bright with curiosity, darted between them.

Maddie seized Ronnie in a tight embrace. "You old married lady, you," she said, her eyes flicking to Wes. "Introduce me to Mr. Mysterious."

"Maddie, this is Wes Brody, my new husband," Ronnie said. "Wes, my cousin Maddie Moss, and her husband, Jack Daly."

Wes watched Maddie's face carefully, but she made no reaction to his name. Neither had Jack. He shook hands with the others, his knees weak with relief.

The moment of truth would come. But not tonight.

Wes and Jack were talking about Jack's ocean-cleaning, plastic-eating enzyme formula, so Maddie leaned close to her. "Ron!" she murmured. "He's great. Handsome, energetic, funny. And he seems real. Like Jareth never did."

Ronnie winced. "Can we pretend that relationship never happened?"

"Oh, don't be touchy. Jareth led you into Wes's arms, so he was good for that much. So what's up with the two of you?" Maddie lifted a well-shaped dark eyebrow. "Are you guys actually involved?"

Ronnie's blush spoke for her. Maddie's smile widened to a grin.

"I'm having so much fun," Ronnie confided in a whisper. "He's wonderful, but I hardly know him. My first thought was only about covering MossTech's ass, but then I started to realize that he's special in his own right. I just hope I haven't overloaded this relationship. We should be getting drinks, flirting, playing it cool. But we're married, for God's sake."

"I don't think it's overloaded," Maddie said. "I have a good feeling."

"Let's not think about it too hard, Mads," Ronnie begged. "I don't want to scare it away. Don't ask me any tough questions about him yet, okay?"

"I understand how you feel, but you know what? That guy is crazy for you. I can tell. I never got that sense from He-Who-Must-Not-Be-Named. He thought he was God's gift. I won't last long without asking questions, Ron. It's my nature."

"Oh, speaking of questions," Ronnie said. "Remember that photo album Aunt Elaine gave me when I graduated, with the pictures of Mom and Dad? Do you know where those came from? Does Aunt Elaine have a stash of my mom's stuff?"

"Well, yes." Maddie looked puzzled. "She rented a storage unit for the stuff that was shipped from Sri Lanka after the bombing. Didn't you know about it?"

Ronnie's neck prickled. "A storage unit? With Mom's stuff?"

Wes looked over them. "Storage unit?"

"Yes, of Naomi's stuff," Maddie explained. "She sent a container on a boat from Sri Lanka before she was killed. Gran went out of her way to intercept it. She knew Jerome would've burned it, and she wanted to preserve whatever she could for you. She would have stored it at her own house, but she wanted to keep it safe from Jerome."

"Yes, he tried to destroy everything that belonged to her."

"There wasn't a lot in there, as I recall," Maddie said. "Gran took me there when you and I were seniors in high school. She wanted help looking through the boxes for photographs for a graduation present for you. There were lots of books, some furniture. Old file folders. Random stuff. Clothes and shoes. Dishes, fabric, ceramics. Things like that."

"But why didn't Aunt Elaine tell me?" Ronnie asked.

"I think she intended to." Maddie sounded bemused. "But after we graduated, you took off like a shot, and stayed gone for a long time. Then Grandpa Bertram died, and I think Gran forgot all about it. Why did you think of it now?"

Ronnie glanced at Wes, who took her hand. "Because of a conversation we had," she said. "About reconciling with the past."

Wes spoke up. "I lost my dad when I was just a couple of years older than Ronnie was when she lost her mom," he said. "A couple of years ago, I found some old journals of his. It meant a lot to me. Like he was reaching across time."

"What a lovely thought," Maddie said. "All I remember

is that the storage place was somewhere in Greenwood. Gran should have the address, and the key."

"Okay. I'll ask her tomorrow."

Maddie's eyebrows climbed. "So you're going to introduce him to Gran?"

"Should I be afraid?" Wes asked.

"Not in the least," Maddie said. "You saved MossTech. And she disliked Jareth. You're a much better bargain."

Wes inclined his head. "I'm gratified that you think so."

"Why can't we talk to Caleb and Marcus? They'll be thrilled."

"Not yet," Ronnie said. "There's plenty of time to tell them later. Same with Dad. Someone's going to tell him about this, if they haven't already, but no need to rush it. He's going to be so angry."

"Angry?" Wes looked around. "Angry why?"

Ronnie, Jack and Maddie exchanged glances, and snickered.

"He's always angry," Maddie explained. "It's his default state. Keep that in mind when you meet him. That way you won't take it personally."

"Okay," Wes said. "Thanks for the tip."

At that moment, the waiter came to the table with a bucket of ice and a bottle of champagne sticking out. Maddie pulled out the bottle and filled three flutes with the sparkling wine. "And now, my dear cousin, and my new cousin-in-law, I must make an important announcement," Maddie said, beaming. "I've been bursting to tell you."

"Oh, God. Are you pregnant?" Ronnie exclaimed.

"Twelve weeks," Maddie said. "We were waiting to be sure, but everything looks good. We don't know if it's a girl or a boy yet."

Many tearful hugs and much excited babbling ensued. It made her heart melt.

"I want to be there when you tell Aunt Elaine," she said. "I want to see her face."

"Soon," Maddie said. "After my next ultrasound. Not a word when you see her tomorrow. Tell me if you find anything interesting in the storage unit, okay?"

"As soon as possible," Ronnie assured her. "I'll call you."

"Let's go tomorrow," Wes said. "As soon as you get the address and key."

"You don't have to go with me," Ronnie said. "It'll be dusty and boring. Probably sad."

"All the more reason. You can't do a sad thing alone. Not on my watch."

There was a moment of startled silence. Maddie gave him an approving smile.

"Excellent," she said. "And for that show of touching solidarity, you get a piece of the best chocolate-pecan pie you will ever taste."

In the midst of their laughter, Ronnie felt his hand under the table, squeezing hers.

It felt so good to have someone holding her hand, having her back. She'd tried not to need that with Jareth. To be self-reliant. Not jealous of what her cousins had found. The laughter, the tenderness, the trust, the ease. And now, a baby, too.

Suddenly, it seemed as if maybe she'd been blessed by that wild magic, too. It seemed greedy and dangerous to hope that it was real. Like asking for trouble.

But she couldn't seem to stop herself.

Ten

She was climbing a mountain. Crawling up bare, jagged rocks. Crawling through thorny plants. The wind was cold, and the sky was gray and threatening.

Suddenly, there was an opening in the rocks. She pulled herself up, and stepped through it, into a hanging valley. The grass a brilliant green. The clouds had broken into puffy white columns, with deep blue behind them. The ground was thick with flowers, and the fragrant breeze made the grass ripple, changing its nap like velvet when it was stroked. She gazed at the heart-stopping beauty in awe...

The squeak of the bedroom door made her eyes open. Wes poked his head in.

He smiled apologetically. "Didn't mean to wake you," he said. "I just wanted to check and see if you were awake and ready for breakfast. Go back to sleep."

She smiled, lazily. "I was having a really good dream."

He ventured inside, smiling. "Sorry I interrupted it."

She thought of the unbelievable pleasure that he'd showed her after they got back from Café Kuna as her eyes traveled over his magnificent body. "Reality is even better."

"Good to hear," he said. "Since you're awake, you should know that I went out and got breakfast from the coffee shop down the street. On the table is fresh orange juice, breakfast sandwiches, breakfast pastries and French roast with half-and-half."

Her belly rumbled, making them laugh, and Ronnie sat up, tossing her hair back. "That sounds delicious," she said, stretching, arms over her head. "I'm hungry."

He studied her naked chest with hot-eyed fascination. "Before I lose my head, the mission I set myself was to fuel you for the mission. Operation Reconcile with the Past."

Ronnie sauntered across the bedroom, taking her bathrobe from the hook. His eyes felt good on her body as she shrugged it on. She'd always felt self-conscious with Jareth when she was naked. Like he was judging, comparing, assessing her assets and her flaws.

Well, duh. Because he had been, constantly. Wes made her tingle and glow.

"First, coffee," she told him. "Must have coffee."

"On the double," he said.

Soon she was at the breakfast table, being freshly pampered. The sandwiches were delicious. Eggs with crispy bacon and melted Gruyère on crisply toasted English muffins. Gooey pecan-crusted cinnamon rolls. Lemon-blueberry scones. Tangy, fresh-squeezed orange juice. A big cup of strong, fragrant dark roast, with a shot of cream, just how she liked it. He'd noticed and remembered. How sweet.

He'd even gotten a bunch of sunflowers for the table. Flashy, cheerful, gorgeous.

It felt wonderful, having him in her own pretty space, sipping coffee. The sky was an ominous gray, and it was going to rain today, but she was inclined to see the beauty in any natural phenomenon that came along today. It was a survival skill that all Seattleites developed, with their constantly overcast skies and omnipresent drizzle.

After she finished licking the pecan goop off her fingers, she sighed with satisfaction. "I'm ready to face the past. I'll call Aunt Elaine."

Aunt Elaine picked up the call quickly. "For heaven's sake, it's time you called!" she scolded. "Just a text to say you're married, and not another word? Where are you?"

"I'm in Seattle, at my condo. I was wondering if we could drop by this morning."

"By all means, come right along! I'll be waiting. Don't dawdle!"

Wes poured more coffee for her. "So I couldn't help but notice that you didn't specify that the other half of 'us' is not Jareth," he observed.

"Nope," she said. "That's an explanation I'd prefer to make once, in person."

"Fair enough," he agreed.

It didn't take long to get through the late-morning traffic to Aunt Elaine's gracious Victorian mansion in Windermere. Ronnie loved the place far more than her father's house. All her happy childhood memories had been formed at this house.

They parked in the big, round driveway and they walked through the garden, past the leaping fountains, the manicured flower beds. Wes looked strained.

"Relax," she told him. "She'll be disposed to like you. You're singlehandedly rescuing her from the consequences of her own silliness, to say nothing of mine. And what's more, you're not Jareth. She'll be easier to win over than my cousins."

"Why is that?" he asked. "What would your cousins have against me?"

She snorted. "You're a man, that's what," she said. "They're suspicious of any man who shows an interest in me or Maddie. They have this thing about protecting us from evil predators. It's sweet of them, but it gets tiresome."

The door was opened by Lizette, the tall, slim fifty-ish woman with black bobbed hair who butlered for Aunt Elaine. Ronnie embraced her warmly. She'd known Lizette since she was fifteen, since the last butler retired, and she'd always liked her.

"Welcome back!" Lizette said. "You look wonderful. Mrs. Moss was so delighted about you visiting this morning. She's waiting in the library. Who's your friend?"

"Lizette, this is Wes Brody," Ronnie announced. "My husband."

Lizette blinked, nonplussed. "But aren't you…? Didn't you…?"

"No," Ronnie said. "There was a last-minute change of plan."

"Welcome!" Lizette recovered her professional aplomb quickly and shook Wes's hand. "I tell you what, Ronnie. I'll let you introduce your own husband to Mrs. Moss. I'll just get the coffee and cookies ready."

Aunt Elaine was sitting in state in the library, in her favorite wingback chair, the one with a view of the portrait of her husband, Ronnie's uncle Bertram. Elaine looked over with a big smile—which froze when she saw Wes, and not Jareth.

She got up with the help of her cane. "Ronnie, darling,"

she said. "I assumed that you were coming here with your husband, so that I could congratulate you. Though I will not forgive you for cheating us out of a proper wedding. A party afterward is not the same thing, my dear. So where is your husband? And who is this young man?"

"I'm not married to Jareth, Aunt," Ronnie said.

Elaine's face stiffened. "So your text wasn't true? You're not married after all?"

"No, that's not what I said," Ronnie explained. "I am married." She nodded toward Wes. "To him. Aunt Elaine, meet Wes Brody. My husband."

Elaine's jaw dropped. "Good God, Ronnie," she said, pressing her hand to her chest. "A little warning."

"Jareth refused to go through with it," Ronnie said. "So Wes stepped in."

Aunt Elaine gave Wes a searching stare. "Well, well. We owe him a debt of gratitude. Come on over here and sit down, Mr.…what was your name again?"

"Wes Brody. I'm glad to meet you, Mrs. Moss. Please call me Wes."

"Then you must call me Elaine. Lizette is bringing coffee and some of her marvelous Scottish shortbreads. Settle in, young man." She leaned forward, patting the chair next to her own. "Tell me all about yourself." She smiled, but her eyes had a glint of pure steel. "And I…mean…everything."

Over the next hour or two, Elaine Moss put Wes's nerves brutally to the test. When that woman said "everything," she meant everything. He told her about his past, his education, his mother, his work, his health history, his religious beliefs, his political stance, his knowledge of current events, his scientific literacy. Until his voice cracked.

The only facts she did not forcibly excavate were the

details of his father's occupation. He mentioned that his father died when he was ten, and she had the delicacy to leave it alone. Random luck, because lying to her would not be easy, with those laser-bright eyes boring into his face. The woman would have made a kick-ass CIA interrogator. And all gracefully clothed in the guise of polite, friendly interest.

Ronnie watched the show, a subtle gleam of amusement in her eyes.

On the plus side, Elaine had shown no sign of recognizing his name. So Caleb and Tilda had kept the drama to themselves. It was a good thing that he hadn't pressed charges against Tilda for stealing the file. Everyone would have known his name. Ronnie would never have gotten anywhere near him.

But that wasn't the reason he'd passed on pressing charges. Truth was, he'd refrained because of Annika. He liked and respected Tilda Riley, though he'd been furious at her at the time. But she had done what she did for love, however dumb and wrongheaded it was. Not for spite, or revenge, or greed, or the other classic bad reasons. And she had a sweet little girl who would be motherless if Tilda got locked up.

He was a big sap, and he wasn't taking an innocent little kid's mother away from her if he could help it. Mom and Dad would never have approved.

Lizette's coffee and shortbreads were a welcome diversion. He crunched one of the buttery, delicious cookies as he looked around the luxurious library. It was a large, bright, airy room, with high vaulted ceilings, and beautiful shelves of antique books. Portraits were hung at intervals between the bookshelves.

"Is this the family portrait gallery?" he asked.

"That's right," Elaine said. "This one is my late husband, Bertram." The old lady gestured at a portrait of a stern, handsome man in the prime of his life.

Then she pointed at a black-and-white photograph of a beautiful young dark-haired woman on a swing. "That's a photograph of my late daughter Susanna. Caleb, Marcus and Maddie's mother. I never had a chance to get a portrait painted of her. She never stayed still long enough. She never married, but she brought her children home for me to raise."

Wes recognized the subject of the next one. A striking painting in oil of a stunning redhead. He turned to Ronnie. "That one is you, right? It's amazing."

Ronnie shook her head with a little smile. "That's not me."

"That's Naomi," Elaine said. "Ronnie's mother. Uncanny, isn't it?"

"She could be Ronnie's twin," Wes said. "She's stunning."

Ronnie gazed at the portrait. "Hah. I know about your gift for blarney."

"Not about this," he said. "I could not overstate your beauty if I tried."

"I agree." Elaine gave him an approving look. "And that's not all she got from Naomi. Her mother was a brilliant scientist and an innovative thinker. She was kind, compassionate, principled. All good things. Veronica inherited them all."

"I'm a lucky man," he said.

"You certainly are." Elaine looked at Ronnie. "You'll want to take this portrait to your own home when you start a dynasty. It's a precious memento of your mother."

"Ah, yes. About that," Ronnie said. "Aunt Elaine, Maddie said that she once went with you to a storage unit in Greenwood where you kept some of my mother's things."

Elaine's brows rose. "Oh. Yes. I meant to tell you about that, many times. But either you were rushing off to the four corners of the globe, or Jerome was breathing down my neck. There was always something, so I never got around to it."

"It seems pretty important," she said, keeping her tone gentle.

"Well, not really," Elaine said. "You see, I went through it. Truth to tell, there's not much there. At least not much that has any relevance. I remember some dishes, some furniture. Clothes and shoes, decades out of date. She sent a container off on a slow boat before the bombing happened. I picked out anything that might have some personal meaning for you. Letters, photos, jewelry. I think we got the best of it already. The rest doesn't amount to that much. It's just odds and ends, sweetheart. I stored if off the property to keep Jerome from sniffing around and finding it."

"I'd like to look at it, if you don't mind."

"Good heavens, of course not. It belongs to you, of course. I'm sorry I didn't tell you about it. Excuse me, and I'll get the key for the storage unit right now. I have to dig around a bit. Back in a tick."

Once Elaine left the room, Wes sagged in his chair. "Whoa," he said fervently. "She is a piece of work."

"Yes, she's something," Ronnie agreed. "She definitely likes you."

"Likes me? I've been wrung out like a dishrag! How would I feel like if she disliked me?"

"She wrings us out, too," Ronnie assured him. "I think she's relieved. She and I acted in anger after my father misbehaved at Maddie's wedding, with that decision to put me into the mandate. When we cooled off, we both regretted it."

"Yeah? What did he do to deserve it?"

"Maddie and Jack had left the signing of the marriage certificate for the last minute, for dramatic effect. Right before midnight. My dad made the paperwork disappear before they could sign anything."

"Yikes," he said. "But clearly, his tactic didn't work. How did they pull that off?"

"They got privately married before the public ceremony," Ronnie said. "They left nothing to chance. Dad was beside himself. I haven't spoken to him since."

"Life is short," Wes said thoughtfully. "It's a shame, to be estranged from family."

"Oh, I doubt he misses me," she said. "But enough about him. I'm curious to see that storage unit, even if it's just dusty garbage."

"Hell, yeah," he said. "I can't wait."

Ronnie waved that away. "Oh, please. I don't expect you to root around in moldy boxes. You don't have to prove yourself to me. Go relax. I'll do it on my own and tell you what I find when I come home."

"I'm not letting you face those feelings alone. When I found my dad's journal, it was wrenching. I want to be there for you."

"Oh, that's lovely, honey! You should let him go with you! By all means."

They turned to see Aunt Elaine in the door of the library. "Sorry, love," her aunt said. "Was that a private moment?"

"Um…a little bit," Ronnie murmured.

"Oops. My bad." Elaine sounded unrepentant. "When a man offers to help with heavy, dusty boxes and possibly spiders, for goodness' sake, let him do it. What are men for, anyway?"

Wes choked on his laughter and stood, taking a bow. "At your service," he said.

"That's the spirit," Elaine said. "You'll do, Wes Brody."

"I hope so," he said. "She's incredibly special. She'll be hard to live up to."

Elaine's face softened. "I'm glad to hear you say that, and I hope that you mean it, because she is special. She deserves a man who's grateful. Jareth was never grateful, and that bothered me. Intensely."

"Aunt Elaine, please," Ronnie pleaded. "You're embarrassing me."

"Sorry, but I can't help it. It's what you deserve." Elaine locked eyes with Wes. "Buckle up, new guy," she said. "Whoever you are and whatever you've done, you will have to up your game to be worthy of her."

Wes inclined his head. The nod felt almost ceremonial. "I'm ready."

Elaine held out a small manila envelope to Ronnie. "That you go, darling. There's a key inside, and a card with the address of the storage place. Unit 824. I hope you find something that makes the trip worthwhile."

Ronnie took the envelope and tucked it in her purse. "Thank you, Aunt Elaine."

Aunt Elaine gave her a hug and turned to Wes. "And you," she said. "I hope you live up to your unexpected good fortune."

"Aunt Elaine!" Ronnie protested. "Give it a rest!"

"Oh, he can take it, honey," Elaine said. "I find that refreshing. He's sharp, too. Jareth was always too busy listening to himself talk to get my barbs. This one's different. He never misses a beat."

"I hope that's a good thing," Wes said wryly.

"It's certainly a more interesting thing." Elaine had a hint of humor in her voice. "I look forward to hosting dinner when all the kids get home. My goodness, what a gathering of talent that will be."

Wes forced a smile. "I look forward to it."

"And not that it's essential, but you are a fine specimen to add to our collection of ridiculous good looks," she said, with obvious satisfaction. "What a lineup. Something for every possible taste."

"Aunt!" Ronnie gasped. "That is so inappropriate!"

"Oh, pfft," Aunt Elaine scoffed. "I'm old and dotty, sweetheart. I get to be inappropriate when I feel like it. It's one of the very few advantages of advanced age."

They made their goodbyes, and got into the car, where Wes sat, staring blankly out the windshield at a hydrangea bush.

"Um… Wes?" Ronnie ventured. "Are you okay? Traumatized? Clobbered?"

He laughed and shook his head. "It was exhilarating. She's intense, but I like her."

Ronnie looked relieved. "Excellent, because she is important to me."

He concentrated on getting the car in gear before she could see the look in his eyes. He knew exactly what Elaine would think of him when the truth came out.

So now he had yet another reason to dread that moment.

They made their way to the Greenwood address on the card, Fillmore and Sons U-Store. It was a large complex, ringed by a chain-link fence.

At the glassed-in front office near the drive-through gate was a young woman with bleached blond hair and tattooed forearms. She looked up from her novel and her eyes stuck on him appreciatively.

"Excuse me," Ronnie said, her tone sharper than usual. "We need to get into unit 824. We have a key. Which way do we go?"

"Through this door, turn right, and go all the way to

the last aisle before you turn left," the blonde girl said. "It should be halfway down that aisle."

It was starting to rain, and the wind was gusting hard, but they found the unit quickly. Ronnie stood staring at the door as if she were afraid of it. Gathering her courage.

Wes waited. The moment could not be rushed. Not with memories and ghosts rustling around them in the wind.

As if in answer to his thought, thunder rolled in the distance, and the rain got heavier, drops pattering down and marking the concrete.

She shot him a rueful smile. "Sorry," she whispered. "Just working up the nerve."

"Take your time," he said gently.

But as she fit the key into the lock, his own heartbeat sped up. His palms sweated.

Not cool. He could not display intense, inappropriate interest in the contents of Ronnie's mother's boxes. She would feel it, as intuitive as she was. And he did not want to ruin this. For him, or for her. It was too important.

He breathed to lessen his stress response as she pushed the door open.

Eleven

Ronnie stepped into stale darkness. There was a light switch by the door. She flicked it on, revealing a square, blank room, smelling of dust. A pile of boxes and a clump of plastic-wrapped furniture were positioned in the center.

There it was. She didn't know what she'd expected. She knew there would be no bolt of heavenly light from above, no angel chorus. So why the clammy hands, the racing heart, the butterflies? What the hell was she looking for?

Something to feed her hungry heart.

It made her feel so vulnerable, but at least Wes was with her. She could endure being seen in this naked, fragile state by Wes. Who knew why.

The rain was getting harder, so she stepped forward, making space for Wes to follow her in. She walked over to the stack, and around it. There were a few pieces of furniture. A plastic-wrapped wingback chair, the plastic long since decayed into shreds, thick with dust. A coffee table of a dark, carved wood that looked like it might be beautiful under the grime. Many larger boxes, some smaller ones.

They had all been opened and then resealed with packing tape. Presumably on Aunt Elaine's and Maddie's foray years ago, looking for photographs.

Her knees were wobbly, but this was a job that needed doing, with driving, focused attention, or else she'd drown in it. She seized one of the boxes on the top and tried lifting it. It was very heavy.

"Hey!" Wes said. "Hold it right there."

She looked at him over her shoulder. "Huh? Why?"

"Let me do the heavy lifting. Didn't you hear your aunt? What are men for but lifting dusty boxes and dealing with spiders?"

Ronnie laughed. "I'm actually quite strong, you know. I work out."

"I noticed," he said. "I've inspected every inch of you. I'm in awe."

"Stop your blathering. I also once wrote a paper in college on tropical arachnids. I'm not scared of a few barn spiders."

"Even so," he said firmly, hoisting up the box. "Indulge me. What does it cost you? One tiny, throwaway gesture, to make me feel useful and manly."

She laughed at him as she peeled off the tape that held the box closed.

It was full of books. Drip irrigation, hydroponics, ethical biofuels. Genetically modified seeds, the future of agricultural plastics.

"Let me open boxes at the same time," he suggested. "We can inventory them twice as fast. If I find something which strikes me as personal, I'll draw your attention to it." He reached into his coat pocket and pulled out a pen. "We'll label each box's contents when we're done."

It sounded like a plan, so they got right to it. She sat on the floor and went through the books in the box. Some pages were marked, notes taken in her mother's small, elegant cursive script.

She opened a book about drip irrigation techniques, and something fluttered down onto her lap. A bookmark.

Her heart jolted, in a flash of memory. It was a picture that she had drawn herself. The violets that had been blooming in the garden outside. She had tried to render the clump of flowers exactly, and then color it with her colored pens. Her dad's butler at the time, the benevolent old Mr. Braxton, had taken it to have it laminated so that she could send it to her mother in Sri Lanka as a bookmark.

Her mother had mailed her a similar bookmark, also laminated. A drawing Mom had drawn for her, of a Kadupul, the Queen of the Night. A beautiful, stately pink blossom with a yellow center, native to Sri Lanka. She'd painted it with watercolors.

Ronnie had kept that bookmark tacked to the wall over her bed until she went to college. She still had it, tucked into the photo album with her pictures of her mother.

It took a couple of minutes for the blur of tears to clear from her eyes.

"You found something?" Wes asked.

She held out the bookmark to him. "A bookmark that I made and sent to her when she was in Sri Lanka. Mr. Braxton, the butler, helped me laminate it."

Wes leaned over and took the bookmark carefully in his hand. "It's beautiful," he said. "You drew this when you were seven? It's incredibly detailed."

She started to speak, then gave it up, and worked on making her chin stop shaking.

Wes handed the bookmark to Ronnie and rested his

hand on her shoulder. "See?" he said gently. "Already worth it. You reached across time, and she reached back."

Ronnie let out a soggy laugh. "Stop it. Or I warn you, I'll cry."

"It's okay to cry," he said. "I cried when I read my dad's journal. You'll feel better if you do. That's another gift."

Ronnie looked away as her face dissolved again.

After that little meltdown, they settled in. Box after box of file folders, project reports, documents, correspondence, all regarding the many agricultural projects that her mother had been overseeing at the time.

The next few boxes were full of glassware, dishes. Then there was a box of beautiful teapots. Some looked very old. She lifted out a silver-plated one, with spots on it that were worn thin and stained dark from age. It was decorated with semiprecious stones in claw settings and had a handle made of yellowed horn.

She turned it around in her hand, understanding why her mother had decided to ship it home. It felt good, to resonate to the same beauty that Mom had.

"I'll take this one home today, and brew some tea in it," she said.

"Great idea," he said. "Hey, look at these. It's been just books up to now, but this one has textiles."

Ronnie knelt and pulled out the one on the top, unwrapping the plastic wrapping. It was a handloom piece, made of silk and delicately embroidered with a complicated pattern, all in shades of blue. "Pretty," she said, digging deeper. "These are gorgeous. I have to do something with these."

And so it went. Many, many boxes of things which time had made irrelevant, mixed in with small, random treasures.

The rainy afternoon faded into twilight. By then, she'd

set aside a couple of big boxes of things to take home. Some of the lengths of cloths, a gorgeous set of mother of pearl brushes, combs and a hand mirror, several intricately carved wooden boxes, a set of wooden animals, wrapped in brown paper, and tucked into the middle of a bunch of genetics journals. There was a piece of paper taped to the top, and "Ronnie-babe" written on it, in her mother's beautiful cursive handwriting.

Wes never complained, as twilight stretched into evening. She got up, rubbing her stiff knees. Wes was peeling open a fresh box and leafing swiftly through the files.

"This must be crushingly boring for you," she said.

"Wrong. There is nowhere in the world I'd rather be right now." He pulled an envelope from the box and looked up at her. "Ronnie?" he said. "Look at this."

She hurried over to him "What did you find?"

He passed her a battered manila envelope. On the front, in black marker, was "Letters from Ronnie." It had a wreath of doodled hearts all around it.

Her eyes fogged up as she pulled out the sheaf of letters. "Oh, my God," she whispered. "I wrote every week, and she kept them all." She shuffled through them. "I started every single one with 'How are you? I am fine.'"

Wes leaned over to look at them. "I bet she loved getting these letters."

Ronnie traced the hearts her mom had drawn on the envelope with her finger. Such an offhand, thoughtless doodle. She might not have done it consciously at all. And it had taken on such a huge significance, twenty-three years later.

Throwaway moments, lost in time. As precious as pearls.

She felt Wes's hand on her shoulder. "Hey," he said. "I

know you're very focused, but you should have a cup of tea. Or dinner. You haven't eaten since those shortbreads."

Ronnie snuffled into a tissue. "Neither have you."

"Okay, fine. I admit, I'm hungry. Shall we break for a while? Come back tomorrow? We can take the things you set aside with us."

"They're heavy. We can bring a cart on another day."

"Let me bring them to the car now. You need those little animals on your shelf tonight. That bookmark gets tucked into the corkboard over your desk, and you need that teapot, to brew some tea after dinner. Speaking of dinner. Shall we order out?"

"Great idea. Thai Dream is near my place. They're great. Do you like Thai?"

"Love it," he said. "My mouth is watering already."

"Look at their online menu, and order in the car as we're heading home," she suggested. "I have an account there, and they deliver quickly."

"Sounds great. Let's make a run for it. It's still raining hard."

They made it out to the car getting only minimally soaked. Ronnie put the heat on while Wes took charge of ordering what sounded like a delicious and abundant meal from Thai Dream. The food arrived right after they got home. Wes carried up her boxes while Ronnie received the fragrant, heavy bags filled with Thai Dream's bounty. The timing was good because the rain had begun to pound very heavily.

Once inside, they set the table and popped open ice-cold beers. They feasted on dumplings, skewers of chicken with peanut sauce, rice noodles, grilled sea bass with a ginger sauce, beef and basil, curried shrimp, calamari. It was delicious. Reaching across time was hungry work.

Ronnie's smartphone buzzed as they were polishing

off the calamari. She glanced at the display. "Excuse me, but this is one of my team," she told him. "I need to take this. Word must be getting around about the show being canceled."

"Go right ahead," he said. "I know there's a lot going on for you."

She hit Talk. "Hi, Elliott."

"Is it true?" Elliott wailed. "Are they insane?"

"Yes, they are, and I'm so sorry," she said. "Jareth and I didn't get married after all, so he canceled me out of spite."

"But it was so good! And everyone was making money hand over fist!"

"Yes, I know, I know. It's awful."

"We have to see if we can take it to another production company," Elliott said. "Avery and I are hopping on an early flight to Seattle. We made an appointment with an IP lawyer that Jane recommended. She's already studying our contract with Fadden Boyle, and she'll meet with us tomorrow afternoon at one. Can you be there?"

Her eyes strayed to Wes, hesitating for a second. "Yes, of course."

"Great. I'll text you the address. I think it's walking distance from your condo. Let's meet at noon, for coffee, before we go up to see her. There's no time to waste. I would hate to lose *Secret Life*'s momentum."

"Fingers crossed," Ronnie said. "Till tomorrow, then, Elliott."

She laid the phone down. "I have to leave you for a few hours tomorrow," she said. "My team wants to strategize. We're talking to an IP lawyer."

"Excellent," he said. "Don't worry about me. I've got plenty to do. I'm a big boy."

"You certainly are," she murmured.

They locked eyes, and she gazed straight at him, savoring the delicious hum of sexual tension between them. God, how she loved that. The intense awareness. The heat, rising. The mind connection, shining in the air. The hunger, growing, deepening.

Wes stood and went to the boxes that he'd carried inside. He took out the silver-plated teapot, and carried it to the sink, rinsing off the dust, and polishing it with a tea towel. Ronnie searched through her tea drawer for the jasmine tea and put the kettle on.

They brewed tea in the beautiful little pot, drinking the fragrant, steaming brew out of the delicate, gem-studded silver cups.

"The teapot looks good in here," he said. "I'm glad you have it."

"Yes, it's wonderful," she said. "Thank you, for encouraging me to do this. It feels incredible, to have her things around me. Like being kissed."

His smile was very sweet. "Anything that makes you feel good is all right by me."

Ronnie grabbed his hand. "You helped me make the leap. You know how it feels."

His eyes were somber. "You're welcome," he said. "It's an honor to be of service to you. Like I said to your aunt. I meant it."

She couldn't seem to speak, so she squeezed his hand.

"Trying to live up to you will make me a better man," he went on.

That made her intensely self-conscious. "Come on, Wes. Now you're overdoing it. I'm not some celestial being. I'm very fallible."

"I am not overdoing it." He lifted her hand to his lips, pressed slow, deliberate kisses to her knuckles. "It's straight from the heart."

The air turned electric. All she heard was the rain outside, a thrum against glass. She could hardly breathe for the shimmer, the ache of anticipation that glowed in every part of her body. It deepened, wanting to burst open like a flower and be entirely known.

Maybe she pulled him, maybe he pulled her, but soon they were twined together. Hungry, eager, pleading, demanding. Both ready to give everything to the other. Both demanding everything in return.

Such contradictions. She didn't know him at all, and yet, he knew her better than anyone ever had. After two days, she felt more real and authentic with him than she ever been before. She loved feeling so spontaneous, passionate, joyful, sensual. Bold and brave. Even…happy.

Oh, God. She was almost afraid to think it. Definitely afraid to feel it.

Wes lifted her up, her arms around his neck, her legs around his waist, every part of her melting hot with pleasure, every part that touched him coming wildly alive. She lifted herself, moving against him as he carried her into the bedroom, cupping her bottom.

He kicked off his shoes before setting her down, pulling aside the bedclothes. The skylight over her bed was a heavy drum of rain. The sound felt cleansing.

She pulled her clothes off, as he did with his own, and pulled him on top of her, kissing him eagerly while he caressed her most sensitive flesh with his incredible, unerring skill, delving into her, slowly stroking. Just the right spot, just the right way, swirling and pressing, pushing her closer and closer to…oh yes.

The whole world was lost in a long, blinding pulse of pleasure.

When she gathered her senses into one place, Wes was on top of her, inside of her. His warmth covered her whole body. Inside her, poised and waiting.

She gave him a lazy smile of encouragement, arching her spine, canting her hips.

"What are you waiting for?" she whispered.

"For you to say that," he said, laughing.

And they were off. Deep, slick, marvelous. He surged inside her, as she clutched his shoulders, legs folded high, nails dug into his shoulders, gasping. Egging him on.

He brought her to orgasm three more times with his masterful skill, explosive and deep and wrenching. After the third one, she drifted back to him kissing her forehead, his hand cradling her head, stroking her damp hair. "Can I?" he asked, hoarsely.

"God, yes."

He let go, and so did she, clutching him and sobbing as they launched over the edge. Soaring together, endlessly.

Afterward, they got rid of what clothing clung to bodies and arranged the covers over themselves. It was all they had the strength for.

Then it was just cuddling. Lazily kissing, stroking, exploring, memorizing. Holding each other, as close as they could.

She draped herself over his big body, playing with his chest hair. Every detail of him was something to be marveled at. She had never been so relaxed. Images drifted through her head, of the day's discoveries. The bookmark, inside drip irrigation techniques. Doodled hearts on the envelope. The teapot, the wooden animals. Small things, seemingly insignificant, but they were caresses from an invisible, benevolent entity.

As a little girl, she'd liked to imagine that her mother was watching her from heaven. Or perhaps was even closer, like a ghost. As she got older, her rational mind had decided that fantasy was childish and silly. She'd locked it behind a heavy door.

But she hadn't killed it. It was alive, and as soft and open as she felt, that heavy door would not stay closed. It was wide open, and astonishing truths were rushing out.

That anything was possible. That love was eternal.

Maybe Mom had helped bring Wes to her so that Wes could bring her back to Mom. So many memories were waking up. The love she'd felt, the feelings she'd buried, the loss, the pain. A heart hurt when it came back to life. It burned like a coal, but it was worth the pain. As the rain pattered gently on the glass above them, as she inhaled Wes's hot, salty scent, her face against his chest, she no longer felt afraid of it. That was Mom's gift to her. It would shine inside her forever.

Maybe. In any case, it was a lovely fantasy, and it hurt no one.

She let it carry her gently away.

Twelve

Nothing. There was nothing in Naomi Moss's boxes that pertained to the toxic-mold disaster or the subsequent cover-up.

His mother had pounded away at MossTech and their army of lawyers for years. Peg Brody had raged and railed until she exhausted herself, but the case against his dad had been watertight.

Or rather, it had been until Wes found the file, and his dad's journal. Over a decade after Mom's death.

Wes set the final box down right where they had left it the night before and stretched, wiping his hands on his jeans.

He'd marked the boxes he'd searched the day before. Today he'd gone through every box that he hadn't gone through himself yesterday. Page by page. Item by item.

There was nothing in this storage unit that could exonerate his father's memory or incriminate the senior Mosses.

And all he felt about it was intense relief. That burden has been lifted from him. He would get no justice for his dad's disgrace, or his mom's heartbreak—that was true—but at least he was not obliged to attack the Moss family.

That would have killed him inside, now that he was bonded with Ronnie.

Of course, his love affair with her was doomed. The truth would come out as soon as Tilda and Caleb came back. He was screwed, no matter what he had or hadn't done.

He wished he'd never found his dad's journal and the lab notes in the Colombo house. That he'd met Ronnie Moss at some investor function or other and chatted her up like a normal guy. No agenda other than desire. Free to woo her with all the skill and style and charm that he had in his arsenal. And if he got lucky, marriage. A real one. A life with her. A family, tough as that would be with two busy careers. In sickness and in health.

And of course, in honor and in disgrace, like the Brodys did it. Mom had never lost faith in her man, no matter how they slandered him.

He wanted that life with Ronnie so badly. As much as Fate would allow. His parents had been cheated of that, and now he'd cheated himself of it, too. His dad's disgrace had tormented him all his life. He'd hoped that putting it right would give them all peace.

But everything had its price, and the price of his quest for truth was Ronnie. The sweetest thing life had to offer him. And oh God, was he sorry.

Now all that was left for him to do was to find the courage to come clean. The last thing he could give her. Brutal honesty.

He shook out the kinks, and switched off the light, then locked up with the key he'd copied. Ronnie had left it on the kitchen bar, luckily for him, because he would not have the stomach to fish in her purse for it. Not that swiping a key that had been left in the open was any less a betrayal. But there were lines he wouldn't cross.

He strolled past the front office and heard a voice behind him. "Hey, Mr. Moss?"

Whoa. That whipped his head around. "Are you talking to me?"

"Yeah!" It was the blonde girl, coming to the door of the glassed-in front office. She wore short sleeves today, leaving the tree tattoos on her arms on full display.

"My name's not Moss," he told her.

"Oh." She looked confused. "But you're unit 824, right? Moss is the name on it."

"Yes, that's correct," he said. "It belongs to Veronica Moss."

"Okay. I just need to tell everyone from unit 820 through 836 that we had a problem with the rain gutters clogging the drain after the storm last night, and there was a little flooding this morning. Was there any water in your unit?"

"Just a trickle near the door. I swept it out into the drain outside. It didn't get near the boxes."

"Okay. I was just told to call and let everyone know that the problem has been fixed, and the gutters are clean. Will you tell her?"

"Sure. Thanks, I appreciate that."

He got into the Mercedes SUV that he'd leased that afternoon, after their leisurely brunch at Café Kuna. One hand feasting on eggs Benedict and strawberries with cream, the other hand twined with Ronnie's slender hand, which needed an engagement ring.

Pearls, definitely. Glowing with the magic and the mystery of the sea.

It was money down the drain for sure. A foolish sacrifice upon the altar of guilt. When the truth came out, she would throw that ring in his face, and he would deserve it.

But he wanted to honor her with a ring worthy of her beauty. He wanted that moment with her, no matter what came after. He still hoped that somehow, he could convince her that his feelings were real, and the ring was tangible, costly evidence of his sincerity. Or maybe it would just look to her like more crass manipulation.

Screw it. He'd blunder forward in the dark as best he could. With a ring.

After a day of reading all of Naomi's correspondence, articles, reports, he'd concluded that the woman was just how Elaine had described her: intelligent, principled, committed to her work and to being of service. He liked Naomi Moss. She was a dedicated scientist, a devoted mother, a loving wife.

His father's journal had documented his confusion. He'd liked Naomi, too, and he hadn't wanted to believe that she could be behind that cover-up. He'd steeled himself to do the right thing if she was a criminal. Wes had memorized those passages.

Confronted Naomi M. today and demanded the truth. She promised to tell me everything, but only in person. Won't talk on the phone. Seems paranoid. She's sending copies of the documentation home in case something "happens" to her. Can't wait to be done with this crap and get back to Wes and Peg. I am not cut out for intrigue.

After what Wes had read today, he doubted that Naomi Moss had framed his dad. It was a shame that he couldn't have obtained this game-changing information before he'd ruined any possible future with Ronnie, but at least he wouldn't be throwing mud on Ronnie's memories of her mother. He of all people knew how bad that felt.

And despite her bossiness, he liked Elaine Moss. She'd

been half a world away, running a far-flung company with her husband, raising three rambunctious grandkids. She'd been in no position to fabricate a frame job, or plot John Padraig's downfall.

He had to let go, and hope that his parents would forgive him. He was sure that they would, if they knew how he felt. Both of them were gone. He couldn't help them, or save them. There was no peace to be found by following this path. He couldn't change the past.

But dammit, he wanted a shot at the future.

So he was letting this go. He actually was. Damn.

The realization made him giddy and disoriented. Everything was changing. The ground shifting under his feet.

Tonight, he'd cook Ronnie a fabulous dinner. Then, he would book a room in the most beautiful and romantic place that he could find that was within a couple of hours' drive of the city. Tomorrow, he'd shop for the ring. He would present it to her once they were at their destination, and throw himself on her mercy. There had to be a way to make her understand.

He loved her. He wanted a life with her. He wanted to offer her everything that he had, everything that he was. He'd do anything, give up anything for her.

Even his obsession for justice.

Thirteen

Ronnie had just parked her car when her smartphone buzzed. Lizette's name was on the display. Her aunt's butler.

"Hi, Lizette. Is everything okay with Aunt Elaine?"

"Everything's fine," Lizette said. "This isn't about Mrs. Moss. She's doing well."

"Great," she said. "So what's up?"

"Well, I got to thinking. When I heard that you'd asked for the keys to that storage unit, I remembered a conversation that I had years ago with Braxton, before he retired. It was at some big family event, maybe Christmas, and Braxton hinted about how Jerome went off the rails after your mother died and burned all her things. Papers, photographs and what have you. Braxton disapproved of that tantrum very strongly."

"Yes, I remember that tantrum," Ronnie said. "All too well."

"Well, anyhow, Braxton hinted that he hadn't let Jerome find everything. He'd kept some things aside that Jerome didn't know about. Braxton died a couple years after they hired Olsen, and Olsen might not have ever known about these things Braxton was keeping for you. So I called him yesterday, and I asked him to take a look in the nooks and crannies where a butler might hide a stash. And he called me back. He found it!"

"Oh," Ronnie said, her heart thudding. "Oh, my goodness."

"I know, right? So anyhow, call Olsen. He's very pleased with himself."

"I will. Thank you, Lizette. It's so nice of you to chase that down for me."

"Honey, it's my pleasure. I'm glad that my inquiry bore fruit. Tell me more when you find out what it is. Come visit and bring that lovely tall drink of water with you."

She laughed. "Will do, Lizette."

She sat there, a fine tremor of excitement and emotion vibrating through her.

Signs and symbols were gathering around her. She was trained in science, and didn't usually indulge in magical thinking, but right now, she felt as if she were in one of those ancient folk tales. The orphan girl with the magical tree that rained down gifts.

Someone was watching over her. Someone who loved her.

And what did it matter? Real or not, fantasy or not, she would just enjoy it and be grateful. To whatever or whoever was showering her with love and luck.

Olsen picked up on the first ring. "Veronica! Hello! I'm so glad you called."

"Hi, Olsen. Lizette told me you had found a box of my mother's things?"

"I did! In a crawl space up in the attic. A beautiful carved wooden chest, full of your baby things, and photographs. It has Veronica carved into the top. I would never have found it in a million years if Lizette hadn't told me to look for it."

"I'll come by and pick it up. Could I swing by tomorrow?"

"Of course. I'll be here, waiting for you."

She practically floated up to her condo. Delicious smells met her nose as she walked inside, and music was playing. Roddy Hepner's new hit single, "If You'd Only Take A Chance On Me." She set her purse on the shelf and entered the kitchen.

Wes smiled over his shoulder from the stove. "Good timing," he said. "I just decanted a nice pinot. It's been breathing the last few minutes, waiting for you." He set aside the wooden spoon, poured a glass of wine and handed it to her. "Try this."

Ronnie sipped it with a sigh of pleasure. "You've been busy."

"Oh, yeah. I leased a car, and I did some shopping and cooking. I also hatched tentative plans for a romantic honeymoon adventure. Pending your approval and availability, of course."

"I'm intrigued," she said. "Tell me more."

"I will, but first, come and have some dinner."

He ushered her into the dining area, and she gazed around with delight at the spectacle. Candles flickered on the table. A spike of calla lilies was the centerpiece, and a spread of goodies was laid out on many plates. Sliced cheeses, tiny little fresh mozzarella knots, plump red olives, sun-dried tomatoes and roasted eggplants.

"Sit down. Relax with your wine. Start nibbling while I drain the *paccheri*."

Ronnie did as he suggested. She hadn't eaten for a long time, and the wine was perfect. Everything looked and tasted fabulous. There was hot, crusty bread to go with it. A fresh salad, gleaming with olive oil.

After a couple minutes, Wes carried in two plates heaped with fresh *paccheri*, like big, floppy fresh macaroni noodles, chewy and delicious, dressed with a creamy, orange pinkish sauce, sprinkled with basil and grated pecorino cheese.

"We'll start with this while the steak is resting," he said.

"It looks wonderful," she said. "What's in that sauce?"

"Roasted red and yellow peppers. Once they soften in the oven, I peel and deseed them, sauté them with garlic and butter, and then purée and mixed them with fresh basil and some heavy cream. And the cheese at the end, of course."

She took a bite and moaned in bliss. "Wes, you're an artist."

"I know," he agreed. "I've always liked cooking."

The pasta was delicious, as was the tender grilled flatiron steak, the salad. To finish was a tiny, heart-shaped cheesecake, perfect for two, decorated on top with gleaming raspberries, blueberries and blackberries. "This, I bought," he admitted. "I didn't have time for pastry tonight. But I'm equal to it. I make a Christmas bread pudding out of gingerbread that would blow your mind. Cream sauce with a slosh of good whiskey in it. My mom's holiday request, every Christmas. It was her favorite."

"I can't wait to taste it," she told him. "I'm not much of a cook myself. Eggs and toast and a sandwich, at best. Takeout and yogurt, usually. And fruit."

"Only the most delicious morsels shall pass your rosy lips when I am at your side."

She was charmed by his nonsense. It was seductive,

being met when she came home by food, warmth, music, welcome. A glass of wine, a kiss. Someone who was happy to see her. It was an exquisite luxury. Some part of her felt like she didn't deserve it. She didn't dare let herself get used to it. Too sweet to be real. Too good to be true.

"So how did it go today?" Wes asked.

She nibbled her cheesecake, trying to take the smallest bites she could, just to make it last. "It was good to see my team, but the situation doesn't look good. According to this lawyer, our agent wasn't aggressive enough at protecting my interests. The way our contract is worded, if Jareth and his production team feel like messing with us, they could block us from taking the show elsewhere."

"Even if they refuse to produce it themselves?"

"Even then. Even if they did, I don't want to work with Jareth. I don't want him responsible for my livelihood, or for him to have control of my creative projects."

"I'm tempted to have a little conversation with him myself. Just to clear the air."

"Don't you dare," she warned him. "Don't get near him. All this stuff has absolutely nothing to do with you."

"Okay, don't worry," he soothed. "I won't worry my pretty little head. I'll stay in my proper place with my hands folded. Pinkie swear."

"Oh, stop it."

He nudged his chair closer. "Let's change the subject to something more cheerful and frivolous," he said. "I have an indecent proposition. Have you got meetings planned with your team for the next few days?"

"Not until next week. Elliott and Avery had to get back to LA to finish some other projects, and then we'll meet in LA. I told them that I needed a few days to decompress."

"Awesome," Wes said. "Because there's this resort I found. It's called Cloud Top. Only a few guests at a time allowed. Each suite has a terrace out in front with complete privacy and a view of the canyon, with hot mineral water piped into a private tub sunk into the rocks. If we get there in time, we can watch the sunset, naked and sipping prosecco, up to our nipples in hot mineral water. Here, look at the catalog."

He slid a tablet toward her. Ronnie scrolled through the stunning photos. The brochure showed all the different rooms and the terraces outside, the pools of steaming water. There was a sense of infinite space, soothing silence, exquisite luxury.

"It looks magical," she said.

"Good, because I took the liberty of booking five days there. Just you and me, far away from the jabbering voices and the grabby hands. In perfect privacy."

"Um…wow."

"I know this is a big ask," he said. "You're a busy woman, and a whole lot of people want a piece of you. I won't expect all your attention all the time. But for the next few days I'd really love to get you all to myself." He paused, looking at one of the photos. "Besides, can you imagine the fun we could have in one of those hot pools?"

"Yes, actually," she said. "When were you thinking of leaving?"

"How about tomorrow, late morning? We could check in tomorrow afternoon and watch the sunset. Dinner in our room. A long, luxurious soak. Hours of kissing. Time to learn more about you. What you dream about, what you like, what you hate, what you want. I want more data. More time. More Ronnie. As much as I can grab."

"Actually, you had me at 'indecent proposition,'" she said. "It's a fabulous idea."

"Excellent. I have to take care of an errand in the morning before we go."

"I have a couple of things to take care of, too," she said. "I need to stop by my father's house. My dad's butler, Olsen, told me that he found a box of my baby things. I absolutely want to collect that, as soon as possible. Just to protect it from my dad."

"I'd love to see where you grew up," he said. "Part of my data-gathering project."

Ronnie stood, shaking her hair loose and unbuttoning the top button of her white silk blouse. "I've got some data for you to collect, Wes." She unbuttoned the second button. Then the third. "Are you taking notes?"

"No need," he said. "I couldn't forget a single detail if I tried."

Ronnie finished the buttons, the cuffs. Peeled off the blouse. Unhooked the bra.

"Ronnie," he whispered. "You're so damn beautiful. It hurts to look at you."

"Suffer, then," she said, keeping her voice light. "But don't you dare look away."

That got a laugh from him. He stripped off his sweatshirt and she almost purred at the sight of his naked torso. So solid, so well proportioned. Too good to be true.

If something seems too good to be true, that's because it probably is.

Her father's cynical maxim floated into her head before she could block it. She wanted to slap it away, like a pesky fly. Or a wasp. This one stung.

And what was worse, there was a part of her that believed it. She'd always be carrying that doubt. A constant double vision. No matter how happy Wes made her, there was always that haunting certainty that anything so improbably sweet and fun and sensual and lovely had to be fleeting. Ephemeral. It was a natural law. Like gravity, like entropy.

It was the hard, painful stuff that stuck around, that stood the test of time. Guilt. Anger. Sorrow. You could count on those. They were as faithful as the dawn.

And so? Was that any reason to hold back? Life was short. Wes was here, right now. Tossing away his pants, standing there, stark naked, fully erect. Smoldering at her.

Now was not the time to pout about the ephemeral nature of love. Now was the time to take her satisfaction. She stepped out of her heels and shucked her pants. Snagged her panties with both thumbs and stripped them swiftly off.

Then she tossed away her comforter, and stretched out on the cool sheets, naked. She gazed up at him with sultry eyes. "Get over here, you," she said huskily.

He lost no time in obliging her.

Fourteen

"May I look at this one?" Wes asked.

"Certainly." The jeweler's eyes sparkled as she passed the pearl ring to Wes to examine more closely.

Yes. This was the one. It was a narrow platinum band with pavé diamonds all the way around, adorned by three natural pearls, each of a slightly different size. One was faintly pink, one was a rainbow-tinted, iridescent gray and one was a glowing, bronzy gold tone. A delicate ribbon of platinum studded with diamond brilliants held them together like a ribbon. Elegant, stunning, unique. Perfect for Ronnie.

It was also wildly expensive, but hey. If ever there was a time to make an extravagant statement, this was it. And he had plenty of money. What the hell.

The plan was to get Ronnie up to Cloud Top, soften her up with steaming mineral water, a sunset and champagne. Then he'd get on his knees, offer her the ring. Along with his heart, and his soul. He would blurt out the whole ugly, ungainly truth about his quest for justice. The lengths it had brought him to.

Of course, he couldn't buy a woman like Ronnie with a ring, or any sort of material goods. But symbols mattered. Sacrifice mattered.

He sized it on his own pinkie finger, having snooped into Ronnie's jewelry for just this purpose, just to be sure he was getting the size right.

Yes. It stuck exactly halfway up the second joint of his pinkie. Perfect.

"I'll take it," he said.

The woman beamed at him, as well she might, considering that she probably worked on commission. He'd looked at hundreds of rings today. He was lucky that he had a few points of reference. One, pearls. Two, a low setting, smooth, so as not to snag her nice cashmere knits. Three, it needed to be sublime. Gorgeous. Worthy of her divine beauty. The toughest requirement of all.

Once the transaction had been made, as well as the saleswoman's day—hell, probably her week—he tucked the small package into his bag and headed to his car. Everything was in place. Now it was balls to the wall.

The need to be honest with her had become urgent, driving. More painful with every hour he spent with her. He'd tell her how much he hoped for her forgiveness, her grace. The ring would say some of that nonverbally. The language of gemstones, held out by a man on his knees. Ring in one hand, and his naked, unprotected heart in the other.

Just take it. It belongs to you. Forever and always.

Please. Have mercy.

Oh, wow. Mom's textiles were gorgeous.

Ronnie sorted through the silk handloom and batik

pieces that were packed into one of the boxes that they had left behind in the storage area.

An idea had come to her last night, while dozing in Wes's embrace. She'd been looking at his chest, focused on the cheerful bold pattern of her duvet cover that she'd bought from a catalog. She'd suddenly thought of the beautiful pieces of fabric art that her mother had chosen to take home. There were maybe fifteen or sixteen of them that she had counted so far. They would be fabulous duvet covers.

She'd picked out two for herself, and four more, one each for her cousins and one for her aunt. Maddie and Jack got one with all the colors of the changing ocean, a nod to Jack's ocean-cleaning-enzyme formula. Tilda and Caleb's had the colors of the sky: pale blue, dark blue, stormy darker grays, for Tilda's meteorological tool, Far Eye. Eve and Marcus got green, to honor Eve's Corzo project, which they all hoped would help feed the world. The fiery-toned sunset-colored one was for Aunt Elaine. For herself, the sunflower gold, and the peony pink.

It made her happy to imagine her house beautified by things that her mother had handpicked. Naomi, once again reaching across time, giving a subtle kiss to her grown-up daughter. It felt intimate. Fanciful, maybe, but she was going to indulge herself.

She packed the box. It wasn't heavy, just cloth inside. As she went out, she noticed moisture near the door, but she'd be cleaning this place out soon. The problem was barely worth addressing. She locked up.

The blonde at the front desk jumped up when she saw her walking past. "Excuse me. You're Ms. Moss, right? The one with unit 824?"

Ronnie turned. "Yes, that's right. Can I help you?"

The blonde woman's eyes rolled in relief. "Okay, I was

just checking, because I messed up yesterday, when I called your husband Mr. Moss, and I wondered if—"

"My husband?" Ronnie repeated. "Yesterday?"

"So, like, he told you about the leak, right?"

Ronnie felt bewildered. "Leak? No one told me anything."

The blonde woman looked dismayed. "I told him to tell you! There was a blocked rain gutter, and the water went under the door of some of the units. We fixed it, so it won't happen again. But I was supposed to call everyone."

"I noticed a little water, but it wasn't near the boxes. But my husband wasn't here yesterday. You must've mixed him up with someone else."

"Oh yes, he was!" the young woman said. "It was him. Pardon my saying so, but a guy like that makes an impression on the eyeballs."

"True," Ronnie said wryly. "But he couldn't have been impressed on your eyeballs yesterday because we were here on Tuesday together. Not yesterday."

"Nope. I know he was because I told him about the water damage. The rainstorm was Tuesday night, and yesterday was Wednesday, I crossed 824 off the list of units I needed to call about."

"That's strange," Ronnie said. "But don't sweat it. I'll ask him. In any case, I know about the leak, and it's no biggie. Have a good day."

"Okay," the girl said doubtfully. "Have a good day yourself."

Huh. Strange. Ronnie tried to put it out of her head. She went about her errands quickly, to the sewing studio, where she'd gotten some clothes designed. She laid out her specs for the larger pieces to be cleaned, restored and turned into six sets of king-size duvet covers, each one backed with a high-thread-count linen backing, made from the predominant color in each piece. An aqua blue, a gray, a dark forest green, a rusty orange, a pale pink, and a bright, sunshiny yellow.

But she enjoyed herself less than she should have while comparing color swatches, talking design, feeling closer to Mom. Because that interchange had been so strange.

Yesterday? How in the hell…? Maybe the blonde had just vaped something hallucinogenic on her coffee break. But something felt off.

She saw Wes's newly leased SUV was parked in front of her condo, and Wes met her at the door, with a sensual kiss. "Hi," she said, as soon as she could come up for air.

"Hi. I missed you. So I did my thing. How about you? We good to go?"

"I'm just bringing the bag I packed this morning." She'd just thrown in sweaters, active-wear pants and good shoes for mountain walks, plus sexy unmentionables. She hoped to spend the majority of her time wearing those items. Or nothing.

"Already packed into the SUV," Wes said promptly. "So that's all?"

"That's all for the luggage," she said. "There's just one thing I need to ask you."

"Ask away," he said.

"I stopped at the storage unit this morning, to pick a few things up," she said.

He looked distressed. "You should've told me. You know I like to be there with you, to help with carrying boxes and wrangling spiders."

"The box wasn't heavy, just fabric. I took them to be made into duvet covers. I want to give my cousins a set. A memento of Aunt Naomi. Plus one for Aunt Elaine."

"That's a great idea," he said. "They'll be beautiful."

"The woman at the counter says that she saw you there

yesterday," she went on. "Evidently you guys had some sort of interchange about the water damage, which happened on Tuesday night. So…were you there?"

Wes frowned. "Yes, I was."

Ronnie's unease ripened into alarm. "Why on earth would you go there without telling me?"

He shrugged. "It's embarrassing, but yesterday after you left, I called about leasing a car, and when I went for my wallet for my credit card, I realized that I'd left my bag in the storage unit. It had my wallet, with my license, my cards, my cash. I didn't notice because I was carrying the boxes. You'd left the unit key on the bar, so I figured, why bother you? I called a car, went to the storage place for my bag, locked up and headed to the car dealership. I would have told you, but it was just logistics."

She relaxed. "Okay. I still wish you had said something."

"Sorry. I should have. I forgot. It would've come to me eventually."

"Okay," she said.

"So, next stop, the family seat. Lead the way. I feel like you're going to take us to some freaky Gothic pile on a windswept cliff. Or Bluebeard's castle."

She snickered. "That might be overstating it slightly. Dad's not a killer, just a garden-variety misogynist and curmudgeon. But he's in London, so our stop should be drama free. No telltale drops of blood, no one hanging by their hair in a locked tower room. Still, I want to rescue my box of keepsakes as soon as possible."

She looked into his smiling dark eyes and decided that she wasn't going to second-guess this. She'd milk it for all it was worth, not ruin it by being suspicious. Maybe she was a fatuous fool, but at least she'd be a blissful, happy, sexually fulfilled fatuous fool.

Fifteen

Wes was still shaking when they got on the road. Frantically wondering whether he had just hammered those coffin nails in even further by what he'd said to her.

More lies. But the timing was all wrong. He hadn't been ready, braced, fortified. He'd gotten so attached to the fantasy of going down on one knee at a luxury resort, pearl ring in hand. This was so delicate. It had to be carefully managed.

But he might have ruined everything. One more lie could be the final blow, if there had ever been any hope in the first place.

Ronnie's mood visibly altered as they got closer to her childhood home, as if a shadow had fallen over her.

"Are you okay?" he asked. "Are you sure that you want to do this right now?"

"Yes," she said. "I want everything that belonged to my

mother in my possession. I don't want to risk my father getting his hands on it."

They drew up to the tall, ornate wrought-iron gate, behind which was a stunning, ostentatious late-nineteenth-century mansion. Wes whistled softly. "Whoa."

"Yes, it's over-the-top," Ronnie said. "A rich, corrupt timber baron had this built as a wedding present for his extremely spoiled daughter at the end of the nineteenth century. She expanded it, and her children expanded again in the roaring twenties."

"It's impressive," he said. "But you sound like you don't approve of it."

Ronnie shrugged. "It's got bad memories for me. If I spend any amount of time here, I get depressed and anxious. This house will eventually be mine, I suppose. It'll go on the market before you can even blink."

"I hear you." Wes pulled the car to a halt.

A tall, balding man in his late fifties came out to greet them. Veronica greeted him warmly. "Olsen, let me present my husband, Wes Brody."

Olsen gave him a curious once-over. "I'm glad to meet you. Lizette told me about your news! I was so surprised. And…ah… Jareth?"

"Thought better of it," she said. "It's for the best. Wes suits me better."

Olsen grinned, pumping Wes's hand. "I'm so glad to hear that," he said. "Lizette spoke well of you. Come on in. The box is in the library."

The interior of the house was as spectacular as the exterior. Gleaming wood paneling, carved detailing, ornate molding, furnished with priceless antique furniture and fine art. Stained glass windows were in every room. The front hall had a beautiful Belle Epoque crystal chandelier. The grounds outside were exquisitely landscaped.

They were ushered into a huge library, with bookshelves that went up two stories high, colorful frescoes on the ceilings. A walkway stretched around the room halfway up, and sliding ladders were on both levels.

"What a room," Wes said. "It's stunning."

"Have a seat," Olsen encouraged, waving them toward the couch. On the table in front of it was a little beautiful wooden chest. Veronica was carved into the top.

Ronnie leaned over and touched it, her eyes shiny. "Wow," she whispered.

"I'll…ah…give you some privacy," Olsen said, hurrying out of the room.

"Would you like me to give you some privacy, too?" Wes asked gently. "I can wait right outside, if you want. For however long you need."

"No," she said swiftly. "Please, don't go. I want you right here with me."

"Whatever you want. I'm here for you."

She shot him a wan smile, then unlatched the clasp and lifted the lid.

The box was full of baby things, as Lizette had said. Ronnie lifted items out, one by one. White baby shoes, with satin roses. A white eyelet bib. A tarnished silver spoon. A crocheted lamb's-wool baby blanket. Onesies. A handful of small board books. She leafed through one of them, about a baby monkey who was looking for his mother.

She found an envelope full of photographs. Her as a newborn. Her at three months, four months, six months. Ronnie in her mother's arms, in her father's.

Ronnie held that picture up to examine it. "Huh," she murmured. "I can't remember ever seeing that expression on his face when he was looking at me."

"How could he help it?" Wes asked. "You were such a cute baby."

She held up another one, of Naomi Moss leaning toward her husband, both of them hugging Ronnie, who looked about three. All of them were laughing.

"So there were some good times, back in the day," Wes said. "That picture wouldn't have been possible otherwise. Those smiles can't be faked."

Ronnie's eyes were wet. "I'm not sure if that makes things better, or worse."

"This is your mom, reaching out across time," he said. "I'm going to go out on a limb here and suggest that it's better. Things are trending better. Trust your mom."

She slanted him a look. "That's a sweet thought, but you haven't met my dad yet."

"You have a point," he admitted. "And I admit, I'm biased. I want things to be better for you. Not just better. The absolute best. You deserve it, and I want that for you with every fiber of my being."

He'd never been so sincere, or so terrified. So much hung on a thread.

Ronnie tucked the photos into the envelope. "Thank you," she said. "There are other treasures in here to pore over, but not here, not now. I can only take this house in microdoses, and I'm already over my limit." She shot him a teasing smile. "Besides, I'm excited to get to our romantic hideaway resort."

"Then let's be on our way." He hoisted up the chest. "I'll take this out to the car."

Olsen went before him, opening all the doors for Wes on his way to the entry hall. Wes waited by the door as Ronnie gave Olsen a warm hug.

"Thanks so much for finding that box," she told him. "I

know you must've spent hours crawling around in dusty hidey-holes looking for it. It means the world to me."

"I'm delighted that I did," Olsen told her. "I'm so glad that Lizette suggested it."

There was a thudding and a clatter outside, a shadow flickering outside the frosted windowpanes in the big front door, and the door swung suddenly open.

A sour-faced old man in a raincoat and hat stood in the doorway. His eyes narrowed as they fastened onto Wes.

"What the hell do you think you're doing here?" he growled.

"Dad!" Ronnie exclaimed. "I thought you were in London."

"I came back when I got the news." Her father kept staring at Wes. "I had to see what was going on with my own eyes. I certainly can't count on you to tell me the truth."

"That's unfair, Dad," Ronnie said. "What news? Who did you get it from?"

"You meant to keep it a secret, then?"

Ronnie sighed. There was no point in scolding her dad, or even fighting back. It just made things worse. Her dad never backed down, even when he was in the wrong. Which was always. "How did you find out?" she repeated.

"Jareth called me," he said.

That surprised her. "Jareth? I didn't know you two were engaged in any sort of independent dialogue."

"When it involves important information about you, we are."

Ronnie gasped, as it all came clear. "You got Jareth to screw me over in Vegas, right? I should have recognized your distinctive touch."

"Jareth isn't stupid, Veronica. He knew that my leadership at MossTech would increase its value by orders of magnitude. And after forty years of hard work and sacrifice, it was my turn to be CEO."

"Yes, and you would have taken MossTech public, which Uncle Bertram never wanted," she said. "Or my aunt or cousins. You'd just be making a group of rich shareholders richer."

"Stop mouthing off old platitudes," her father snapped. "It was refreshing to deal with Jareth. Finally, someone in the family who reasons with his head. So much for that, eh? What have we here?" He strode closer to Wes. "Who is this person?" he demanded. "Did you even bother to check? Or did you pick him because he was good in bed?"

"Watch it, Mr. Moss," Wes said. "No one speaks to my wife that way."

Her father's mouth twisted. "Do not scold me in my own house. What have you got there in that box? If you got it here, leave it here. It belongs to me."

Olsen stepped forward, his face grayish. "Sir, I assumed, since Miss Veronica's name was carved on the top of the box, that it belonged to—"

"You are wrong in that assumption, Olsen. Put it down!"

"No," Wes said, with steely calm. "The box is Ronnie's. You can't have it."

Her father's face turned red. "You son of a bitch. How dare you."

"It's just a baby box, Dad!" Ronnie yelled. "There is nothing that would be even remotely interesting to you! Baby shoes, blankets, onesies, board books! Just let me have it, for God's sake! What the hell do you care?"

"I thought I got rid of all that garbage," he said.

"Well, this one slipped through your fingers, and I am taking it," she told him.

Wes's gaze did not waver.

Her dad let out a grunt of disgust. "Fine. Take it, and

good riddance. But that's the last thing you'll ever get from me. You're out, Veronica. You will not inherit a penny from me." He shot Wes a triumphant glance. "Not such a good bargain now, is she?"

"Holy God, Ronnie," Wes said. "This guy is unreal. Let's go."

"Yes, go on," her father sneered. "Run away. I'm sure that's exactly what you'll do, now that she's disinherited. Unemployed, too, from what I hear."

"So you agree with Jareth?" Her voice thin and colorless. "You think it's appropriate for him to cancel my show? Just to punish me?"

"Somebody has to," her father snapped. "You cruise along, doing as you please, never thinking of consequences. It's your aunt's fault. She always encouraged you."

"Thank God," Ronnie muttered. "Only reason I survived."

"And getting your name added to Elaine's mandate? You could have handed me control of MossTech, but no. You chose to give me your middle finger. And this person?" He gestured at Wes. "You look familiar. What's your name?"

"Weston Brody," Wes said.

"Humph. Don't know it." Her father scowled fiercely at Wes. "So you knew this man for what, two hours, before you married him? You're just like your mother. She couldn't resist the lure of sexual novelty either."

She opened her mouth to tell him what she thought of that, but Wes's gentle touch on her shoulder made her jump.

"Ronnie," he said. "There's no point. Don't even try. It's time to go."

She let out a slow breath and nodded. "Yes, you're right. Let's go now." She glanced at Olsen. "I'm so sorry about this," she said.

Olsen's face was tense, but he gave her a grave nod as

he opened the door. "It's all right," he said, his face stoic. "Whatever happens. It's for the best."

They walked out to the car, ignoring her father's muttering and fuming.

Wes stowed the wooden chest carefully in the trunk. The silence was heavy as he drove. They'd been on the highway for forty minutes before she could speak at all.

"Wes," she said. "I'm so sorry."

"You're not the one who should be apologizing," he said.

"I let him get to me," she said. "Usually, when I interact with him, I'm braced for it. But today, he caught me by surprise. You'd think that I'd be used to it, right?"

"You should never have had to get used to treatment like that," Wes said. "He doesn't deserve to be near you."

"I doubt he intends to ever speak to me again," she said. To her dismay, her chin started to shake. "Oh, dammit." She dug for a tissue.

"It's okay," he said. "You're entitled. I'd be trembling under the bed if I got treated like that by a parent. Who's supposed to love and protect and support you."

"Wes," she muttered, wiping her eyes. "You're not helping."

"Go ahead and cry," he said. "It's like taking a shower, but inside your head."

She followed his advice. Not that she had any choice. She turned her face away, and let the tears move through her. It exhausted her, and afterward, she drifted off.

She was pulled back to wakefulness by Wes's gentle touch on her shoulder.

"Sweetheart?" His deep voice was like the brush of silken fur. "We're here."

She stretched and yawned and looked around.

They were in another world. The trees so tall, the air

intensely sweet, the colors so vivid. Every breath of chilly, pine-and-fir-scented air helped clear her muddled head.

The resort was like nothing she'd ever seen. The rooms were partly built into the rock shelf itself, as was the restaurant, which was cantilevered out over the canyon. It was a wonderland. Like being on Mount Olympus. A mythical landscape.

When they closed the door to their suite, Wes laid the wooden chest on the table, and followed her out to admire the view and the steaming pool of water on the patio a few steps below. The terrace was part raw, smooth stone, and part dark, textured gray slate. They were shielded on either side by thickets of sapling pines and firs. Only someone on the cliff across the canyon would ever see them, and only with binoculars.

"This place is incredible," Ronnie said. "I can't believe I never heard of it."

"It's new," he told her. "I only know about it because I invested money in it. It used to be the luxury hideaway of some eccentric software billionaire. He had a bad divorce, and the wife ended up with this place, so she sold it to a hotelier who turned it into a luxury resort. Speaking of luxury, the kitchen opens in a half an hour. Shall we go try out the Michelin-star chef? She specializes in fusion cuisine. After that, we retire for the evening. You and me, steaming hot water, moonlight?"

"Sounds great," she said.

A few minutes to freshen up, and they headed for the dining room, watching a spectacular sunset from the wall of windows, nibbling from a spread of gorgeous finger food. It was spectacular, but her appetite was off. She felt hollowed out.

"You're very quiet," Wes said. "Can I help? Can I do my clown act for you?"

"You can hardly help it," she told him, laughing. "It's hardwired into you. Oh, and by the way, thanks. For standing up to him. That was no clown act. That was a class act."

"Well, duh," he said. "Of course."

"Jareth always defended my dad," she said. "He would point out all the ways that it was my fault. Ways that I could be more compliant, more acceptable. As if I hadn't been trying for my entire goddamn life."

"Jareth is an ass-kissing, gaslighting troll. If I saw him, I'd slug him."

"No, you will not," Ronnie warned.

Wes mock pouted. "Aww. Can I key his car, at least?"

The phone buzzed in her purse. She pulled it out and gave him a pained look. "It's Dad," she said. "As if I would speak to him tonight. Like hell." She tapped the screen. "Decline. Take that, Dad."

"Turn it off," he said. "Take a night just for you."

"Don't mind if I do," she said. "I'll turn the ringer off. That'll show him."

She laid the phone on the table when she was done, nudging it away, and sipped her wine. "So, Wes," she said. "My fortunes have changed today. Does it make any difference to you that I've been cut out of the Moss inheritance?"

"Yes," he said. "As a matter fact, it does."

Whoo, boy. She hadn't expected that. Ronnie's belly clenched. "Well, thanks for your honesty, at least."

"No, no, you don't understand. It's the best news I've had since all this began."

"Excuse me? Exactly how could being disinherited be good news?"

"Because finally I can look you in the eye and say that I don't give a damn about the Moss fortune, and you actually might believe me. If you're disinherited and penniless, you can see that I'm sincere."

Ronnie laughed. "Silver linings, huh? 'Penniless' might be overstating it a little. I've saved money all these years of working, and I've bought property. And I'm definitely employable. Also, Uncle Bertram left me a few shares in the company when he died, so I'll never be destitute. But still. It's a huge step down, in terms of wealth."

"Who cares?" he said lightly. "I'm loaded, babe. Not that I really ever cared. It just happened, because I'm good at what I do. Plus, my small superpower is that I'm not afraid of taking risks. That's because I genuinely never gave a shit whether I lost it all or not. But that's over for me. For the first time in my life, I've got something precious. Something that I'm scared to death of losing. I don't want to screw this up."

She seized his hand. "I can't imagine how you could screw this up, Wes."

"You're very generous," he said. "I hope you can continue to be generous when I end up…disappointing you."

She laughed, trying to lighten the moment. "Gee," she teased. "Do you have any immediate plans to disappoint me?"

"It's inevitable," Wes said. "It's a mathematical certainty. People are flawed. They mess up. They miss the mark. Though I can't see any flaw in you yet."

She squeezed his hand. "That's sweet, but it's only a matter of time. Of course I'm flawed. We all are. But today, you were my hero. Are you ready to go to the room?"

"Oh, God, yes." He leaned over the table. Their lips met, a sweet, searching kiss, so full of tenderness and exquisite care. One hand holding her hand, the other stroking her face as if he could hardly believe she was real.

She leaned into it. His kiss made her so soft and open, aching for him. She leaned back, gasping for air. "Right now," she said, breathlessly.

Sixteen

Wes's mind raced when the door to the suite closed behind them. Was this the big moment? The best moment? The ring was still in his bag, not in his pocket, and the bag was in the bedroom, and Ronnie was so sweetly passionate and on fire. He didn't want to interrupt the wonderful erotic momentum.

He wanted to worship her, pleasure her, persuade her. She was a miraculous creature, and he'd compromised that, and it just made him so…damn…*angry.*

"What?" She was panting. "What's the matter? Is something wrong?"

"No, no," he assured her. "It's wonderful. I'm just kind of emotional tonight."

Her expression softened. "Oh, me too," she said. "I'm glad that I'm not the only one." She pulled off her sweater.

They yanked off their clothes, eager for that rush of electric joy that went with skin on hot skin. Wes tossed the covers back on the bed and turned as Ronnie gave him a hard shove on the chest. He yielded to the pressure, pitching backward onto the bed, bouncing.

She climbed on top of him, her silky thighs clamped around his, her slender hands stroking his shaft, making him shiver and moan. She braced her other arm against his chest. Her radiant smile made his heart twist and burn with longing. Her hair draped around them like a fragrant satin curtain. She rained soft kisses on his forehead, his cheekbones. Too much. He couldn't be so close to her, so tuned to her, and not be completely honest with her. It was killing him. "Ronnie," he whispered.

"Mmm?" She stroked her velvety soft cheek against his, then kissed it.

"I have to tell you… We have to… Oh, my God, Ronnie."

She rose up, undulating over him, sliding and wiggling along the length of his shaft. Anointing him with her sweet, hot, wet balm. "Yes?" she asked sweetly. "You were saying?"

"I need to tell you…that… I…that…ah…oh God."

His voice trailed off, dumbstruck, as she reared up, nudging the tip of his penis inside her slick opening. Hot, clinging. She arched, poised for a long moment as the anticipation built…and then, slowly sank down and enveloped his aching shaft into the delicious, clutching heat of her perfect body.

And that was it. Couldn't speak or think. All he could do was watch the stunning spectacle of Ronnie Moss, moving over him. First slow, graceful, a sensual spectacle. Then it got more intense as she sought her own pleasure. Riding him, all the way to blinding completion. When the delicious clutching flutters around his penis eased, he rolled her onto her back, and lost himself inside her. Wild, wonderful, deep…then the explosion, wiping away his fear and dread. At least for that sweet, blinding instant.

They lay there, damp and panting. Relaxing as the sweat dried, and their galloping heartbeats slowed. And the dread crept in. It would not leave him alone.

Some time later, Ronnie disengaged herself, and disappeared into the bathroom. She came out moments later, winding her hair up into a knot, fastening it with a clip. She slid open the door at the patio. Puffs of steam rose from the pool and into the moonlit air.

"I'm going to soak in this pool and look at the moon," she said. "Join me?"

There was only one possible answer to that question. He followed her immediately, hypnotized by the beauty of her elegant, sinuous nude body as she paced around the hot pool, every line, every curve, painted by moonlight and shadow.

She stepped into the pool, descending to her waist. The sound of the water sloshing and trickling sounded incredibly sensual. She sank onto the bench with a sigh.

He followed her in, sinking down, drifting over to float right in front of her.

He was giving himself one more night of perfection. Tomorrow morning, he would tell her everything, and they would face reality together. No matter what happened.

He pulled her into his arms. This might be all he ever got of the shining miracle that was Ronnie Moss. He damn well better make this night count.

Wes ran as fast as he could along rocky, uneven ground. Pounding feet, heart in his mouth, life-or-death urgency, either toward something or away from something. A chasm yawned in front of him, immeasurably deep. He reeled, teetering. Couldn't stop. His momentum had pitched him over the edge, and he couldn't even see the bottom, it was so far below, lost in the mist. Rocks and dirt pitched off with him. He yelled—

A strong hand caught his wrist and pulled him up. Easily, as if he were only ten years old. It was his dad. His eyes looked worried as he set Wes onto his feet.

*Wes lunged to grab him...*but the light was pressing on his eyelids. When he opened his eyes, they were wet with tears.

He pressed his face to the pillow and looked around. The room was bright. The sun was well up. They had gotten to sleep late.

Ronnie wasn't in the bed. He sat up, looking around, and saw her cross-legged on the floor, sitting in a square of sunshine from the window. She wore a white, fluffy hotel bathrobe over her sexy teddy nightgown. Her hair streamed over her shoulders. Her mother's baby box was open in front of her. Small objects were arrayed before her, on a clean towel that she'd spread out onto the carpet.

She was holding up a tiny, multicolored knit baby jumper. A pair of miniscule pink socks. A hairband, with silk flowers on it. A black velvet baby coat. Tiny pink hair clips.

Wes got up, shrugging on his own robe, and went over to kneel next to her.

Ronnie gave him a smile, but her eyes were wet. "Hey there," she said, her voice husky with tears. "Don't mind me. I'm just over here, yanking on my own heartstrings."

"I hope it's a good feeling," he said.

"Yes," she assured him. "It aches, but it also makes me feel loved." She held an object up to him. "Look at this. From the day I was born."

Wes examined it. It was two plastic ratchet-closed hospital bracelets, linked to each other. The big one had Naomi

Moss printed on it, the little one Veronica Moss. Wes cradled it in his hand, as if it were alive.

"Beautiful," he said. "An artifact of love."

"Yes," she said. "Yes, exactly." She reached for a tissue, in the pocket of her robe, and blew her nose noisily. "I would never have found these, if not for you. And despite all the ugliness with Dad, it's just so healing."

Wes looked into her eyes, and it came into focus, in a blinding moment of realization. This was it. This was his moment. He would never have a better time to redress his mistakes. Never a moment when her heart was softer, her mind more open and disposed to forgive his transgressions. Never a better time to beg for mercy.

He had to man up and do this thing.

Right. Freaking. Now.

He went to the bag where he'd stowed the pearl ring, then crossed over to Ronnie with the box in his hand. He sat next to her on the floor.

"Ronnie," he said. "These last few days since I met you have been the best days I've ever had. In my entire life."

Ronnie dabbed at her eyes, smiling at him. "Me too."

"I know we're already married, so we skipped over the part where I try to convince you that I'm the man who should stand by you for the rest of your life. To make a family with. Grow old with. The whole thing. The real deal."

Ronnie blinked at him. "Wes…are you…um…?"

"Yes," he said. "I'm proposing to you. Sort of. Insofar as an already married man can propose to his wife. I want you with me forever. And I want you to have…this."

He flipped open the ring box and held it up, holding his breath.

Ronnie gasped. "Oh, Wes."

"Will you wear it?"

She nodded. He took the ring out and slid it onto her finger, nestling it up to the wedding band. The two rings together looked great on her.

"It's so beautiful," she said. "Pearls. You sneaky bastard."

"It looks perfect on you," he said. "But if you wanted to look at some other designs, I'm sure that the jeweler could swap it out with—"

"Not a chance. It's the most gorgeous ring I've ever seen. Look no further."

Wes let out a sigh of relief, and then took a fresh deep breath. "I'm so glad," he said. "Because there's another thing I need to talk to you about. An important thing."

"Yeah? So? Let's have it."

"Yeah. It's kind of hard to say. I'm nervous about how you're going to take it. And it's hard to find a place to start that makes sense," he said haltingly.

She grabbed his hand, squeezed it. "We have time. I'm not going anywhere."

God, he hoped that generous attitude would continue when he finally got to the point. "Thanks," he said, swallowing hard. "It's about my dad. How he—"

Rat—tat—tat—tat. A brisk knock sounded on the door, making them jump.

Goddammit. Wes's teeth ground. "Did I really forget to put the Do Not Disturb sign on the door?" he muttered.

Ronnie rolled her eyes and got up, pulling her robe closed and tying the sash as she went to the door. "Who is it?" she called.

"Ms. Moss and Mr. Brody?" It was a male voice behind the door. "I'm very sorry to disturb you, but I have a smartphone that one of you left in the dining room last night. The cleaning crew found it this morning. I thought you might want it."

"I believe that must be mine," Ronnie said, opening the door. She took the phone, murmuring her thanks to the hotel employee. She looked down at it as she closed the door.

"That explains that," she said. "I was feeling both grateful and puzzled that no one was bugging me today while I had my sentimental moment with the baby box. So I'll just switch this thing off, and you can tell me what you were going to…"

Ronnie's voice trailed off. She froze in place, staring at the phone screen.

Wes felt the energy in the air change, and a chill gripped the pit of his stomach.

"What?" he asked. "Is something wrong?"

"Six missed calls from my dad, five from Maddie, four from Lizette. Something's happened. None from Aunt Elaine. She always calls when there's a crisis. Not this time."

"Which suggests that Elaine herself is the crisis," he said.

"Yes. Excuse me, but I have to get back to them." She tapped the screen, sitting on the bed. "Lizette? It's… Yeah. Sorry I didn't get back to you sooner… Oh God. When?" She pressed her fingers to her mouth, her slim shoulders hunched. "Yes, I understand. I'm glad they're on their way. Which hospital? Of course. It should take us two and a half, three hours tops, to get back to the city… Yes, of course. We'll come right away. Thanks, Lizette. I'm so glad you were with her."

Ronnie let the phone drop. She met his eyes. "Heart attack," she said, her voice strangled. "After dinner last night. They tried and tried to call me. She's at the University of Washington Medical Center. Having surgery. Right now."

She clapped her hand to her mouth, leaped up and bolted into the bathroom. He heard retching sounds. Then running water, as she splashed her face in the sink.

She came out, and plugged her phone in. "I'll get as much charge onto this thing as I can while I'm packing." She knelt, swiftly stowing all the baby artifacts into the wooden box. She gave him an impatient look as she jerked on her hiking pants and wound her hair into a quick braid. "Wes?" she said. "Please? Move!"

That jolted him out of his dismayed paralysis. "Of course. Right away."

He got dressed in record time, ashamed of himself. Feeling put-upon about his confession being interrupted when Ronnie's aunt was fighting for her life. But dear God, the timing. He couldn't tell her now. Her mind was consumed with worry for her aunt. Which was just as it should be. He'd waited too long.

All he could do now was grit his teeth and wait for another chance.

Ronnie spotted Maddie in the waiting room of the surgery ward. Her cousin met her with a tight hug. "I'm so glad you're here," Maddie whispered. "The boys are on their way home as fast as they can get here, and Jack's been here for me. And Jerome, of course," she added, a hint of irony in her voice. "But I wanted you."

"How is she?" Ronnie asked.

"Still on the table," Maddie said. "It's bad. Evidently her doctors have been planning this bypass surgery for a while, but she neglected to tell us about it. They're doing quadruple bypass and a valve replacement. Gran is as tough as nails, though. We just have to grit our teeth and hope."

"Sorry I didn't call," Ronnie said. "I left my phone in the resort restaurant."

"Resort, huh? Sounds festive. I'm glad you were having fun, at least, before all this happened. I'm so sorry to have interrupted the honeymoon."

"Are you kidding? Aunt Elaine is everything to me. We can honeymoon for as long as we like later on."

"Yeah, absolutely," Maddie agreed. "Jack and I decided that if it's a girl, she'll be Elaine. We'll call her Lainie. I'll tell her as soon as she wakes up. We were waiting for the ultrasound, but I'm not waiting for anything, ever again."

Maddie dissolved into tears, and they hugged again. Then she glimpsed her father approaching, over Maddie's heaving shoulder. Her belly clenched, bracing for whatever.

Wes moved closer, too. Instinctively protective. How sweet of him.

"Aww. How touching," her dad drawled. "Twelve hours of radio silence, entirely ignoring all our frantic calls, and you finally deign to come to your ailing aunt's side."

"I didn't get the messages until today," she said.

Ronnie let them catch her up on all the details that the surgeon had shared so far. They took turns as the hours ground by, taking breaks for air, coffee, sandwiches from time to time. At one point, Wes accompanied her to the hospital cafeteria, but instead of getting in line at the bar, he took her arm and led her through the lobby and outside, into the chilly evening air, under the big porticos.

Wes squeezed her shoulders gently with both hands. "Ronnie, I know this is a bad time," he said. "But remember this morning? I was about to tell you some things that I think you should know about me."

"Oh, Wes. I'm fried and distracted right now. Let's just stick with the present emergency and save the reflections about the past for later. When I can give you the focused attention that you deserve. Forgive me for putting you off, okay?"

“I understand how you feel, but please.” Wes’s voice vibrated with tension. “I think it’s important, to say this to you now. Even in the face of Elaine’s emergency. Maybe especially in the face of it.”

Ronnie sighed and nodded. “Okay. If it’s that important, then let’s hear it.”

“I’ll be quick.” He grabbed her hands and kissed them. “Thank you. So, like I was saying this morning, this is about my dad. Twenty-three years ago, he was in—”

“Wes Brody?” They jerked their heads around, at the loud, accusing tone behind them. “What the hell? Get your hands off my cousin!”

Caleb and Tilda Moss stood there, staring at them.

Seventeen

So. This was the way it had to be. Wes let out a sigh as the certainty of his doom settled into his guts. He squeezed Ronnie's hands one last time, just in case it was the last time she permitted him to touch her and turned to face Caleb and Tilda. "Hello, Caleb," he said grimly. "Tilda."

"Wait." Ronnie's eyes were bewildered as she looked at them. "You guys know each other?"

"You could say that," Wes said.

"Yeah, I know this scheming son of a bitch," Caleb said. "He has no business touching you, Ron. He tried to attack MossTech with a faked file that implicated our family in a crime from years ago. Grandpa Bertram, Gran, Jerome. Even your mother."

Ronnie turned to Wes, horrified. "That can't be true," she said. "Is that true?"

Wes tried to swallow, but there was a burning lump in his throat. "It's complicated," he said. "It's true, I had a fact-finding agenda at the beginning. But as soon as I started getting to know you, that changed, and I started to—"

"No. No, stop it right there. I don't want to hear another word."

"Ronnie, please. I was trying to tell you. I tried this morning, before you made the call to Lizette. I tried again, just now."

"So that's why you encouraged me to find my mother's things," she whispered. "Not for the healing love, and her hand reaching out across time to caress me. It was so that you could snoop and pry in our family's private documents."

"Ronnie—"

"Oh God." She backed up a step. "All those tender moments. Completely faked."

"I never faked anything," he protested. "Not for one second."

"And the other day, you didn't go back to that storage unit to get your bag. You took my key, and you snooped through my mother's boxes. To hurt me."

"No," he said. "I would never hurt you."

"Bullshit! Every damn thing you've ever said to me was a lie."

"That's not true." He reached out, but Ronnie slapped his hand away. "I had to see if the papers were there," he said desperately. "I was looking for the documents that would exonerate my dad."

"Exonerate who? What the hell are you talking about?"

"The toxic-mold disaster," Wes said. "The one in the file Caleb mentioned. It happened. People died. Someone tried to cover it up, and they blamed everything on my dad, who had died in the bombing. Along with your mom."

Ronnie's face was blank. "But I don't remember hearing about anyone named Brody," she said. "The name of the man who died with her was John Padraig."

"He was my stepdad."

"Stepdad?" Ronnie's tone was accusing. "What stepdad?"

"He was the only father I ever knew. I called him Dad. I was a baby when my mother met him. I was a mistake made when she was nineteen. Then she met my dad, and they fell in love. They intended to get married eventually, and he intended to adopt me and give me his name, but he never got around to it. Then time ran out for him. He died in that blast, and the whole mess got pinned on him. It broke my mom's heart."

"I see." Ronnie's mouth shook. "So you decided to break mine to make it even?"

"Absolutely not," he said forcefully. "Never."

"I understand wanting the truth," she said. "Ironic, though, that you sought the truth by lying to me. Continually. Even while we were making love."

Caleb and Tilda exchanged shocked glances. "What the hell is going on?" Caleb demanded. "And where is Jareth?"

"Jareth is history. He bailed on me. I married Wes instead. God help me."

"Oh, dear God," Tilda said, her voice small.

"Yes. Jareth and Dad planned it out, for him to choke at the last minute and make me miss the deadline. I thought it was all over." She gestured at Wes. "Then he happened along, seemingly by chance. He offered himself up to help me fulfill the mandate. So generous, right? All he wanted was the entertainment value and the pleasure of my company. You are a world-class liar, Wes. And I am an empty-headed fool."

"I wasn't lying," he said. "I knew I was screwed when you turned out to be the woman of my dreams."

"Oh, stop it. You're just doing your bullshit blather out of habit. It's not necessary to keep up the pretense anymore, so stop."

"Please, Ronnie," he said. "Try to imagine being in my position. If someone had accused your mother of horrible crimes, wouldn't you do anything to find the truth?"

"Don't speak of my mother again," she said. "You were digging for dirt in her private papers, to throw at her memory. Now you're asking for understanding?"

"I wasn't trying to hurt anyone," he insisted. "I just had to see if what was in my dad's journal was true. She told him that she'd copied her documentation and sent it home with her things, in case anything happened to her. Dad thought she was being overdramatic. That last journal entry was dated the day they both died."

"Where is this journal?" Ronnie demanded. "Can I see it?"

"No," Wes said. "Tilda burned it."

Tilda winced. "Wes, you should have told me all this. I had no idea your father was involved."

"The documentation in that file showed the cover-up," Wes said. "I didn't start questioning that until now. But my father didn't want Naomi to be guilty. He wanted to get to the bottom of it. I don't think she's guilty, either. Not anymore."

Ronnie brushed the backs of her hands across her eyes, but they were still wet, glittering with shock and tears. "And why on earth would you change your mind about my mother now?"

"Because I read her letters," Wes said simply. "Naomi wasn't a venal, money-grubbing hack who didn't care about people dying from toxic mold. That was someone else. But not my dad."

"You still have that transcript, right?" Tilda said. "There

was a printed transcript in the file copy that you gave me last year."

"Yes, but it doesn't hold up as proof," Wes said. "It just points to Naomi's shipment home. My last signpost."

"Oh God," Ronnie said. "So you and Tilda and my dad all knew about this file, and you never saw fit to tell me?"

Caleb looked pained. "I'm sorry, Ronnie," he said. "I thought it was better to just let it be. I didn't tell Marcus or Gran either."

"I'd like to see the transcript," Ronnie said stiffly.

Wes pulled out his phone, attached the file and sent it to her email address. "Done," he said.

"Forward it to Caleb and me, too, Ron," Tilda said.

Ronnie tapped at her phone, her mouth tight. "So I take it the other day, at the storage unit, that you did search my mother's things."

"Yes," he admitted. "Everything."

"And did you find anything incriminating or exonerating?"

"Nothing," he said. "Just evidence that she was dedicated and altruistic, and working hard. That she was far from home, and missing her husband and her little girl. I liked her."

"Don't," Ronnie said stiffly. "Those letters weren't yours to read. She isn't yours to like."

"I'm sorry."

He stood there, locked in misery while Ronnie blew her nose and squared her shoulders, staring at him with blazing eyes. "This wasn't a complete loss for you," she said. "You set your doubts to rest. You will never find anything else that belonged to my mother, so you have no reason to linger. I'm surprised you didn't disappear after you finished at the storage unit. Why drag out the charade? Were you just enjoying the sex?"

God, it hurt to breathe. "No, I stayed for you. I never wanted to leave you, ever again. I still don't. I'm sorry I didn't tell you sooner. I kept waiting for the perfect time, and I missed my window."

"There was never a window, Wes," she said. "There's never a good time to find out that you've been lied to and screwed over."

"I couldn't think of any other way," he said. "Not after what happened with Tilda and Caleb. But I've been regretting it since that first night."

Ronnie looked at Caleb. "I wish you told me this whole story," she said.

"I was trying to keep things calm," Caleb said. "Once everything was burned, what was the point of getting everyone all upset?"

"If I had known his name, I wouldn't have run into his arms like an idiot," Ronnie said.

"I'm sorry, Ron," Caleb said. "I never meant to hurt you."

"Neither did I," Wes said.

Caleb glared at him. "Shut up."

Wes ignored him, eyes locked on Ronnie. "I love you," he said.

Ronnie shook her head. "You're not credible, Wes," she said. "Just go. And for God sake, take this." She tugged the pearl ring off, and held it out, but she got tired of his refusal to take it. She grabbed his hand, and slapped the ring into his palm.

"What about the marriage mandate?" Wes asked. "Are you just going to give MossTech to Jerome?"

Ronnie gave Caleb a stricken glance.

"It doesn't have to be that way," Wes said. "Even if you don't want me near you, we can leave things as they are. Please. I want to do at least that much for you."

Caleb and Tilda gave each other a searching look, and in unison, shook their heads.

Caleb looked at Ronnie. "Cut him loose," Caleb said. "You can't continue with this marriage after what he's done. Not even at a distance. None of us would ask that of you, even if you were willing."

"I'm so sorry," Ronnie said. "I wrecked everything."

"It wasn't your fault," Tilda said. "You never deceived anyone. Let Jerome do his worst. We've all been braced to let MossTech go for months."

Ronnie turned to Wes, head high. "We're done," she said. "You'll hear from my lawyers about filing for a divorce. Goodbye."

She spun around, and marched back into the hospital, spine elegantly straight.

Caleb and Tilda might have said something before they followed her in, and they might not. He couldn't hear them over the roaring in his ears, and wouldn't have understood if he had. He just stood there and clutched the pearl ring so tightly, the diamond band practically carved itself into his palm. Trying to take it in. The doomsday, rock-bottom, worst-case scenario.

The worst of all possible worlds. That was the one he had to live in.

Eighteen

Four months later...

Ronnie shivered on the cot in the doctor's examining room. She'd been there in the chilly room for over forty minutes waiting for the bloodwork.

Her symptoms were annoyingly vague, and all of it could be attributed to stress. Blood pressure so low, she felt dizzy and queasy. Heartburn, short breath, swelling, spotty periods, waves of intense fatigue. She just felt… weird. Not herself. Probably just stress, from being miserable, hurt, humiliated. It was enough to drive anyone off the deep end.

At least Aunt Elaine was recovering. She was almost back to her former self.

Ronnie just hoped that whatever she had wasn't alarming. Aunt Elaine's heart attack was enough stress for now. Plus, she wanted to focus on happier things, like the babies. Tilda was pregnant, Eve, too. Maddie was coming right along, just two months to go. A whole crop of gorgeous Moss babies would soon be rolling around together on Aunt Elaine's fine Persian rugs. She didn't want to be the buzzkill lonely-hearts spinster aunt with the chronic health problems, angling for attention.

Stop whining. Crybaby. Suck it up.

Her dad's voice in her head. She should not feel ashamed about going to the doctor when she felt sick. She should have been in here weeks ago.

Dr. Vindaman came in, a short woman with a black braid and a brisk manner.

"Hi, Dr. Vindaman. Did they check my hormone levels?" Ronnie asked. "I wondered if it could be premature menopause. The symptoms seemed consistent."

Dr. Vindaman frowned. "Someone has been doing some amateur medical research online, eh?"

Veronica shrugged. "In my own defense, I do know quite a bit about human biology."

"I don't doubt it," Dr. Vindaman said. "My twin girls love your show. Is there going to be a new season?"

"That's up in the air," Ronnie told her. "I had a falling-out with the production company, so I'm not sure where it's going to end up."

"Well, that is a shame. Lie down on the cot. I'm going to do an abdominal ultrasound."

"Ultrasound?" Ronnie was startled. "Is something wrong?"

"Don't worry," Dr. Vindaman soothed. "Just ruling things out. Go on. Lie back and expose your lower abdomen for me."

In a few minutes, the ticklish wand was sliding through the thick, viscous goo all over her belly, but the monitor was turned to an angle where Ronnie could not see it.

After a few moments of this, she was ready to snap. "Dr. Vindaman," she pleaded. "Throw me a bone. What are you looking for?"

The doctor didn't answer for a long moment. The machine clickety-clicked as she took picture after picture. "One moment," she said, her voice abstracted. "Hang on."

Finally, she turned to Ronnie and swiveled the monitor so that she could see it. "Take a look," she said. "I think we can safely rule out premature menopause."

Ronnie looked at the screen, and her jaw dropped. Oh. *God.*

The image morphed and shifted according to how the doctor was moving the wand, but Ronnie had seen enough of her friends' sonograms to recognize what she was looking at. Which was to say…a total readjustment of her entire existence.

Her vision went dark for an instant.

"Look here," Dr. Vindaman said. "There's the head, the arms, the legs, spine. Too early to tell the sex. Another couple weeks. If you want to know, of course."

"But…but… I'm on the pill." Her voice was a thin thread of sound.

"Yes, I know." The doctor's tone was ironic. "I prescribed it for you. Were you taking antibiotics? Did you maybe forget a day, or two days?"

She thought about it. "I had an upset stomach on the day that my aunt had the heart attack. I threw up after taking the pill. I couldn't keep anything down the next day, either."

"Was that approximately sixteen weeks ago?"

"Yes," she said.

"Well, then. That was it." Dr. Vindaman looked concerned. "Is it a bad time?"

"Uh…well, I'm very surprised," she said. "Unprepared.

I don't have a partner. I broke up with the man I was seeing. I certainly don't want to co-parent with him."

"I see." The doctor's voice was gentle. "So you've got some big decisions ahead. Take a couple days. Talk to your family. You can get dressed."

Ronnie thanked the doctor and said goodbye like an automaton. She didn't remember the drive home, or walking into her own condo. Time lost all meaning as she sat in the dining room, hours crawling by. Rain trickled down the window that looked out over the waterfront. There was a cup of peppermint tea in front of her, long since gone cold. The only thing her roiling stomach could stand.

She was stupefied. A baby. Wes's baby.

Her mind raced around in circles. Images, memories, feelings. Longing for what might have been. What should have been. A tornado of emotions. After it passed, her face and throat ached, but a strong, clear certainty had risen up inside her.

She wanted this baby. That both thrilled and energized her.

But what about Wes? It wouldn't stay secret. People noticed her, photographed her, wrote about her. Her pregnancy would be remarked upon. Wes would do the math.

He would want to know his own child. And as angry as she felt, she did not want to deprive her child of a father. She'd grown up without a mother. She wouldn't wish that on anyone. Still, interacting with him was going to be so awkward, considering that she missed him so badly, she hadn't been able to breathe for four months. Everything reminded her of him. Everything hurt. And now, she would have the ultimate in reminders. For the rest of her natural life.

Out of nowhere, she felt a sensation that could almost

be described as hunger, rather than nausea. It had been so long, she barely recognized it.

She had to figure out how to nourish herself and this baby. She got to work, and sat down to a turkey sandwich on toast. She'd gotten through more than half of it when her smartphone buzzed. Elliott's name was on the display. She set the sandwich down.

"Hey, Elliott. What's up?"

"Um…your showbiz career?" Elliott's voice vibrated with excitement. "That's what's up, love! Things are turning around at last, and it is about time!"

"Excuse me?" she said. "What on earth are you talking about?"

"Avery got a call," Elliott said. "From Orion's Eye. It's a new streaming service. They just got a massive infusion of cash from a venture capitalist, and his only stipulation was that they produce *The Secret Life of Cells*!"

"What venture capitalist?"

"I don't know," Elliott said. "Do we care? Is it relevant? Whoever he is, I want to kiss him right on the mouth!"

"But Elliott, we can't take it to another platform," Ronnie reminded him. "Fadden Boyle will never let us out of that contract clause. We've been through this before. We have to rebrand and start from scratch, and even then, it will be tricky."

"And that, my love, is where you are dead wrong! They're letting us go!"

"Huh?" She jerked up in her chair, startled. "Really? What happened?"

"I was hoping you'd tell me. Jane said that Jareth told her we were free to take the show elsewhere. Then he told her to, and I quote, 'Tell Ronnie to call off the dogs.'"

Ronnie gasped, as realization hit. "Oh, my God!"

"So you do know!" Elliott crowed. "You've been holding out on me! Do tell!"

"Sorry, can't right now. We'll talk soon. Thanks for giving me the news."

Ronnie set the phone on the table, freshly rattled. What the hell…?

Slowly, she picked up the phone and pulled Wes's number from her contact list. Silently pleading with her heart to slow down before she hit Call.

Wes picked up swiftly. "Ronnie?"

"Hi, Wes," she said.

He was silent for a long moment. "It's good to hear your voice," he said.

Oh, God, it was good to hear his voice, too. It was beautiful. She cleared her throat. "So I heard that a mysterious venture capitalist has been prodding Orion's Eye to produce Season Four of *The Secret Life of Cells*."

"Yeah? Smart guy. Excellent investment."

"I also heard from Jareth's production company. They're letting us have the show back. And Jareth says, 'Call off the dogs.'"

"Did he?" Wes laughed under his breath. "And of course, you thought of me."

"What did you do to him? I told you to leave him alone."

"It pissed me off that he was sitting on your beautiful show like a spiteful toad," Wes said. "So I reminded him of the video I made. Remember when he threatened to destroy your career? I told him I'd send that video to some famous influencers, bloggers, vloggers, podcasters. I'm friendly with all of them, and they would make his life hell. It's not like I hit him, or anything entertaining like that."

She was struggling not to smile. Damn the man. "Wes, I can fight my own battles."

"Okay. Won't happen again. I would have run the idea

past you, if you'd been speaking to me. But you weren't returning my emails or my texts, so I was forced to make decisions without guidance. We all have our limits."

Ronnie stifled a snort of laughter, and then thought of the baby. She had to tell him. But not on the phone. "Anyhow," she said. "Thanks for doing that for me."

"I wasn't doing you any favors. *The Secret Life of Cells* is an incredible property. I was just taking advantage of inside info about an amazing opportunity. So don't thank me. I'm going to make money off that move. So are you, incidentally."

"Well," she said. "Okay. Fine. Even so. Thanks, just the same."

"Whatever," he said. "Can I come over? I really want to talk."

"Wes… I don't think that I can—"

"I have your mom's baby box. Are you at home? I could come over now."

Panic stabbed through her. She couldn't. Not today, with her mind still blown from this momentous news, her eyes red and swollen, in such a vulnerable state. No way. The idea of holding his baby in her arms… Oh God.

"Not today," she said, her voice choked. "Not here."

"I'll be a perfect gentleman," he said. "The divorce was finalized a month ago. You have no agenda, I have no agenda. All I want is to talk to you. Please, Ronnie."

Ronnie pondered that as she walked around the kitchen. It was true; they had to talk. But not at her place, and not all alone. She missed him too damn much. She might disgrace herself.

She needed her angry, indignant family around her, to make her strong. Keep her honest.

"Not at my place. Aunt Elaine's. Tomorrow. The family will all be there for lunch."

Wes made a noncommittal sound. "Your aunt won't be thrilled to see me."

"Probably not, but you'll both live," Ronnie said. "Everyone will live. Come there tomorrow at noon, if you want to talk to me. Goodbye, Wes."

She put the phone down, and stared at her own reflection in the window, her hand on her belly. Trying not to imagine, or hope, for some scenario where they could be together. She'd worked so hard to let it all go, and just the sound of his voice knocked her back to square one.

She breathed down the butterflies, which were going nuts, and suddenly, she felt it. Like the butterflies, but deeper. A delicate, ticklish flutter deep and low inside her. That wasn't nervous knots. That was a tiny live being, for which she was entirely responsible. It was miraculous, beautiful. Terrifying.

She sat and ate the rest of her sandwich. Every last bite.

Nineteen

Lizette answered the front door of Elaine Moss's mansion, at twelve on the dot. Her face was tight-lipped. Entirely different from the smiling woman who had served him her shortbread cookies just a few short months ago.

He walked in, waiting by the door. "Where shall I put Ronnie's box?"

"On the chest by the wall," Lizette instructed coldly. "Follow me, please."

She led him into the first large salon. Two people were in there. Marcus Moss, and his wife, Eve Seaton. Eve was a brunette with long, glossy curls, and Marcus Moss was even taller than Wes. Black hair, chiseled features. Biracial, the rumor mill said. Half-Asian. His mouth was tight with anger. Eve studied him coldly, arms crossed.

"This is the guy?" Marcus asked Lizette.

"Yep, he's the one," she said crisply.

"You have a lot of damn nerve, coming here," Marcus said to him.

Wes was stoic. "Ronnie said to come. I'd go to the gates of hell if she told me to."

"I'll drop kick you right through the gates of hell if you upset her," Marcus said.

Huh. His very presence would probably upset her. But after losing Ronnie, the gates of hell held no terror for him, and her family's anger was the least of his problems.

All the Mosses were trickling in, for his or her own chance to give him the fisheye. There was Tilda, and Annika, a beautiful little girl with long dark hair who ducked and wove between the older Mosses to get to the front. Annika glared at him. "Is this the guy who was mean to Aunt Ronnie?"

"Annika, go to the dining room," Tilda said.

"If you're mean to Ronnie, I'll kick your butt," Annika warned him.

"You will do no such thing, young lady," Tilda said. "Go straight upstairs."

Caleb appeared in the doorway, then Jack, with Maddie behind him. She was visibly pregnant, and as radiantly pretty as ever, but he got no smiles from her this time.

Whoa. That was a whole lot of glacial hostility to process.

"He's here?" Elaine Moss's imperious voice, behind them. "Excellent. Get out of my way, all of you. Let me get a look at him."

Elaine sailed through them in her wheelchair like the parting of the Red Sea. Her piercing gaze seemed less hostile than that of her younger relatives.

"Hello, Mrs. Moss," he said. "I'm glad to see you looking better."

"No thanks to you," Elaine said crisply.

He just waited, trying not to break eye contact. In fact, she did look pretty good, considering. Thin and pale, but her white hair stuck straight up with its usual vigor, and her eyes were sharp, studying him hard. She held an ebony cane across her lap.

"Marcus is right," Elaine said. "Coming to this house, knowing that all of us would spit in your eye, that does take nerve. I always did like that quality in a man."

"Gran!" Caleb sounded shocked. "What the hell are you saying?"

"Shush," Elaine said. "Young man, behave yourself with Ronnie, or we will destroy you. And if there's any butt-kicking to be done, I will be the one doing it." She lifted her cane, shaking it. "Don't think I'm just some helpless invalid. Clear?"

"As crystal, ma'am," he said.

Elaine harrumphed. "All right, then. She's in the library." When he didn't jump to it, she made an impatient sound. "What are you waiting for? You know the way. Go on."

He made haste to obey, passionately relieved to get the hell out of there, while at the same time, paradoxically glad that Ronnie had their fierce, unwavering support. They were a steady and dependable resource for her. He wished that he had family like that.

Then again. There was always a downside. Like that marriage mandate, for instance. Hey, he might be a loner, but he'd been spared a lot of drama. Trade-offs.

He slowed at the door to the library. *Do it, Brody.* He shoved the heavy, intricately carved wooden door open.

Ronnie was silhouetted against the window. She wore slim black pants and a long, textured sweater made of every shade of green. "Hello, Ronnie," he said.

She turned, and it cut him to the heart how beautiful

she was. Too pale. Her brilliant blue eyes had smudgy shadows under them.

"Wes," she said. "Did my family behave themselves?"

"As well as could be expected," he said. "Not too terrible."

The silence was painful. There was so much he was desperate to say, but she would never accept it. He cleared his throat. "Your mom's baby box. Lizette said to leave it in the foyer."

"Thank you," she said. "I'm glad to have it back. It's precious to me."

"I was pleased to see your aunt in fighting form," he offered. "She threatened to kick my ass if I misbehaved. As did Annika. And Marcus."

Another ghost of a smile. "They are silly and overprotective."

"As well they should be," he said. "Not silly at all. I'm glad they look out for you."

"So, Wes. I appreciate your help bringing us to the attention of the Orion's Eye platform. And for prying our intellectual property free of Boyle Fadden's contract, even if your tactics were those of a Mafia don. My team is over the moon."

"I told you, it wasn't a favor. I only—"

"Yes, yes, I know. Just a business move, completely self-interested, yada yada. But still. Thanks."

"You're welcome."

"What else did you need to say to me, Wes?" she asked. "Because this is really hard."

He nodded. "I know, but I just have to say it. I love you. Always will. I can't stop thinking about you. I can't let go of the idea of being with you forever."

Her mouth shook. "Wes, don't. I'm sorry, but…don't."

His heart sank. “Absolutely never? That’s still your position?”

“I see your point of view,” she said. “I know that seeing your father’s memory desecrated drove you to act the way you did. If I were in your position, I might have done exactly the same thing.”

“I’m glad you understand,” he said cautiously.

“Yes,” she said. “But if I’d done what you did, the price would be the same. It would just be me paying it, instead of you. It’s not for free.”

“I see,” he ground out.

“It hurts too much, that all those wonderful memories I have were never real. On some level, it was all just theater for you.”

“No, Ronnie. It was the realest thing I’ve ever felt. It knocked me on my ass.”

“You know I have feelings for you,” she said. “But what happened left me raw inside. Everything hurts. I’m just one big walking flinch. I don’t know how I could trust you again. It’s not from lack of wanting to. It’s because I can’t.”

The hope that he’d tried to keep hidden even from himself abruptly deflated, leaving him feeling empty and flat. “I understand,” he said dully.

“But I have something important to tell you,” she said.

Wes waited, and waited some more, vaguely alarmed. “What?” he demanded. “Is something wrong? Is everything okay with you?”

“I’m fine, but there’s a new development,” she said.

He guessed it, all at once, and felt like the floor had just dropped out beneath his feet. “No way.”

She nodded, putting her hand on her belly.

He gasped for breath. “Holy shit, Ronnie.”

She reached into a big pocket in the front of her sweater and held out a small sheaf of ultrasound photographs.

"Four months," she said. "The day of Aunt Elaine's surgery. I threw up that morning, after I took the pill. The next day, I was so miserable, I couldn't keep anything down. That did the trick."

Wes took the scraps of paper and studied them. Minutes ticked by.

He struggled to speak normally. "I take it you want to keep this baby?"

"Yes," she said quietly. "Absolutely."

"Does your family know?"

"Not yet," she said. "I found out yesterday."

"I want to know my child," Wes told her.

"I figured that you would."

"So you agree to let me participate? You won't try to cut me out?"

Her hair swung forward to hide her face. "We'll…we'll work something out."

The emotional charge made it impossible to look at her, so he turned away, just to look at something else, anything else. As chance would have it, he found himself gazing at the portrait of Naomi Moss. He did not allow himself to flinch. Just looked straight at the remarkable portrait.

"It's incredible how you resemble her," he said.

Ronnie walked over to him and looked up at the portrait. "I'm glad it survived," she said. "It chills me to think how close Dad came to burning it when the shipment arrived. Aunt Elaine said the only thing that slowed him down was how big and bulky it was. He didn't have an ax handy to chop it up and feed it into the fireplace. That gave Aunt Elaine and Uncle Bertram a window of opportunity to spirit it away."

Wes looked at her. "When the shipment arrived?" he said.

"Mom's things, from Sri Lanka. Elaine told me the story

when she was recuperating, in the hospital. Brushes with death make you reflect on the past, evidently."

Hairs prickled up on his neck. "This painting was in that container?" he repeated. "The one that came from Sri Lanka, after the bombing?"

"Yes. It's an Aaron Holmes. He was the hot portraitist at the time. He was vacationing there. Dad made him an offer he couldn't refuse. Dad's small superpower."

Well, hell. Wes stared up at the gleam of sly humor in Naomi Moss's blue eyes. Her expression seemed to say, *Seriously? You still don't get it?*

Of course, it no longer mattered if he got it or not. He couldn't act on it now.

But Ronnie plucked that right out of the airwaves. "What is it?" she demanded. "What are you thinking?"

Wes gestured at the portrait. "What do you think, Ronnie? Knowing me?"

Ronnie's eyes widened. "For real? You're thinking that Mom hid the documentation in her portrait? That's so cloak-and-dagger. Only you, Wes."

"I know, but it's the last place to look." He shrugged. "If you don't want to, well, tough. Too bad for me. I'll always wonder, but that's my cross to bear."

Ronnie stared up at her mother's portrait. "There's no reason for me not to check it out," she said.

His heart thudded. "No?" he asked. "Really?"

"Not for you," she said. "For me. For us. If Mom put anything in there, it wouldn't be anything she was ashamed of. It would be exactly the opposite."

"Your call," he said. "I learned my lesson. Naomi is not for me to mess with, or look at, or even like."

Ronnie reached up to seize the portrait. "All things considered, maybe I'd better look into this thing preemptively," she said. "Or God knows what scheme you'll come up with to get your paws on it."

He let out a rusty laugh as he helped her lift it down, turning it so that the portrait side was to the wall, and pulled his out his pocketknife. "Do you think I'll try to seduce your Aunt Elaine to get the run of the house?"

"Do not flatter yourself, Mr. Brody. You're not my type."

They turned, startled, to see Aunt Elaine being pushed through the library door by Jerome. He looked outraged when he saw the portrait off the wall.

"What are you doing?" he demanded. "Put that back where it was!"

"Wes thinks that Mom might have stored information in it," Ronnie said.

"You're letting yourself be manipulated by that bastard?" Jerome roared.

"There's no reason not to check," Ronnie said. She looked at Wes. "Go on."

Wes started gently loosening the nails that held the canvas to the frame.

"I can't believe this!" Jerome bellowed. "It's insane! I won't allow it!"

"Jerome, shut up, for God's sake," Elaine snapped. "Let's see what happens. Go on, then. Proceed."

Wes pried the frame loose of the canvas, taking care not to damage it. He lifted the canvas free of the frame and turned it around. There was a square of cardboard backing behind it, once white, now yellowed. A manila envelope was taped to it, and three letter-size envelopes. One was addressed to Jerome, one to Ronnie, and one to Elaine and Bertram.

Wes set the piece of cardboard backing on the table and stepped back to let Ronnie do the honors. Ronnie's cousins had made their way into the library and were crowded around watching. The room was hushed. Even Annika was quiet, eyes big and worried, sensing the gravity of the moment.

Ronnie detached the large envelope, and the three letters. She opened the manila envelope and looked inside. "It's full of floppy disks," she said. "Does anybody know someone with equipment that can read a format this old?"

"Give them to me," Maddie said. "I'll get right on it."

Ronnie gave the envelope to Maddie, then passed Elaine her letter, and Jerome his. Jerome's face looked stricken. He held it by his fingertips, as if it might bite him.

Ronnie settled on Elaine's wingback chair and opened her letter.

Twenty

She was intensely aware of everyone watching. Only Wes had turned his face politely away. The handwriting of her letter was different than other examples she'd seen of her mother's handwriting. Not cursive, printed much larger. Meant to be read by her seven-year-old self. Her eyes began to blur almost instantly as she read it.

Dearest Ronnie,
Sweetheart, if you're reading this, it's because the saddest thing has happened, and I won't be coming home.

I hope you never see this. I hope you see me instead. I'll hug you and kiss you, and someday, when you're grown up, I'll tell you how scared I was, and we'll laugh about it.

But just in case, I'll tell you right now that I love

you. I'll never stop. Wherever I am in the universe, I'll be blessing you forever.

I know this will be hard for Daddy. Try to be strong if he gets sad. I sent a letter to Aunt Elaine and Uncle Bertram, and another one to Daddy, telling them everything that happened. They'll explain it to you when you're bigger.

I wish you love, baby. Be bold. Don't let real love slip away. Try to forgive. It's always worth the effort.

I love you to the ends of the known universe and beyond.

All my love,
Mommy

She could hear her mother's voice. Her heart felt like it would burst.

"Her letter lays it all out." Elaine's voice quavered. "It was Raimund. The payoffs, the corruption, the cover-up, the falsified data. Probably the bomb, as well."

"Who is Raimund?" Ronnie asked.

"Raimund Oswalt, our chief operating officer back then," Elaine said. "Naomi says, *'Tomorrow I'm meeting John Padraig and giving him copies of the data, just in case. I confronted Raimund yesterday, and someone cut the brake line of my car, which I then drove into a ditch. I'm afraid to talk to anyone but Padraig. If anything happens to me, ask Padraig for the real story. The data is in the floppy disks.'*" Her hands, holding the letter, dropped to her lap. "Oh, Naomi," she whispered. "Oh, honey."

"Where is this Raimund Oswalt?" Wes asked.

"Dead," her father said flatly. "He died of cancer five years ago. So I can't even crush him for killing my wife. He's out of my reach. Goddamn him."

Ronnie turned to her father, shocked by his eyes. He

looked as if he'd been mortally wounded. "Dad?" she whispered. "Are you all right?"

"No. Raimund told me she was having an affair with Padraig. And I believed him. I paid him a fat salary and bonuses, year after year. After he killed my Naomi."

"Oh, Dad," Ronnie said. "I'm so sorry."

"I let her down," he said brokenly. "I let you down, too, Veronica. I've always let you down."

She couldn't in all honesty tell him that it wasn't true, but her heart had been softened by Mom's letter. "Maybe, before," she said. "But we can start from where we are now. We can try again and do better. Right? That's what Mom would have wanted."

Her dad nodded jerkily and covered his face with his hand.

Ronnie stared down at her letter. It was blistered with her tears.

Don't let real love slip away, Mom had said. Was that what she was doing? Was that why it felt so wrong? There had been so much pain and misunderstanding. Mom's messages of love, hidden almost in plain sight for twenty-three years, had never quite reached them…until now.

She didn't want to choose pride over love. God knows, she should have learned her lesson by now.

Elaine stood, leaning on the ebony cane. "It would seem, Mr. Brody, that we owe you an apology," she announced. "To your parents, as well, God rest their souls. On behalf of MossTech, and everyone involved, I am deeply sorry."

Wes inclined his head. "Thank you," he said. "I accept your apology. And now, if you'll excuse me, I will be on my way."

Panic exploded inside of Ronnie. "You're going now?" She felt almost frantic. "Right now? When we've finally figured it all out?"

Wes gestured at the dismantled painting, the scattered envelopes, her aunt, crying into a handkerchief, her father, who had turned away, hunched and shaking.

"It's time, babe," he said gently. "Look around yourself. The place is trashed, everyone's in turmoil. My work here is done."

"Oh, stop," she said sharply. "Don't joke about this."

"I'm in no mood to joke," he said. "This is huge, Ronnie. We proved that our parents were exactly what we believed them to be. Not crooks, but good, solid people, loving their families, doing their jobs to the best of their ability. I call that a win. I'm not going to get greedy. We'll be in touch about that…ah…that other thing we mentioned." He backed toward the door, giving her a sad, crooked little smile.

"Don't go!" She grabbed his wrist, hearing her mother's voice in her head.

Don't let real love slip away. Try to forgive. It's always worth the effort.

"Don't go," she said again, fingers clamped around his wrist.

Wes turned to look at her. "Why?" he asked quietly. "Why should I stay?"

"Because…because things are different now. Everything's changed."

"Has it?" His eyes met hers, clear and challenging. "How so?"

"My mom told me in her letter to be bold," she said. "She said not to let love slip away. To try to forgive. It's good advice, and I'm taking it. I think that she brought us together. She wanted me to be happy. I want to be happy. And you make me happy."

Joy lit up in his eyes. "I do?"

"Yes," she said forcefully. "Yes, like nothing else in the

world. I love you. I want you. I'll be bold, like she said. I want this. I want to give to you and take from you and just be with you. Do you promise me that you won't lie to me? Ever again?"

"Never," Wes said fiercely. "I never wanted to. It hurt, to lie to you. Never again. I swear it."

"Good," she said. "Stay with me, then. Stay with me forever."

"Yes," he muttered, as they came together. "Oh God, yes."

They clung to each other, then Wes shifted a little. "Careful," he said softly. "We've got to watch out for the baby."

"Don't be silly," she replied. "The baby will be fine. Just hold me."

Stunned silence. "Excuse me?" Aunt Elaine said. "Did I hear you say…baby?"

Ronnie barely noticed the pandemonium that followed. She saw, heard, felt, only Wes. Her family's babbling and exclaiming could not penetrate. She wound her arms around his neck and hung on tight. At long last, her family got the hint, and cleared out of the library, all of them still talking and exclaiming. The door clicked smartly shut behind them.

Ahhh. Sweet, blessed silence.

Wes kissed her cheek, her jaw. His lips were hot and hungry against her sensitive throat. Sweet, melting, dragging kisses. "Let's lock the door," he suggested.

She grinned, lit up with pure, incandescent happiness. "An excellent idea."

Epilogue

"That's her," the obstetrics nurse said. "Elaine Susannah Daly."

Elaine peered through the glass at her great-grandbaby, Maddie and Jack's gorgeous newborn girl. Eight pounds even, curly black hair, wiggling madly. She was the perfect baby, with her sweet little fat cheeks, and her tiny pink rosebud of a mouth.

"Oh, my goodness," she whispered. "She's so precious."

Annika jumped up and down. "Can I hold Lainie? I promise I'll be so careful!"

"All in good time, sweetheart," Elaine said, gazing raptly at the baby.

The rest of them crowded around, gazing at Lainie with soft eyes. Wes and Ronnie were there, Marcus and Eve, Caleb and Tilda and Annika. The sight of them all together made her heart thud in her chest. What a wild gamble she'd made. At the end, she'd lost, but in the great balance of things, in the long run, she'd won.

Still. She couldn't take the credit for the happiness and prosperity of her grandchildren and her niece. That was the result of their own courage and enterprise.

Not that she would ever, in a million years, admit such a thing to them.

"Elaine. Congratulations. Your family line continues."

It was Jerome's cool, dragging voice behind her. Elaine braced herself out of habit, but Jerome wasn't quite as abrasive as he used to be. Not since that trip that he and Caleb had taken to Sri Lanka, to meet with the relatives of the victims of the toxic-mold disaster.

They were in the process of making what reparations they could. That process had been very good for Jerome's general mood.

"Congratulations to you, too, Jerome," Elaine said. "You're next."

He snorted. "So are you satisfied with the result of your machinations?"

"I paid for it," she admitted. "But it was worth it. Just look at her." She gestured at the baby, and then at the rest of her family. "Aren't they a sight to behold? Our new generation. Babies, tumbling all around us in a few months."

"It'll be noisy and chaotic," Jerome observed. "You even managed to get Veronica married and pregnant. Your plotting and scheming knows no bounds."

"The timing wasn't ideal." Elaine tried not to sound bitter. "Reconciling a month after the divorce, and remarrying in another Elvis chapel in Vegas? Good God."

"At least she invited us the second time around," Jerome observed. "Ridiculous affair."

"True, but we had fun," Elaine said. "You know what,

Jerome? All in all, I'm satisfied. Even if I lost MossTech to you, I'm fine. We're all fine."

"Yes," Jerome said. "I agree. We're fine."

"Of course you're fine." Elaine's voice was wry. "You got MossTech."

"About that," Jerome said. "I thought about it, in Sri Lanka, and I've come to a decision."

"What decision?" she asked. "You are going public, of course?"

Jerome gazed at the baby. "No," he said. "I've transferred my shares of MossTech to the kids. Equally. They'll be the caretakers of MossTech's legacy now."

Elaine stared at him, open-mouthed.

"Dad," Ronnie said. "Are you serious?"

"When have I ever joked?" he asked. "Naomi gave me good advice in her letter. Twenty-three years late, but still good. She told me I had a good family, and that I should trust them. She was right. So that's what I'll do."

Wes and Ronnie exchanged startled glances. "Dad. That's…incredible."

"Besides," Jerome went on, his voice dour. "I'll be a grandfather soon, and I'm sure that will take up a considerable amount of my time and attention."

Wes's face froze in stark alarm at that prospect, but Ronnie seized her father in a fierce hug, pressing a kiss to his lean, seamed cheek. "Thanks, Dad."

"I won't be any good at it, you know," Jerome warned her. "Grandfathering, I mean. You know me. I'm impatient and bad-tempered. And stiff as a board."

"Nonsense," Elaine said briskly. "As long as you're making an effort, you'll do fine. You'll learn."

She and Jerome looked around the room. Maddie was with Jack in the recovery room, but Caleb was there with Tilda, whose belly was starting to show, and Marcus with

Eve, and Ronnie and Wes, and her beautiful Annika. Her precious treasures. So lovely.

"Quite the harvest," Jerome said, in an undertone just for her ears. "Better than we deserve, eh? After all our shenanigans."

Elaine smiled. "Probably, but what the hell. We'll take it and run with it."

* * * * *

SNOWED IN SECRETS

JULES BENNETT

For my girls, Grace and Madelyn.
Thank you for teaching me the true meaning
of unconditional love.

One

"Hey, Merle."

Sara Hawthorne greeted the owner of the Quiet Distil with a hug, then eased back, offering the elderly widower a smile. Not all of Angel's Share's clients were close like Merle Allen. But he'd been a loyal customer from day one and was more like a friend than a customer.

When Sara and her two sisters, Delilah and Elise, had started their distillery years ago, Merle had been one of their biggest cheerleaders. He'd told them as soon as they open that inaugural ten-year barrel of bourbon, he wanted first dibs. Sara liked to pop into his bourbon bar every few weeks to visit and just unwind.

And it was the desperate need for unwinding she searched for now. Between the holidays and her personal life, she had to find a few minutes just to herself.

"How's my favorite distiller?" Merle asked as he rested his hand on the glossy mahogany bar.

"I think you say that to my sisters, too." She laughed, leaning against the end of the bar top.

Merle shrugged. "You're all my favorite, what can I say?" His bright blue eyes crinkled around the edges as he chuckled, then pointed toward one of the VIP lounge areas. "Why don't you go on in and have a seat? I'll bring you something to take your mind off your troubles."

Sara tipped her head. "What makes you think I have troubles?"

He smiled as he shook his head and turned to move in behind the counter. "I own a bar. I know heartache when I see it. Now go on and settle in."

Since Sara figured Merle was rather experienced in recognizing a wounded heart, she obeyed. Per usual, she headed toward her favorite lounge area located all the way in the back of the bourbon bar.

Merle had been smart with the way he approached the interior of this place. Each of the rooms was different in motif and decor, but she always loved the cozy warmth of the White Dog Room. White Dog referred to the term of bourbon before it aged, but all of the rooms at the Quiet Distil had appropriate terminology-themed spaces and ambiance that catered to both male and female customers.

As Sara made her way toward the back of the bar, she passed the Rye and Mash Rooms. Both of those were nearly full with couples or friend groups laughing and enjoying their spirits. Another pang hit Sara as she continued down the wide hallway flanked with warm lighting made to resemble old gas lanterns.

On the skirts of pain in her heart came a healthy dose of guilt. She was happy for her sisters—thrilled, actually. They'd each found the love and happiness of their lives. Elise was off on her tropical honeymoon in Fiji with Antonio and Delilah had reunited with Camden after they'd teetered on the brink of divorce.

The ache Sara had lived with for too long threatened to turn her into a green-eyed monster. There was no need to be upset or jealous, that had never been in her nature anyway. Sara knew her time would come to find love, she was sure of it. And waiting for that proverbial knight in shining armor would be worth the time and energy she put into daydreaming…she hoped. Not that she ever needed anyone to save her, but she wouldn't mind a shoulder to lean on every now and again.

She wanted to hold hands in the car, snuggle on the couch after working all day, and talk about absolutely nothing and everything. She wanted forehead kisses and random "I love you" texts in the middle of the day.

Sara slid open the old oak doors and figured the White Dog Room would be just as crowded as the others, but there was only one couple occupying one of the tufted white leather sofas, so she would have a little privacy after all.

Perfect. She just wanted to gather her thoughts and take a little break from life. There had been a whirlwind to get Elise and Antonio married at the castle and Sara was so pleased with how everything turned out for their special day.

Angel's Share's wedding venue was officially open and another chapter in their business venture could be checked off. They were moving ahead through so many layers within their business and excelling at each one.

Angel's Share Distillery started twelve years ago in an old abandoned castle nestled in the hills of Benton Springs, Kentucky. The sisters had loved that unique place from the start and knew buying the historical property would set them apart from other distilleries. Not to mention, theirs was the only female-owned distillery in the country. Anything they could do to get a leg up on their competitors, they had to do. Standing out in this male-dominated field was a must for them to continue their success.

Sara turned toward the opposite side of the room and moved to the back. It was then that her breath caught in her throat and her knees grew weak.

She'd never experienced such a bold flash of lust in all of her life. But the man on the sofa nearly stole her breath. She certainly hadn't seen him at first glance, though she had no clue how she could have missed such a striking guy. The dark hair, the shadowy beard, black dress pants, crisp white shirt and black vest. He might as well have just popped out of a 1930s movie set. There was something to be said about a classy man who exuded confidence and elegance.

Mercy sakes, she blinked and glanced away for fear that she'd get caught staring. Surely a man who looked like that constantly got ogled and she wasn't the first. Also a man who looked like that wouldn't be in a bourbon bar on a Saturday night all alone. Likely his date had gone to the restroom, so Sara wasn't going to go anywhere near that section, either. Which left her options toward the front of the room.

"I thought I'd find you in your favorite place."

She turned to see Merle with a small charcuterie board of cheeses and fruit and nuts, plus a paddle with four different tumblers. He knew she loved the simplicity of the White Dog Room and she'd actually never even ventured into the others on her visits. She couldn't help but smile as she started to take the items from his grasp.

"No, ma'am." He shook his head and took a step back. "You tell me where you want to sit and I'll take it there."

Sara glanced around the spacious room, her eyes immediately catching the sexy stranger in the corner. His mouth lifted in a smirk and she had a rush of arousal she certainly hadn't expected. Well, well, well.

Lust was one thing, but that curl of desire was on an entirely different level.

He held her gaze and continued to charm her with only a grin. Sara had to believe there was no date in the restroom. How was this guy all alone?

The way he stared back at her as he came to his feet had Sara squaring her shoulders and ignoring any nervous twinges.

"What about over there?" she asked Merle, pointing to the sofa the stranger sat on.

"Oh, do you know him?" Merle asked.

No, but I'm about to.

The intriguing stranger closed the distance between them and turned his attention to Merle.

"Could I get another Angel's Share ten-year?" he asked.

Oh, not only did he partake of her distillery bourbon, he had a voice smooth as whiskey to go with the mysterious exterior—as if she needed more reasons to be drawn to him.

"Of course, sir."

"I'll take this," Sara said, reaching for the charcuterie board. "Thanks, Merle."

"You let me know if you need anything else." Merle tipped his head in a nod and went to check on the couple on the opposite side of the room.

Sara shifted her focus back to the stranger and offered a smile. "Care to share this board with me?" she asked.

The guy's brows shot up and he shrugged. "It does seem like a good bit of food."

"Merle is a sweetheart," she explained. "He's always feeding me when I come in."

The striking man turned and headed back to the sofa he'd just left. Once the board and the sample drinks were on the honey-colored table, the stranger took his cell that had been on the sofa and slid it into his pocket.

"Have a seat." He gestured to the area right beside where he'd been sitting. "I take it you know the owner well?"

Sara took a seat, but left some space between them. He might be sexy and had piqued her interest, but he was still a stranger. Besides, as much as she wanted to find her happily-ever-after, she didn't think that would be in a bar and she sure as hell didn't want to come off as desperate.

"You could say that," she replied, then extended her hand in greeting. "My name is Jane."

At the last second she decided to use her middle name instead. In case he turned out to be weird, she didn't want him knowing who she really was.

He smiled, then reached for her hand and slid his thumb over her knuckles. He held on to her hand as he continued to keep his eyes locked on hers.

"You can call me Parker."

Sara eased her hand from his before she got lost in that deep voice, those dark eyes and that firm grip that made her wonder if he was as powerful as he appeared. What would a man like this do for a living? Traveling and dressed nice with shoes that had those classic red bottoms. Real estate? Architect? Definitely some type of business, but what?

She tipped her head and narrowed her eyes. "Parker is not your real name."

"Maybe, maybe not."

The mysterious man wanted to remain just that.

Unable to help herself, Sara smiled and found she actually enjoyed this odd meetup. Sounded sexy to her, but she still had to be cautious.

Another employee of the Quiet Distil came in carrying Parker's drink. Sara eased back onto the sofa, getting more comfortable with this situation. There was nothing to worry about. They were in a public place, they were having fun, and she was smiling and enjoying herself. What more could she ask for in an evening?

"Sir." The new hire sat the drink on the table and stepped back. "Is there anything else I can get either of you?"

Sara shook her head, her eyes still locked on Parker's and his on hers.

"We're good here," Parker stated without glancing up.

Once they were alone again, Sara reached for one of the samples Merle had given her. He always gave her different bourbons and whiskeys to try. Just because she was co-owner of Angel's Share, didn't mean she shouldn't stay abreast of her competition. It was good to see what else was out there and how her own company compared.

"So, what should we talk about? Careers? Favorite colors?" she asked, swirling the amber contents of her glass.

Parker laughed. "I'd rather know what you're doing here alone looking like you're carrying a whole host of problems."

For a virtual stranger to see something, Sara wondered what she must have looked like when she came in. She hadn't been surprised when Merle noticed because she was in here often enough and he knew her quite well. But this guy? Maybe he wasn't a businessman at all. Perhaps he was some sort of doctor or therapist.

Great. That would certainly kill any mood if a hunky guy tried to get into her head and decipher all of her past. She wouldn't put that on someone she'd just met.

"Do I look like I'm sad?" she asked, pasting on her sauciest smile, hoping to dodge the statement entirely.

"You look like you don't want to be," he countered.

Well, so much for that sassy grin and the dodge.

"Everyone has their secrets, and I'd like to keep mine close to my chest."

Parker nodded in agreement, or perhaps that was understanding. Either way, he shifted his focus to the contents of his glass as he gave a gentle swirl. She studied his dark, disheveled hair, those thick black brows and the fan of his heavy lashes. How did one person have so much sexuality and mysteriousness surrounding them?

She was glad she'd chosen to sit in this room and come over to his corner. Spending the evening alone hadn't necessarily appealed to her, but she also hadn't wanted to just stay home. Finding someone at the Quiet Distil was definitely an added perk to her day.

"You like bourbon?" he asked, his eyes darting back up to her.

"What's not to love?" she replied. "That little bit of smoky char, the smooth, rich flavor from the oak barrel, the way it warms you from the inside out."

"You seem to be quite the connoisseur." His crooked smile had the corners of his eyes crinkling, which only made him even sexier. "So what is it that you do?"

Sara lifted her snifter. "Drink bourbon. What about you?"

"Wait in bars for sexy women to come through."

"And does that usually work out well for you?"

Parker shrugged. "I'll let you know in a few hours."

Well, wasn't he a smooth one? Maybe that's why she found him so fascinating. Attractive, mysterious and clearly just as interested in her. A little flirting would be good for her. She hadn't had a date in a few months, and not that this was a date, but close enough. She hadn't really had time to find a date, let alone go on one.

A little banter, a little drinking…there was absolutely no harm and Sara believed this was exactly what she needed. With her sisters always with their significant others and not as free for social time as they used to be, Sara was clearly going to have to make her own fun and start her own traditions.

"I actually work in events," she told him, keeping her career super vague to keep up the element of mystery. "I make sure people have the time of their lives and then I get paid for it."

"Sounds like you love it."

"Nothing better," she agreed. "And my favorite color is white, you know, in case you want just a touch of personality."

Parker's dark brows drew in as he jerked back. "White? I've never met anyone who said white."

"You've never met anyone like me." She sipped her bourbon and offered a smile. "White is underrated, and it's the color of all the things I love. Most carbs, the wedding dress I have pictured in my head, the clouds when I daydream."

Parker laughed and shook his head. That burst of deep, robust laughter sent shivers through her. Flirty chatting was one thing, but the moment she started getting those giddy feelings, she really needed to dial it back a notch. She'd known this guy for all of twenty minutes. Just because he dressed well, had that whole dark vibe going on and smelled extremely sexy didn't mean anything was going to come from this encounter…though she wouldn't mind knowing how long he was in town for and maybe seeing him again.

Sara knew in her heart there was someone out there

for her. She knew without a doubt that as soon as she saw "the one," she would be immediately swept off her feet and head over heels. She had all the clichés logged into her mind and was more than ready for that day to happen.

But until then, she'd just enjoy her time with chance encounters such as this one.

"Interesting take on your favorite color," he told her. "So, these events that you do, I assume you work with weddings since you said wedding dresses and you make people happy."

"I actually just finished working on a wedding."

Elise had made a beautiful bride and no matter that wedding planner wasn't Sara's job, she took that position very seriously when helping to pull off the big day for her sister. Sara had worked damn hard on that memorable event, and her spreadsheets and articulate planning had made the entire wedding come off without a hitch. Now she and her sisters were ready to start booking outside weddings and other venues. This was just another manner in which Angel's Share was set apart from so many other distilleries. Who wouldn't want to get married in an old historic castle?

Maybe one day for her…

"Yet you're single."

Parker's statement shifted her focus back to his intense gaze.

"How do you know I'm not married?" she asked.

He pointed to her hands. "You have jewelry on, yet nothing on your ring finger. You also don't seem like the type to leave a husband at home to come out to a bourbon bar and chat with random strangers."

"Maybe I just left that off my list of hobbies."

Once again, Parker laughed. "Touché."

"I actually hold marriage in high regard," she amended.

"I'm not married, but when I do get married, I hope to still come out to amazing places like this, just with my husband."

"He will be a lucky man."

Sara sat her empty tumbler back in the empty slot on the tray and chose another.

"If he exists," she murmured.

As she eased back against the sofa with a new sample, she took the time to survey Parker once again, this time not caring one bit that he noticed. A man like that wanted to be looked at, he took great care in his appearance and had to know he looked drop-dead sexy.

"Do you practice that look in the mirror?" he asked.

"What look is that?"

Parker stretched his arm along the sofa and behind her back as he eased a little closer.

"The seductive stare."

"Is that the look I'm giving?" she asked.

"Oh, I think you know exactly what you're doing," he told her, leaning just a bit closer. "The question is, what would you do if I took you up on that offer?"

Two

What the hell was he doing? He didn't have time to entertain any extracurricular activities. He owed his editor a favor and once that was done, Ian Ford could actually start writing his novel. He'd saved enough money and made wise investments over the years to stay home and focus on his dream of writing his first book. Hopefully that would lead to more and spawn a new career.

Ian only had to be in Benton Springs, Kentucky, for two weeks, max. He'd do his interviews, conduct all the research needed to complete this piece, type it all out in silence and solitude, and then have everything wrapped up and turned in before the new year.

A perfect plan for the perfect ending to his illustrious career with *Elite*.

"Who says I'm offering?"

Jane's question pulled him back to the moment. Ian couldn't help but laugh.

"Maybe not with words, but that silent stare is more than inviting."

She lifted one slender shoulder, causing her silky black hair to slide around. Ian pressed his fingertips together, resisting the urge to reach out and see if those strands were as soft as they appeared. He'd been too damn long without a woman and in an instant this striking vixen had captured his attention in a way no one had done in years.

"I practiced the look in the car before I came in."

The way she continued to smirk in a sultry way with one brow tipped and her mouth in a soft grin, Ian wasn't quite sure if she was serious or not.

Regardless, he was a sucker. Damn it. He didn't come to town to be sidetracked by a seductive woman on day one. But turning away from her now would be impossible. She stirred a desire in him he sure as hell hadn't expected. This awakening wasn't something to be ignored.

She cocked her head, clearly waiting on a reply. Those strands brushed along his fingertips and another stir of arousal churned within. And here he thought he'd hate this trip to Kentucky in the dead of winter.

Ian didn't resist her again. He slid her strands through his fingers, and yes, they were just as satiny as he'd imagined. Now his mind went to her full lips and wondered how long he'd be able to resist those.

"How long are you in town?" she asked.

Thrown by her question, Ian gathered his thoughts. "Not long. I assume you live here?"

"Best place in the entire world, especially at Christmastime."

He shifted even closer now as he continued to tease the strands of her hair between his fingers. Red flags waved all around inside his head, but he completely ignored them.

He wanted more from her, not quite sure what yet. He also wasn't about to give up his anonymity…not for anybody.

"And have you traveled around the world?"

Jane smiled and there was no way to ignore another punch of desire to his gut. He couldn't figure out if she knew her potency and used it to cast men under her spell or if she was innocent and had no idea…but a woman who looked like every fantasy come to life couldn't be too innocent.

"Not much, but enough to know I belong here."

"You seem to know what you want."

Jane's eyes dropped to his mouth, then back up. Without a word, she reached for his tumbler on the table.

"I've always known what I wanted," she informed him, swirling the contents of his glass.

And she didn't mean his drink, if that heavy-lidded stare told him anything.

There was something extremely sexy about a bold woman, a woman who didn't play coy or bat her lashes and giggle. Not that he was looking for anything, but Jane was too intriguing and mysterious to simply ignore.

Some women who demanded attention were right up in your face, more than eager to talk about themselves. But Jane demanded attention in such a stealthy way that he found her absolutely refreshing. Her appearance, the way she held eye contact, the easy banter.

No, there was no way he could just get up and walk out. He would stay here as long as she did, and closing the place down didn't seem like such a bad idea right now.

Once the bourbon samples and the charcuterie board were gone, Ian still remained close as he listened to Jane discuss her favorite hangout spots in Benton Springs. All of them revolved around bourbon, which wasn't surprising. This part of the country took its spirits very seriously.

Even nondrinkers enjoyed the atmosphere of the low-key bars and restaurants that were rich with the history of the rolling Kentucky hills. Ian almost wished he had more time to spend here, but two weeks was more than enough…especially with the threat of snow.

There was a reason he'd moved south to Miami. Winters in the north had destroyed his life and he'd vowed never to be here again. Yet here he was as a favor to a dear friend, but after this he would never subject himself to icy roads again.

Ian reached up and slid his finger along his scar just beneath the stubble along his jaw. The jagged skin was always the reminder of where he'd come from…and what he'd lost.

A chime sounded from her purse and Jane smiled as she reached around to dig in her bag. The intrusion was a welcome one because staying stuck in his head was a miserable place to be.

"Excuse me," she told him. "You never know when there's an emergency."

Ian studied the way her slender fingers slid over the screen, the little smile that danced around her mouth as she read the message. With a soft sigh, she slid the device into the side pocket and shifted back to face him.

"Sorry about that. I didn't realize it had gotten so late." She glanced around the room and laughed. "And now we're the only ones here. I didn't even see that other couple leave."

No, he hadn't, either, but he hadn't once thought about the time or anyone else in the bar. He also hadn't thought about work or the anxiety that had been eating at him coming back to the snowy north for the first time in twenty years.

"I'd say they're getting ready to close," she stated. "As much as I hate to go, I probably should head out."

She came to her feet and shifted her hair over one shoulder before she reached down to grab her bag. Then those dark eyes landed on his once again and he knew he wasn't ready for their time to come to an end. He had not planned on the unforeseen events of this night, nor had he planned on what to do once they needed to leave.

"This has been a nice surprise," she told him.

Ian stood, leaving very little distance between them. Her eyes widened, but she didn't step back. She smiled after a beat and tipped her head.

Once again, Ian found himself reaching for her. This time, he trailed his fingertip along the side of her face, tucking her hair behind her ear, then gliding his hand on down her jawline. She didn't look away, didn't blink. He had her full attention.

"I'm usually not a fan of surprises," he murmured. "But I might just have to change my stance on that topic."

"I love them," she told him, her voice a little breathier than before.

"I'm not ready to end this night."

He hadn't meant to voice his thought, but the words slipped out and now hovered in the minuscule space between them. No regrets. That was something Ian never did, so now he would just see how the rest of the night played out.

"Who said this had to end?" she countered.

That desire churned in his gut once more, and he couldn't help but recognize the fact that he was spiraling completely out of control here and for the first time in his life, he didn't care. For a man who prided himself on never letting anyone or anything rule his emotions, he wasn't doing a very good job of holding on to that self-control. And while he wasn't about to completely lose himself here, he had to at least explore what the hell had him so intrigued and mesmerized.

"I rented a house for my visit if you'd like to continue the party there," he informed her. "We can stay out on the patio so you feel safe since I am a stranger."

Jane's smile widened. "I'll follow in my car."

Before Sara left the parking lot of the Quiet Distil, she fired off a text to Delilah telling her she was going to meet a guy for a drink and she'd send her location shortly. Just because the guy was sexy, fascinating and every girl's fantasy didn't mean she could be foolish. She still had to stay safe, and he'd reassured her they'd remain outside. The fact that he wanted her to feel safe only added to his charm.

Part of her wanted to know more, though. She wanted his real name, where he was from, all of the basic information. But he was just passing through and clearly wasn't looking for more.

Well, she was looking for more, but until the day came, she'd simply enjoy herself along the way. What other choice did she have? Wallow in misery? That wasn't in her makeup.

Just because she was the last woman standing in regard to relationships in her family didn't mean she would grow to be some old lonely woman. Good things come to those who wait…right?

Sara really wanted to stop living by cheesy clichés and start making the most of her life the way she'd always envisioned it. Complaining wouldn't change anything, but she was human and on occasion she could be cranky.

Not tonight, though. How could anyone be in a bad mood when a charismatic stranger, who was more than easy on the eyes, gave such an inviting proposal? There was no denying the attraction and had she turned him down, she would have always wondered what she'd missed out on.

The fact that they weren't sharing personal details only made their impromptu meeting even more thrilling. She'd never been so mysterious with a man before and going by her middle name still kept her grounded, but she couldn't lie. Having the facade around her made her feel a little saucy, even a little flirtier than she'd ever been. She could be anyone she wanted tonight and right now, she was feeling more powerful and audacious than ever before.

Sara followed Parker's taillights as he made another turn down the snowy road. She rarely made it to this part of the county. Her home was on the other side, but lovely temporary rental homes were all over this area. People came from around the world to see the unique history nestled in these foothills and visit all of the distilleries. The distillery business had exploded over the last several years and the timing of her and her sisters' launching Angel's Share couldn't have been better.

For the moment, most things in her life were falling into place…save for the lack of a partner and the fact that she'd found out her adoptive mother was actually her biological aunt and her birth father was out there somewhere.

Sara blew out a sigh and pulled into the drive behind Parker. She was not about to let her personal life's issues ruin this moment. She still couldn't believe she'd followed a stranger to his home, but she fired off the location to Delilah, feeling safer already.

The two-story cottage with a wraparound porch seemed so quaint and almost…innocent. Seeing something so normal and average put this situation into a more realistic perspective. Flirting in a bar was one thing, but now, they would be alone and even though the promise of not going inside was made, that didn't mean things wouldn't progress. She'd never been one for a fling, but she wouldn't turn up her nose at one, either.

There was something so mystifying about Parker. He had been so gallant and self-assured without being a jerk. She hadn't dated jerks in the past, honestly, but nobody had ever really grabbed her attention for more than a few dates. And clearly she wasn't looking to date Parker, but she almost wished he'd be in town longer so they could explore this instant attraction. Something this fierce and powerful had never happened to her before.

Which was all the more reason to enjoy tonight…whatever may come her way.

She'd just set her cell back in her purse when her door opened. The dome light came on and she instantly turned to face her host as the cold blast hit her. He stood at the opening, looking down at her with a crooked grin that some might say was a little naughty and a whole lot cocky. She had a feeling she might get a better glimpse into the real Parker, but how much did he want to reveal? How much did she?

"Are you thinking about leaving?" he asked, resting one hand on the top of her car and the other on the open door.

"Not at all," she informed him. "I texted a couple people to let them know where I was in case you decide to get weird."

He stared for a moment before shaking his head and extending his hand.

"I will never understand what women go through with always worrying about safety measures."

She slid her hand into his as he assisted her from the car. That strong hold sent another round of tingles through her entire body. The building anticipation of what would happen during her visit also kept her stomach in knots—

in the absolute best way, though. And the fact that he acknowledged her legitimate concern was definitely another check mark in his favor.

“If I didn’t feel safe, I wouldn’t be here,” she said as she slid from her car. “But I still want to protect myself.”

“Nothing will happen to you here.”

The conviction in his tone made her feel secure in her decision to join him at his place. She definitely never would have invited him back to her place. At least this was neutral ground, since he was passing through.

Parker’s fingertips trailed up her arm and back down as he laced his fingers with hers. She allowed him to lead her toward the path that led around to the back of the house. When he unlatched the gate, she hesitated for just a moment.

Parker’s attention turned to her as he stopped as well. “The patio is beautiful with a nice view, and I promise we will be warm. I will leave this gate open, but if you’d rather sit on the front porch, that’s fine, too. Just tell me where you’re comfortable.”

Why did he say all the right things? Clearly there was a woman in his life at some point who had taught him manners and morals. A mother? A sister? A special friend? There was so much she wanted to ask and explore with this man.

Sara offered a smile instead. “Lead the way. I’d love to see this view.”

With her hand still firmly in his, he led her the rest of the way down the snow-covered path and around the back of the house. Sara gasped and stilled once more as she took in the beauty.

“I thought you might enjoy the ambiance out here,” he told her.

Parker released her hand and stepped aside so she could

take in the serenity of the property. The front of the home had been plain, but the back more than made up for that. A large porch, complete with a covered hot tub, a large garden area with benches and a pergola, and twinkling lights draped all over the place as if they had their own little stars shining just for them. Everything was covered in a fresh white blanket of snow, which only made the scenery seem somewhat magical.

"Let's head up to the porch," he told her. "It's freezing out here."

Sara laughed as he tugged her toward the steps, but then carefully held on to her so she didn't slip. Clearly he wasn't from around here, because she loved this weather. Yes, it might be cold, but in December what did he expect? She'd hate living somewhere where she decorated her home for Christmas wearing flip-flops. This was the weather she wanted for the holidays.

"I didn't expect such beauty back here," she told him as they reached the spacious covered patio.

Sara swiped the dampness of the snowflakes from her face and her hair, then sat her purse on the closest chair. When she focused once again on Parker, he was simply standing there staring down at her. Glistening flakes clung to his long, inky lashes and dotted white all over his dark hair. And that mouth. His mouth seemed to just beg her to reach out and touch…so she did.

With her eyes locked firmly on his, Sara reached out and slid her thumb across his bottom lip. His eyes locked solely on her as the snow continued to whirl around, trapping them in some winter wonderland of beauty and romance.

But this wasn't romance. This was merely two strangers who weren't ready to end their night.

Just when she started to pull back, Parker reached up

and gripped her wrist, holding her in place. With one step, he closed the distance between them.

"Is this when you kiss me?" she asked.

"This is when you kiss me," he corrected.

Three

Sara wasn't about to waste another moment, not when she'd been staring at that mouth all night. Lifting up onto her toes, she leaned in and slid her lips over his. Lightly at first, wanting to take in just a slight touch to get familiar with him.

But in an instant, Parker wrapped his arms around her waist and tugged her against his hard, strong body. Something snapped inside her as well as she thrust her fingers through his hair. The warmth of his body warded off any of the chill that surrounded them. Parker coaxed her lips apart and took the kiss to another level and she simply couldn't get enough. What had started as fun banter only hours ago had moved at a faster pace than she'd ever gone before.

Was this a mistake? Was this heated fling too good to be true?

No and no. She deserved a sliver of happiness, even if it was all temporary. With the shock of finding out her biological history, losing the only woman she'd known as a mother, and her sisters finding the loves of their lives, Sara couldn't help but feel alone lately.

While she wasn't one to have a self-pity party, she couldn't help herself right now. Parker was the perfect distraction for everything that weighed heavy. Besides, this was only for one night. What could be the harm in taking advantage of a perfectly delicious opportunity?

Softly, he nipped at her lips before easing back. He ran his hands up and down her arms.

"You're trembling."

Was she? She wasn't even cold—far from it.

Parker took a step back and turned away. "Give me a minute to light these heaters and it will be warm out here in no time."

She remained in place, still trying to process that kiss that seemed like it could be a stepping-stone to so much more. That kiss had been almost like a promise, like he wanted that next level but he'd been gentlemanly enough to not push.

Dee would be so appalled that she was here with a man she'd just met and moving so fast. She would tell her this wasn't safe, she'd tell her she shouldn't settle for a quickie. If Elise were here she'd think the same. That's why Sara didn't check to see if Dee had responded to her texts. It was easy for them to say, but she wasn't settling. She was enjoying herself while this stranger was in town and obviously he wanted to enjoy himself, too.

Parker propped his hands on his hips and stared at the heater near the outdoor seating area. He raked a hand over the back of his neck and shook his head. As he bent down, he cursed beneath his breath.

"Do you need help?" she offered.

"I've never seen a heater like this. It can't be that hard to figure out."

Sara made her way over, bent down beside him, turned the knob, clicked the ignite button and had a flame in seconds.

"It's not," she agreed.

He shot her a glance with one dark brow raised. "Show-off."

"Maybe," she said with a shrug.

She stood back up and held his gaze as he slowly rose, too. His dark stare never wavered and that energy she'd felt with him only moments ago seemed to just get stronger. How should she react to this? Tearing his clothes off seemed a little too forceful, but damn it. She had a need she couldn't explain.

"I can run inside and grab a couple of blankets," he suggested.

"That would be nice."

Sara took a seat on the sofa closest to the heater and curled deeper into her coat as Parker punched in a code on the panel to get into the house. At this point she didn't know if she was shivering from anticipation or arousal, but it wasn't the cold.

Moments later, he returned with a large comforter.

"All I could find was what was on the bed." He laughed. "Do you want a drink?"

"I'm good, but thanks."

The last thing she needed was a drink, because she didn't know how long she was staying. If she had more alcohol, she wouldn't be able to drive to leave and she didn't want to hinder her thoughts or actions, especially where Parker was concerned. So either way, she needed to remain nice and sober.

"When I found this place online, the large covered patio

is what sold me." He took a seat next to her and spread the blanket out over both of them before shifting to face her. "A hot tub in the winter just seemed like the perfect way to relax."

"I've never had a hot tub." Sara tucked her hands beneath the comforter and adjusted so she could face him, too. "Have you been in this one yet?"

"Not yet. You up for it?"

Sara jerked back. "Is that why I'm here? A little skinny-dipping session?"

"You're here because you want to be here," he corrected, then shrugged. "Anything else is up to you."

Skinny-dipping in a hot tub with snow fluttering all around them was that level of romance she'd been wanting, even dreaming about. But there was no romance with a man she'd only known a few hours. That was quite a stretch of the imagination even for her.

"You're too tempting," she murmured.

The corners of his mouth kicked up in a grin she found all too thrilling and promising.

"I always welcome compliments."

Sara rolled her eyes. "I have a feeling you don't need help in the compliment department."

Something dark came over his face, she couldn't quite pinpoint it, but there was a sadness she hadn't seen before. In a flash, the pain vanished. Maybe she hadn't seen anything at all or perhaps he had his own demons he battled.

Regardless, she wasn't here to dig deeper into his life, just like she didn't need him looking further into hers.

"I've never been in a hot tub, nor have I ever been skinny-dipping," she admitted.

His eyes widened. "Never? You must have a grueling job if you don't make time for a little fun."

"I'm having fun now."

Parker stretched his arm along the back of the sofa and toyed with the ends of her hair just like he'd done back at the Quiet Distil. He seemed to be getting quite comfortable with her, which made her feel safe.

"You have a thing for my hair."

His eyes held hers. "I have a thing for you."

"Something we have in common."

His brows rose. "You have a thing for you, too?"

"You know what I mean," she joked.

He shifted once more and his hand brushed hers beneath the blanket. She thought he might lace their fingers together, but he flattened his palm on her thigh, which only sent another burst of heat through her. At this rate, she wouldn't need the blanket, the heater or the hot tub.

Though the mental image of the two of them naked in the bubbling water did nothing to squelch her rapidly growing desire. Had she seriously just met him only hours ago?

"Are you in town through Christmas?" she asked.

"No. I'm only here for two weeks, or less if I finish my job early."

"Any family to spend the holidays with?"

He cocked his head. "No personal questions, remember?"

She remembered, but she couldn't help herself.

"I've never done this before," she admitted. "I mean, I've talked to strangers and gotten to know them, but I've never kept everything so secretive. I'm not sure what to ask here."

"Who said we have to talk? Just enjoy the night."

Enjoying the night sounded so promising and intriguing.

"Do you like to travel?" she asked.

Parker's low laugh sent tingles through her. "You just can't help yourself, can you?"

Sara shrugged. "Not really."

He turned further into her, that hand on her thigh slid to her opposite hip as he shifted her more toward him. Sara stared up into his chocolate eyes, the glow from the heater and the porch lights reflecting all the amber flecks. The man was simply beautiful in both the dark and mysterious way and the charming, handsome sense. There had to be flaws, nobody was perfect, but she hadn't seen any yet and she wasn't about to start looking. She planned on enjoying the evening just like he'd told her to.

And since she didn't know what to talk about, she closed that distance between them and covered his lips with hers. Parker's grip on her hip tightened and he didn't disappoint in that kiss. He threaded his other hand through her hair and tugged softly, tipping her head back so he could have full access.

Damn, that man knew how to turn a kiss into a full-body experience.

With her hands still beneath the blanket, she reached for him. One hand on his chest and the other on his thigh. She wanted to touch, but didn't know what invisible line she should or shouldn't cross. They'd been dancing around the inevitable for hours. She wasn't naive about why she'd decided to come here. She had wanted him from that first glance and from his actions, there was no doubt he wanted the same thing.

This was absolutely drastic and completely out of character for her…which is what made this moment so much more thrilling. She wanted to be bold, she wanted to live her life in a more exciting way than ever before. If this past year had taught her anything, it was that she needed to always be in the moment.

Which was precisely what she was doing.

Sara slid her hand up over his shoulder and framed his

jaw as she opened fully for him. His fingertips released their grip just enough to travel on up to the button of her coat. He had her coat undone in no time and eased back just enough to look down into her eyes.

He said nothing—he didn't have to. Sara kept her gaze locked onto his and shrugged out of her coat, letting it fall behind her.

"Please at least tell me you're not married or have someone waiting for you back home," she murmured.

"I have no family."

His statement hit that wounded spot in her heart, but she couldn't focus on his backstory now. That wasn't what this night was about.

"This is crazy," she whispered with a soft laugh.

Parker smoothed her hair back and framed her face with his hands. The way he looked at her as if he could read her every thought or see deep into her soul only captivated her even more.

"There's no pressure. Anything that happens or doesn't is up to you and fine with me."

"I said it was crazy, not that I wanted to stop."

Sara flattened her palms on his chest and eased him back until she was the one hovering over him. Parker's eyes widened with excitement and arousal. Clearly she'd caught him off guard and apparently he didn't mind a dominant woman.

"Unless you want to stop." She lifted her knee onto the sofa and came up on it to lean even further over him. "I can go anytime."

Instantly his hands encircled her waist as he tugged her toward his chest.

"I like you right here."

Her lips were merely a breath away, so she kissed him again. She didn't recall enjoying kissing this much with anyone before. A kiss with Parker was definitely something to thoroughly relish and since this was all temporary, she wanted to get in as much as she could.

When his bare hands slid beneath the edge of her sweater, another round of shivers coursed through her, but this was so much more intense than any before. Having his skin against hers in an innocent yet intimate way put her desire on a whole other level.

Was all of this passion and desire stemming from the shadowy guise they were under? Or was there really some unexplainable, intriguing chemistry between them?

Sara rested her hands on his shoulders and let him explore her mouth and her body. She wanted rid of these clothes. She honestly couldn't even remember what bra and panties she had on because being with a man had been the last thing on her mind when she went out tonight.

Regardless, she didn't think her undergarments would hinder this union and she was tired of waiting for him to make the next move. Part of her was glad he was being so accommodating and making her feel safe, but she wished like hell he'd just jerk her clothes off.

Sara eased back and gripped the hem of her sweater. Slowly, she eased it up and over her head, tossing it to the side.

From the way Parker's eyes roamed over her chest and torso, the material of her bra was definitely a nonissue.

But that stare didn't last long. In the next moment there was a flurry of hands and clothes were flying. The blanket fell to the floor without a care along with their unwanted garments. The cool air hit her skin, but she didn't care. The warmth from the heater and Parker was all she needed.

In her haste to try to look somewhat sexy and remove everything, she hadn't realized Parker had procured protection until she saw him holding the package in one hand and tossing his wallet to the floor with the other.

Obviously something she should have been asking about, but now it was done and she didn't have to. At least one of them had their common sense about them.

His eyes locked onto hers and she stilled.

"Be sure," he told her.

Without a word, she took the foil pack and tore it open. Once the protection was in place, she straddled his lap and rested her hands on his shoulders. The second his gaze locked onto hers, she joined their bodies and couldn't stop herself from moaning. Sara stilled for just a second to take in the intensity of the moment. She closed her eyes and dropped her head back, welcoming each satiating emotion to consume her.

Parker's hands slid up her bare thighs, over her hips, and settled at the dip in her waist as he started to move beneath her. Sara had no choice but to match his rhythm.

"Look at me," he commanded.

That low, throaty demand had her refocusing her attention on his face. The desire and fierceness staring back at her sent another burst of arousal spiraling through her. How could someone be so powerful, yet so gentle at the same time?

Parker's hands came up to frame her face as he pulled her mouth down to his. His pace quickened the second his lips met hers. He consumed her completely. Her every thought, her every emotion. She'd never had a man make her feel so out of control, yet so powerful at the same time. He'd let her take the lead, he'd waited on her to give any sign she wasn't ready for this, but all the while he'd also made her feel sexy, wanted, needed.

Parker reached around and fisted his hand in her hair, giving it a slight tug. She pulled her lips from his as he trailed his mouth down her neck and to the swell of her breasts. If she thought she'd been pleasured before, that was nothing compared to what Parker was doing to her now. His hands and mouth seemed to be exploring her everywhere at once. She wasn't opposed to her new lover's skills.

His hips pumped faster and she kept up the frantic pace. Her body seemed to curl from the inside out with a need that took over and had her crying out, digging her nails into his bare skin and resting her forehead against his. The climax slammed into her as fierce and fast as this man had come into her life. She didn't care that she cried out or moaned. There was no controlling her reactions or sensations.

Parker's grip tightened. Seconds later, his entire body shook as the muscle in his jaw clenched. Sara slowly came down off her high, just in time to appreciate the view. For the first time since she'd met him only hours ago, Parker let his control slip. His lips thinned as he continued to clench his teeth. Sara placed her hand on the side of his face, loving the feel of that coarse hair beneath her palm.

Who knew she was a beard girl?

Her thumb slid over the puckered scar barely peeking from the hair on his jawline. Parker circled her wrist with his fingers and eased her hand aside. His eyes were solely on her now and his body had relaxed beneath hers. The quiet of the night surrounded them and reality was like a smack to the face.

Damn it. This is why she never wanted to do flings or one-night stands. This is why she wanted a significant other. Because when the sex was over, they could talk or just relax together and not feel the need for words. But considering they didn't know each other, there was only an awkward silence that surrounded them and she had no idea what to do next.

So she started by getting off of his lap and pretending she didn't just have a life-altering experience that would fuel her fantasies forever.

She hadn't been cold on this cozy patio until now, but standing before him naked with every vulnerability exposed, a chill spiraled through her. Sara glanced around for her clothes and saw her underwear sticking out from under the comforter. No need to get hypothermia along with her night of other firsts.

"Regrets already?" he questioned.

Without glancing his way, she plucked one article at a time up off the floor and willed herself not to rush. She had to be casual and calm…two emotions she was certainly not feeling right now.

"I don't do regrets," she stated with her back to him as she tried to remember what had happened to her bra. "But it's time for me to go."

Parker came to his feet. He shifted behind her and Sara stilled. His warmth seemed to reach her before his hand slid to her waist. Her breath caught in her throat as he eased his fingers across her abdomen and his palm flattened against her. With a gentle tug, he pulled her back against his bare chest. Sara closed her eyes and knew she was losing this battle…whatever this battle was at this point. She'd lost herself this evening…and she wasn't sorry.

"Stay for a while," he whispered, his warm breath washing over her and sending a whole host of postcoital shivers.

"I can't stay all night."

"I didn't ask for all night," he corrected. "We haven't tried the hot tub yet."

Sara laughed and glanced over her shoulder. "You're ready for another round?"

Parker smoothed her hair from her face and circled her waist with his hands. He lifted her until she was flush against him and he carried her toward the hot tub on the other side of the patio.

“I will be,” he assured her. “You’re not leaving all tense like that. Apparently I didn’t do a good job of relaxing you.”

Parker eased her hands apart, sending the pile of her clothes back to the floor. After removing the cover, he lifted her over the edge of the hot tub like she weighed nothing at all…which was pretty damn hot. The warmth of the water sent shivers through her. She always loved a nice hot bath, and this was just another level of pleasure.

Sara moved toward one of the built-in seats and eased down. Parker tapped a couple of buttons and jets hit her back. When he climbed in with her, her body started completely over with arousal and desire. How was that even possible? Moments ago she was ready to leave and take her memories with her… Looks like she had more memories to make here.

Parker’s hands rested on either side of her shoulders as he leaned down to meet her gaze.

“I plan on taking more time with you,” he told her. “Unless you really wanted to leave.”

He took one hand, disappearing beneath the water. Suddenly his fingertips eased between her legs. Sara gasped and eased further down into the water.

“I think I can stay a bit longer.”

A naughty smile crept over his lips. “I thought you might.”

Four

"It's a miracle you're still alive."

Delilah was always the dramatic sister, always the careful one who worried. And with Elise out of town with Antonio on their honeymoon, Dee clearly thought she needed to take up the slack of the absent sister.

"It's not a miracle." Sara came to stand behind her desk and smoothed down her cropped blazer. "I had a one-night stand. They happen."

"Not to you," Delilah fired back. "You're the happily-ever-after girl, not the happy-for-now girl."

"Well, maybe I am while I'm waiting for 'the one' to drop into my life." A pang of envy pierced her…and not for the first time. "I texted you my whereabouts and when I was safely back home. So stop acting like my mother."

Delilah jerked back and immediately Sara regretted her words. She blew out a sigh. The three girls had all been in the foster care system as infants, then all adopted by Milly Hawthorne as she tracked down each one. The single woman raised them as her own—it wasn't until her death nearly a year ago that they found out she had actually been their biological aunt and Milly's sister had been their mother. All this time the girls thought they were all adopted sisters and really good friends, but they actually shared a mother.

Their fathers, though, that was another story because they all had different dads. The girls had so many questions, but their mother had passed while in prison serving time for drug possession and now with Milly gone, they were left to their own devices to find their own answers.

"I'm sorry." Sara shifted her hair over her shoulder, her nerves getting the best of her. "I didn't mean that. I know you care, but I assure you that I'm not naive and I'm not careless. I'm a single woman who is just having fun."

Delilah stared for another minute before she offered a wide grin.

"Since you're safe and you didn't get abducted, how much fun did you have exactly? I almost came to your house yesterday, but Cam stopped me. He said you were a grown woman having a bit of fun."

Fun, indeed. The images of Parker and her on the patio sofa and in the hot tub flooded her mind…as if she'd been able to think of anything else since she'd left Saturday night. She'd never gotten his real name, never knew his story or where he was from. But, oh mercy, did she have the memories that would last a lifetime. Her body still tingled.

"I'll take your sly grin and silence as a good indicator of how your night went."

Sara smiled at her sister and shrugged. "I'm less nervous for my interview now that I have something else occupying my thoughts."

"I still cannot believe Ian Ford is doing a piece on Angel's Share." Delilah shook her head and rested her hands on the back of the leather chair across from Sara's desk. "You better hope like hell he doesn't tarnish our reputation."

"He won't."

She hoped.

"Ian is notorious for making or breaking people and businesses," Delilah went on. "We've got too much at stake for him to put a black cloud over our name here."

"There will be no black cloud," Sara stated. "I promise, he will not be able to construe my words in any manner other than bright and shiny."

"Speaking of, what are you wearing to the Christmas at the Castle?"

Their very first holiday gala was right around the corner and as of this moment, Sara had about three dresses she wanted to wear. Of course other days, she hated all the dresses and wanted to start completely over and have someone else tell her what to wear.

"I have no idea. I can't decide if I want to do festive and bright or classy and dark or wintery white. I went ahead and made us all an appointment at Queen so we can shop together once Elise is back."

"Excuse me."

Sara's office door opened and her assistant, Molly, poked her head in. "Mr. Ford is here to see you."

Sara glanced to the time on her computer and realized she and Delilah had been talking for a while and Mr. Ford was a punctual man—though she expected nothing less. No time for nerves or second guesses now.

"Send him on in," Sara replied with a smile.

"I'm not ready for my part of the interview," Delilah

whispered, her eyes wide with worry. "I'm not scheduled to talk to him until the end of the week."

Sara shrugged. "Looks like you're going to meet him now."

She came around her desk and smoothed her hair behind her shoulders, making sure her smile remained firmly in place. Despite the nerves in her belly, she needed to put on a strong front and she was actually glad time had gotten away from them, because she wanted Delilah by her side and there was no time for her sister to scurry out now.

Ian Ford was well-known in the journalism industry. But unless you met the man face-to-face, nobody really knew what he looked like. Any social media account he had was all about his work and zero photographs. Supposedly, he never did public appearances. Ian must have to jump through hoops to keep his image protected…but why? He exuded mystery, which was just all part of his allure…or so his publisher likely thought. It mostly just annoyed the hell out of Sara because she'd tried everything to find him online and absolutely nothing came up.

Looked like she was about to see the man behind the facade.

Her office door opened once again and Sara nearly fell back against her desk. Ian Ford was no stranger. She'd seen him before…she'd seen every inch of him, in fact.

When his eyes met hers, there was no emotion. Absolutely nothing from those secretive dark eyes of his.

As if "Parker" hadn't seen every inch of her as well.

Hell. Oh, hell no.

So "Jane" was actually Sara Hawthorne, co-owner of Angel's Share, and the sole reason for his trip up north.

Fan-freakin'-tastic.

As if he didn't have the weight of the proverbial world

on his shoulders already, the one time he gives in to temptation and has a one-night stand, he discovers it is with his subject.

Nothing like looking like a total ass of a professional with one foot out the door of his publisher. He said he'd do Nigel one last favor with this piece…but sleeping with the subject sure as hell was not what either of them had in mind. This is precisely why he always chose his own subject matter and he never traveled for business.

"I'm Delilah." The striking woman off to the side stepped forward with her hand extended. "We're so thrilled to have you here. Our sister, Elise, is out of the country right now. Sara is the best one out of all of us, though. You're definitely in good hands."

Ian forced his gaze away from the clearly shocked Sara and shook Delilah's hand. The sisters looked nothing alike. There was definitely a story there, and he planned on finding out every secret and bit of backstory with each of these women…more so with Sara, but those findings wouldn't be going in his article.

"It's a pleasure," he told her, shaking her hand, then stepping back to turn his attention to Sara. "Are we doing a joint interview or sticking with the itinerary?"

Delilah waved her hand in the air. "I'm stepping out. We were talking business and got carried away with time. I am looking forward to our talk later in the week."

Ian nodded. "As am I."

Delilah glanced to her sister. "Sara, I'll get with you later."

Then she walked out of the office, leaving with a soft click of the door.

"Did you know who I was?" Sara growled the second they were alone.

Her dark eyes narrowed into slits, showing him a totally different side than the Sara—or Jane—that he knew.

"Of course not. You told me your name was Jane."

"Jane is my middle name."

Ian laughed. "Parker is my middle name."

Sara started to smile, but quickly recovered, narrowing her eyes again. "You want me to believe you didn't go online to see the sisters who own Angel's Share?"

"Of course I did, but the picture on the site is the three of you in front of the castle and the span is large. And your individual bios all have the Angel's Share logo instead of a photo. So, no. I had no idea you were the person I was interviewing when we met the other night."

She continued to glare and shoot invisible daggers like *he* had done something wrong here. She sure as hell didn't think he was doing anything wrong the other night…she'd even begged for more.

Filled with a new level of frustration and annoyance, Ian shrugged. "Believe what you want. This assignment came to me when I thought I was done with *Elite*, but I'm doing this as a favor to my editor. Then I'm done. I'll do a kick-ass job, but I don't need to scroll through your social media trying to uncover who each of the sisters are. I believe in getting that knowledge firsthand."

"You got that on Saturday night."

"Sara, I didn't know who you were," Ian said, trying to keep his frustration in check.

"Well, I tried to find pictures of you," she retorted, crossing her arms over her chest.

Ian willed himself to keep his gaze locked onto hers and not check out how perfectly deliciously that bright blue suit hugged her curves. He could still feel those curves beneath his hands, could still feel her delicate touch and hear her soft moans from the passion they shared.

Damn it. He needed to get a grip. Maybe he could find a way to wrap up this interview a little early so he wasn't subjected to temptation any longer than necessary.

"Why are there no photos anywhere?"

Her question pulled him back to the moment and the fact that she might be sexy, but she was still seething.

"I've never seen someone who literally cannot be found anywhere online," she added in disbelief.

Yeah, and he paid an exorbitant amount to keep his anonymity. There was no way in hell he was going to get into all the reasons why. He'd never let anyone in on his personal life and all of his issues, so there was certainly no chance of him exposing his vulnerabilities with his one-night stand.

"Are we doing the interview in here?" he asked, forcing her hand into professionalism. "Or are you showing me around the distillery?"

Sara stared him down for another moment before dropping her arms and blowing out a sigh. That anger clearly transitioning to frustration.

"Listen, we need to discuss the other night before we just dive headfirst into work."

Ian rested his hands on his hips and really wished he'd done that research on each of the women of Angel's Share. Since this was to be his last piece for *Elite*, he didn't necessarily believe he needed to hone in on each remarkable woman.

He hadn't recognized Sara at the Quiet Distil because she was out of her element and he'd never seen a close-up picture of her, so there was nothing he could do at this point. He couldn't turn back time or have a redo of Saturday night.

He also couldn't have regrets about that night…he *wouldn't*. Everything about their heated affair had been magical and perfect. And each and every moment would have stayed locked in his memory bank had he not walked into "Jane's" office this morning.

"Nothing to discuss," he corrected. "We hadn't planned on seeing each other again, so now we just pretend it didn't happen and focus on work, which is the only reason I'm here."

Oh, those dark eyes seemed to grow even blacker. Maybe she could get sexier, because even anger looked damn good on her.

"Forget it happened?" she fired back. "Do you just have some magical switch you turn off and on?"

He wished. If he was actually as stony as people thought, maybe he wouldn't feel so damn much. He'd done a hell of a job compartmentalizing his emotions over the years and he didn't intend to stop now—that's the only way he made it day by day. Despite the passionate evening they'd shared two days ago, that didn't mean they should or would have a replay.

"I'm leaving that night right where it belongs," he informed her. "In the past, where we *both* agreed it would stay."

She pursed her lips and his body betrayed him. Despite his words, he'd thought of little else since she left his place and seeing those red lips puckered only reminded him of just how damn much he'd enjoyed that mouth.

Getting aroused during the job had never been an issue before…then again, he'd never taken a stranger back to his place for a one-night stand, either. Relationships of any kind had never appealed to him. He refused to put his heart on the line for anything or anyone ever again…no matter how temporary. Work was all that he could control, all that really mattered at the end of the day.

"You're completely different from the man I met at the Quiet Distil."

"Same man," he assured her. "Today is just a different aspect of my life."

When she continued to stare as if trying to figure him out, Ian pulled in a deep breath. There was no way he'd let anyone try to get inside his world, so she might as well not even try. Yes, they had an amazing night that shouldn't still be in his every waking thought, but that was his problem. He was only here as a courtesy and commitment to his editor, nothing more.

"Just like that, huh?" she murmured.

Ian shrugged. "There's no other way to move on, and we both agreed at the time that night was a one-time thing. So, are we doing the interview in here or would you like to show me around first?"

He waited on more backlash, but Sara squared her shoulders and tipped that defiant chin. Damn, she shouldn't be sexier when she was angry, but she was. Again, his problem and something he would deal with on his own. Once he could shift her into that subject zone and see her only as his job, he'd be just fine. Right?

"I need some fresh air." She circled her desk and crossed her office, then grabbed her coat off a peg near the door. "We'll walk the grounds and I'll give you the history of Angel's Share."

He had a feeling the brisk air was the least of his worries, because the iciness from Sara Hawthorne already had him feeling frigid.

Five

"And that brings us back to the main entrance of the castle."

Sara had given every detail and fact she'd ever learned or discovered about Angel's Share from the time it was built all the way up until now. She was nearly frozen, but she deserved to be punished after her poor professional skills in thinking Ian might carry over any feelings he had from the other night.

She wasn't naive, but this entire situation made her feel like a teenager getting dumped for the first time. Totally blindsided from a situation she'd invested too many thoughts into.

Maybe if she hadn't been caught so off guard, she wouldn't have nearly passed out when he stepped into her office. Thankfully Delilah hadn't noticed anything off, or if she did, she was saving that conversation for later.

As they crossed the stone path and the iconic drawbridge leading to the front entrance, Ian reached out and opened the door for her. He gestured her in ahead of him and she gladly stepped inside to get out of the winter elements. At least he still had manners, even if he was still pretending that they hadn't thoroughly enjoyed pleasuring each other only two short days ago.

The warmth from the castle enveloped her as soon as she stepped over that threshold. The old stone fireplace off to the right wasn't just for aesthetics and an amazing backdrop for photo shoots. The heat instantly made guests feel cozy during the cold months in Kentucky. Plus with the beauty of the fresh greenery draped over anything that was stationary, the wintery ambiance had an even cozier vibe.

Several workers moved about from one direction to another, a few stopped to chat, while others seemed to be on a mission. Sara was so proud of all they'd accomplished, not just for her and her sisters, but the fact that they employed over one hundred local folks. This truly was like one big happy family.

"Is there usually this much activity during the day?" Ian asked as he came to stand next to her.

"Not typically, but with the Christmas at the Castle gala in just two weeks, we're a little busier than usual. More decor, definitely more trees and garlands and lights. Mistletoe, too. Can't have a Christmas party without it."

"Is this gala something you do every year?"

"This will be our first, but one we hope to make an annual tradition."

Ian glanced back down to his notepad and jotted more notes. He'd barely looked at her since leaving her office earlier. He certainly hadn't touched her or made any personal references. No personal questions, either.

This whole charade was really getting old. It was impossible for her to just fake all of this nonsense. Yes, they were both professionals in their fields and, yes, Ian Ford was a celebrity journalist, but at the end of the day, they were both real people. Well, she was. She was starting to wonder if he was hard-hearted or simply robotic. This was definitely not the man she'd been with the other night. This Ian Ford was exactly like she'd imagined: cold, stoic, all business…boring.

The man from Saturday night was the complete opposite. Sexy, intriguing, attentive, passionate. There had been nothing icy about "Parker."

Then again, they'd both been someone else that night. She'd faked being bold and assertive and now she was her true self. Perhaps he'd done the same. Maybe this stony man before her was the real Ian. Shame that, because she wouldn't mind meeting "Parker" again. Parker made her want to be that bold woman, that woman who wasn't afraid to go after what she wanted.

"You're staring."

His statement forced her attention back to him and she blinked to return to the moment. He hadn't even looked up from his notes and he'd known she was staring. Lovely. Could she be any less professional?

"I'm not staring," she corrected, though she totally had been. "I'm waiting on you to finish up before we move on."

His lips thinned as he continued writing and Sara blinked as she glanced away. The last thing she needed to be looking at was his lips. She needed to focus on this interview because despite what had already transpired between them, Ian was going to write a piece on Angel's Share and with the launch of their ten-year bourbon just months ago and their rise to fame and success, she couldn't afford to have a black cloud hovering over them.

Elise, Delilah, and Sara all invested so much into this business—Milly, too. Their adoptive mother had cheered them every step of the way and, unfortunately, had passed just short of the ten-year bourbon rollout. But Sara knew she was smiling down on them and proud of what her girls had accomplished.

Sara just wished Milly would have disclosed the truth while she'd been alive. Why not just come out and say that she's their biological aunt? That her sister was their mother and the woman had a drug problem? Not telling them might have protected them for so long, but ultimately the pain still entered in once they discovered the truth.

"You still with me?"

Sara shifted her focus back to Ian, who stared at her with his brows drawn together. Great, now she'd zoned out on him. He probably thought she wanted to be anywhere but in this moment...which was partly true.

With a deep breath, Sara pulled herself together and eased out of her coat.

"Are you ready to head back to my office and start the interview? Or would you like to break for lunch?"

"Where is a good place around here to grab something?" he asked.

She folded her coat over her arm and started walking toward her office on the second floor. He fell in step beside her and part of her wanted to tell him a few places to go, to give herself a break from his presence, but that damn voice in her head kept nagging at her. Anybody else, whom she hadn't slept with, she would offer for them to stay and she'd have something brought in. She should treat him no differently.

"I actually have a favorite and one call will have anything you want delivered." They reached the landing and started to turn, but she stopped and looked up at him. "I figure being from the south, you don't want to go out in the cold any more than you have to, and I just had you in and out for the past two hours."

The muscle in his jaw clenched. "I'm actually from Ohio, but I've lived in Florida for years. I don't like the cold."

Why was he so intense? Something in her innocent question pushed a trigger within him and she shouldn't want to know more…but she did. She had a feeling trying to figure this man out would be about as easy as cuddling up with a porcupine.

"Let's get to my office and we'll order in," she suggested. "We can have a working lunch…unless you want to ask personal questions."

"I don't."

Of course not. Well, she couldn't compartmentalize as easily as he could, so he'd just have to live with it. She wasn't going to walk on eggshells or be someone else just because he was uncomfortable.

They reached her office door and she punched in the code, then gestured him in ahead of her. Once inside, she closed the door and turned to face him.

There it was. That crackling tension she'd felt at the Quiet Distil. He had that damn stare that made her wonder if he could see into her soul. He hadn't moved far into the room, actually stood only a few feet away from her. He'd said he didn't want to discuss that night, but his eyes said he wouldn't mind an encore performance.

Sara pulled in a deep breath and turned to hang her coat on the peg by her door.

"Let me have your coat," she told him, looping her tag over the hanger.

When she shifted back around, Ian had removed his coat, and her breath caught in her throat. He had on another one of those vests with his dress shirt and dress pants—

dove gray this time. Why did he have to look like he just walked off a movie set from the 1930s? And why did the man's wardrobe turn her on so much?

Ian handed over the garment and Sara reached out, her hand immediately grabbing his instead of the coat. Her eyes darted up to his and she wasn't surprised to find him staring right back.

Without a word, she snagged the coat and hung it next to hers. Sara needed to gather her words before she addressed all of this tension because she couldn't handle the rest of the week the way this morning had gone. Being close, talking business, pretending like they hadn't shared flirty banter and a heated night.

"You told me you did weddings."

Sara jerked back at his statement before she'd ever even had a chance to say anything.

"That's not what I said at all," she countered. "I said I helped with weddings, which I had just done for my sister and we are currently working on one for the governor's daughter in the spring. And don't get so high and mighty when you didn't give me your real name. If we'd done that off the bat, none of this would have happened."

Something even darker came over his eyes as he closed the distance between them. Sara's breath caught in her throat and she had to force herself not to move, not to reach out to see if that icy exterior melted beneath her touch. She waited.

"None of this would have happened," he murmured, his eyes dropping to her mouth. "Do you have regrets?"

"No."

How could she have any shame or guilt over one of the most thrilling nights of her life? All she regretted was how this reunion was playing out.

"We need to discuss what happened so we can move on," she insisted.

Ian's lips thinned. "What do you want to talk about so badly? Does that night replay over and over in your head? Are you wondering how we can work together on this article and not rip at each other's clothes? Are you wondering if I'll make a move?"

Well…yes, actually. Yes to all of those questions, but the way he worded them made her sound desperate and she might be achy and needy, but she definitely wasn't desperate.

And she wasn't the only one having a difficult time. She might not know him well, but she wasn't blind. The way he'd stared at her, the way he'd been so attentive the other night, there was no way he could turn off those feelings. She refused to believe it.

Maybe when he'd first arrived this morning she'd thought him stony, but he'd stepped into her office moments ago and looked at her as if ripping her clothes off was precisely what he'd been wanting to do.

"Is that what *you* want?" she asked. "To make a move?"

The muscle in his jaw clenched, drawing her attention to that puckered scar. His beard covered a good bit of the old injury, but the jagged edge peeked out above the dark hair. She'd also felt the uneven skin beneath her touch the other night.

Unable to resist, Sara reached up and trailed her fingertip along his jaw.

"You're a mysterious man," she whispered. "With a past I can't help but wonder about."

That flash of desire quickly vanished as Ian took a step back, then another, then ultimately turned to head across her office. Was he trying to purposely keep this wall of division between them? Because he seemed like he was having a hell of a time battling his self-control.

"Keep wondering," he commanded with his back to her as he stared out the arched window.

Sara clenched her hand at her side, trying to hold tight to that warmth from his body. She shouldn't want more. She should ignore her urges and move on. Ian clearly waged a war between his own wants and he seemed to have no problem pushing her aside.

That shouldn't cause a piercing pain, but…

Sara smoothed her hair away from her face and took a deep breath before heading toward her desk. She was supposed to be ordering them a lunch, not rehashing Saturday night or even hoping for something more. Ian wasn't a "something more" type of guy, he'd made that much very clear.

Obviously two people could be physically compatible, but that's where it ended. She wasn't naive, she knew what the other night was and wasn't. She'd just been caught so off guard and there was so much more she wanted to know about Ian. She had so many questions, but from the look of his rigid shoulders and the silence that had settled heavy between them, Sara would have to keep wondering…just like he'd suggested.

Six

"Well, how did it go?"

Sara glanced up from her phone to her sister standing in the doorway.

Settling back into her desk chair, Sara shrugged. "It went."

"That doesn't sound promising." Delilah stepped into Sara's office and closed the door at her back. "Was he a jerk? Did he ask difficult questions? Do you think he's planning to ruin us with the article?"

"No, no and no."

Delilah came to a stop as her brows drew in. "Then what was the problem?"

Sara didn't know if she should reveal the full truth now, or tell her later when Elise came back, or if she should just keep everything a secret. But there had already been so many secrets in their lives that Sara didn't want to add to them.

If Sara had learned anything over the past year, it was that family was more important than ever. She desperately needed someone's advice before she had a total meltdown. There were too many raw, fresh emotions swirling around inside her and she trusted two people with her life…and one was on her honeymoon. That left Delilah.

"I slept with Ian."

Dee's face completely morphed into shock, confusion and anger all at once. Her eyes widened, those sculpted brows shot up and her mouth dropped. She remained still, too still, as she continued to stare.

"What the hell, Sara? You just met the man this morning."

Sara chewed the inside of her cheek for a moment. "We met before."

Delilah blinked, then gasped. "No. Please tell me he's not the man from the other night."

"Okay. I won't tell you that."

Dee closed her eyes and blew out a frustrated sigh. Maybe Sara shouldn't have said anything, but she was hoping once the initial shock wore off, her sister could offer some sound advice.

Granted, Sara was still in shock herself, so she shouldn't be expecting a miracle here.

"You've got to be kidding me," Dee muttered as she crossed the office and sank into the leather club chair across from Sara's desk. "Of all the people in the world you choose for a one-night stand, you chose Ian freakin' Ford?"

"It's not like I knew who he was," Sara defended. "You know the man is so elusive. It never crossed my mind he was the stranger I flirted with at the bourbon bar."

Delilah pinched the bridge of her nose and the lighting caught the emerald-cut diamond on her ring finger. As if

Sara needed that visual reminder of just how Delilah's life was on the path Sara wanted to be on.

"Okay, we need to fix this," Dee stated, dropping her hands into her lap.

"And how do we do that?" Sara asked. "I can't un-sex him."

"Now is not the time for jokes," Delilah scolded.

"That wasn't a joke. I literally have no idea what to do."

"Well, did you guys at least address the issue?"

A vivid image of him hovering over her, looking like he wanted to kiss her, flashed through her mind. But she'd ruined anything Ian had been about to say or do when she reached up and touched his scar. What was the story there? Was the scar the sole reason for the beard? Another way for him to hide? Or was that what started his need for anonymity?

So many questions that she couldn't have answered, but that didn't stop her from wondering. She couldn't get Ian out of her mind for a variety of reasons…mainly her Saturday night experience that still had her tingling.

"Sara. Snap out of it."

Sara blinked and leaned forward, resting her elbows on top of her desk.

"No, we didn't discuss it because he didn't want to." The man had closed up for the rest of the day and they only discussed business. "I brought up that night a couple of times and he only wanted to move forward."

"That's typically how a one-night stand works."

Sara rolled her eyes. "I'm aware. I mean, I'd never had one before, but I assumed. Still, these are unique circumstances and I thought we should clear the air or something. Anything would be better than just ignoring it."

Delilah didn't reply. Silence hovered between them and Sara waited on her sister to give some solid, sound advice that would make all of this awkward tension between Ian and Sara go away. They had several days left together to go through the entire bourbon process, not to mention the other spirits Angel's Share sold. They were going over every aspect of the company from conception up until now. Ian wanted all the answers, and that could only boil down to hours of alone time.

Which was the last thing she needed with a man who made her toes curl when he simply sent a stare her way.

Why this guy? Why did she have to get so wrapped up with the one person who should be off-limits? Had she met him in a professional setting first, Sara would have just thought he was some arrogant jerk. Sexy and intriguing in that dark, stealthy way, but a jerk nonetheless.

"So now what?" Dee asked after a moment.

"That's sort of what I was hoping you'd tell me," Sara replied. "I mean, clearly we have a kick-ass company and we're growing each day. I'm not at all worried about the professional side of this situation."

"Maybe you should just take his lead and move on," Dee suggested.

Sara mulled that thought over in her mind and finally nodded. "You're right. Trying to get him to talk or rehash it all would only make me look desperate."

"Please don't tell me you want to sleep with him again? That was a one and done, right?"

Sara laughed. "Of course. Now that I know who he is, I definitely can't sleep with him again."

"If he wasn't Ian Ford, you'd be right after him."

Sara shrugged. "If circumstances were different, you bet I would. Parker was a totally different man than Ian."

Delilah's brows lifted. "Parker?"

"The name he gave me at the Quiet Distil. I was Jane and he was Parker. We both used our middle names."

Delilah closed her eyes and shook her head. “One-night stand and role-playing. Lovely.”

Sara couldn’t help but laugh. “We weren’t role-playing. We just didn’t want to go into personal details since we hadn’t planned on seeing each other again. Granted, we didn’t plan on sleeping together, either. We were just flirting and talking, then the bar closed, and then there was a hot tub.”

Delilah held up her hands. “No details necessary. I get it.”

Sara’s cell vibrated on her desk and she glanced to see Ian’s name pop up. Her eyes darted to Delilah, who had also redirected her attention toward the cell.

“Well, well, well,” Delilah crooned. “Perhaps he wants to chat after all.”

Sara didn’t want to snatch up the phone like some teen who needed the attention from a popular boy. She’d never chased after a man in her life and she sure as hell didn’t intend to start now. Oh, she might have been a little assertive with Ian the other night, but that was merely going after what she wanted.

Determined, that’s what Milly always called her. A pang of nostalgia hit her at the thought of the only mother she’d ever known. This would be one of those circumstances where she could use some motherly advice.

“Aren’t you going to see what he wants?”

Sara glanced from her sister to the phone. She eased into her seat and turned slightly back and forth, weighing her decision and how she wanted to proceed with this web she had spun around herself.

“I will. He’s not going anywhere.”

Delilah sighed and pushed to her feet, instantly reaching for the cell. “Well, I want to know what he says.”

Dee snatched the device before Sara could and all Sara

could do at this point was hold her breath. She watched Delilah's face for any sign of what Ian had sent, but all Dee did was chew on her bottom lip.

"Well? What is it?"

"You acted like you didn't care," Delilah reminded her. "Now you want to know?"

Sara stood and rounded her desk, grabbing the cell from her sister. She read the message herself.

I will be in at 1:00 tomorrow

That's it? That's all he wanted to tell her? Wait a second! They'd set their start time for 9:00 a.m. He was now pushing it back several hours.

Okay, fine. Whatever. So he was a professional and not texting her for a booty call. Shouldn't she be glad he didn't think of her that way?

Probably. But she wouldn't mind if he did. Just one more time.

"Sorry, sis." Delilah rested her hand on Sara's arm. "That man has a workaholic reputation for a reason. He's all business, all the time."

"Not all the time," Sara muttered.

Clearly he was in the zone and nothing would pull Ian Ford from this work bubble he'd encased himself in…not even the opportunity for another passionate night.

His loss.

Seven

The online meeting with Nigel had run over and Ian was even later than he had planned getting back to Angel's Share. He figured Sara was still upset with him over… well, everything, so what was one more thing?

This entire interview and article had been a mistake from the second he'd said yes, but Nigel was impossible to say no to. The man had given Ian his crack into journalism when Ian first moved to Miami. Nigel was so much more than a boss or a mentor; he was probably Ian's closest friend. His only friend, really.

Ian had no plans on leaving Miami once he was finished at *Elite* and he had no plans on ending his relationship with Nigel. Ian had become restless with his work lately, always trying to find something more, but nothing was filling that void. Nigel understood and was actually the one to recommend Ian write a book.

Being able to write while working remotely and alone

was the only way he wanted to live. He'd gotten comfortable with his lifestyle and just because he needed a fresh restart in his career didn't mean he was ready to change his habits.

Yet he'd gone completely against everything he stood for when he'd picked up Sara in that damn bourbon bar. And maybe the circumstances wouldn't be so bad if she wasn't his subject and if he still didn't want the hell out of her. Seeing her in her element yesterday had only added to her appeal. She'd been so professional and business-oriented. She loved her job and her passion for everything she'd built had come to light.

Having seen her passionate side in business and her pleasure in private had him wondering how often she revealed both sides to the same man.

Ian stepped inside the main entrance of Angel's Share and instantly found himself feeling at home. How ridiculous was that? He'd only been to this distillery once and already he thought he belonged?

Perhaps those unwanted, unexpected emotions stemmed from all the Christmas decor with the fresh evergreens and all the twinkling lights that reminded him of how his mother would decorate. Or maybe there was something about Sara herself that had touched on a warmth inside him he hadn't known existed.

No matter what, Ian knew for certain he wouldn't be staying here long, so he might as well just shove these emotions out of his head and his heart. He was here for a job, not to get all nostalgic. The memories he'd suppressed needed to stay buried because nothing would mess him up more than reliving that nightmare all over again.

"Mr. Ford?"

Ian turned to Delilah, who was crossing the lobby. She had a wide smile on her face, her dark hair smoothed over one shoulder, and a red pantsuit. There was something to be said for having three strong, powerful women running a successful business. They'd set themselves up for a unique success that was unmatched in the industry.

"It's so great to see you again." She greeted him with a firm handshake. "Sara is handling a minor hiccup at the moment, so I will be taking you to our VIP room for an exclusive tasting. You will get all the perks of one of our elite clients so you can see exactly how we conduct our business."

"That sounds interesting. I'm definitely up for a tasting. I actually tried one of your batches at the Quiet Distil the other evening."

Delilah started walking and Ian fell into step beside her as they made their way toward the staircase. As they started to climb to the second story, Ian wondered if Sara actually had an emergency or if she was avoiding him. He'd be lying if he didn't admit he was a little disappointed. He'd wanted his experience to be overseen by Sara. He wanted to see her as much as he could while he was here. Perhaps that made him a glutton, but he couldn't just ignore the fact that he found her way too damn intriguing.

Delilah led Ian down a corridor and up another flight of steps until they reached a room surrounded with stone walls. This part of the castle definitely had to be an original portion, but they'd modernized the area with glass shelving that housed their various bottles of bourbon and their specialty gin. They also displayed their tumbler sets with the Angel's Share logo etched into the glasses.

Everything about this distillery exuded class and money. Was it any wonder the nation, hell, the world, had fallen in love with these three women? He'd spent the morning on the phone with other distillers to get their take on Angel's

Share. No deep dark secrets revealed, just a good dose of healthy envy over Angel's Share's accomplishments.

Delilah gestured for him to take a seat in the leather chair opposite where she stood. The raw-edged table between them had a nice, neat row of testers lined up. Ian unbuttoned his coat and slid it off.

"I'll take that for you," Delilah offered. "My apologies. I should have grabbed that first thing."

"No problem at all."

Something clearly occupied her mind and he wondered if that same something was what kept Sara from coming in here now. He wondered if the problem was business or personal, but had to quickly remind himself that neither circumstance was his concern.

Delilah skirted the table and took his coat, then hung it on a small hook near the door where they came in. Ian waited until she was back before he took a seat in the club chair.

"We'll start from your left and move our way down to the right," she started. "This first one is our ten-year that we unveiled just a few months ago."

"I believe that is the one I had the other evening." Ian reached for the glass and swirled the contents. "The aroma is amazing."

He took one sip, letting the flavors come to life against his taste buds, then he took another.

"Yes," he confirmed. "I had this at the Quiet Distil."

"Where you met Sara."

Ian's eyes darted up to Delilah's and she merely held his gaze without a smile, without any emotion whatsoever.

Okay, that was certainly a plot twist he hadn't expected in his day. Obviously Sara had said something to her sister, but Ian didn't know what all she had told her, so he'd be best to keep things light here.

"We did meet there," he agreed. "We had no clue who the other person was, but we had some great conversations."

Delilah pursed her lips as she quirked a brow.

Oh, yeah. She knew the whole story. Damn it.

How could he keep up his image, his reputation, his *professionalism* if he was going around having sex with the subject before they even got started?

Ian sat the shot glass back down and weighed his next words carefully.

"I have to assume by that disapproving frown, you are fully aware of what happened."

"I'm aware." Delilah flattened her palms onto the table as she leaned in slightly. "I'm not getting into any of that, but what I do want to address is our business. I'm hoping you're professional enough to keep that personal interaction out of your article."

Ian scoffed. "You think I'd mention what happened?"

Delilah shook her head. "No, but I don't want that to hinder your view of Angel's Share or any of us."

Delilah had to be the peacemaker and she clearly seemed worried about what all he'd put into his project. Did she think that he would be harsh simply because Sara picked him up in a bar?

Okay, maybe he picked her up, but whatever.

"I'm professional enough," he assured her. "Just like I assume you didn't tamper with these drinks now that you know I slept with your sister."

Delilah stared for a moment before she laughed and pulled over a stool. "Now that it's settled we are both professionals, let's keep this sampling on track."

"That's it?" he asked. "You're not going to warn me about hurting your sister or say something about how amazing she is?"

Delilah crossed her legs and placed her hands on her lap. "We both know Sara is one of a kind in the very best of ways. She's giving, comforting, always seeing the bright side of things…everything that embodies the perfect human. I'm more jaded with life, but Sara can also be a little naive at times. She truly sees the good in everyone, but I won't warn you. She's a grown woman and while she may have stars in her eyes and be looking for that happily-ever-after, she would never forgive me if she thought I was even having this conversation with you."

"Then why are you?" he asked, reaching for the next glass.

Delilah shrugged. "Because I care about Sara and Angel's Share. Family is everything to us and even though she can certainly take care of herself, that doesn't mean I can't play the protective older sister at times."

Ian sipped on the bourbon and welcomed the warmth and smoky flavor.

"Sara's lucky to have you," he finally told her.

"We're lucky to have each other," Delilah corrected. "Do you have siblings?"

His personal life was sure as hell not the area he wanted to delve into.

"I'm an only child." He sat the glass back down. "Which bourbon was that?"

"That is the special recipe we came up with for one of the pubs in Spain." Delilah pointed to the next one. "This was also created for Rodriguez's. Those restaurants are owned by Elise's husband."

"The sister that just got married?"

Delilah nodded. "Yes. His family has a string of upscale pubs and restaurants in Spain. That's actually how he and my sister met. He came here to look into bourbons."

"And found more than he was looking for."

"I'm sorry I'm late."

Ian turned toward the door and was glad he was sitting down. Sara came striding in wearing a body-hugging green pencil dress and nude heels, which only made her shapely legs look even sexier. With her hair flowing around her shoulders and that red lipstick, Ian wondered if he should just stick with Delilah for the day to avoid further temptation.

"Are you doing a tasting or filling him in on the family secrets?" Sara asked as she came to stand beside her sister.

"A little of both."

Delilah and Sara shot each other a look that had to be some sibling, silent-speaking communication thing. He'd never had that and didn't understand a bond so deep. But he understood love and family, and these two had something special.

"I can finish if you have something else to do," Delilah offered.

Sara glanced to Ian and his gut tightened with that instant arousal…just like the other night when they'd first met.

"I've got this."

Sara continued to hold his gaze as she replied to her sister.

"Are you sure, Sara—"

"We're fine, and that issue I had will have to be discussed later."

Ian watched as the women exchanged another look and the journalist in him wanted to know the details and what had been so important. He'd originally thought Sara was trying to dodge him or any interaction, but after seeing the smoldering look she'd given him, he had to believe something had happened behind the scenes.

Delilah nodded and focused back on Ian. "I look forward to my interview so we can continue our discussion."

Ian couldn't help but stifle a laugh because that almost sounded like a threat…or a promise, he really couldn't tell. Regardless, he gave a nod because he never backed down from a challenge. He had a feeling each of these women would challenge him in a variety of ways.

The click of Delilah's heels echoed in the spacious room as she let herself out. The moment the door closed, Ian met Sara's intense stare.

"What held you up?"

He shouldn't have asked—he actually wasn't going to, but the question just slipped out. He wasn't sorry, though. He did want to know what was going on even if none of this was his concern. That's how he'd gotten such a stellar reputation. He asked the questions people didn't want to answer and somehow got them talking.

"I had a personal matter that needed my immediate attention."

She crossed her arms over her chest and glanced down to the shot glasses. "Looks like you have a few more to go."

"In a minute," he told her. "Something kept you from our appointment and you still seem a little flustered."

"Our appointment?" she questioned with the quirk of one arched dark brow. "Would that be the appointment you changed on me last night?"

"I had a last-minute meeting with my boss at noon that couldn't be moved."

"My appointment couldn't be moved either."

Sara squared her shoulders and didn't blink, as if silently daring him to keep on this topic. He wasn't a stupid man, but he was determined and tenacious. Maybe he wouldn't dig into her personal life right this second, but he would get there and she likely wouldn't even know he'd done so. He wasn't the top journalist in the field for nothing.

"I was just learning about the batches of Angel's Share that are going to Spain."

Sara blinked, clearly taken off guard at his change of the subject. Or perhaps she was surprised he gave in.

"Yes, my brother-in-law was thrilled to have several options to offer his customers. I heard Dee telling you about him."

"So he and Elise fell in love over tastings?" he asked, reaching for another glass.

Sara let out a soft laugh that shouldn't send warmth spreading through him…but that sweet sound was impossible to dismiss.

"I believe they fell in love when they were locked in our cellar during a thunderstorm and power outage."

Ian eased forward a little more and held on to the glass, but was much more interested in hearing this story. "I'm not sure one night together can constitute as love."

"For them it did," she countered, her stare never wavering.

Maybe he should have kept on the topic of her personal life instead of dancing around the topic of a one-night stand. Or love. That sure as hell was one area he didn't want to get into.

Ian sipped the next sample, needing time to figure out exactly how to approach Sara and the work he should be doing here. He'd never been in a position like this before and it was damn uncomfortable wanting a woman and knowing she was off-limits.

He should have made her off-limits from the start, but he'd been in a vulnerable spot that night and in she walked—wearing the same troubled look he'd seen in the mirror. He'd thought they could just keep each other company over a few drinks. He should have known that would be a mistake, considering that was so far out of his comfort zone.

Why Sara? Why couldn't he have met anyone else from Benton Springs and shared a passionate night? Then he wouldn't be so tied up in knots and struggling to keep his professional persona in place.

"Why don't you ever let anyone see the man behind the words?"

Sara's question hit him like a punch to the gut. Nobody was ever so bold with him and she continued to stare like she wasn't about to back down. Well, too damn bad.

"If your personal life is off-limits, so is mine."

Her brow quirked and Sara merely nodded in understanding. The silence settled between them, heavy and thick like the tension that had encompassed them from the moment he realized who she actually was.

Sara blew out a sigh and closed her eyes for the briefest of moments before leveling his gaze once again.

"Perhaps I should have Delilah finish the tastings," she suggested. "This is getting more difficult."

Ian listened to her words, but there was something she wasn't saying. Reading body language was second nature to him in his line of work. He'd always had to read between the lines and take hints from how people responded, or didn't respond, to him.

Sara had a look in her eyes he hadn't seen before. And while he hadn't known her long, he had a feeling the woman he met that first night was the true Sara. That woman had been bold, vibrant, persistent. And while this Sara was all of those things, today there was a look in her eyes he hadn't noticed. Something haunted her or kept that light from shining like before.

And he wasn't about to let her just gloss it over or pretend. She didn't have to be all business right now because clearly an underlying element had rattled her world.

"Let's get out of here," he stated.

Sara blinked and jerked back. "Excuse me?"

Yeah, he had no idea where he was going with this, either, he just knew these walls were closing in on him and she looked like she needed a break. He would be here for a while still, so taking a few hours away from work for both of them might be just what they needed to get back on track.

Ian came to his feet and gestured toward the door. "Let's go."

He didn't wait on her to reply as he headed to snatch his coat from the hanger and head out. Now he just had to figure out what the hell his plans were.

Eight

Sara had no idea how she ended up in the front seat of Ian's rental SUV, but here they were maneuvering through the snow-lined streets of Benton Springs. They'd barely said two words since leaving the distillery and when Delilah had given her a questioning look as they'd been walking out, Sara had merely shrugged.

"Is there a point to this trip?" she finally asked.

He shot her a brief look. "To maintain our sanity."

"Is that a problem for you? Because I'm perfectly fine."

Ian snorted, but said nothing. Maybe he noticed she wasn't fine, but she had to at least put up a good front. No matter what had transpired between them, they were still in a working relationship. And as much as she hated to admit it, she was at his mercy. She was the business owner who had the obligation to cater to her client. This man was an award-winning journalist and she wanted nothing but glowing words in regard to Angel's Share.

The snow started coming down a little harder and she noted Ian slowed; his grip on the wheel had gotten tighter if his white knuckles were any indicator.

"Do you need to pull over and let me drive?" she offered. "I'm used to this unpredictable weather. Warm one day, freak snowstorm the next."

He didn't take his eyes off the road or speak, he merely shook his head. Obviously he wanted to concentrate and needed silence. Whatever. A skiff of snow was no big deal to her, but for someone from Miami, it could be concerning.

When Ian pulled into the lot of her favorite coffee shop, Sara unfastened her seat belt.

"We had coffee right in my office," she informed him.

"We also needed to get out of that atmosphere," he retorted.

Ian opened his door and an immediate blast of cold air filled the interior. He muttered a curse and something about freezing his ass off before the door closed behind him. Like a gentleman, he rounded the hood and opened her door, then extended his hand to help her down.

"Careful," he warned. "There's a little patch of ice here."

Before she could even take a step, Ian wrapped his arm around her waist and lifted her from the ground. He carried her at his side and carefully set her down on the sidewalk.

Why did her heart have to flutter at this gesture? He was merely making sure she didn't embarrass herself by falling, he wasn't playing some chivalrous modern-day knight. He was much too brooding to play the good guy in any situation.

"You been here before?" he asked, nodding toward Rise and Grind.

"All the time. One of my friends from high school opened this place about ten years ago."

Ian shook his head. “I should’ve known you’d be friends with the owner. Is there a business around this town that you aren’t in close contact with the owner?”

Sara thought for a moment, then shook her head. “Not really. We’re actually a small town and very supportive of one another.”

Snow started to fall once again, dotting Ian’s dark hair. The striking contrast captivated her attention and she watched as each flake melted.

“You’re staring.”

Sara blinked and smiled. “I don’t think you mind, do you? I’m freezing. Let’s get inside.”

He reached for her hand and she knew without a doubt it was to assist her over the snow piles, but part of her loved that strength and warmth from his touch. She shouldn’t, *couldn’t*, find this man so enchanting. He was not the fairy-tale ending she was looking for. He was a one-night stand and a temporary fling. Nothing more.

And one of these times she’d believe those lies she kept telling herself.

Ian reached for the door and ushered her inside. The cozy atmosphere always boosted her mood. The fresh aroma of coffee, the fire in the old stone fireplace, the dark rich wood floors and the leather chairs could be seen as masculine, but Sara always found Rise and Grind to be a place of strength. Maybe that came from the caffeine, but the decor really spoke to her as something classy, timeless.

Much like the man beside her. She’d never seen him in anything other than a vest, matching dress pants and a white button-up shirt. That was so damn classy and sexy, she was having a difficult time remembering why they shouldn’t keep exploring what they’d started the other night.

“Are we staying or getting drinks to go?” she asked.

Ian glanced out the window as snow continued to swirl around. "I didn't realize the weather was going to get this bad."

Sara watched the flurries and shrugged. "You've been in the south too long. This is nothing. Let's grab a seat. They have the absolute best bacon cheddar scones."

As she headed to the counter, Sara noted they weren't all that busy. Hopefully her favorite spot in the back was available. The barista took her order and Sara turned to see Ian still staring out the window.

"Ian?"

He jerked his attention back to her and crossed the open space. After a moment, he ordered and pulled out his wallet.

"I'll get it," she told him.

His eyes darted down to her and he shook his head. "I invited you, I'll get it."

"This isn't a date."

Her response was greeted with a sneer. "We're well beyond dating, don't you think?"

That low tone and sexy glimmer in his eye had shivers racing throughout her body. She pulled her coat tighter around her waist and stepped aside as he paid. Once he was done, she turned and moved around the stone fireplace and found the leather sofa in the back unoccupied. There wasn't anyone in this area, actually, and Sara wondered if being alone with Ian was a good idea or not. But they were still in a public place and what else could happen? They'd already slept together.

Sara removed her coat and placed it over the arm of the sofa before she took a seat.

"Relax." She patted the cushion beside her. "The weather is fine and they will bring our order. So sit down before you give me anxiety."

Ian raked a hand over the back of his neck and Sara wondered what could be bother him that much. The weather? It was just a few snowflakes. Certainly nothing to get worked up about. December in Kentucky was unpredictable so those who lived here just learned to roll with whatever Mother Nature handed them.

"Ian. Relax," she repeated.

Finally, he glanced to her and nodded. He took a seat, but not too close as he remained on the edge of the cushion with his elbows resting on his knees.

"You were more relaxed back at the distillery," she told him. "Maybe leaving wasn't the best idea."

"I'm fine," he assured her. "Snow just makes me nervous."

"I can tell. If you're not comfortable driving when we leave, I can. I've never lived anywhere else, so I'm used to this."

"No," he insisted. "You're not driving. It's far too dangerous."

Dangerous? That's not at all what she would use to describe the conditions, but before she could say anything else, the barista brought their drinks and scones.

Sara met the eyes of the server. "Thank you, Megan."

"Sure thing, Sara. Let me know if you guys need anything else."

"Oh, there is a to-go order I'd like to place," Sara added. Might as well get some items to take with her to snack on later.

Once Megan took the order and Ian and Sara were alone again, Sara reached for her scone, which already had her mouth watering.

"Are you always so personable?"

Ian's question caught her off guard as she glanced to him. "Personable?" she asked.

"Calling people by their names," he explained. "You did that at the bourbon bar and here. I assume you're just as chipper and energetic with your clients and staff."

Sara couldn't help but laugh. "I try to make people around me feel comfortable and important."

Ian merely grunted.

"Clearly you work too much by yourself if that's a foreign concept," she added.

"Not so much foreign," he corrected, reaching for his black coffee. "You and I just have entirely different views of how to accomplish success."

Sara rolled his words around inside her head and finally nodded. "I suppose you're right. We're both good at what we do. You're just disgruntled and I'm positive."

She broke off a piece of her scone, but not before catching his narrowed side-eye.

"I'm not disgruntled," he corrected. "I'd call it realistic."

"Jaded."

"Experienced."

Sara chewed her bite and figured going in circles with Ian wouldn't get either of them anywhere. She enjoyed her scone while Ian sipped on his coffee. They might be total opposites when it came to their outlook and paths they traveled to success, but the underlying physical similarities couldn't be dismissed.

"My mother used to make scones."

Ian's words were so low she barely heard them. When she glanced his way, he was staring at the pastry and she had a feeling he'd just been caught thinking out loud. She wanted to know more, wanted to use this opening he'd presented her to jump straight through and learn all she could about such an intriguing man.

"Did she love to bake?" Sara asked softly, shifting in her seat to face him.

He blinked and took a sip of his coffee. Sara wondered if he'd shut this conversation down before it could truly get started. But to her surprise, he went on.

"She actually ran a bakery in my hometown. Helen's Bakery. She named it after my grandmother who taught her to bake."

"Sounds like a family trait. Did you pick up any skills?"

Ian shook his head. "I tried, but the only thing I found to excel at in the kitchen is eating. My poor mom tried to teach me, but I never got the hang of recipes."

"She must be proud of you for your accomplishments, though."

His lips thinned and the muscle in his jaw ticked. "She passed when I was a teen."

Sara's heart clenched at the sorrow lacing his voice. She knew that hurt, that indescribable pain that came from losing the one person in your life who held your whole world together.

"Losing such an important part of yourself is difficult," she told him. "And I obviously never knew your mother, but I bet she'd be proud of the man you are today."

Ian stared at her, his brows raised just a fraction, but enough to give Sara insight to the fact he'd never had that thought before.

"You've done so much in your career," she added. "Any mother would be honored to have you as her son."

"I guess she would be," he murmured after a moment. "But we're supposed to be discussing you and your business."

"No reason we can't throw a bit of your backstory in there as well." Sara reached for her hot mocha and held on to the warm cup. "Maybe I'd like to know more."

Ian shook his head. "No reason for you to learn more about me. You already know more than most people."

"Wow, you really are a recluse."

"You say that as if it's a bad thing."

Sara couldn't help but laugh. "It sounds lonely and depressing."

"I've been pretty damn happy most of my life."

Sara stared at his dark eyes and he might say the right words, but there was no masking that pain. She recognized heartache.

"You look miserable," she told him. "I can see why you're so great with words on paper, but in person, you can't lie."

"We're supposed to be talking about you," he countered.

"You also can't change the subject."

"I can."

Sara didn't want to argue. She believed him when he said she knew more than most people. There wasn't a doubt in her mind that he held all of his emotions and memories close to his chest. Perhaps that's why he hid behind his computer. Maybe he got into the journalism field so he could focus on other people's problems or lives instead of dealing with his own.

"You're over there trying to figure out my mind," Ian stated after a moment. "Don't waste your time."

"Maybe I like trying to figure other people out," she retorted. "Maybe you *need* someone to figure you out to help you move on from the hurt."

He sat his mug down before sliding his arm across the back of the sofa and leaning further into her. Those coal-like eyes held her still, her breath catching in her throat. Clearly she'd struck a nerve, but that's what happened when too many feelings were suppressed.

"I don't need anything or anyone," he growled. "One night of sex doesn't give you any power over me or the pass to gain access into my world."

Those words were harsh, but Sara had thick skin. She'd pushed and poked, wanting to know more, but she'd gone too far. Still, that didn't give him the right to be hateful.

"Our night together has nothing to do with why I was asking," she defended, still holding his gaze. "I know what it's like to hurt and to not know how to express myself. I know what it's like to lose someone who meant everything, and I sure as hell know that closing in on yourself is not the answer."

He stared for another moment before easing back.

"We've already established we tend to go through life on different paths."

"Maybe this date wasn't the best idea," she suggested.

"It's not a date," he corrected. "We both needed out of that space and to clear our minds."

Sara snorted. "Do you feel better?"

Ian's lips twitched as if he was holding back a smile. "The coffee was good."

"If you're not eating that scone, I will."

Now he did smile as he gestured to the pastry. "Go right ahead. I haven't had one in years."

Since his mother died—at least she assumed that's the rest of the sentence he didn't say out loud. Before Sara could respond or even snag the scone from the dainty plate, her cell chimed from her bag.

"Excuse me."

She turned and opened her purse to find her cell. She'd had a call this morning with the private investigator and there might be a tip on the location of her biological father. She'd been shaken up, knowing she was just one step closer to discovering his identity…*her* identity.

Did the PI already have an answer? Would Sara be able to make that life-altering decision of whether or not she wanted to meet the man? Did he even know she existed?

There were so many questions and she couldn't even grasp all the thoughts swirling around in her mind.

The cell chimed once again.

"Are you getting that?" Ian asked, pulling her from her thoughts.

Sara's hand shook as she reached for the phone and shot Ian a glance. Her eyes darted to the screen, only to see Delilah's name. A wave of disappointment rippled through her, but she had to be patient. She'd gone over thirty years not knowing who her father was. A few more days or even months wouldn't matter.

"Hey, Dee," she answered. "What's up?"

"Where are you?"

"Rise and Grind. Why? Need a mocha latte?"

"I'd love one, but the roads are getting kind of bad all of a sudden. I heard some customers talking and Cam just came by to give me a lift home. We're going to have to close early and I didn't know where you were."

Sara came to her feet and walked toward the front of the coffee shop. Sure enough, those flurries were coming faster and fatter than before. Cars were creeping by on the street. She recalled how nervous Ian had been when there had only been a little skiff of snow.

"I'm with Ian in his rental, but I can just have him take me home."

"Okay. Be careful. Cam and I will shut things down here."

"Thanks, and you be careful, too."

Sara had no idea the weather was supposed to take a turn, but clearly she'd been preoccupied arguing with Ian. She battled between wanting to wring his neck or rip off his clothes. There was no in between.

After she disconnected the call, she made her way back

to Ian, who had a worried look on his face. Those thick brows were drawn in and his eyes locked onto hers.

"Something wrong?" he asked as she approached.

"No, but we should head out." Sara picked up the scone plate and decided she needed a to-go box. "Let me grab my other order on the way out, too."

"Is there a rush?"

Sara shrugged as she grabbed her purse and shouldered it. "The weather took a turn, so we should probably head home before the roads become too bad."

Ian muttered a curse under his breath and helped her gather their dishes to take to the bin next to the counter. Sara grabbed a box from the barista, now filled with sandwiches and scones, and shrugged into her coat, wishing she would have thought to get her scarf and gloves. She'd been too surprised that Ian demanded a field trip, her thought process hadn't been working right.

"I'll drive," she told him as they reached the door. She reached her hand out toward him. "Keys."

Ian jerked his attention from the glass doors to her. "Hell no. My name is on that rental. I'll drive."

"Listen, you live at the beach and I've lived here my whole life. I swear, if something happens to your vehicle, I'll take care of it, but I'm used to this weather."

He looked like he wanted to argue, but she raised her brows and held his gaze, silently daring him to keep arguing. Why was it that was all they could do besides sex? The man could be infuriating, but she was not backing down.

"Where are we going?" he asked. "My house is on the other side of town and the distillery is too far with those curvy roads."

Yeah, she'd already thought of all that…which only left one option.

"We're going to my house."

Nine

What the hell was actually happening here?

Ian barely resisted the urge to grip the door or the console as Sara maneuvered through the streets heading toward her home. She claimed her house was the closest of their options, but they'd been driving ten minutes and he was more than ready to get out before he embarrassed himself by having a panic attack.

The SUV slid as Sara took a curve and Ian's breath caught in his throat.

"We're good," she assured him in that soothing tone of hers. "There's a sheet of ice beneath that fresh snow from when we had rain and then the temps dropped. The snow is actually helping to give us some traction."

He didn't say anything—he *couldn't* say anything. Flashes of another freak snowstorm with another woman driving threatened to consume him. Hell, those images *were* consuming him. He needed to get out of this vehicle now.

"Almost there," she murmured.

Ian didn't know how she remained so damn calm when they were fishtailing down the road. One jerk of the wheel or one car sliding toward them could alter everything and put them both at risk.

"Are you going to hyperventilate?"

Ian shook his head, still unable to find words. He wanted to close his eyes, but part of him felt the need to know what was happening around him. Not that he had any control here…nor had he the night his mother was killed.

That's what terrified him most of all. The lack of control and no way to undo the damage of his past. He just had to live with it every day, like a lead weight he'd been carrying around for years that he couldn't shake off.

"We're here."

Sara eased into a tree-lined drive. The path had no tracks and seemed long, so long that he couldn't see the house yet.

"You're safe," she told him. "Even if we slide off the driveway, we're just in my yard."

Ian released a breath he hadn't realized he'd been holding. He kept his eyes fixed out the windshield and finally spotted a two-story dark blue home with a stone porch. The charming style sent a wave of calm through him. He didn't know why the sight of her house settled him, but it did. They were done traveling for now and he'd worry about how to get to his own place later.

After Sara pulled into the garage, she killed the engine and shifted to face him.

"I knew you didn't like the weather earlier, but I had no idea this was a true phobia."

"It's not a phobia."

She tipped her head and leveled his stare. "I realize you don't like to admit you might actually have human emotions, but there's nothing wrong with being afraid of something."

"I'm fine."

Could this get any more humiliating?

Sara let out the most unladylike growl and jerked the door handle. She snagged the to-go box from the center console and hopped out of the vehicle and promptly marched right inside her home. With the door into her house standing wide open, he assumed she was going to let him inside, even though she was clearly frustrated.

He wasn't about to admit his nagging worries to a virtual stranger. He still wanted to preserve his pride and those deepest fears.

Ian made his way into the house and closed the door behind him. The utility room was neat and tidy with labels for everything from dirty laundry to the detergent. He wasn't at all surprised that Sara liked things nice and orderly.

He made his way on into the kitchen where she stood at the large island. Her palms were flat on the granite with the to-go box between her hands. She stared out the back window as fat flakes continued to swirl. Being alone with her in her house might not have been his first choice, but he sure as hell knew his anxiety wouldn't have allowed him to make it all the way to the other side of town to his house.

"I'm afraid of being alone."

Sara's soft words slid between them as she kept her eyes fixed away from him.

"You live alone, though, right?" he asked.

Now she blinked and redirected her focus. "I do, but my fear is of always being alone. I bought this house with every intention of filling it with a family. My family. Each year that goes by, I wonder if I was too optimistic."

Ian never thought of being alone or that he'd likely be that way forever. The idea of giving a piece of himself to anyone and opening up the possibilities of pain and loss again wasn't worth the risk.

But someone like Sara would want that familial lifestyle. He could see her expertly juggling a high-profile career with a husband and children.

An unexpected pang of jealousy hit him at the idea of some faceless man in her life. Ian already hated the bastard. How did one night of passion make him have such irrational thoughts? Hadn't he told her that their night didn't give a pass into his life? The same should be true for hers because there was no way in hell he would fill that role for Sara. No, he was leaving town as soon as the article was done and he could go back to the warmth of Miami where he could start the next chapter in his career.

At least, that was the plan. But it sounded so…cold.

"You're still young." Ian came to stand on the other side of the island, needing that barrier between them. "There's plenty of time to meet 'the one' and have a family."

Sara chewed on her lip as if trying to figure out a timeline. She shrugged from her coat and hung it over the high-back barstool.

"Let me have your coat," she told him. "I'm not sure how long we'll be hunkered down here, but hopefully the plow and the salt trucks will come through and you can get back to your place this evening."

Yeah, because the alternative would be spending the night here and he knew full well how that would turn out. He prided himself on being in control in all aspects of his life, but when it came to Sara, she flipped that switch to Off and he was at her mercy.

Did she even know? There was an innocent power she held and he doubted she had any clue that she could have any man she wanted. That family she so desired? All she'd have to do is snap her fingers and any man would come running into her life, ready to give her everything she'd ever dreamed of.

Not him, but any other man.

If he were looking to settle down, Sara would be perfect wife material. She understood the work ethic, she had a drive for success and she valued those close in her life.

Added to all of that, she was sexy as hell and he didn't think he'd ever find a better lover.

Suddenly hotter, Ian removed his coat and walked around the island to hang it on the stool next to Sara's. His arm brushed hers as he shifted. Ian's fingers curled around the back of the stool as he grappled. He prided himself on dominating every situation, yet he couldn't get a handle on his own emotions. He was still too raw, too vulnerable from the circumstances that led him to her house. He had to get that day, those images, out of his mind if he was going to be able to stay strong during his unexpected visit.

"Do you want to tell me about earlier?" she asked gently, her dark eyes boring into his.

He'd swear she could see right into his soul, and perhaps that's what she was trying to do, but he needed to keep that door shut.

"We already moved on from that topic," he reminded her.

"Being vulnerable isn't a problem." She reached out and laid her hand over his. "I'm a pretty good listener and I wouldn't tell anyone. We all have secrets and sometimes the best way to move on is to get the weight off your chest."

He stared at her, knowing she believed every word she said. But that simple touch of her hand clicked something inside him and the dead last thing he wanted to do was chat about the past that still haunted him twenty years later.

Ian jerked his hand from beneath hers and took a step back. "I can wait out in the truck until it's safe to go."

When he started to walk by, Sara grabbed hold of his elbow. His forearm brushed the edge of her breast and he noted the pulse on her neck quickening. The intensity threatened to consume him, to push him even further into her world, and he couldn't mentally afford to get lost in this trap.

Sex the other night had muddled everything since they'd met initially in her office. They'd started every aspect of their working and professional relationship off on the wrong foot and he'd been scrambling to regain his footing since.

"This is a bad idea," he growled, glancing from her hand to her face.

"We're just talking. Isn't that what we're supposed to be doing anyway? That is why you're here."

Wasn't she cute, messing with his mind like this? He couldn't fall for her charm or her compassion or her sex appeal. Why did she have to be everything all wrapped up in one neat, tidy package?

"Listen, we'll work on the interview if that makes you more comfortable." She dropped her hand, but didn't move away. "We can settle in the living room and you can ask whatever else you need to know."

Ian laughed. "We're not even close to everything I want to know."

Sara's smile widened and another kick of lust hit his gut. Yeah, being alone with this woman was nothing but trouble and he'd originally thought she was naive and had no clue…now he was starting to believe she knew precisely what she was doing and she was driving him out of his ever-loving mind.

* * *

"You could say that Elise is definitely the brains of the group," Sara stated, tucking her feet up beside her on the sofa. "Delilah is the guarded one, but she's softened a little since getting back together with Cam."

"And they were divorced?" Ian asked from the opposite end of the couch as he typed notes into his phone.

"Not yet. Nobody had signed the papers." Sara sighed. "Those two were always meant to be together. They met and had a whirlwind affair and next thing I knew, they were getting married. I guess they just knew from the start."

Ian sat his cell down and stretched his arm along the back cushion. "Delilah said Elise met her husband at Angel's Share and then something about getting locked in the basement."

Sara couldn't help but laugh. "Yes, Antonio came to the States to look for distilleries and wineries to partner with for his family's chain of restaurants in Spain. Long story short, he and Elise got locked in the cellar of the castle together during a rainstorm and now they're on their honeymoon."

Ian's eyes widened. "You ladies work fast."

There went that pang of remorse once again. "Two of us, anyway."

Maybe she wouldn't marry. Perhaps she'd be like Milly and just care for others. Milly had a happy, satisfying life…didn't she? Sara never recalled her mother wanting to marry or have a serious relationship. She dated very rarely, but with raising three girls and making sure their lives were enriched, maybe Milly just didn't have the time.

"Don't go there," Ian scolded. "Stop worrying about when you'll get married. It will happen if that's what you want. I firmly believe you don't let obstacles get in your way."

Sara blinked and pulled herself back to the moment. "I definitely don't, but I was just thinking about Milly."

"That's your mother who just passed."

Sara nodded. "She never married. I never thought about that until now, that she was always so busy making us happy and pushing us to fulfill our dreams. I just wonder what her dreams were."

"Maybe that was her dream," he countered. "To see her children happy."

The thought warmed Sara and she smiled. "You sound as if you knew her."

"It's easy to see the type of woman she was when there are three successful, powerful women living out her legacy."

Damn. He did have a way with words. Who knew this interview would be a balm to her wounded soul?

Not only his words, but his presence. It had been a long time since a man sat on her living room sofa and talked. Even if this moment was by chance because of the weather, she didn't mind. The soft glow from her Christmas tree and mantel lights gave the room an even cozier vibe. There was a content blanket that seemed to cover her right now and she couldn't help but wish this moment would never end.

"So why a distillery?" Ian asked. "You said yesterday the male-dominated bourbon industry is the main reason you three wanted to dive into it. Tell me why."

"We wanted to bring something different, yet something that we knew would be a success. Kentucky loves bourbon and they love rich history. Opening a distillery in an old, abandoned castle seemed like a no-brainer."

As he put notes into his phone, Sara went on. "I can

rephrase that if you want something more eloquent for your piece."

Those thin lips quirked again. She couldn't help but stare…and remember. He'd been such a giving lover. Her desire for him was stronger now than ever before. Seeing him humanized earlier had really added a surprising element to all the layers that seemed to make up this mystifying man.

"You're staring."

Sara shrugged. "You're attractive. What else do you want me to do? Close my eyes?"

Ian's bark of laughter caught her off guard. She wasn't going to apologize for enjoying the view. Clearly she wouldn't be doing more than that because he'd made it clear they were, as Dee stated, "a one and done." Granted everything about this was unique and completely out of the norm, but Sara couldn't help but wonder how they'd be now that they knew each other even more.

Ian might not be "the one" she was waiting for, but she had to live her life and enjoy herself until that person came into her world.

"What made you take me back to your house the other night?"

She hadn't meant to ask that, but now that the words were out, she wasn't sorry. Because she'd gotten a good glimpse of the man and his personality, and taking a strange woman home was not in his character.

"I rarely deny myself anything and it had been too long since a woman intrigued me the way you did."

Well…that was eye-opening and a useful nugget of information.

"I expected you to fully dodge that question," she admitted.

The fire in her gas fireplace kicked on, immediately

giving her cozy living room those warm, inviting vibes—not to mention romantic. As if she needed more of a push to romanticize this entire situation. She was sinking deeper and deeper with a temporary man and Sara knew she had to safeguard her heart and her mind, but she was having a difficult time grasping that concept.

"I believe in honesty, but I don't always answer when I'm not comfortable."

"And you're comfortable with me?" she asked.

"Surprisingly, I am."

Another useful piece to lock away. She was chipping away at his steely exterior and those guarded walls.

Sara pulled her old cardigan tighter around her and rested her head on the back cushion. Before she realized it, a yawn escaped and she covered her mouth in a vain attempt to mask her exhaustion.

"Go lie down," he told her. "I'm fine here."

"I'm not just taking a nap with a guest in my house," she scoffed.

"Why not? It's not like we've done anything normal since meeting, anyway."

"True," she agreed. "But I'm fine. I think my body is used to just going at warp speed, so when I'm still for too long, it thinks I should be asleep."

"Maybe—"

Sara's celled chimed from the pocket of her old sweater. She'd changed before they'd settled into the living room in her favorite leggings, Milly's cardigan and a pair of fuzzy socks. Definitely not the sexy look she'd given Ian on their first encounter.

She pulled the phone out and glanced to the screen. Her heart clenched as the name stared back at her.

"I need to take this."

Ian waved her on. "Go ahead."

With a shaky hand, Sara gripped her cell and came to her feet. She needed to have this conversation in private because she had no clue what information she was about to receive or how she would react.

She tapped the screen as she moved into her office and closed the double doors.

"Hello."

"Sara, I have something."

Her heart beat faster at the words she'd been waiting to hear for a while now.

"What is it? You found my father?"

"I found him."

Sara's knees weakened and she sank right to the floor. She concentrated on what her investigator continued to say at the same time as she tried to breathe deeply and not pass out.

Since the moment she and her sisters had discovered they were actually half sisters and not just the very best of friends, Sara had been searching for her birth father. Elise hadn't wanted to find hers and Delilah was still on the fence about meeting the man who'd fathered her after Cam tracked him down.

But Sara wanted to know. She had that yearning to get her own backstory. Yes, she had an amazing life with Elise and Delilah and she'd had the best upbringing with Milly… but there was still a void she wanted to fill.

"He does have a family," the investigator went on. "I was wrong about his name being James, though. Your father's name is Trenton Mills and he lives in Knoxville. He's a schoolteacher there and his son just graduated from high school last year. His wife is the principal at the same school. They seem to be a very tight-knit family from everything I've uncovered."

Family. That word meant so many different things

and looked so many different ways. Yet there was love at the root.

"I wonder if he even knows about me," she murmured.

"I never approached him, but I can do more digging or I can hand over all I know along with his contact information."

Sara closed her eyes and attempted to push back the unshed tears. Swallowing the burn in her throat, she replied, "I'll take the information, please. I can take it from here."

"I had a feeling you'd say that. I'll email everything now."

"Thank you. Seriously. I can't thank you enough."

"I'm always glad when I help someone."

Sara ended the call and immediately went to her email. She kept refreshing until minutes later, the file showed up and she instantly dug into it.

There were photographs. So many images, and she wanted to devour them all at once. She'd definitely pull these up on her computer later and print everything out, but she couldn't wait, so the small phone screen would have to suffice.

She scrolled through quickly, then went back to the beginning and stared at each one, dissecting for any glimpse of a similarity. She definitely had her father's eyes and mouth…so did her brother.

A cry caught in her throat as the first tear slipped down her cheek. She had a brother who likely didn't know she existed. For all Sara knew, her father had no idea, either.

Was it right for her to be so selfish and disrupt his life? Would he want to know she was out there? How did someone so successful and grounded get involved with a habitual drug user like Sara's biological mother? There were still so many questions, but all she wanted to know was if he would want the truth about her. That's all that mattered now.

She'd have to talk to Dee and Elise because she needed their support more than ever, but she was ready to open this new chapter in her life book.

Ten

Ian tapped on the office door. When the wood gave beneath his knuckles, he eased the door open and spotted Sara on the floor. She turned to look up at him and those red-rimmed eyes and tear tracks down her cheeks had him bursting in and immediately at her side.

"What's wrong? What happened?" he demanded.

He sank to his knees and glanced to her phone. She'd been looking at images of a family he didn't recognize, but he wanted to know what the hell happened from her taking a call almost an hour ago, until now when she'd clearly been having an emotional moment on the floor.

"Oh, my word." Her damp eyes widened as she shoved her cell back into her sweater pocket. "I forgot all about you."

"Well, that never helps a man's ego," he joked, hoping to lighten the mood. Ian shifted to sit more comfortably at her side on the rug. "Is everything all right? Did you get bad news?"

Sara shook her head. "I got amazing news, but I just don't know how to process everything. And I was so wrapped up in everything, I lost track of time and touch with reality. I'm so sorry, Ian."

Relief settled inside him. "Don't be sorry. I started to worry when you didn't come back and then when I saw you on the floor crying… Damn it. Don't scare me like that."

Sara patted the side of his face, her fingertips brushing his scar.

"See? You do care and aren't so coldhearted."

That touch, so simple and playful, yet so arousing, struck a nerve he'd thought for sure he'd severed.

Ian reached up and grabbed her hand, curling his fingers around her delicate ones. Sara's eyes widened, and her mouth dropped open as she continued to stare at him.

"Is that how you see me?" he asked. "Cold?"

"I— Well. No."

Damn right he wasn't cold. He was so hot right now, he should have waited in his vehicle like he suggested hours ago, but here he was alone and on the floor with Sara… the woman who wouldn't get out of his mind. Even when he was alone, she was there, always in the forefront and demanding his attention.

"Are you going to kiss me?" she whispered, her gaze dropping to his lips.

"Is that what you want, Sara? You want me to kiss you? To make you remember the other night?"

She inched closer. "I want you to make the other night happen again."

Hell. There was no way he could deny her…or himself. They'd danced around this moment since they reunited in her office. But she was vulnerable. Whatever happened with that phone call had taken her to a new place and he didn't want to be a regret.

Ian pulled her hand away from his face and tugged her closer until she fell against his chest. He searched her eyes for any sign of doubt, but only saw desire.

"Are you using me to forget your trouble?" he asked.

"Maybe. Is that a problem?"

Not a problem, but he was surprised that there was a sliver of disappointment. He never wanted connections or ties to anyone or anything. He sure as hell wasn't looking for any of that now, either. But something about her being so casual confused him.

Perhaps he was just caught off guard because she was unlike any woman he'd ever met. Maybe what he needed at this point in his life was a simple, sexy distraction, and Sara wasn't asking for anything more…at least not from him.

"You're thinking an awfully long time," Sara stated as she started to ease back.

Ian held tight and rested his forehead against hers.

"Occupational hazard," he explained. "I process everything before acting."

A smile danced around her pale pink lips. "And did you process everything on Saturday when you took me back to your place?"

Ian couldn't help but chuckle. "I sure as hell processed everything about you and my decision."

"Then I guess it's decided." Sara moved her hand from his and looped her arms around his neck as she crawled into his lap. "We need to make sure you made the right decision then and now."

Oh, he was pretty damn sure he'd made the right decision both times, but he was done talking. Whatever was going on in Sara's personal life had nothing to do with him and if she needed the escape from reality, he'd be the one offering it. He couldn't explain the territorial tendency when it came to this woman, but he wasn't about to explore those unwanted emotions now.

"And maybe you need to use me as well," she added. "You were pretty stressed earlier. There's nowhere to go for now, so..."

No. There was nowhere to go and he was going to take full advantage of this snowstorm.

Ian slid his hands around Sara's waist, easing his fingertips beneath the hem of her tank. Her warmth penetrated him in ways he'd never experienced before her. How could just one simple touch be both erotic and soothing? He was here in this moment for the physical aspect of this relationship...nothing more. He couldn't afford more.

When Sara arched into him and dropped her head back, Ian seized the opportunity. He'd been dying to taste her since the last time they were together. He trailed his lips over the smooth column of her throat until he reached her chin. Sara shifted and met his lips with her own as she threaded her fingers through his hair.

Liquid fire. That's the only term Ian could use to describe the way Sara reacted in his arms. No doubt she was good for a bruised, battered soul, not to mention pretty damn nice for his ego.

But she was more. Much more than he'd ever admit out loud...so he squelched the thoughts before he could get too carried away. There were so many layers to intimacy, and he only wanted the superficial.

"You're thinking too hard again," she murmured against his lips. "Relax."

"This floor is damn hard," he grunted. "I'm not young anymore."

Sara laughed and pulled away as she came to her feet.

When she extended her hand and smiled down at him, Ian's heart did a flip that irritated the hell out of him. There was no room for heart flips or any other bonding emotion.

Ian reached for her hand and rose, but immediately lifted her into his arms. Sara's playful squeal reminded him of just how opposite they were. At first he was confused by their differences, but she was starting to grow on him...which could prove to be dangerous.

The plush, pale yellow couch in the corner would have to work. He wasn't about to use a hard surface like the desk or the floor. She deserved better, but the bed was out. For one thing, he didn't know where her bedroom was, and for another, crossing that threshold would take them to a level he would never be ready for.

His eyes landed on the couch and he nearly groaned.

"What do you have so many damn throw pillows for?"

Sara locked her ankles behind his back and circled his neck with her arms as she glanced across the room to the silver-and-white pillows, all with Christmas patterns or some holiday wording.

"Because I'm a woman and I like pretty accessories. Don't ask questions. Just go with it."

Of course she liked pretty things. She was simple in that way and wanted her world to be festive and fun. He never knew that manner of thinking and had never really gotten to know anyone like that, either.

He'd known Sara less than a week and she'd already changed something inside him. Who the hell knew the person he'd be once he finally left Benton Springs?

Ian dropped Sara onto the pillow-covered couch and stood over her. Damn, but she was breathtaking with her dark hair spread all around her and her smiling lips swollen from his kisses.

"I love when you look at me like that."

Ian stilled. How had he been looking at her? What could she possibly have seen?

He wasn't about to ask because he didn't want to know the answer…especially when she tacked on the *L* word to the sentence.

Ian unbuttoned his vest and let it fall to the floor. He started working the buttons on his shirt, moving slowly to enjoy Sara's watchful gaze. He couldn't deny he thoroughly enjoyed having her look at him like he was the only thing in the world that mattered. He didn't have that in his personal life. Didn't know he wanted something like that until now.

An unwanted emotional tug pulled at his heart and Ian knew he'd have to work like hell not to lose control. He had no idea how Sara could have this hold over him in such a short amount of time and she likely had no clue the power she possessed.

"There you go thinking again," she murmured as she sat up. "Those worry lines between your brows get even deeper. What has you so bothered?"

You.

"The fact that you're still wearing so many clothes." He ridded himself of his shirt and went to the buckle of his belt. "Or am I the only one getting ready for this party?"

Sara cocked her head. "I am enjoying the show, but I'm starting to feel overdressed."

She took off her cardigan, then reached for the hem of her tank, keeping her gaze locked onto his. Ian continued to shed his clothes as he stared down at her, but when she came to her feet, Ian had to take a step back.

As much as he enjoyed having her half-dressed, he wanted her completely bare. The urgency of his need and ache had him reaching for her pants and helping her out of them and her undergarments in record time.

Ian slid his hands over the flare of her bare hips and settled in that dip in her waist as he stepped toward her. Her breasts grazed his chest and another punch of arousal coursed through him.

"Protection?" she asked, looping her arms around his neck. "I don't have any. It's not like I bring men back here."

For reasons he didn't want to explore, Ian liked knowing she didn't have anyone regular in her life. That territorial feeling came over him again. He wanted to keep her all to himself...but that wasn't possible. They lived in two different worlds and had completely different outlooks on life.

All they had was here and now.

"I don't have any with me," he told her. "I didn't think I'd end up here when I set out this morning."

Sara pursed her lips and another wave of need pumped through him.

"I'm clean," she murmured. "But if you want to stop, I—"

Ian captured her lips. No way could he stop now unless she put on the brakes.

His grip on her waist tightened as he pulled her body flush with his and deepened the kiss. Carefully, Ian lifted her off the floor and turned. When the back of his knees bumped the edge of the sofa, Ian eased down. Sara straddled his lap and settled over him as she pulled from the kiss and stared down.

"I'm clean, too," he assured her. "I'd never do anything to hurt you."

And he'd never wanted to be with someone without protection, either. Sara was doing something to him, something he couldn't reason with in his own mind.

Sara's smile spread across her face as she slowly joined their bodies, all the while keeping her heavy-lidded gaze on his.

The little minx knew just how potent she was. Clearly she wasn't as innocent as he'd thought and that fact made her even more desirable than before. The juxtaposition of her personalities was surprising and maybe even a little challenging. No matter what version of Sara he was presented with, he couldn't resist.

The moment they were joined as one, Sara dropped her head back and arched her body. He remembered from the other evening how sexy she looked in this pose, but he wanted something else. There was so much more to explore with her and now that they had nowhere to go and could take their time, he wanted to do just that.

Ian banded an arm around her waist and shifted until he had her flat on her back. He loomed over her as she locked her ankles behind his back. All of that dark hair fanned around her, her eyes had a hunger in them that he knew matched his own, and then she reached for him. Her hands framed his face as her lips parted, silently urging him to kiss her.

He gripped the arm of the sofa just above her head and reached back to grab hold of her thigh. Then he moved. His hips jerked against hers and he covered her mouth. He wanted all of her at the same time. He wanted to consume everything within her and be all she thought of, all she wanted.

Sara's body danced with his and her urgency was apparent as she moaned into his mouth. Ian pulled her leg a little higher, giving her a more intense experience. She tore her mouth from his and cried out, bowing back and trembling all around him.

Ian stilled, wanting to feel her come completely undone around him. Coupled with seeing her passion explode, Ian had to use all of his self-control to let her finish. He didn't want to miss a single moment of her pleasure.

The moment Sara's body started to settle, he moved again. Faster this time as he worked toward his own release. Her fingertips trailed over his lips, down his throat and over his bare chest. His body couldn't take another second and he welcomed the rush.

Sara murmured something as her hands continued to roam, but he couldn't make it out. His desire had been too strong, his release too intense, to concentrate on anything else.

The moment he came down from the high, Ian rested his elbows on either side of Sara's head and smoothed her hair from her face. She stared up at him with her heart in her eyes and Ian had to close his and pretend he didn't just see straight into her soul.

"I'm glad you're here," she whispered.

Yeah. He couldn't say the words, but he was, too.

Now how the hell was he supposed to deal with that nugget of information? He didn't belong, he didn't *want* to belong, anywhere. Yet here he was, sliding right into a world he didn't want.

Eleven

"So what comes after this project?"

Sara stretched her legs out on the sofa and propped her feet on Ian's lap. They'd never made it out of her office, but they were both now wearing his clothes. He'd put back on his dress pants, but left them unbuttoned, and she'd thrown on his shirt. She'd be lying if she didn't admit she loved the smell of him on her. It took all of her willpower not to turn her nose into the collar and inhale deeply.

"When you leave Benton Springs, what will you do next?" she added. "You seem to travel the world, from all I've seen with your articles."

Ian rested his hand on her ankle and curled those long fingers around her foot. When he started to massage, Sara nearly groaned, but refrained from that as well. She wanted to learn even more about him. The snow was still coming down and she'd sent off texts checking on the employees and the distillery. Everything was under control, so the only thing that needed her attention right now was Ian.

The information about her father wouldn't be going anywhere and that was something she wanted to share in person with her sisters. Elise would be back from her honeymoon tomorrow, so long as the weather cooperated, and Sara would call a family meeting.

"I'll head back to Miami but I'll be gone from *Elite* before the piece comes out. It's time for a change."

Sara laid her arm across the back cushion and tipped her head. "What makes you want to do something else?"

With a shrug, Ian shifted and faced her. He adjusted her feet in his lap and started back up the massage.

"I'm getting restless," he admitted. "I can't pinpoint why, but my time with *Elite* has come to an end. Nigel opened this door for me years ago and I owe everything to him, but even he agrees that I need to move on."

"So what's your goal? Go back to traveling the world? Take a break from work?"

Ian seemed to be thinking as he studied his hands moving over her bare feet. Maybe he didn't want to share his plans, it wasn't like they had any ties or he owed her any explanation.

"You don't have to tell me," she quickly added. "I'm not trying to be some nosy girlfriend. I mean, I'm not your girlfriend, I'm just—"

"Relax," he told her. "I didn't think you were turning clingy on me. I actually have always wanted to write a book."

"Really? That's amazing."

He gave a nonchalant shrug like writing a book was no big deal.

"I've been all over the world and I'd like to focus on

nonfiction from things I've learned from my travels. Who knows, maybe I could write more than one?"

"Do you plan on moving?" she asked.

"I love Miami. It's been my home since I was a teenager."

"After your mom passed?"

Ian's hands stilled on her as his eyes locked onto hers. His silence proved that she had crossed the line into territory he didn't want to get into. Loss could make people close in on themselves and there was no "getting over" such a hardship. But she couldn't help but wonder if he ever talked about her to anybody. Who was in Ian's life that he could confide in or use as a shoulder when needed?

Knowing what she did about Ian, the man likely thought he would be just fine making it through his life by writing about others. He wouldn't need to lean on anyone if there was nothing going on in his own world. Throwing himself into his work and getting wrapped up in each of his projects had likely fulfilled his life all these years.

But he was restless and she knew he was still trying to find something to fill that void his mother had left.

"Forget I asked," she finally stated with a wave of her hand. "We'll talk about something else, but keep up that massaging."

His shoulders relaxed and he resumed rubbing the arch of her foot.

"Would you like to stick around for the gala?" she asked. "Should be a fun night and hopefully no freak snowstorm cancels our plans."

"Today's storm has me ready to head back to Miami as soon as possible, but I still have things to do here." He rested his hands on the top of her feet and leaned forward a bit. "I might be persuaded to stick around and leave after the gala."

Why did that make her so giddy inside? Ian sticking around a little longer didn't mean anything…he was still a temporary fling whether that lasted one week or three weeks. He wasn't staying and they weren't building anything permanent here.

Still, she couldn't help but be excited that she had more time with him, and she fully intended to take advantage of their days together.

"You could always just stay here for the rest of your trip."

When his eyes widened, Sara chewed the inside of her cheek and waited. She hadn't actually meant to say that out loud, but she couldn't take the words back now so she wasn't even going to try to defend them.

"Is that so you can take advantage of me whenever you want?" he asked, a naughty grin dancing around his lips.

Sara shrugged. "Guilty."

At least he wasn't appalled by her request and he hadn't come out and just turned her down…which meant he was thinking about it. Another burst of exhilaration shot through her at the idea of Ian spending his days at the distillery and his nights in her bed.

"You have a spare room?"

His question confused her.

"I have three spare bedrooms. I just assumed—"

"I'll stay, but I won't share your personal room. That's too intimate."

He had a serious issue with any type of bonding or connection, but she would respect his wishes and try to be compassionate about his reasoning.

"Fine by me," she told him. "Once the roads are safe again, we'll go get your stuff."

"We won't have the hot tub," he reminded her.

Sara pulled her feet from his lap and stood. She came

to stand before him, then placed one knee on either side of his hips as she straddled his lap.

"Maybe when we go get your things, we can enjoy it one last time," she suggested.

His hands cupped her backside as he rocked her body against his. "You do have the best ideas."

He leaned up to cover her lips with his. She'd never invited a man to live with her before and she didn't know why she had asked Ian, but she wanted to be with him as much as she could for as long as she could. Their time together was dwindling and there was no reason they couldn't have a little fun until their time ran out.

"Well, you look gorgeous and rested."

Elise breezed into the conference room at the distillery and was all smiles. Sara was so happy to see her sisters in love and moving in a new direction. Elise truly did look like she'd rested and relaxed, and that glowing tan only made Sara a tad jealous that her sister had been on some tropical beach.

"I feel refreshed, but still jet-lagged," Elise admitted. "That snowstorm really screwed up our flights, but I guess spending extra days in paradise wasn't a bad thing."

Yeah, Sara hadn't minded those extra days, either, with her new houseguest, but that was definitely not a conversation she was going to get into. There were much more pressing matters to discuss and her heated fling wasn't even in the top three.

"Sorry I'm late." Delilah stepped in right behind Elise. "Cam thought it was a great idea to surprise me with a puppy and I was up all night. Not to mention the shoes I was going to wear had been peed in, so…how's everyone?"

"A puppy! Why didn't you send us any pics?" Sara demanded. "Let me see. What's the name?"

"What's the breed?" Elise chimed in.

Delilah sat her travel coffee mug and her purse on the table and wrapped an arm around Elise. "I'm so glad you're back. You look even more gorgeous and I didn't think that was possible. Anyway, her name is Milly. Is that okay?"

Sara gasped. "Yes, of course! She would have loved that."

Delilah tapped on her cell and scrolled, then turned the phone to face her sisters. "There's several pictures and some videos. She might not sleep and she potties all over the place, but we're working on it and she's just so cute, I can't be mad."

"I can't tell if she's a Lab or what she is," Elise murmured.

"Cam got her from the local animal shelter." Delilah smoothed her dark hair behind her ears and peeked around to see the screen. "He said he'd been thinking of surprising me for a while, but we're usually so busy with our workloads. He's really lightened his cases and spends much more time at home now. He thinks this will be a good segue into a baby."

"What?" Elise's hold on the phone fumbled and Sara caught it. "You guys are thinking of a baby?"

Delilah nodded. "We've talked about it, but nothing is certain. I'm more open to it than I was and the idea of my own family is kind of growing on me."

"You would make a wonderful mother," Sara added. "That's so exciting and I'm going to need to come over and see this pup. She is precious."

"Sure, anytime." Delilah took her cell and sat it down on the table before grabbing her coffee. "So, what's the urgent talk we need to have, Sara? Your text sounded urgent last night."

Sara's stomach knotted as she pulled in a deep breath.

Her sisters were so supportive of her decision to find her father, and she knew they'd be happy for her. She was more afraid of what would come once she set out to meet the man.

"My investigator found my father," she told them.

Both of her sisters' mouths dropped open, so Sara hurried on.

"He lives in Knoxville and he has a family of his own." She moved to the head of the table where she had a folder of all the information and photographs she'd been emailed. "I have a good bit here I wanted to share with you guys."

Her sisters were quickly at her side as Sara flipped open the folder. Right there on top was a photograph of her dad, his wife and their son.

"Oh, wow," Elise muttered. "Sara, you look just like him."

"I thought so, too." Emotions threatened to clog her throat, so Sara swallowed and forged ahead. "It's crazy knowing I have another family and that I actually look like someone. Isn't that silly? I'm excited that I have the same chin as another human being."

"When you're adopted and aren't sure where you came from, that's not silly at all," Elise defended. "You should be excited. So, are you going to call him or try to see him?"

Sara moved to pull out the leather chair and sank into it. Her attention landed back on the photograph and she chewed on her lip while so many thoughts swirled around in her head.

"I do want to reach out, but I don't know the best approach," she confessed. "It's such a life-altering bomb to drop on him. Do I email so he can take time to think of a response? Or do I call so he can put a voice to a person?"

"I would call," Delilah told her. "You know Cam got that information on my father and I've never reached out.

I'm not sure I'm going to, but that's just where I'm at. This is your journey so do what's best for you. I think I would make a call because an email is so impersonal."

"Agreed." Elise reached for Sara's hand and gave a reassuring squeeze. "We're here no matter when or how you decide to reach out. This is so exciting, though. I'm really happy for you."

Elise had been adamant that she didn't want to know about her biological father, and Dee had the information, but hadn't done anything with it. Sara couldn't help herself. She had a yearning to learn more about her past and see if there were any more similarities other than physical.

"I guess I'll call, then." Sara blew out a sigh and tried to ignore the nerves swirling around in her belly. "I hope I don't disrupt his life. I mean, what if he knew about me and disregarded the fact that my mother was pregnant?"

Elise shuffled through the papers in the folder, handing some to Delilah as well. Sara waited while her sisters looked over the contents. There wasn't a ton of information to take in, but the necessary basics and much more than she'd ever had before.

"The man has devoted his life to teaching and volunteering with after-school activities," Delilah finally stated. "I'd say he loves children so there's a good chance he didn't know about you."

"I'm so confused, though," Sara replied. "How could someone like this get caught up with someone like our mother? A drug addict who was in and out of rehab for years."

"Our mother did have some clean and sober moments." Elise sat her papers down and took a seat next to Sara. "Maybe that's when they met."

That would have to be the case here. The man in front of Sara seemed to be the total opposite of everything they knew about their biological mother. Sara didn't have ill feelings toward her mother. Sara had never gotten a chance to meet the woman since she passed in prison after being incarcerated for drugs. People made mistakes and Sara just wished her mother had been able to straighten her life out and raise the three girls she'd given birth to.

But Milly had stepped in and adopted all three girls, raising them as her own. Sara had a great childhood with memories that would last her a lifetime.

"Am I being greedy?" she asked. "Wanting more, I mean."

"There's nothing greedy about you." Elise snorted. "And there's nothing wrong with you making a phone call. If he doesn't want to meet you, then you will know. But if he does, that opens up a whole other life for you that could be even more amazing."

That possibility had her anticipation spiking. The hope that she would have more family to love and create memories with had her tearing up.

"Oh, damn it." Delilah went to the accent table near the door and grabbed the box of tissues. "Don't cry because then we will and we all have a full day ahead of us. We're ugly criers, remember?"

Sara laughed and sniffed. "I'm aware."

She took a tissue that was offered and dabbed beneath her eyes so she didn't ruin her makeup.

"Okay. Let's move on," Sara suggested. "Elise, how was the honeymoon? Gorgeous and relaxing?"

Her newlywed sister beamed. "It was absolutely everything fairy tales are made of."

"You deserve that," Delilah chimed in as she took her own seat. "We all deserve happiness and I think we're all moving in the direction of the greatest times of our lives."

Sara smiled and clutched her tissue. "I agree."

She couldn't help but think of the man back at her home whom she'd shared the most erotic few days with. They'd gotten his stuff from his rental, made some serious use of that hot tub one last time, and he'd settled into her guest bedroom…the one right next to hers.

"So, should we discuss the gala?" Elise asked. "I just need to be brought up to speed on where we stand on final details."

Sara pulled herself back to reality and reached for her laptop over the stack of papers. After firing up her list, she ran down everything that still needed attention.

"We need to finalize the desserts for the caterer," she told her sisters. "The rest of the food is done."

"It's Christmas, so we have to do a red velvet cupcake or cookie or something," Elise stated. "Other than that, I don't care."

"We need a classic white," Sara added.

"Chocolate," Dee told them. "You can't have a party and not have something chocolate."

Elise shrugged. "I guess just let them know we need those three flavors and to do what they think. A variety would be great and I think finger-type desserts are best. Something easy for the waitstaff to serve either in delicate clear glasses or a cookie sort."

Sara typed in her notes and would call later today. She went over the parking and valet and the decorators' last-minute questions. Once that was all taken care of, she eased back in her seat, feeling accomplished already and they'd only been in their meeting an hour.

"Ian is coming today, right?" Elise asked.

Sara nodded. "He should be here around eleven to interview both of you."

Delilah made a little humming noise that had Sara shifting her attention. "What was that?"

Delilah shook her head. "Oh, nothing. Just didn't know if you wanted to fill Elise in on Mr. Ford."

Sara narrowed her eyes at her sister. "I was going to get to that, tattletale."

Elise stood up and walked to the door and closed it, then turned back to her sisters. "I have a feeling we're going to need privacy for this chat."

"I really was going to tell you what happened." *And is currently happening.* "There were just other things to get to first."

Elise reclaimed her chair and crossed her arms over her chest as she stared back at Sara. Her fiery red hair around her shoulders made her seem a little intimidating, but really, the woman couldn't say a word. She'd just married one of their clients after her own heated affair when they'd been locked in the castle basement.

"Ian and I have a mutual understanding—"

"You had sex," Elise finished. "I'm assuming that's what you're dancing around. So was it a one-time thing or is this ongoing?"

"One time."

"He moved in with me."

Delilah and Sara spoke at once and Sara cringed when both sisters gasped in her direction.

"Moved in with you?" Delilah questioned. "Are you out of your mind? He's not staying, Sara. You can't get tangled up in the man who is writing the most important piece our distillery has ever known."

"I know he's not staying, but it's ridiculous for him to have a rental when we're enjoying each other's company."

Why was she defending herself? She was a grown woman living her life to the fullest. Anything going on between her and Ian was their business.

"I'm only letting you guys know because I don't keep secrets," she added. "I'm not looking for permission or acceptance."

Sara leveled a stare at Delilah before she turned to Elise to do the same. Silence settled heavily among them and she absolutely hated any animosity or turmoil with the two people she treasured most in this world. But she also had to stand up for herself and do what she thought was best in her own life.

"We just worry." Elise dropped her arms and eased forward in her chair. "You all worried about me when Antonio came into my life. It's just natural."

Sara softened and sank back into her seat. "I know, I know. We love each other and that's just the way things are. But I swear, I know what I'm doing and I'm well aware Ian isn't the staying type."

"She's not very convincing," Delilah whispered in Elise's direction.

"I was in denial, too," Elise replied.

Sara's focus shifted from one sister to the other as they chattered back and forth.

Sara smacked her hands on the table. "I'm right here."

"And falling fast for a total stranger who will break your heart," Delilah scolded. "Just be careful and guard yourself. That's all we ask."

Yeah, well, she could only guard so much. She was human and formed attachments, but she was also being smart. She knew what this was and wasn't. And maybe she was enjoying herself and getting caught up in the moment, but that's how she lived her life. She wanted to take in each second and be happy instead of looking to the end and sadness.

"Regardless of how we end things, none of this will affect the piece Ian is writing on Angel's Share."

Her sisters didn't look so convinced, but Sara knew Ian would write an amazing piece and he would be honest. There was nothing not to like here and he hadn't had a bad experience. So far he'd loved the tastings and he was fascinated with the grounds and the history of an old castle nestled in the Kentucky hills. She knew he planned to talk to their rivals, but Sara wasn't worried about that, either. Competition was natural in any industry.

Sara wasn't going to keep discussing this any further. Her sisters would just have to trust her judgment and once they talked with Ian later, they could see for themselves that he was a genuine guy. He might be reserved and quiet, but he wasn't deceitful or working on some other plot. He wasn't using her because there was nothing for him to gain and he'd had no idea who she was when they first met.

There was that very realistic voice that wouldn't shut up, though. Ian would be leaving and she would have to just accept that they weren't a couple. No matter the secrets they shared or the memories they made, this moment in time would be locked here forever and nothing would ever be added.

Twelve

"The whole setup and story is so remarkable."

Ian followed Elise and Delilah into the conference room after they'd given him a mock tour. They'd wanted him to get the same experience that a customer coming through would have. It was different from the behind-the-scenes tour Sara had given him when he'd first arrived. He'd quizzed them on various aspects of their part of the business as they'd walked and talked. They'd stayed out of the way of actual tours happening, but Ian was impressed with the number of people that came through Angel's Share during any given day.

"We'd like to finish up in here." Delilah gestured for him to go in and have a seat at the long table that stretched out from the exposed stone wall. "Then we'll set you free."

Ian rolled out one of the leather chairs and waited until the ladies came in and took a seat before he relaxed. Though he felt like he was about to face a firing squad, he attempted to maintain his posture and eye contact. No way in hell was he about to look weak in front of Sara's sisters.

"I've enjoyed my time today," he admitted. "I was anxious to get to know the two of you after spending so much time with Sara. You're all quite different, but each powerful in your own department. Everything works together like one cohesive unit. Flawless, really."

"Flawless." Elise smiled and nodded. "I like that because there are certainly days that don't feel flawless. I hope when we're stressed and scrambling to cover issues that arise that our clients never notice."

"No business is perfect," he told them. "May I speak with some employees to get their perspective on such a successful operation?"

"Of course," Elise replied. "We have nothing to hide."

He wasn't quite ready to ease back in his seat and breathe a sigh of relief. With the way Elise and Delilah were glaring at him across the table, he had a feeling they were about to get into the personal side of this gathering. There was no way Sara's sisters would let this opportunity pass them by to grill him or threaten him.

Regardless of the reason he initially came to Benton Springs, that had changed drastically the moment he'd met "Jane." Now he had to deal with her loyal family and faithful watchers. She was lucky to have them and very likely knew that.

Part of him had a twinge of jealousy that she had such close-knit relationships and family. The other part of him was terrified he'd gotten tangled into such a web, because getting out would be a hell of a mess.

"I can save you the time." He had to attempt to regain control of this situation…and his life with this family. "You brought me here to quiz me or threaten me about Sara."

Elise smirked, but Delilah remained staring. Tough crowd here.

"You moved in with our sister after knowing each other for only a few days," Elise started.

Damn. Sara told them he was staying with her? Clearly they had no secrets among them, but it sounded much more permanent than the situation actually was.

"I'm staying with her through the end of next week when I leave, but she has tried to convince me to stay for the gala, so maybe just a bit longer. I'm in the guest room, we're not playing house, and anything else you want to know should come from Sara."

"She's a hopeless romantic," Delilah told him. "She's waiting for some knight to ride up to the castle."

Ian couldn't help but laugh. "She's the last woman who would need to be rescued from anything. From what I've seen, she can definitely hold her own."

Elise leaned forward and rested her hands on the table. Why did Ian suddenly feel like he was being interviewed for a position he hadn't even applied for?

"She wants to be rescued from reality," Elise told him. "She can hold her own, but she's always had this dream of a big family and that all starts with the man of her dreams."

"She knows I'm not that man." Above all else, that had to be crystal clear. "We're adults spending time together and I'm working on this article. There's nothing more to read into this."

Sara was strong, determined, sexy and independent. There wasn't a doubt in his mind that she would hate her sisters acting like she was anything less.

Ian came to his feet. "No disrespect, ladies, but if we are done with the business portion, I'm going to head out. If there's a problem with this situation, you should take that up with your sister instead of talking to me like she's incapable of making her own decisions. You might be worried for her, but I assure you she can handle her own."

He scooted the seat back and started for the door. Before he crossed the threshold, he heard them murmur.

"I like him."

"Yeah. So do I."

And that might be the most terrifying part of his day. He wasn't trying to win these ladies over. He was here for a job, damn it. When did this project shift from business to personal and how the hell had he lost so much control?

Sara sat in her car in her driveway and stared at the number on her cell. All she had to do was hit the final button. She'd been waiting for nearly ten minutes now. There was no going back once she pressed it and this one simple call would change so many lives forever.

She'd never been so nervous in her life. Her hands shook, her stomach rolled. She was just going to have to do it before she completely lost her nerve.

Without thinking, she pressed the button and put the call through her car. She couldn't hold on to the phone right now, she had too many nerves. The first ring seemed to echo through her vehicle. She closed her eyes as the call went on to the second ring.

Maybe the voice mail would kick on and she could just hang up and call when she had more courage.

"Hello."

Her eyes flew open at the male voice that answered. But that male voice belonged to her father.

"Hi, um, Mr. Mills?"

"Yes. Who is this?"

"My name is Sara Hawthorne. You don't know me and I'm not selling anything, so please don't hang up." She reached up and gripped the steering wheel, needing something to cling to. "I have reason to believe you are my biological father."

Silence. There was no noise coming through the speakers now, but at least he hadn't hung up.

"There was no easy way to lead into that," she quickly rambled on. "My mother was Carla Akers from Benton Springs, Kentucky."

Trenton muttered the name beneath his breath as if his past had just come out of nowhere. She couldn't imagine what was rolling through his mind right now, but she wanted to put him at ease.

"I'm sure there's no good time to just spring that news on someone," she added. "And I don't want to ruin or disrupt your life. I guess I just wanted to know if there's any chance at all that we could meet."

"I—I don't even know what to say. What was your name again?"

"Sara. Sara Hawthorne. I live in Benton Springs. I believe you used to live here for a short time, as well."

"Do you have proof? You have to understand I'm not only caught off guard, I'm skeptical."

Sara released the steering wheel and started to normalize her breathing. He was talking to her and that's all she could have asked for. She really hadn't known what to expect, but so far, she was still hopeful.

"I just recently found out who my birth mother was," she explained. "I was raised by her sister. I hired an investigator to find you and she does have proof. Of course we could do a DNA test, but I've seen a photo of you and, well, I look just like you."

More silence. This poor man was trying to process so much in a short amount of time.

"You don't have to answer me now about meeting," she went on. "And I promise I don't want anything from you other than to know if you'd like to see me. I don't need money or anything else. I just…needed to talk to you."

"I don't know what to say. This is a lot to take in and I can't just assume."

"Of course not," she agreed, still holding on to hope. "Listen, you have my number now. If I never hear from you, I'll know you just want to move on and I understand. But if you decide you want to meet, to just see if this is real or not, I'm here. No pressure."

Again, Trenton's end was completely silent and the tension coupled with the unknown had Sara almost regretting her decision to call.

"I didn't mean to interrupt your life and I apologize if I did that." She closed her eyes once again and dropped her head back against the headrest. "I'll just… I'll let you go. Thanks for listening to me."

She disconnected the call before she could beg or demand an answer. Tears clogged her throat as the impact of the last several days caught up with her. Or maybe the emotions came because the control was out of her hands now. Whatever happened, or didn't happen, would be up to Trenton.

Sara took a minute to let the tears flow. She deserved a self-pity party, especially now that she had privacy. There was so much going on in her life. She'd taken some of the biggest leaps just in the past week between getting involved with Ian and calling her father. Never did she dream she'd be in this position where her feelings were all over the place.

But sometimes taking those big leaps had bigger rewards. So tears were fine for now, but she needed to get hold of herself and concentrate on what she could control.

Sara wiped her tears and pulled in a deep breath. She couldn't help but wonder how long she should wait for a call or if she should just come to the realization that maybe her father didn't want to upend the family life he'd built. Regardless, she was proud of herself for reaching out and stating her case.

As she stepped from her car and headed toward the house, she realized Ian wasn't here. She'd left the distillery nearly an hour ago and he'd been gone long before that. She hadn't talked to him since his interviews with her sisters and all they said was things went well.

Something must have happened for them to have been tight-lipped.

No matter, Sara still wondered where Ian had gone to. He certainly didn't owe her any explanations or need to check in, but she was curious. There was really no protocol for this temporary living arrangement so all she could do was go about her evening and not focus on all the balls she had up in the air.

Thirteen

The moment Ian walked in the front door, some delicious aroma hit him. Something warm and yeasty…a scent that definitely reminded him of his childhood. Instant memories flooded him of his mother in the kitchen or him hanging out in the back of her bakery. She always loved trying new recipes and he was her favorite taste-tester.

He couldn't help but smile and Ian wondered when the last time he smiled about that memory was. Usually when he thought of his mother, an onslaught of guilty emotions threatened to consume him. But for now, there was a sense of peace.

He must be sleep-deprived, because how the hell else could he explain that a damn smell made him happy? That was absurd.

Or maybe that was just another way Sara had infiltrated his world. He hadn't even given her his entire backstory, yet she was slowly healing his shattered heart.

Ian carried his bag to the back of the house toward the kitchen. His stomach growled as he headed past the steps and down the hall. Music and some off-key singing also greeted him. The minute he crossed over the threshold, he stilled.

Sara stood with her back to him just swaying to the classic tunes as she attempted to sing with Ol' Blue Eyes. She stirred something in a pot without a care in the world except her duet with Frank. Ian leaned against the doorjamb and watched those swaying hips. Never in his life did he think he'd want to come home to a woman in his space, but he couldn't lie that…

No. He shouldn't be getting swept up in this moment. This wasn't his home and Sara wasn't his woman. Falling into some familial fantasy was ridiculous.

Sara tapped her spoon on the edge of the pan and spun around—her singing immediately coming to an abrupt halt.

"Oh, sorry. I didn't hear the door alarm over the music." She shut the melody off and turned back to face him, pasting on a wide smile. "I didn't know if you'd be hungry when you came in, so I just made some cheesy potato soup and sourdough bread. Nothing fancy, but I like comfort foods when it's cold outside."

Sara reached for the towel hanging on her oven door and wiped her hands. Then she brushed her hair away from her face and rushed to grab some bowls from the cabinet.

"You don't have to eat, but it's here if you're hungry. I'm not sure what all you got into today, so…"

Ian stepped farther into the kitchen and placed his bag on one of the stools at the island. Sara started muttering something else and trying to get dinner set up, but her hands shook and she looked like she was on the verge of tears.

What the hell had happened today?

He stepped in behind her and wrapped his arms around her waist, pulling her back against his chest.

"Relax," he murmured. "You don't need to do anything extra for me, especially when you've had a hell of a day."

Her body went lax against his as she sat the bowl on the counter.

"I don't know what happened," he went on, "but I've got you."

He didn't know where these reassuring words were coming from, but she clearly needed them…and maybe he needed this, too. His emotions since walking through the door had been up and down, but Sara had some inner turmoil that was causing her to panic.

"How do you even know how my day was?" she asked.

"Because you're on edge and can't stand still."

Sara turned and wrapped her arms around his neck. Her lips grazed his skin as her warm breath tickled the side of his face. Something seemed to just click into place, but he had no clue what because he hadn't been looking for anything to "click." Maybe he was just feeling that sense of pride for being in the right place at the right time. Clearly Sara needed someone right now and he wasn't sorry he was that guy.

"I have a bad feeling I'm about to dump my entire life story on you," she sniffed against the side of his neck.

"Was that a warning for me to run?" he asked.

"This is your only chance to save yourself."

Ian tightened his hold. "I'm not worried about me. Let's hear it."

A moment later, Sara broke down. He hadn't expected tears before the story, but there was obvious pain she was working through.

Ian reached behind her and turned off the burner, then

bent down and lifted her. With one arm behind her back and one beneath her knees, he carried her to the adjoining living area and sank down onto the couch. He cradled her against him and attempted to soothe her with soft strokes up and down her back. The way she trembled against him had his heart clenching and he wished like hell he could do something to fix this, but he wasn't quite clear what "this" was.

The glow from the Christmas tree and the flames in the fireplace kept the room in soft lighting. He couldn't see her face, but he slid her stray strands over her shoulder and let her take this moment. Everyone had a breaking point, even him. He just always kept himself in check unless he was alone. And even at that, he hadn't had a private moment in years. He couldn't allow himself to go to that dark place in his mind because he truly feared he'd never recover if he accepted the fact that he was responsible for his mother's death.

Oh, the doctors and social workers told him the accident wasn't his fault, but if he hadn't been arguing with his mother and had her distracted on that snowy road, perhaps she'd still be alive.

Sara sniffed once again and eased up. Her damp eyes met his and that helpless feeling rolling through him was most certainly unwelcome. She trusted him with her emotions or she wouldn't be so vulnerable and open. Which made this moment even more amazing. She was brave enough to trust him with her fears and there was no place else he'd rather be than right here, right now.

"I really didn't mean to just cut loose like that."

Ian shrugged. "It's better than your singing."

Sara swatted his chest and laughed…which was the exact response he'd been hoping for. She needed to have just a little of that pressure removed from her shoulders and that was the only way he knew to do it.

"I wasn't expecting an audience," she informed him as she swiped the moisture from her cheeks.

When she started to scramble off his lap, Ian tightened his hold around her waist. "Talk to me."

She pulled in a deep breath and shook her head. "It's just all caught up with me and you found me at a weak moment. I'm sure you know nothing about being weak."

"You're not weak, you're human, and we're not talking about me right now."

"You never want to talk about you," she countered. "That's how I know you're not weak. I have a roller coaster of a day, hell a week, and I lose it."

"You're entitled to lose it. Did something happen with your sisters? Did they tell you about my visit?"

Sara's eyes narrowed. "They didn't say anything, which makes me nervous. What happened?"

No way in hell was Ian going to get into that little conversation he'd had with Elise and Delilah. That was between Sara and them.

"We had a good interview," he replied. "So if the issue isn't them, what is it? Does it have anything to do with that phone call of yours the other day?"

Sara nodded. "You know my sisters and I are all adopted? Well, what we found out a few months ago is that our adoptive mother, Milly, was actually our aunt. Her sister was our biological mom."

"That must have been quite a surprise."

"That wasn't even the most shocking part," Sara went on. "We found out our mom had been in and out of rehabs, had given birth to the three of us and, I'm sure I don't need to tell you, we all have different fathers."

Ian smiled. "That's apparent, but you all are very strong

women, so you must have gotten that from your mother's side of the family."

"We definitely got our strong will from Milly. She raised us to be who we are today, but she never told us the truth. We can only assume to spare us the pain of knowing who our mother was or the mistakes she'd made."

Ian could see that being a very strong possibility. He ran his hand up and down her thigh, silently urging her to keep going.

"Elise never wanted to know who her biological father was and Delilah got the information on hers, but never reached out." Sara swiped at her eyes once more and then started drawing a pattern on the back of his hand. "I hired an investigator and that's who called the other day with the contact info for my father. As you saw I was a bit overwhelmed on my office floor and maybe even more so today."

Ian waited for her to keep going. At least she'd stopped crying and she wasn't shaking. Her fingertip continued a circular pattern and she seemed mesmerized as she continued speaking.

"I called Trenton Mills today," she murmured. "He's a teacher in Knoxville with a wife and a son. He's got a family and when I called him, he was so taken off guard, I think I ruined his life."

Ian turned his hand over and laced his fingers with hers. "You didn't ruin his life," he told her. "Look at me."

Her tear-filled eyes came up to his and he raised his brows to drive his point home.

"You didn't," he repeated. "The man is going to be shocked and maybe not so welcoming right off the bat. If he held a conversation with you, then that's a good sign. How did you leave things with him before you hung up?"

"I said if he wanted to meet, he could call me. Basically

I gave him an out and said that if he didn't want anything to do with me, I would understand if I didn't hear from him."

Ian pulled her against his chest and held tight. "That's all you can do. Give him time to process everything. Who knows, it's Christmas so maybe he'll call and you'll get the greatest gift."

"I've already thought of that. I couldn't ask for more than just one more talk with him. Even if he calls, I just liked hearing his voice." A soft laugh escaped her. "That probably sounds crazy."

"Not at all. I never knew my father, either, so I get it."

Sara trailed her hand up over his shoulder, her fingertips brushed along his jawline as she spoke. "Did you ever look for him?"

"No. After my mother passed, I pretty much remained in foster care for the next six months and then I took what little savings my mom had and money from the sale of her bakery and I moved south. I wanted as far away as possible."

Away from the memories, away from the nightmares that had plagued him for months. It had taken a total reset once he'd gotten to Miami. He'd promised himself the minute he stepped foot into the town that his new life would not involve emotions or attachments. The closest thing he had to a relationship was Nigel.

"And you've been pushing people away since."

Sara's words penetrated the moment and pierced that wall he'd put up around his heart. He never spoke about his past, ever. Yet with Sara, he found himself actually wanting to.

What the hell was happening here?

"Maybe I have," he admitted. "Life has been easier that way."

Sara pressed her palm to his chest and lifted her head. “That’s the saddest thing I’ve ever heard.”

“Do I look sad?”

She stared at him for a moment, then ran the tip of her finger between his brows. “You do.”

Well, damn. He hadn’t expected her to say that. He’d worked so hard on being strong, resilient, maybe even stony. But he’d never wanted to come across as sad because if anyone saw that, they would offer pity and that’s the last thing he ever wanted from anyone.

“I’m sad because I’m hungry,” he countered, needing to get the focus off of his backstory. “What do you say we eat?”

She offered a slight smile. “I’ll get the table set.”

“No.” That was another level of intimacy he couldn’t enter into, not even with her. “Let’s eat in here and watch a movie.”

Sara quirked a brow, but ultimately nodded. “Deal. Get the movie set up and I’ll get everything else.”

He thought he’d get some pushback on that one, but thankfully he didn’t. Maybe a casual dinner and movie would help soothe both of their souls tonight.

Fourteen

"That was the worst movie I've ever seen." Sara moved her feet from Ian's lap and stood to stretch. "I should have never let you choose."

"But you did and you're a better person for watching. There's nothing like old Westerns."

Sara snorted. "You got that right. I thought we'd watch something old like a nice black-and-white with Ingrid Bergman or Rita Hayworth."

"You didn't put a request in." Ian rose to his full height and stared down at her. "But you did make a hell of a dinner."

"Soup and bread? You really need higher expectations."

He took a step closer and rested his hands on her shoulders. "I've found my expectations are changing, perhaps better than they've ever been."

Those talented fingers started kneading her knots and Sara couldn't help the groan that escaped her.

"If your nonfiction book doesn't work out you could make some serious money being a masseur."

He was constantly rubbing on her: feet, thighs, shoulders. She wasn't about to complain, either. The man had magic hands…in the bedroom and out. Not that they'd made it to her bedroom, he still put the brakes on that.

"Do you have an early day tomorrow?" he asked.

"Not really. The busiest part of the distillery right now is rush orders for the holidays. I'm working on planning the governor's daughter's wedding for the spring and getting the rest of the venue options locked in for other weddings. Elise's day has blown up our social media even though she just had an intimate ceremony."

Ian threaded his fingers through her hair and tipped her head back. "We're supposed to get more snow tonight and I didn't like the idea of you out too early."

Sara grinned and slid her arms around his waist. "And here I thought you just wanted to keep me in your bed."

"That, too," he confirmed.

He dipped his head and grazed his lips over hers. Sara closed her eyes and let him lead the moment. Maybe she could take half a day off tomorrow. There was nothing she couldn't work on from home and she'd already finalized the last-minute Christmas at the Castle details. All there was to do now was… Ian.

She reached for the button on his dress shirt and wondered if the man owned any casual clothes. He'd shed the vest, though, so now all she had to do was get him out of this shirt and his pants.

She, on the other hand, had changed immediately when she'd gotten home and Ian probably wondered why she looked homeless in her own house. But her favorite cozy sweats and off the shoulder sweater were perfect for a wintery night in.

The only light they had now was the fireplace and the crisp white lights from her Christmas tree. And once she peeled that shirt off of him, she wondered why she hadn't thought to capture that chiseled body more in this glowing effect.

"You look at me like…"

"What?" she asked, glancing up. "Like I want to devour you? That's because I do."

"That will have to wait because I'm taking my time with you tonight."

Oh, that sounded like the most delicious warning and promise all rolled into one.

Sara took a step back and quickly removed her clothes, leaving her standing in only a white cami and matching boy shorts.

Ian's eyes traveled over her like he was taking in the sight for the very first time. But in all honesty, they had always been rushed and frantic and eager to pleasure each other. Tonight was different. Tonight *felt* different.

That vise around her heart tightened and Sara knew she was going to be in trouble, but she couldn't stop how she felt any more than she could stop wanting this man. So she might as well just go with it and worry about the ramifications later.

"How do you make everything look so damn sexy?" he murmured, reaching for her.

"I'm just me," she said, shrugging, not really knowing how to answer that.

"Yeah." He pulled her close and tipped her head back to grip her chin. "That's what makes you so damn irresistible."

Sara let him take over, let him do whatever he wanted, because she wanted to forget. She wanted to erase the fear that stemmed from the phone call with her father, and she needed to eradicate the sickening feeling that Ian would be out of her life much too soon…because she wanted to hold on to him forever.

Ian had just sat down at Sara's kitchen island with his laptop and his first cup of coffee for the morning when his cell rang. Nigel's name came up on the screen and Ian popped in his earphones, then tapped the speaker so he could have his hands free.

"Morning," he greeted. "What's up?"

"Just checking in," Nigel claimed. "I hadn't heard from you in a few days. You ready to move back north or will you be returning?"

Ian chuckled. "I'm ready to hang up this coat and get back to the sunshine and heat."

"Glad to hear it. I mean, you're moving on no matter what, but I like knowing you're not leaving me completely." Nigel let out a sigh and continued. "Seriously, though, how does everything look? Are you on track for the first-of-the-year deadline?"

"I am. I've been compiling notes and writing the piece as I go."

After his interesting interaction with Elise and Delilah yesterday, he'd spent the rest of the day at Rise and Grind. He'd ultimately tried the scones and his past and present collided. He could see a bridge between the two and he had Sara to thank for something so trivial, yet meaningful. He'd also found the perfect quiet corner to get some much-needed work done.

"I'm likely staying for the Christmas at the Castle gala at the distillery, but I should be back just before Christmas."

"So you'll be here for dinner at my house? Because Beth is making your favorite trifle dessert."

Ian had spent every Christmas with Nigel since he'd come to Miami. Where else would he be?

"Tell her I wouldn't miss it. And this piece on Angel's Share might actually come in early."

"In a hurry to be done here at *Elite*?" Nigel joked. "You've never had a project early in your entire career."

"This one is different," Ian admitted, toying with the handle on his coffee mug. Of course the embossed front was the distillery logo. "This place is fascinating."

"And the women?"

"Also fascinating."

"So fascinating you canceled the rental?" Nigel asked.

Sara swept into the kitchen and padded straight to the coffeepot. She'd just gotten out of the shower and that familiar floral aroma left a trail behind her. She sat her mug down to fill and shot him a naughty grin over her shoulder.

Apparently all of last night and this morning had put her in a good mood. He was in a pretty good place in his life, as well.

"How did you find that out?" Ian asked, refocusing on Nigel's question.

"Considering the magazine was paying for your travels, the invoice and cancellation were brought to my attention from accounting."

All the more reason he needed to get away from a regular job. He could do what he wanted, when he wanted. Not that Nigel cared, but Ian didn't care for being questioned on his actions.

"I found something better."

Sara went to the fridge and bent over, looking for her creamer. The little T-shirt she'd thrown on moved up her thighs and Ian merely sat back and admired the view. Even with her silly, fluffy pink slippers, she looked so adorable and too damn perfect.

All of this was starting to feel too perfect…but it couldn't be. This wasn't what he came here for and he had other aspirations. Settling down in one place, with hellish weather, was not his idea of a good time. It all sounded like a trap.

"And does she know you're not the staying kind?" Nigel asked.

"Yeah. That's been discussed."

Nigel let out a grunt, of acknowledgment or disapproval, Ian wasn't certain. No matter what his friend and boss thought, Ian didn't do bonds or commitments or anything else that was outside of furthering his career. Granted, his career as a journalist had taken off years ago and he was at the top of his game now, but he was so set in his ways and just fine with the life he'd created.

"You sound different."

Nigel's statement interjected right through Ian's thoughts.

"Different? How?"

"I can't put my finger on it. You almost sound…happy."

Ian ground his teeth as he stared across the kitchen to Sara as she poured the perfect amount of creamer.

"Why do people keep thinking I'm not happy?" he demanded.

Sara tossed another look over her shoulder and merely shrugged with a smile.

"Because you've always been like a robot just going through daily motions," Nigel explained. "Living your life and simply being alive are completely different things."

Sara stirred her coffee and blew before taking that first sip. When she closed her eyes and sipped again, Nigel's words somehow made perfect sense. Sara lived her life. She enjoyed each and every aspect including something as mundane as morning brew.

"Everyone is different," Ian replied.

No way was he getting into anything too deep this early in the day and especially with Sara standing within earshot. Nigel had a wife, children and an incredibly successful company. Ian was thrilled for the man, but that didn't mean that lifestyle was meant for Ian.

"I'll be back after the gala," Ian informed him. "Don't worry about this project. I've got everything covered."

"It's not the project I'm worried about."

Ian disconnected the call and reached for his mug. He was a big boy and, while he appreciated the love and respect from Nigel, Ian didn't need life or love advice.

Love. What a ridiculous term to even try to fit into his life. He wouldn't even understand how to love a woman, not the way one deserved. And Sara absolutely deserved the best. Maybe if he'd met her when he'd been younger and he hadn't created such a jaded world for himself… but there was no sense in even allowing his thoughts to travel down that path. He was passing through and considered himself damn lucky to have met someone like Sara Hawthorne.

"Are you staying here all day?"

Sara stood on the other side of the island, cupping her mug with both hands and staring at him, waiting for him to come back to reality.

"If it's snowing, I'm not moving from this spot."

Sara rolled her eyes. "You really have a problem with this and I'm going to break you of it."

Ian shook his head. "Doubtful. There's a reason I've lived in Miami most of my life."

"Yeah, fear," she countered. "But since you don't want to discuss your past, which I respect, I have to deal with the Ian I know now and I'm here to help you."

What was it with her and Nigel wanting to help him all

of a sudden? What part of his actions or his life did they see that they deemed necessary to "fix"?

"Why don't you go on to work and I'll stay here and get some things done on my end?" he suggested.

Sara's smile spread across her face, but instead of looking wholesome and adorable like always, she seemed almost…maniacal.

"You can stay here," she agreed. "But I need to run out and I'll be right back."

She dashed from the kitchen and Ian instantly had a pit in his stomach. Whatever she had planned, he had a feeling he was not going to like this.

Fifteen

"You've got to be kidding me."

Sara clapped her gloved hands and laughed at Ian's face. The poor man looked like he was getting ready for a root canal without the Novocain. But she wanted to tackle whatever demons he had, and since she didn't really know what he was dealing with, this was all she could think of.

"Come on. Like you never went sleigh riding as a kid?" she asked.

Ian nodded. "Of course I did, when I was little and not afraid to break a bone."

"Don't be so dramatic," she scolded. "You're not going to break a bone."

"Maybe not, but splitting these snow pants is a real possibility," he growled.

"Yeah, well, Camden is just a little shorter than you and

that's the only place I could think of to get you snow gear spur-of-the-moment."

Delilah had thought Sara was an absolute fool for taking the day off and playing in the snow with Ian. But thankfully Sara wasn't asking for opinions and only wanted to borrow Cam's clothes.

"I'm worried about my nether regions," Ian added.

"I'm here to make sure you have fun and I'll watch out for those regions," she joked. "Neither of us wants harm to come to that territory."

Ian turned and looked at the slope going down her backyard, then shifted back to her.

"How about a snowball fight instead?" he suggested. "It's damn cold out here and that sounds quicker, and less stress on the seam of these pants."

"Snowball fight is after the sleigh ride." She picked up the two-person sled and settled it into the snow. "Hop on and then I'll get in between your legs."

He eyed her another minute like he was about to argue, but she just pointed to the sleigh.

"How the hell did I lose control?" he muttered as he awkwardly sank and fell into the sled.

Snow crunched and gave way beneath her boots as she made her way to her spot. After settling in, she grabbed the rope in front.

"Ready?" she called.

"No."

Too bad. She rocked her body and pushed off the snow with one hand while steering the sled with the other. Ian's arms banded around her waist as the crisp snow rushed up to her face. Thankfully she had her scarf wrapped around her and her hat pulled low. The rush of the slide had Sara squealing, but she had a feeling Ian sat behind her with his eyes closed.

She tugged on the rope to the side, hoping to go just a bit farther down the slope, but her plan went askew. The sled tipped, sending her and Ian into the snow on their sides.

Laughing, Sara pushed her way up to her knees and glanced to Ian, who was still lying in the snow. He'd rolled to his back and stared up at the sky.

"Nobody would believe this if they could see me," he muttered. "Not one person."

"What? That you're having fun?"

"Is that what this is called?"

Sara gathered up snow in her glove and packed it tight before launching the ball at his chest. Ian wasted no time in forming his own and tossing them right back. But he had a faster process than she did and all she could do was laugh and use the sled as a shield.

"I'm waving the white flag," she yelled. "You win."

"Does that mean we're going back inside?"

She peered around the sled. "You don't want to do the hill again? Just one more time? You can take the lead."

The snowball in his hand dropped in front of him as he stared back at her. She'd never seen him in any element other than professional, but he looked good here. Too good. He'd slid fluidly into her world and she'd watched every step of the way, disregarding any warning bells that had gone off in her head.

She'd made a grave mistake and fallen for Ian Ford.

Why the hell had she ever thought she could compartmentalize her emotions? She threw every part of herself into every aspect of her life. Having a one-night stand had never been her norm for good reason…because she formed bonds so easily.

And if they'd just shared that one night, maybe she could have gotten him out of her head, but there had been many nights and days and now here she was with her heart on the line.

"Will that make you happy?" he asked. "Just one more time?"

She could do this all day with him and lock each second in her memory bank.

"One more time," she agreed. "Then we'll go inside and get warm by the fire."

"You need a hot tub."

"I'm realizing that more and more."

Sara used the sled as leverage to come to her feet. She slipped a little before regaining her footing, then pointed toward the top of the incline.

"This is the only downside to sledding," she told him. "Climbing back up."

"It's the chafing for me."

Sara snorted as she started to climb. "You'll be just fine and back in your work clothes in no time."

She should have grabbed some sweats from Cam as well, but those likely would have been ill-fitting, too. She couldn't reprogram Ian into the man she wanted him to be or the man she thought he could be. She adored who he was, but she wished she could figure out what had made him into such a cautious, wary man who was too strait-laced for his own good.

And he was leaving next week. She'd heard him talking on the phone earlier, and even though she'd known it was coming, that didn't make the fact any less depressing.

All she knew was he was staying through the gala and then he'd be gone. There was no chance of him changing his mind and she wasn't naive enough to believe that a heated fling would make someone uproot their life and start over. This wasn't her fairy tale at all…this was just an amazing moment in time that she'd have to remember forever.

Ian Ford had definitely marked a spot on her heart that could only be reserved for him, and that was okay. She just had a sinking feeling she'd compare every man that came into her life to Ian from here on out and there wasn't a doubt in her mind, there was no comparison.

"You have to get the red," Elise declared.

Sara turned side to side in the mirror and really did love the look of this gold gown, but red was her color and that other one she'd just taken off really did accentuate her figure.

"Agree," Delilah chimed in, stepping up beside Sara on the platform.

Queen was their go-to boutique when they needed upscale dresses. Where else could they shop in private and have champagne served to them?

"Wow." Sara took in Delilah in the white shimmering gown with a high neck and long sleeves. "You look like an angel."

"I have a bad feeling if I wear white, I'll spill red wine all over me, but I do love this one."

Elise came to stand near the platform. The sisters all surveyed one another in the mirror and Sara was so thrilled that they were able to do this, that they'd come this far. Hopes and dreams were continually being made each day they were successful in their business.

"You have to get it," Elise insisted. "Nobody could look that good in that dress except you."

Delilah gave a half turn and looked at the back of the dress, which was scooped low with more shimmer detail. Sara glanced to Elise and took in the black strapless gown with gold beading around the bust.

"That's gorgeous, too," Sara told her sister. "We're all looking pretty damn good. Let me put the red dress back on and let's see how we'll all look as a team."

Sara stepped off the platform and rushed back to her dressing room. Her cell vibrated on the chaise and she paused to check the text from Ian.

Let me know before you come home. I have a surprise and it's not ready.

A surprise? Well, that was unexpected, and she loved surprises. Smiling, she hit Reply.

Can't wait!

So many thoughts ran through her mind as she wrestled out of this gown and into the other. She literally had no clue what he could possibly be doing or have bought her. Was this for an early Christmas? They weren't doing gifts…were they? Maybe she should have gotten him something, too.

Damn it. Now she was confused.

She had no idea what to get him and the only thing she wanted this year was to hear from her father. It had been days since she called and she didn't know how much longer she should give him before she just gave up and moved on.

Sara eased open the door and stepped out of her dressing room just as the associate came in with a tray of champagne and a silver bowl of strawberries.

"Ladies, you all look amazing." She sat the tray down on the white table and offered a wide smile. "Can I grab some accessories and shoe options for each of you?"

"Absolutely." Delilah beamed. "I think these are the dresses we're going with, so bring us whatever you think."

"Give me just a few minutes."

The experienced associate left them alone, and that was the perk of always working with the same woman. She knew their likes and dislikes as well as their sizes. She knew when to help and when to give them privacy. Sara appreciated a smart businesswoman.

"That red is hands down the best one for you," Elise told Sara as she caught her reflection in the mirror. "I'm so excited for this Christmas party, you guys. I want the castle to not only be known for great bourbon, but our amazing events."

They'd set long-term goals and were knocking them off one at a time. Their projected plans were all falling beautifully into place and Sara couldn't believe this was her life, that she actually got to have a dream career with her very best friends.

She hadn't told them about reaching out to her father yet, but she really wanted to share that with them. They could offer her that boost of support because she was desperately wishing he'd text or call…anything at all.

"I have some news to share with you guys." Sara went for a glass of champagne and grabbed one to hold her hands steady. "I called my father and spoke with him."

"What?"

"Are you serious?"

Her sisters spoke at the same time, both of them staring at her with wide eyes and open mouths.

Sara nodded. "Yeah, um, he was shocked, obviously. He didn't hang up on me and listened to what I had to say, so that's something. But he didn't agree to meet with me or anything. I gave him an out and just asked him to think about it and call me if he wanted to know more or meet up."

Delilah reached for her own champagne glass. "How long ago was that?"

"A few days now. I didn't want to say anything yet because I was hoping he'd call or text and then I could tell you guys that. But I couldn't hold it in anymore. I'm so anxious with every sound my phone makes that it's going to be him, but nothing so far."

"Okay, well, you took a big step." Delilah sipped on her champagne and grabbed a glass, passing it to Elise. "I won't promise that he will call, but I would think once he starts thinking about this more and more, he'll want to know you. I wouldn't dismiss this so quickly or worry quite yet."

"Agreed," Elise stated, stepping off the platform. "I assume he'll call, but we don't know this man, so there's no way to gauge his reaction. We're going to all be optimistic. It's Christmas, right? If there's ever a time for miracles and renewal, now is it."

Sara took a drink and hoped her sisters were right. Just hearing them assure her eased some of her nerves. Talking to Ian had helped, too. She hadn't expected him to be such a great listener. She just wished like hell he'd open up to her as well. Was he going to leave town and keep that area of his past a secret? Did anyone know what he'd been through? Obviously his social workers, but did he ever have a counselor or someone he trusted wholeheartedly to help him through those difficult days?

Delilah sat her champagne flute down and glanced back to Elise.

"Don't you want your champagne?" she asked.

Elise glanced from Delilah to Sara. "Yeah, I do. I mean, I love champagne, but..."

Elise burst into tears. "I'm pregnant."

Sara was glad she'd sat her glass down. Pregnant?

"Oh, honey, this is great news." Sara stepped forward and wrapped her arms around her sister. "Our first baby of the family. This is exciting. Is Antonio happy?"

Elise sniffed. "He's already choosing names and paint colors for the nursery and I just found out yesterday."

Sara eased back as Delilah came in for a hug, too.

"You're still in shock, but I'm so excited," Dee stated. "You guys are going to be the best parents and I'm going to be an aunt. I better start shopping."

Sara laughed, already knowing her own credit card was about to take a big hit. But she didn't care. Elise and Antonio were just starting their married lives together and building their family. The next generation was on the way and Sara couldn't be happier or more excited.

The associate stepped back in with boxes of shoes and a variety of jewelry on a tray.

"Oh, is everything all right?" she asked, obviously seeing the tears and hugs.

"We're fine," Sara assured her. "Happy tears."

"Oh, great. Do you need me to help further or should I leave these and give you privacy?"

Delilah stepped back from Elise and offered the associate a smile. "We're good for now, but thank you so much."

Once they were alone again, Delilah cringed. "One of us is always crying when we come here."

"Yeah, last time it was you," Elise teased as she patted her damp cheeks.

Delilah had a minor crying spell when they'd been in to choose dresses for their bourbon launch. In her defense, she and Cam were on the brink of a divorce and she was absolutely heartbroken. Now they were back together and happier than ever…with their new pup, Milly.

"I'm sorry." Elise glanced to Sara and tipped her head. "I didn't mean to dampen your news about your dad. I didn't know when to tell you and I would have just done it later, but Dee handed me champagne and—"

"Do not apologize for being happy," Sara scolded. "We're all going to have ups and downs and I'm not even sure where my news falls on the spectrum."

"This is an exciting time for all of us." Delilah picked up Elise's flute and started sipping. "We're all in another chapter of our lives, but we're doing it together and that's all that matters."

Sara nodded in agreement. "True. I don't know what I'd do without you guys."

"Does that mean you want to talk about Ian and what's going on back at your house?"

Sara stilled and wished she'd taken that extra glass of champagne. Instead, she reached for a strawberry and popped one in her mouth.

"She's not going to answer that," Elise replied. "Which means she's already in too far."

"No way. Love already?" Delilah shook her head. "They haven't known each other very long."

Elise shrugged. "Who am I to judge? I married a man I was trapped in a cellar with."

Sara sighed and stepped up onto the platform to admire the dress she was going to purchase. "I'm not in love," she insisted.

Maybe heavy, heavy like and about a breath away from falling in love, but she wasn't there…yet.

"We're just having fun while he's in town. He's attending the gala and then he'll be on his way. Our write-up in *Elite* will be glowing and amazing and we'll pull in even more business. There's nothing negative about our situation, whether it be personal or professional."

The skeptical looks from her sisters in the mirror only had Sara smiling in return. "Now, let's look at all of these accessories and get more champagne and some sparkling water in here."

Sixteen

This whole idea was preposterous. What was he thinking? He'd never done anything like this before, but he'd woken up and Sara had bustled around to head out the door to meet her sisters for a girls' day and her house had been so quiet.

He hadn't liked the silence. When he'd walked from his guest room just down to the kitchen to work, he'd felt… lonely. That was an emotion he hadn't felt in so long, it was almost foreign.

But he was leaving soon, so he'd have to get used to that solitary lifestyle once again.

Who knew spending almost two weeks in Kentucky with a bubbly woman who was the polar opposite of him would have his entire life turned upside down? How the hell had she managed to reprogram everything he thought he knew or wanted?

He was just getting sidetracked, that's all. He was so

far out of his comfort zone with everything here, his mind was just confused.

But he couldn't deny he was a little anxious for her to get home and see the surprise. He honestly couldn't believe he'd done something so extravagant for anyone, let alone the woman he'd been sleeping with for such a short time. She deserved someone to spoil her, though. He just wished like hell he didn't feel so awkward about this.

Sara was always busy making sure others were comfortable or consoled and he knew she was going through a difficult time with the worry of her father up in the air. While his surprise might make him feel uncomfortable because he'd never done something like this, he figured it would put a smile on her face. He hoped.

When the driveway alarm chimed, Ian saved his work on his laptop and closed it up. He shoved back from the kitchen island where he'd set up a makeshift office area and wondered if he should take her straight to the gift or let her unwind first.

Maybe a glass of wine? She liked wine.

Or should he pour her a bourbon?

Why was he so nervous? This wasn't his girlfriend or his wife about to walk through that door. Knowing Sara, she'd love the gesture and it would make her think of him long after he was gone.

An instant image of another man here with her churned his stomach and pissed him off, actually, but he couldn't have it both ways.

The chime from the door between the garage and the utility room echoed through to the kitchen. Moments later she stepped through and had already shed her coat and bag. She brushed her hair back away from her face and met his eyes across the room.

"Hey," she greeted with that wide smile he'd come to

expect whenever she looked at him. "You gave me absolutely no hints to this surprise and it's been bugging me all day. So let me have it."

She held out her hands and danced on her toes like a giddy child and Ian couldn't help but shake his head and laugh. This woman could make any mood lift when she was around. How could anyone be upset or sad when Sara stepped into the room? She demanded happiness and stability in her part of the world. And she deserved everything she could ever want.

"I can't exactly put it in your hands," he informed her. "It's a little larger than that."

Her arms fell to her sides and her brows rose. "Did you get me a dog?"

"No animal at all."

Sara's lips pursed as she scanned the kitchen and then looked over his shoulder toward the living area. Her eyes came back to his.

"You didn't go buy new clothes because you're still wearing your dressy stuff that looks entirely too uncomfortable for a night in."

"No, I didn't buy new clothes. I don't need them."

"That's still up for debate," she stated. "So, where is this gift?"

He opened his mouth, but she held up her hands.

"Wait," she commanded. "I didn't get you anything for Christmas. I didn't think that's where we were at here, but if this is a Christmas present, I'm going to feel terrible."

"I didn't do this for Christmas." He closed the distance between them and took her hands in his. "I did this because I thought you'd like it and you need someone to pamper you."

Those wide, expressive eyes held his. "And is that what you're doing? Pampering me?"

"For as long as I can."

He leaned in and kissed the tip of her nose. "Follow me," he told her, taking her hand and leading her toward the back of the house.

"We're going outside? It's freezing."

"It is," he agreed, still leading the way.

"We're not dressed for sleigh riding and it's dark now."

"You're stating all the obvious." Ian stopped and turned to face her. "You must be nervous."

She chewed on the bottom of her lip. "Intrigued, definitely. But you don't make me nervous."

He reached out and cupped the side of her face, loving when she leaned into his touch. She shouldn't affect him so damn much, but he could look at her and be with her for—

No. Not forever. That thought was absurd and naive. She was remarkable, yes, but he was not the man for her.

"Close your eyes and let me lead you."

After the briefest of hesitations, she closed her eyes and Ian took both of her hands and carefully walked backward. When he reached the double doors, he reached out and flicked the lock open and pushed them both wide. The blast of cold air hit them, but Ian didn't care. Now that he took in the entire space he'd had done for her, he knew he'd made the right decision.

"How much farther? And are you really just going to blast me with snowballs?" she asked.

"I promise, no snow is involved with this surprise."

"Can I open my eyes yet?"

Ian angled Sara just the right way before he released her hands and stepped aside.

"Now."

He kept his focus on Sara, wanting to take in every bit of her reaction…and she didn't disappoint. Between the gasp and her hands flying up to her mouth in shock, he could finally breathe a sigh of relief that he hadn't overstepped his bounds here.

"Ian," she exclaimed. "What have you done? Oh, my word."

"I hope you like it."

She took a step toward the new hot tub that had the jets bubbling and the colored lights illuminating the water. Then she glanced around to the clear bulbs he had draped from the ceiling of the back porch and the steps leading up to the hot tub. On either side of the steps were box pillars that held fat black lanterns for an added glow.

"You did all of this today?" she asked, spinning back around toward him. "I wasn't gone that long, was I?"

"I actually made a couple of calls yesterday and had my plan put into action as soon as you were gone today." He crossed over to her where she stood on the outdoor rug beneath the hot tub steps. "And you were gone about eight hours. Plenty of time to give you a little oasis."

With all the various lighting surrounding them, plus the full moon, Sara's eyes sparkled as she stared back at him.

"I can't believe this," she murmured. "I mean, this was a lot of work. When you said surprise, I thought maybe you got me a pair of earrings or a sweater. Hell, maybe a snow sled. I never, ever expected anything like this."

Ian rested his hands on her shoulders and leaned in a little closer. "Do I strike you as the type of guy who would pick out jewelry or clothes?"

"Honestly, you don't strike me as the guy who would pull out a surprise like this, but I love it." She framed his face with her delicate hands and pressed a kiss to his lips. "I have no idea how you did this in such a short time, but I've never been more surprised or excited."

Tears welled up in her eyes and she blinked them away.

"I don't know the last time anyone surprised me with

something," she admitted. "I mean, I had a surprise Sweet Sixteen party, but as far as a surprise for no reason at all… I don't even know what to say. 'Thank you' seems so small in comparison."

All along he'd thought they were different in so many ways, but he could relate. Surprises weren't something that happened to him, either, and he'd never had anyone he wanted to surprise with something. Being on the giving end was pretty amazing and seeing just how happy she was made the time and the money and the phone calls all worth it. He'd definitely paid a hefty sum to get this done on the spur of the moment, but none of that mattered. He'd pay triple to see her this happy and genuinely surprised.

Genuine. That was the perfect word that summed up Sara. She loved her life, expected nothing in return but loyalty, and gave every bit of herself to those she loved.

She blinked again and a lone tear slid down her cheek and she nestled deeper into his embrace.

"It's cold out here." She laughed. "Maybe we should make use of this hot tub."

He eased back enough to swipe that tear with the pad of his thumb. Rubbing the moisture between his fingertips, Ian placed a kiss on her forehead.

"There are already towels out here in that bin beside the tub," he told her.

Ian started to pull away, but her eyes were wide, her mouth open, like she was still in shock.

"Did I say something wrong?" he asked.

Sara blinked and shook her head. "No, nothing's wrong."

She didn't move for a moment, like she was lost in a thought or in a trance. Ian snapped his fingers in front of her face and she jerked.

"Oh, sorry." She laughed again. "Everything is great, Ian. Let's check out this hot tub."

She immediately started stripping, hopping from one foot to the other.

"Damn, it's really cold out here," she stated.

Ian hurried out of his own clothes and climbed into the hot tub, then reached out his hand to assist her in. The moment Sara joined him, he wrapped her in his arms and they sank deeper into the warm water.

"This is the best way to end the day," she murmured against his lips. "How can I ever repay you for such an amazing gift?"

Ian's body stirred and he laughed. "You can show me your appreciation right now."

"He got me a freakin' hot tub and a redo of my back patio."

Elise and Delilah stared at her like she'd grown two heads.

"And he gave me a forehead kiss," Sara added. "What the hell am I supposed to do now? How can I not fall for him?"

Sara smoothed her curls over her shoulder and really tried not to get worked up, but she couldn't help herself. She hadn't had a chance to tell her sisters and now they were getting ready to open the doors for the gala. But she needed advice and she needed…

She didn't even know what she needed at this point. All she could pinpoint with certainty was that she didn't want Ian to leave and she didn't know if she'd ever be able to get over him once he was gone.

"You're bringing this up now?" Elise demanded.

"I've been busy using the hot tub," Sara replied, smiling.

"We need to have a family meeting to talk about you

and Ian. We're four minutes from opening the doors to our first Christmas at the Castle."

Delilah settled her hand on Sara's arm. "For what it's worth, I really like the guy."

Elise rolled her eyes. "He's great, okay? We tried to ruffle his feathers and he gave it right back to us. We can't help but think he's amazing, but if you're telling me you're in love because he kissed your forehead—"

"No, of course not," Sara groaned. "There are so many things that have made me feel this way and I just don't know what to do with all of these emotions."

"Of all the times for you to discover love." Elise sighed. "Listen, we will talk and give you our best advice, but this will have to wait. I'm a nervous wreck that people won't show, I've been queasy all day because morning sickness clearly doesn't have a watch."

"I'm sorry." Guilt instantly replaced uncertainty and Sara reached for Elise's hand. "For what it's worth, you look stunning and Antonio is a lucky man."

Elise pulled in a deep breath and smiled. "Thanks. I won't be so cranky once I feel better. But I do like Ian, the little time I got to spend with him. And if you like him, if you *love* him, then he deserves to know before he leaves. Trust me on that one."

Yeah, if anyone knew what it was like to potentially lose a man to long distance, it was Elise. Antonio now divided his time between the US and Spain, but mostly spent it here with Elise. Sara figured he'd be here even more during this pregnancy so he could hover over her and make sure she wasn't overdoing it.

"Is Ian coming tonight?" Delilah asked.

Sara nodded. "He was still in town at Rise and Grind when I left the house. We decided to come separately since

I had to be here early and he said he had a great idea for the opening to his book."

"A book?" Elise asked.

"He started his first chapter today." She couldn't believe the man could just sit down and spit out words like that. "That's his goal when he's done at the magazine, but we can discuss all of that later. Let's get this party started."

Sara had nerves, of course, because this was their first holiday party. Would people come? Would they be too busy because it was a chaotic time of year?

But the main source of her uneasiness came from not knowing how Ian would react to seeing her in her dress, how he would react when she opened up about her feelings or how he would react when she confessed she wanted to see where this relationship could go once he left. Maybe they could make this work. He didn't exactly act like he didn't want to be with her, but he'd also made it very clear he was leaving and moving on.

She couldn't just be a way to pass his time…she refused to believe that. He might hold his emotions close to his chest, but there was no way he'd be so giving and caring toward her if she was just a fling.

Then again, they'd never spent the night in her bed and they'd never had a meal at her dinner table. Everything was still casual, still very surface-level romance.

The large double doors opened at the same time and guests started milling in. The waitstaff in all black maneuvered fluidly through the crowd and Sara greeted people as she walked around. Her eyes never stopped scanning for Ian and she figured he'd show up in another of his suits with a vest. Somehow that look just fit him and made him stand out, when he so desperately wanted to hide in the shadows.

Sara lost track of time and how many people she chatted with and welcomed. Some familiar faces, some newcomers who wanted to check out the castle and likely some who wanted an incredible backdrop for their social media holiday pictures.

Across the open ballroom Elise stood by Antonio's side. He had his arm around her waist and they laughed at something another couple was saying. Sara scanned again and found Camden and Delilah, who were also chatting with customers Sara recognized. Her sisters had found their happily-ever-afters and Sara knew hers wasn't far…perhaps hers was in the making right now.

How could she know? How would she be certain when the right one for her came along?

She still didn't see Ian anywhere and Sara knew Rise and Grind had closed hours ago. Maybe he'd changed his mind. Perhaps a large gathering gave him pause and he just couldn't do it…even for her.

She couldn't make him someone he wasn't and she'd fallen for the man he was. But there was a huge part of her that wanted to save him. He lived with a pain she didn't understand and kept locked away and she just wanted to take all of that heartache and replace it with good memories.

If he didn't show, she'd understand, but she'd be disappointed. Regardless of what happened here, she planned on talking to him as soon as she got home. They both deserved for her to be honest about her feelings.

Seventeen

Breathtaking. Stunning. Flawless.

Ian could use so many words to describe Sara and yet none of them came close to capturing her essence.

He'd sneaked in nearly an hour ago and climbed the stairs to stand on the balcony that overlooked the ballroom. Guests came and went from the second story. Many up here were posing for pictures, he'd even been asked to take a few. But he sipped his bourbon and watched as Sara worked the room and did what she loved. This was her life, the smiling and mingling. Sara Hawthorne was a natural-born charmer. She loved being around people, she thrived in this atmosphere.

And he stood up here hiding.

It didn't matter how much he wanted to fit into her life, and even thinking that seemed absurd, but this was not where he belonged. She didn't know about him, not everything. She deserved someone who would stand by her side, just like her sisters' husbands. Sara would want a man she could be proud of.

They'd started this relationship in a bar. Who the hell meets their soul mate in a bar?

But Sara wasn't his soul mate. She was the woman who'd made him want to be a better man. She'd made him open his eyes to the life around him. She'd made him have fun, and he'd made some of the happiest memories of his life. He'd never forget her, but after tonight, he would be heading back to Miami. His flight left in the morning and no matter how many times he thought about moving it, he knew he couldn't keep putting off the inevitable.

Sara turned, the slight train of the red dress trailing behind her. He loved the sight of her bare, but seeing her in red had him doing a double take when he'd first spotted her. And from up here, he'd seen many men do the same. There was no denying she was a striking woman and he couldn't fault anyone for wanting another look.

She walked from one end of the ballroom to the other and happened to turn again…and she glanced up. Her gaze caught his and that wide smile came in an instant. So did the punch of lust that she continued to deliver with each glance.

Sara gathered the material of her skirt and started up the curved steps. Ian gripped his tumbler and pushed off the railing to go meet her.

"How long have you been here?" she asked the moment she reached him. "I've been trying to watch for you."

"You were busy when I came in," he explained. "I've been admiring your beauty from up here. That dress…"

She held her arms wide and did a slow spin.

"You like?" she asked. "I was hoping you would."

The fact that she wondered how he would react to how she looked told him they were both far deeper into this relationship than he ever intended. Hell, he'd had no intentions, yet here they were.

Ian took her hands in his and stepped closer. "Other than in your hot tub the other night, you've never looked more beautiful."

She tipped her head and smiled as if him bringing that up in public embarrassed her. She sure as hell didn't seem embarrassed the other night.

"I'd like to talk to you," she told him. "I mean, not right here, but I have something I want to tell you."

That hope in her eyes had his gut tightening. He couldn't let her think there was something beyond this, and he had a feeling he was already too late.

"Sara—"

"We can talk when we get home."

Home. She said that word so calmly, as if they literally shared a home. But he'd never let himself fully invest himself into her place. He'd had to keep the distance wherever he could.

"My flight is tomorrow morning."

Her eyes widened and she took a slight step back as if he'd caught her off guard, and he likely had. He'd never told her for certain when he was leaving—he'd only said after the gala. But it was time, because the longer he stayed, the more difficult things would be when he actually left.

"I—I didn't realize," she murmured.

Ian waited for her to say more, but she pulled in a deep breath, squared her shoulders and tipped her chin. In an instant, she'd gone from shocked to strong and there wasn't a doubt in his mind that she was trying to hold it together.

"I didn't mean to spring that on you," he explained. "I had thought about moving it, but I'd like to get back before Christmas and I can't stay."

People moved around them. A server interrupted to

see if they needed another drink or an appetizer. Nothing else mattered and there was nothing else Ian wanted except privacy. He hadn't meant to do this here and the last thing he wanted to do was hurt her. No matter when he left, there would be pain for both of them. In a short time, they'd come to mean something to each other. This was more than a fling and it was more than just a subject. But long-term wasn't in his plans and Sara deserved a man who could be everything she wanted and give her everything she deserved.

Sara continued to stare at him, but for the first time since meeting her, he couldn't get a bead on her thoughts—which likely meant she was doing a damn good job of masking this hurt.

"I need to see about our guests," she told him. "And check with the staff to see if they need anything."

So she was going to distance herself now. She was definitely hurt and he was a jerk for causing it. Unfortunately, there was no way around it. This was the reality they were dealt with.

When she started by him, Ian reached out and curled his fingers around the crook of her arm. She paused beside him, her gaze going from his loose grip to his eyes.

"What did you want to tell me?" he asked.

A corner of her mouth kicked up like she wanted to be happy, but the light had gone out.

"That I'm falling in love with you."

She held his gaze another moment before easing away from his touch.

"If you'll excuse me."

Sara left him standing there alone with that bomb she'd just dropped. He wasn't stupid or naive. He'd worried she was falling too fast, but hearing her say the words really gripped at his heart. She'd crossed over to another level that he could never be on.

How did he move on after this? More so, how could she be falling for him? They'd only known each other a few weeks.

Ian blew out a sigh and glanced up toward the ceiling and exposed beams of the castle. And that's when he saw the mistletoe dangling. Wasn't that just ironic? Not kissing beneath the mistletoe had always been said to be bad luck.

Obviously, that wasn't a myth.

Sara stared at her cell, completely caught off guard at the number that had left a voice mail.

He'd called. Her father had called while she'd been at the gala and she'd just looked at her phone when she got back to her car.

She'd hoped Ian would have called or texted…anything, because she hadn't seen him again after they both dropped bold statements.

So there was that disappointment that Ian hadn't reached out, but she was also anxious that her father had. But what had he said? She was almost afraid to push Play. If he called to tell her he never wanted contact again, that would be it.

But surely he wouldn't have called if that was the case, right? He would have just ignored her and never reached out.

Sara adjusted the vents in her car and cranked up the heater, then she hit Play and waited for the familiar voice to come through her car speakers.

"Hi, Sara. Um, it's me. I can't stop thinking about you. My wife and I would like to meet with you. Whenever you're free, we'll make the drive. Call me when you can."

Tears instantly sprang into her eyes and she glanced

at the time. It was much too late to call him now, but she would tomorrow. After all of this time, she was finally going to meet the man who had been missing for her entire life.

She'd connected with her father on the same day the man she'd fallen in love with announced he was leaving town. Maybe that's just how fate wanted to help her heal. Maybe having her father in her life would help her move into the next chapter…the chapter without Ian.

Sara maneuvered through the curvy country roads and headed home. She replayed the message from her father the entire way. She would never get tired of hearing his voice and having him say he wanted to meet her.

When she pulled into her drive and up to the garage, her stomach tightened at the sight of Ian's vehicle. She'd thought he might get his stuff and hit a hotel for his flight tomorrow. She really hadn't known what to expect or if he'd be here when she got back. She wouldn't let her hopes get too high because they were already so low now. She couldn't mentally afford another letdown or more heartache.

She took her time gathering her dress and getting out of the car to head inside. She had no idea what to say or do at this point. Maybe he'd be asleep and she could slip into her room quietly. She really didn't know how she'd react or feel seeing him in private now that they were free to speak their minds. But if he was dead set on leaving, there was nothing she could say to make him stay.

Oh, she could plead her case and fight for what she wanted, but she didn't want to have to beg a man to be with her. She didn't want to make someone stay out of guilt or obligation.

Sara gripped her clutch and her cell and stepped into the utility room. She waited, but heard nothing. As she moved on into the kitchen, her eyes landed on Ian's laptop case and the suitcase at the island.

He'd packed, but he hadn't left. Yet.

The glow from her Christmas lights should be welcoming and heartwarming, but she wasn't feeling too festive right now.

She sat her clutch and phone on the island and gathered her skirt in one hand. Holding on to the edge of the counter, she slid off one heel and then the other, letting them clunk to the floor.

"I couldn't leave."

Sara jerked to see Ian in the arched doorway leading down the hallway. He still wore the black suit he'd had on at the gala, but his hair seemed quite a mess. Clearly he'd spent some time running his fingers through it and she had to admit, she was a little happy that he was just as frustrated.

"You weren't supposed to tell me you love me." His eyes remained down and he propped his hands on his narrow hips. "You weren't supposed to make me feel. I didn't want to feel."

Sara remained in place, saying nothing, because he was obviously working through something all on his own and she had to let him.

"When my mother died, I swore I'd never get attached to anyone again," he went on, still staring down as if seeing something replaying before his eyes. "I see this damn scar on my face every day, the reminder I need that tells me I don't deserve someone else in my life."

Sara started to step toward him, but he held up his hand and met her gaze.

"No," he commanded. "Don't. You need to understand why I can't love you back."

He muttered a curse and then silence settled heavily in the room.

"I make a living out of stringing words together, but nothing is coming to me that sounds right. I'm out of my element here and it's terrifying."

As much as she wanted to say something, Sara nodded and let him continue. He had to work through his demons on his own before she could step in.

"I never knew my father," he started. "My mother was all I had. I loved her more than anything and I knew she'd do anything for me. When I became a teen, I guess I was like all teen boys and wanted to be a little rebellious to see what I could get away with. She would pull me back in and be stern, but loving."

Ian slid off his jacket, tossing it aside, then unbuttoned his cuffs and rolled his sleeves up his forearms. He raked his hands through his hair once more and blew out a sigh.

"We were arguing the day she died. The weather was horrible. Snowy and cold. I had just gotten my license and wanted to drive, but she kept insisting I wasn't ready. But I kept begging and she gave in. We started arguing when I slid the first time on a patch of ice. She wanted me to pull over and I told her I was fine, but then I slid again and..."

His voice cracked at that last word and Sara didn't try to refrain anymore. She took a step forward, then another, until she closed the gap between them.

She framed his face in her hands and swiped when a lone tear slid down right over his scar.

"That accident wasn't your fault," she insisted. "Deep in your heart you know that and I didn't know your mother, but I'm sure she wouldn't want you blaming yourself."

"She wouldn't," he whispered. "But that's not the issue here. I need you to know why I can't get close, why you can't love me, why I can't stay."

Oh, she understood perfectly.

"I needed to tell you all of that before I leave," he added. "I couldn't just go and have you wonder if there was something you did wrong because none of this is you. You're… Hell, Sara. You're everything."

Yes. Yes. Yes.

That's all she needed to hear, because that vulnerable statement was damn near a confession of love. The man just didn't know how to love or he was too afraid.

"Running from what we have won't make it go away." She smoothed his wayward strands from his forehead. "You go back to Miami, and your thoughts and wants will still be with you. I will still be with you."

He closed his eyes and dropped his forehead to hers.

"This isn't how things were supposed to go," he admitted. "I thought I could handle this fling with you, but then I came here and you make me want a home. You make me want things I never thought I deserved."

"And why don't you?" she asked softly. "Because you're human and had an accident? You can't punish yourself for the rest of your life. That's just like if you had died that day. Don't you want to live? To make your mother even more proud than I'm sure she already is?"

"How do you do that?" he whispered.

Sara eased back, dropping her hands to take his.

"Make me feel like this is possible," he clarified.

"Because it is. If you want something, go for it." Sara swallowed her own fear and trudged on. "Do you want what we have, Ian? Do you want to see where this will go? Or do you want to continue hiding and letting life pass you by?"

He squeezed her hands and a blossom of hope filled her.

"You sound like Nigel," he said with a soft chuckle.

"He's always telling me to live my life and stop watching life around me."

"He's a smart man."

Ian's damp eyes held hers and while her heart broke for him, she also had a piece that was so full of love and optimism. This could work, if only he would let it.

"You'd like him and his wife," Ian told her. "Maybe you can come to Miami and meet them sometime."

Sara smiled. "I'd like that."

"And maybe I could stay here. For now."

"I'd like that, too."

He continued to stare at her and she wondered what was going through his mind. All she knew was he was staying, he was giving them a chance, and there was no way they'd fail.

He ran his hands up and down her arms and then cupped her cheek. "When I talked to your sisters they said you'd been waiting for your own fairy tale, that you wanted that knight to come save the day."

Sara would have a talk with them about that later. "That's not exactly what I've said, but I do want a fairy tale."

"You have it." Ian's thumb raked over her bottom lip. "Only you didn't need saving, Sara. You were the one who saved me."

Sara's heart flipped and tears instantly sprang into her eyes. Never in her life had she thought she could save anyone. She'd wanted to fall in love with the right man and she wanted to have that companion forever, but she never thought she was strong enough to save someone's heart.

"I couldn't leave now if I wanted to," he added. "Because I'm falling in love with you, too."

Sara threw her arms around his neck and held tight. "I know you are. I just needed to hear you say it."

"I'll keep saying it, so long as you don't sing anymore."

A laugh escaped her and she pulled back enough to swat at his chest.

"That's rude, but I'll take that deal."

Ian's lips grazed over hers. "You can do anything you want, just promise you'll continue to be patient with me during this."

"I'm not going anywhere," she promised. "But I do have one request."

His brows drew in as he stared down at her. "Anything."

"My father called and wants to meet in person after the holidays." Just the thought had nerves dancing in her stomach. "Will you go with me?"

"I'll be right by your side."

Ian bent down and scooped her up into his arms and headed down the hallway.

"We're sleeping in your room from now on," he told her. "This is just the beginning of our own happily-ever-after."

Epilogue

Ian's hand settled around her waist as Sara snuggled deeper into his side. She couldn't help but smile as Delilah and Cam, Elise and Antonio all gathered in her living room. She'd decided to host a family Christmas Eve dinner and gift exchange. Though they'd all found love this year so what could be better than that?

"I hope someone got me a size seven-day cruise," Elise stated. "That fits me best."

"You just took a honeymoon," Delilah scolded, sitting on the arm of the sofa next to Cam.

Antonio shook his head as he swirled his bourbon. "She's turned into a travel fanatic. She's already in discussions with my mother about going to Spain after the first of the year."

Sara started to reply, but her doorbell rang. She glanced to Ian who had a sneaky smile on his face.

"What did you do?" she asked as she sat her wineglass on the accent table behind the sofa.

Ian merely shrugged. "Go find out."

Nerves curled in her belly, though she knew whatever Ian had done, he'd done out of love. She just couldn't fathom who else they were missing. Maybe he got a dog or perhaps a shipment of wine. She wouldn't be opposed to either of those gifts.

Sara reached the front door and pulled in a breath before turning the knob. But the moment she spotted her guest, Sara gasped. Her eyes immediately filled with tears, but she remained still.

"Merry Christmas."

Trenton Mills—her father—stood on her doorstep with a package in hand and a cautious smile on his face.

"I hope this is okay," he added.

Ian stepped up behind Sara and she turned to him. He offered her the widest grin.

"I thought this was better than anything I could purchase," he stated.

Sara glanced back to her father and laughed through the tears. "This is more than okay and absolutely the greatest gift."

Ian reached out for the package and gestured. "Come on in and welcome to the family."

Trenton held out his hand for Sara to shake and the moment her hand slid into his, the tears fell. He gave a gentle tug and she found herself fully embraced by the man she could now call father.

"We have so much to catch up on," he murmured in her ear. "This is just the beginning."

Yes. Just the beginning.

* * * * *